DEKE BROLIN

RHOL

© COPYRIGHT DOUGLAS BACKUS

ISBN — 13 -978-0987673206

LBTEH PUBLISHING

PART I

RHOL

Chapter One

It was one of the clearest nights Deke Brolin could ever remember seeing. The moon illuminated the forest that surrounded him much like the low light a candle throws in a darkened room.

Most people would've felt uneasy standing in the middle of a forest at night, but not him. This was his last chance to save himself from the desperate life he was leading. Ironically, the same place where he'd found refuge as a boy was also the place that had caused him so much pain. It was a pain so great that it had sent him spiraling down the wrong path. It was the easy way, one in which Deke never really exerted any energy nor reflected on the consequences of his actions as he travelled aimlessly from place to place.

Deke Brolin was at his wit's end and couldn't bear to walk this path any longer. He'd found his way to the crossroads of where it had all begun, and he needed to find some comfort within the place that had left him so conflicted. He'd chosen to be here on this day for a reason.

An old rickety wooden bridge appeared to him in the distance and marked the halfway point of his journey. The weathered bridge had been there for years. It provided safe passage across a small pebbly creek that wound its way through a meadow in the middle of the forest.

Breathing in deeply, Deke savored the smell of the smoke that hung in the air from the long since extinguished fireplaces of the old farm houses that lay scattered around the outskirts of the woods. He loved that smell. Millions of lights pierced the dark sky. The stars were shining so intensely he could've stared at them all night imagining the countless worlds that might exist beyond this one.

This time of year was his favorite. There was always a light frost on the ground that made the moss crinkle under his feet. Ahead of him large Maple's formed what looked like a long tunnel along the path he walked. The tree's seemed desperate to hold onto their leaves as if not wanting to lose their fiery red, yellow and orange colors. For the first time in three years, he felt at peace again if only for this one moment.

The bridge creaked slightly at the added weight it was now forced to endure when Deke sat down upon it and dangled his legs over the side. The sounds of the gurgling brook beneath his feet calmed him, but soon his mind began to drift into the past with memories he wished were long forgotten. Two of the most vivid had changed his fate forever.

Life is really about choices, Deke thought.

He'd made many in his short life, and those choices couldn't be changed now. They'd already weaved their way into his life's path.

His life wasn't always so troubled. Up until he was eight, his life had been good. His parents were caring people. Larry, his father, was a tall, husky man who wore glasses and had an extraordinary zest for life.

Deke laughed to himself thinking about how ridiculous such a large man looked while driving the family car; a red Volkswagen Beatle.

His dad was a school teacher who taught history, and despite his size, he was a great adventurer and outdoorsman with an incredible imagination. His father could do anything in his eyes. He used to tell stories to Deke before bedtime and usually with his own twist. Deke would sit on his dad's lap in the living room of their quiet bungalow while the fire roared away in the large stone fireplace. Sometimes his Dad would find his own story so amusing that he would roar with laughter. His laugh was like no other and echoed throughout the whole neighborhood. His mother Sarah would just giggle and shake her head at him.

She was a very soulful person - tall and strikingly beautiful. She chose to stay at home and take care of the family. She constantly worried about Deke because he was her only child. The thousands of acres of forests behind their house had caused her countless days of anguish. Deke loved the woods and would often disappear within them for the entire day. If he wasn't floating down the nearby creek on a raft, he was climbing trees and building forts.

On most days Deke was allowed to stay out until the street lights came on, but if a minute late his mother would be in a panic. She used to stroke her long blonde hair to calm herself down, and in a matter of minutes, she would be hugging him. She was filled with love, not only for him and his father but for anyone that graced her path. It was remarkable how people in need instantly gravitated toward her.

What an age. Deke recalled.

He was loved more. His parents had made life easy and comfortable. They were always there to teach and nurture him, right up until the time that, well...they died.

A defining moment and...a choice...Deke lamented.

For years he tried to block the memory out, but it would never escape him.

He couldn't recall exactly how the accident happened, but he did remember the car veering off the road and careening down a small embankment. Memories of his mother desperately trying to grab him as the car rolled over caused his hands to clench and his breath to quicken. He swallowed and wondered what might've happened had her loving hands reached him, but they hadn't. A distinct feeling of weightlessness had swept him away from her forever.

Deke remembered pulling himself from the ground and staring at the burning car. He ran as fast as he could and reached his mother first. His dad lay slumped over the steering wheel beside her, unconscious with his legs pinned under a heap of metal.

Deke instinctively shook his head attempting to rid his mind of this all too vivid memory.

"Take care of him," his mother had gently whispered.

He had no idea why, but he heeded her words and ran to help his father. Deke tried to shake his father awake, but it was no use. Using all the strength he could muster he tried to pull his father from the wreck, but it was not to be.

Deke's face fell into his hands. His stomach was twisting and turning as the horrid scene played out in his mind. He felt like a weakling, a failure and tried once again to rid himself of the memory, but his thoughts still haunted him.

He remembered running back to his mother's aid. The thick black smoke was slowly suffocating him. He reached his mother as the flames converged on her. She just smiled at him and stretched her arm out through the car window. She touched his cheek and whispered to him softly for the last time.

"You must go. There's no time. Remember that your father and I love you more than life itself."

He wouldn't leave. He begged her to try and move, but she was gone.

Deke's recollection of what happened next was foggy at best. He was standing a safe distance from the car but had no idea how he had gotten there. Seconds later the car exploded. His knees buckled and his stomach had felt so tight it caused him to roll into a ball. That's how the police found him. They surmised the explosion had somehow thrown him out of harm's way and saved his life.

In Deke's mind, they'd both died because of the choice he had made to save his father first. That decision had defined his life for many years. Following the accident, he had been placed in a foster home as the authorities were unable to find any living relatives. There he became a recluse and an outcast. He was obsessed with the events surrounding his parent's death and what he could've done differently to save them. His memories kept his mind locked in the past and never considering the future...that was until he met Mary Toller. She would become the other defining moment in his life - for Mary was a true friend who would lead him down a bright path, but then through no fault of her own, spiral him back into darkness.

CHAPTER TWO

Deke pulled himself up and walked away from the bridge. It was time. Before long, the trees surrounded him again. The moonlight sliced its way through the tangled branches above him. Falling leaves cast against the moon caused strange shadows to come to life in front of him as he meandered down the path. In the distance, Deke could see that he was nearing his final destination. He wondered if he would find what had saved him from the anguish of his foster home so many years ago or if time had forever changed his sanctuary.

His first foster home had been in the city, a place he'd been unwilling to adjust to. His foster parents eventually gave up on him after enduring an entire year of his stony silence. They tried to find psychiatric care for him, but the State was unwilling to pay for the expense of it. Unable to deal with his mounting issues, they sent Deke away to another foster home in the country. They hoped that perhaps a more familiar surrounding would help.

At least in the country, he was able to find some comfort in the forests and fields that surrounded the small town. Unfortunately, his new foster parents were miserable to live with. The only thing they cared about was the money they received as a supplement for him and the other foster children. Of course, the kids never saw a dime of it and were forced to wear the same clothes and scrounge for food wherever they could.

Despite this, Deke would eventually meet his savior here. She would help him cope with the feelings of guilt that overwhelmed him and show him how to look toward the future, not back into the past. Without her, the memory of his parents' death would have consumed him.

Deke would never forget the day he met her.

He'd not spoken a word since his parents died and had prided himself in avoiding people, but on this particular day, something had made him change his regular route home. Unwittingly, he'd come upon four neighborhood bullies who were surrounding a petite girl. She looked to be the same age as Deke. Tears were streaming from her eyes as the bullies hurled abusive words at her. She tried to escape their circle, but they wouldn't allow it. They kept pushing her, telling her to go back to where she came from, that they didn't need another street urchin around here. Confused and scared, she'd fallen to her knees only to have these animals throw crab apples at her staining her white dress with red circles.

Deke had been stunned by their abuse, their cruelty toward this girl who had obviously just arrived at the foster home. Walking straight through them, he picked the tiny girl up from the ground and without saying a word guided her away pushing two of the assailants aside. His actions had saved the girl, but he was wrestled to the ground and savagely beaten. Help quickly returned with his new friend, but by then the damage had already been done.

Deke paused remembering the touch of her hand on his cheek before he lost consciousness. How could he ever forget? It was reminiscent of his mother.

The girl's name was Mary Toller, and over the three weeks that it took him to recover, he came to learn that she'd never left his side. She would remain there for the next several years.

They found many things in common with each other, one of which was their love for adventures and it was one in particular that eventually changed them forever.

They had happened upon a cornfield on the outer edge of the forest and soon discovered the field contained valuable items discarded and left for lost long ago. Every year when the field was ploughed, they would find new treasures which had emerged on its surface. Some of the artifacts were quite strange, and they imagined them belonging to ancient civilizations. At the end of each day, they would carefully bury their cache in an old stone well, hoping that one day they could use it to escape the confines of their miserable home.

The field became their refuge. Over time they built a fort from logs left strewn around the area. The fort overlooked the entire area. They built it about twenty feet from the ground - in a strategic place so that it doubled as a lookout post. Two enormous branches of a large oak tree supported the structure.

Deke affectionately remembered the times he had spent with Mary in and around that fort. Those years felt timeless, but it was all about to change.

They'd just celebrated their fourteenth birthdays which fell in the same week. On this particular night, Deke had snuck into the kitchen to get some food for Mary and the other children but had been caught by his foster parents. They were incensed and locked down the entire house. Undeterred, he snuck out around the back and climbed the basswood tree up to Mary's window. After getting her attention, Deke had told Mary to meet him at the bridge at seven the next morning so that they could go to the fort.

He spent the remaining part of the night roaming the streets. Only the growing light in the sky made him realize that he had lost track of time. When he arrived home the sun was already visible, so he ran straight to the bridge. When he got there, Mary was nowhere to be found.

He waited at the bridge for a short time and then walked to the fort to look for her. She wasn't there either. Becoming concerned he ran back to the house thinking she may have slept in. She wasn't there either, and Deke's foster parents were in an uproar about her whereabouts; hearing this worried Deke. He tried to tell them about the plan they'd made to meet at the bridge. He begged them to come to the woods and help search for her, but his pleas fell on deaf ears. They locked him away in his room hampering any hope of him finding her.

Deke scowled at the memory of it all. He should've broken away from their grasp that day. If anyone could've found her, it would've been him he angrily thought.

About twelve hours passed before his pretend parents started worrying about their monthly checks and finally called the police. Deke was furious that they waited so long. The police spoke with all the children in the house saving him for last. He told them everything, including the plan to meet Mary at the bridge in the forest.

After a two week search of the area, the police came up with nothing other than a shoe with blood spots on it. Mary's shoe with blood spots on it. They wouldn't tell Deke where they found it and suddenly he became the prime suspect in her disappearance.

The police constantly interviewed him, and everywhere he went people whispered about him being a deviant and a savage. He was angry that they wasted their time on him instead of looking for Mary. They were right though. He was responsible, not in the way they thought, but because he'd been late. He'd let her down. She might well be here walking with him today, had he arrived at the bridge on time.

His guilt consumed him. In his mind only he was to blame. The only friend he had in the world was gone because of him.

When they finally closed the missing person file and presumed her dead Deke walked away from life. He lived on the street, alone and broken travelling long distances, but going nowhere. He became lost in a world of self-loathing - unable to forgive himself.

He travelled from city to city always staying on the outskirts, skulking like an animal in search of food, not wanting to have contact with anyone. After three years of living in isolation, Deke couldn't take it anymore. Something from deep inside of him was guiding him back to the place where it had all started. He never had the chance to say goodbye to her back then. To say farewell to a friend who once saved him, who had loved him for who he was.

He would have his chance now for the path he was walking down suddenly came to an end and a vast field of rich soil gleaming from the night's frost lay before him. He stared out at the place he once called his sanctuary. In a few moments time, it would be his resting place.

Chapter Three

It had not changed a bit. The east and west sides of the field were still divided by a long range of birch trees that jutted out from the woods, stopping about a hundred yards into the field. To the east of this was another pocket of trees which resembled an island surrounded by dirt rather than water. That was his destination.

Deke walked along the line of birch trees. They were beautiful. The moonlight made their bark glow in the dark almost like a beacon for lost travelers. He came to the end of the range and crossed over the field to the island. He hesitated momentarily before walking into the dense bush. A short way in, he found the slightly overgrown path that he and Mary had worn into the ground over the years they'd come to this place.

In the distance, he saw the oak tree that he was looking for and hurried toward it. He smiled when he looked up and saw that their fort was still there. Wasting no time he began to scale the tree's endless branches. When he reached the bottom of the fort, he pushed open the trap door and pulled himself in. Two stumps that were once used as seats were all that remained inside.

Deke sat down, caught his breath and looked around. He spotted the hole in the tree where he and Mary use to hide their binoculars and wondered if they were still there. He reached in and found them, a little rusted, but not in bad shape considering the amount of time that had passed. Deke felt better already. He was home again and could now fulfill the purpose of his trip. He could still read what he and Mary had carved into the tree, but never finished, "Mary and Deke – Soul," he flicked open his pocket knife and finished it "Mates Forever."

It might not have meant a lot to some, but Deke became overwhelmed. He gazed up into the moon and swiped at the light mist that formed above him with each breath he took. He'd come all this way in hopes of getting answers from her. Was she alright? Was she at peace?

Deke paused and reached out to touch the jagged carving in the tree.

Most importantly, did she forgive him? He knew there was only one way to find the answer to these questions.

It was the perfect place for his life's path to end and his new one to begin. He wanted it this way. It would end as he had lived most of his life; alone with his thoughts. It was comforting to know that at this moment he was as close as he could get to the only person who had ever understood him. It felt right, although he did have the distinct feeling that someone was with him, watching him. Perhaps there was someone there, for he could hear a faint sound. The sound was growing louder. It was an unusual noise, kind of like the soft slap a wave makes when it hits the sand.

Deke looked out over the field in the direction of the noise. At first, he saw a dim light, but it quickly faded away leaving him blinded for a short period. It took his eyes a few minutes to readjust to the dark before he saw it.

What was he looking at? Whatever it was, Deke was sure that it hadn't been on the field before his arrival.

It looked as though a large mound of dirt had suddenly appeared in the middle of the field. He stared so intently at the object it almost seemed to move.

Deke fell backward into the fort when he realized it was not his eyes playing tricks on him. It was moving. It began to stand up. He could only make out a silhouette. It was huge. The sun was slowly beginning to rise, but it was still too dark to get a clear view.

Deke nervously swallowed and fumbled for his binoculars. Perhaps he could get a better look using them. His hands were trembling making it difficult to focus, but when he held his breath, it seemed to help. Still, the binoculars didn't provide him with a much better view. He could only make out a shadowy figure that appeared to have long wavy hair.

His curiosity took over. He had to get a better look. He quietly inched his way down the oak tree hoping the sweat forming on the palms of his hands wouldn't cause him to lose his grip. He reached the last branch of the tree - the branch that you had to jump up to reach or drop down to get off. Deke hung from the branch for several seconds before letting go. He winced when he hit the ground crushing the leaves under his feet. He stood there frozen, straining to hear if anyone was coming toward him in search of the noise.

Several minutes passed in silence. So far, so good, Deke thought to himself.

Deke began crawling on all fours, up ahead he noticed a cedar tree on the edge of the field. It looked like a good vantage point. Every instinct he had was telling him to turn back, but his arms kept dragging him closer.

It took time, but eventually, Deke found himself peering through the thick cedar branches. He had hoped the cedars would've provided better camouflage, but it would have to do. He had a clear view now and instantly felt a cold shiver run down his spine. Why had he allowed himself to get this close?

Deke was petrified, afraid to move. The creature was now standing, and it appeared to be about eight feet tall. Its body was the shape of a man's, but it wasn't of human origin. Fur covered its legs, and large boar like tusks protruded from its jaw in a downward direction. Its long black hair slowly swayed back and forth even though there was no wind.

Lying flat on the ground Deke began to slide himself back across the cool dirt, praying that this thing would not hear him trying to make his escape. His plan had not included the assistance of anyone or anything else.

"You can do it, just move slowly," he said to himself.

By the time Deke realized that he'd forgotten to take his binoculars off, it was too late. The sound of the metal scraping noisily over a rock made Deke cringe. Using only his eyes, he glanced upward; the creature was staring right at him. Its pearly white eyes glowed in the pre-dawn light. Its skin was black except for some white script written on its chest, and its hair which was pushed back behind its long protruding ears, sparkled like diamonds. Deke remained frozen to allow his eyes time to adjust to the growing light. Its hair became more pronounced as it moved ever so slightly upward before circling back down again. They weren't diamonds at all. The tiny sparkling dots were eyes. Its long black hair was made up of snakes.

Deke felt his heart pounding against the ground. Fear entrenched him, he jumped up and ran crashing through the woods.

Behind him, the sound of breaking branches was becoming more and more prevalent. The creature was gaining ground. Suddenly, Deke veered off the path and found himself running through the dense bush. It was almost as if he'd been pushed.

A blood-curdling roar sounded out behind him. He felt like his heart was going to explode. He continued running all the while feeling that something was guiding him. Nobody was there, but as he ran, Deke found himself feeling a sudden urge to turn in a different direction. He did, and as he burst through a thicket, only the empty field lay ahead of him. He didn't want to look back. He had nowhere to go, nowhere to run. The creature was right behind him. He could hear it breathing. No, it was laughing.

"What are you?" Deke screamed.

He wouldn't get a response, only the feeling of a sharp shooting pain through his shoulder from being pushed to the ground. Deke's head hit the dirt first, and he screamed aloud when something tore into his face.

Deke Brolin rolled over and grasped at the item protruding from his cheek. He didn't have time to see what it was before he instinctively closed his eyes and covered his face in a feeble attempt to protect himself from the creature who had found its prey.

Chapter Four

Deke opened his eyes and looked around. Everything was blurry. He could feel a sharp burning sensation on his cheek and opened his clenched fist to look at the item that had caused him the pain. It was a small spearhead made out of white stone, somewhat resembling quartz. It was quite a find. He just wished he'd found it, rather than fallen on it. He was slowly coming out of his daze remembering what had happened. He couldn't see or hear any signs of the creature that had been pursuing him, but the surrounding darkness made it hard to see.

Ever so slowly, his eyes began to adjust. A strange feeling overcame him, perhaps brought on by fear combined with the darkness of the damp cave he was sitting in. Deke had no idea how he'd ended up here. The smell of the cave reminded him of an old knapsack he'd left his wet clothes in for over a week. He was patting the ground trying to get a better grasp of his surroundings when he noticed the walls of the cave slightly glimmering from a single beam of light that permeated the darkness. He decided to follow it hoping it would lead him out.

Wobbling slightly, Deke rose to his feet and began to make his way along the sheer rock corridor. Strange carvings of creatures began to appear on the walls of the cave. They resembled nothing he had ever seen before, except for one of them. He was sure it was the thing that had just chased him.

Becoming unnerved he moved further down the wall looking at more of the strange creatures. He wondered who had etched the drawings into the stone; they were so detailed they almost appeared alive. The walls of the cave seemed to be the same type of stone as the spearhead. It must've taken ages to complete them he thought. Whoever had carved them had taken the time to write words beside each one. Perhaps it was some ancient language. He certainly didn't understand it.

Deke continued toward the light wondering where he was and how he had gotten there. Perhaps he had fallen into an underground cavern that had been hidden from sight just as the creature had pounced on him.

When Deke reached the mouth of the cave, his body began to shake. He was standing on the edge of a cliff, and a vast terrain stretched out before him. A mixture of fear and, a sense of wonderment overcame Deke. How had he arrived at such a breathtakingly beautiful place? Vast mountain ranges stretched as far as the eye could see. The mountains surrounded a lush valley that lay thousands of feet below him. There was not a cloud in the sky. Deke surmised that the sun peeking out over the west side of the mountains meant it was the beginning of the day.

Waterfalls cascaded down the mountains in every direction eventually molding together to form one, which emptied into a large lake. The only ripples in the lake were caused by the pounding water as it fell to its final resting place. It was a stunning sight which was only enhanced when beams of sunlight appeared to turn the water into a sea of stars that sparkled on the lake's surface. Unfamiliar trees and vegetation surrounded the entire area. The trees were enormous, towering hundreds of feet high.

From where Deke was standing, there was no way to get down into the valley. He deliberated for a while, admiring the view, but finally decided to return into the darkness of the cave and find another way out.

Deke cautiously walked back in, eventually passing the place he started at. It was becoming darker the further he ventured into the cave which made him uncomfortable with the notion of what might lie ahead.

Even though the air seemed slightly warmer, the hair on his arms rose as if warning him not to go any further. In most situations, Deke would have heeded this warning and turned back, but he didn't think he had much choice.

With no light left to guide him, Deke began to feel the walls of the cave while slowly inching forward. Occasionally, the walls felt damp and furry, but he chose to believe it was moss. He knew that moss needed some sunlight to grow and convinced himself that at some time there must have been enough to suffice.

Deke stopped momentarily to catch his breath. He was beginning to reconsider travelling deeper into the depths of the cave when without warning something grabbed him by the arm. It felt coincidently like moss and it was dragging him further into the cave.

The creature he thought!

Deke broke free and ran blindly through the darkness toward the entrance. He could sense whatever it was, right behind him. The further he ran the lighter it got, but there was still a long way to go. His pulse quickened with every step he took.

Suddenly, something grasped his shirt. Deke screamed in terror, believing that the creature he'd just escaped from was once again upon him. He strained to break free using all the strength he could muster, but it was not enough. Panic was the only thing that provided him with enough energy to try one last time. It worked. The creature's grasp relented, and Deke ran, banging into the walls of the cave he sought to escape. He cursed to himself when his foot caught a stone causing him to fall firmly to the ground.

"I have to make it!" he said to himself.

Deke clawed at the ground attempting to regain his footing, but his fall had allowed the creature to grab him again, this time by his ankle. Once again, he found himself struggling to escape the creature's grasp. Deke could see the rock he'd tripped over. It was just a few feet away. He reached out, stretching his fingers in an attempt to roll the stone into his hand.

Deke could feel its jagged edges cutting into his fingertips as he scratched at the rock, desperately trying to move it toward him. After several attempts, he finally felt it in the palm of his hand. He firmly clenched it and thrust his arm into the darkness toward his captor. He heard a grumble, a thud and then silence. He had connected. Deke scrambled to his feet and ran trying not to look behind him, but unable to resist the odd glance.

It seemed like an hour, but in mere seconds Deke found himself standing on the ledge of the cliff again. Blood was dripping from his hands. He quickly checked himself and confirmed it wasn't his. Looking around in fear, he wondered where to go next.

He was alone and frightened and contemplated jumping into the large lake below him, but he knew the fall would kill him. Even if the lake was deep enough, nobody could survive a jump from this height. Deke's stomach was churning up what was left of his last meal.

"Calm down!" he thought to himself. "Calm down and think!"

Deke frantically looked around, desperately trying to find a safe way off the cliff. Then, in the distant sky, he saw a small dot which seemed to appear out of nowhere. Deke strained his eyes in an attempt to determine what it was. It appeared to be flying or at least floating in the sky in front of the farthest mountain he could see. It began to glow a bright fiery orange and grew larger the longer he looked at it. A quiet tranquility came over him, if only for a moment. It was simply beautiful.

The moment wouldn't last, however, for behind him he could hear strange grumbling sounds. Deke turned abruptly. There was nothing there. He remained transfixed on the cave's entrance waiting for what he knew was coming.

"What is happening? This must be some sort of nightmare!" Deke desperately thought. "It can't be real!"

Maybe he was sick. He was feeling hot, even feverish. "I could be hallucinating," Deke reasoned, wiping the sweat from his forehead.

Suddenly a creature quite unlike the one Deke was expecting, leapt from the darkness of the cave toward him. It had crimson red eyes that appeared shiny and drawn. It was yelling something that he couldn't understand and seemed raging mad. Deke could see it had wings, but they were slowly disappearing, molding into the creature's body. Its flesh twisted and distorted as it continued to move toward him. It was almost rolling now. Deke was in shock, too frightened to move. He was burning up. Sweat dripped down his nose and fell to the ground. He could hear every drop crashing upon the rocks below him.

His instincts to survive consumed him. He turned to run toward the edge of the cliff forgetting that he had nowhere to go. He hadn't expected to be met with the wall of fire which stretched out before him. With nowhere to go, Deke just stood there frozen in time, helplessly awaiting the inevitable. It would be the creature that reached him first, throwing him over the cliff.

Chapter Five

Flames were covering the sky above him, and he was falling to his certain death. Deke closed his eyes and wished he was back at home. He thought of his old life and especially of his father. He wished his dad hadn't left him at such a young age, that he could've been there to teach him the ways of the world. The memory of his father was so vivid that Deke was confident he could hear his father's voice calling out his name. He opened his eyes and was astounded to be looking right at him. It was his father! His father, who he had watched die was desperately holding onto him as they plummeted to their death.

"Deke, imagine your bird!" his father yelled.

Deke couldn't hear a thing through the wind that whistled around his ears. "Deke your bird, remember your bird!" screamed his father.

Deke looked down to see the trees, water and jagged rocks approaching at a rapid pace.

Did he say imagine your bird? What was he talking about and how did his father ever come to be here?

His favorite bird was a falcon he had named Ralph. He'd found Ralph near a creek behind his old house where he had grown up. The Falcon, while diving for prey had misjudged a tree. The bird's wing slammed into a branch, and it had fallen helplessly to the ground. Deke had run to the Falcon's aid and spent the better part of the summer nursing it back to health. He'd released the Falcon in the fall, and as if to say thanks, Ralph insisted on hanging around, dive bombing anyone who came in close quarters with him.

As he thought of Ralph his father's face began to twist and distort, his nose took on the form of a beak, and his eyes flipped backward in his head only to be replaced by round yellow ones. Claws instead of hands were now gripping Deke's body. Deke pushed away in fear and continued falling faster with the ever changing figure steadfastly pursuing him. It wouldn't be long now; he thought bracing himself for the impact.

After several seconds Deke opened his eyes, wondering why he hadn't already felt his body crash down upon the rocks. He was astonished to see he was now flying over and in between rock caverns. A large falcon was gripping onto him, struggling to keep them both afloat.

Deke looked behind him. It just couldn't be, and yet, it was. A dragon was relentlessly pursuing them. It was enormous. Two horns protruded from behind its pointed ears followed by three more on each cheek. Its dark eyes appeared as if they were black pools of water, and its jagged forked tail swung madly to and fro. It was gradually gaining on them as it maneuvered easily through the sky. The creature's wings were a shiny turquoise on top with a brilliant red underneath and were far larger than its scaly body. Claws protruded from the farthest point of each, which the dragon used to destroy anything that came into its flight path. Every few seconds, a stream of flames shot from its gaping jaws, causing the trees around them to explode in a torrent of fire and sparks. The Falcon was screaming for Deke to hold on. Deke didn't quite understand why a bird was talking to him, but at that moment he didn't care.

"We must make the waterfall, it's our only chance!" the Falcon screamed.

Deke could see the waterfall in the distance. There was a long way to go, and the dragon was gaining ground. It was relentless in its bid to destroy them, and soon they would have to leave the cover of the now burning forests.

The Falcon carried Deke between the last of the trees that would provide them cover. They were now flying in the open air. The dragon roared and spewed an orb of flames so large it covered the entire sky behind them. The air became almost unbearably hot as the beast's fiery breath closed in upon them and Deke braced himself in preparation for what was to come. A loud hissing noise startled Deke causing him to lose his grip. He hurtled toward the ground enveloped in a thick fog. Deke didn't see the boy who appeared in front of him in time to stop himself from crashing into him.

Deke sat up and took in his surroundings. The fog still made it difficult to see. In minutes, he realized that wasn't what it was at all, but steam caused by the dragon's fire striking the waterfall. The Falcon had used the passage behind it as an escape route. The hissing noise had merely been the sound of the fire screaming its last breath as the water devoured it.

"We made it!" Deke shouted.

"Yes, barely," Deke heard someone answer.

Deke turned and stared at the boy he'd crashed into. The boy looked the same age as he and was roughly the same size. His eyes were an ashen grey unlike Deke's which were blue. His hair was to his shoulders and was a sandy blond color. The boy was covered in bruises and cuts and had a noticeable gash on his forehead over his right eye.

"Where is the Falcon?" Deke enquired while backing away not quite sure what to expect next.

"The Falcon is gone," the boy replied.

"Who are you?" Deke nervously asked.

"I'm your Paladin. My name is Deodatus, but you can call me Deo for short."

Deke had no idea what a Paladin was and was sure he'd never had one before.

"My Paladin, what is that?" Deke, asked.

"In short Deke a Paladin is another name for a protector, a defender or guardian angel. I have been at your side since you were born."

Deke just stared at the boy. He was obviously daft.

"It's complicated Deke, but just because you couldn't see me doesn't mean I wasn't there. You'll now be seeing things you've never seen before; perhaps things you only imagined existed. You've much to learn."

"More like much to understand about what just happened," Deke thought. The monster in the field, the incident in the cave, his father appearing out of nowhere, a falcon that talked and a dragon whose only purpose was to burn him alive.

"What exactly is happening, where am I and how did I get here?" Deke angrily shouted.

"Deke, I will explain everything to you, but right now you must trust me. We have to go. The dragon, Phanthus will be alerting ground patrols as we speak. This place is no longer safe."

Deke yelled in frustration. "I'm not going anywhere! I want to know where I am!"

"You're in Rhol, Deke. Now quickly, follow me."

Chapter Six

The clouds soaked up the last remaining sunlight making the evening sky radiate in a brilliant orange. When lines of red began to form on the horizon, Phanthus knew it would be dark in a matter of moments. This wouldn't have bothered him generally, but on this day he knew that the sooner the darkness came, the sooner he would have to face Solharn, the Dark Angel.

Solharn would not be pleased when Phanthus conveyed the message that the little human had escaped him. In all of his years on Rhol, he had never seen a creature such as the one that had saved the boy. In the end, it wouldn't matter. Solharn wouldn't accept any excuse. Still, Phanthus would have to report something.

He was pondering this when he caught a glimpse of Kaltaures soldiers scouring the ground near a fallen village. By the sight of the smoldering lumber strewn about, Phanthus surmised the attack must have taken place that morning. Phanthus watched as they scoured the village for anyone that may have survived their attack. What vile creatures he thought. They had no regard for the fallen. A true warrior respected even the death of his enemies.

Ω

Leal was located on the outskirts of the Valley of Aura. It was a beautiful village, surrounded by several miles of field and dense forest. Its quaint streets were lined with log houses built from trees in the neighboring woods. Pipher grass surrounded the area, kept short by several hundred Garin, which freely roamed the fields. Garin were small creatures, but with unusually wiry hair, that was bluish grey. Their tails were longer than their bodies, and they liked to use them as a whip on predators, or for that matter, any unsuspecting person whom they found to be annoying. They were used mainly for grooming the fields. Because of the Pipher grass, their milk was a light blue color. It was quite tasty but not easy to come by. The Garin were very irritable. Most Lealians preferred to drink water rather than endure the sting of their tails.

Colorful wild flowers of all shapes and sizes grew in and around Leal from the farthest fields to the doorsteps of their homes. The Garin didn't like the taste of them, which was fine with the Lealians since the Garin helped themselves to everything else.

In the middle of the village stood a tall building which had been erected centuries ago by Lealian masons. It was said that every rock used to construct its hallowed walls was blessed before having been carefully positioned into place. It was a sacred temple to the Lealian's and comfortably housed their entire village.

Lealians were different than most other inhabitants of Rhol. They had a life span of five hundred years or more and that had allowed them to gain great knowledge over the years. Their populace was not large, for a Lealian woman could have only one child in her lifetime. Because their numbers were small the Lealians had an unwavering loyalty to one another; there was no bickering between them, no stealing, and no unfaithfulness. They lived together, helped each other, and they tolerated no disrespect.

They were peaceful people willing to help anyone in need, but when provoked they were fierce fighters. Over the centuries they had fought in many wars to protect the world they lived in. With those wars came a profound knowledge of life that was passed down to their children, who passed it on to theirs. The Lealians were famous archers and swordsmen who handcrafted all their weapons. Bows and arrows were made from Orler trees indigenous to their village. The lumber of an Orler tree was the most sought after wood in Rhol, not only durable but strong. Many believed it contained magical powers. The tree itself was small, never growing more than eight feet tall and a few inches around. In many parts of Rhol, the Orler tree was thought to be extinct, but the Lealians had nurtured several over the centuries and hidden them throughout the forests of Rhol.

Even after the kingdom fell, the Lealians maintained the utmost loyalty to Queen Elissa, the ruler of Rhol. While many other inhabitants of Rhol hid far and abroad, the Lealians continued to wage war against Solharn. Even after Solharn created the black plague, killing thousands, the Lealians had refused to surrender in their bid to defeat him. They were mighty warriors who instilled terror into anyone who would fight for the Dark Angel. Solharn created the black plague, in the hopes of diminishing their numbers, but it was not to be for the Lealians were immune from it.

Not a Lealian living today would ever forget the day they were told to retreat. It was not in a Lealian's heart to sheath their weapons while a war still raged on, but they would be forced to do just that. Solharn's power was becoming too great. Queen Elissa knew she would not be able to sustain her Rule much longer. With this in mind, she protected the Lealian village by surrounding it with an impenetrable force. She ordered the Lealians never to leave the boundaries of Leal until the time was right, lest it would be the end of Rhol. She did not explain how they would know when this time was, just that they would. The Lealians knew their Queen would be helpless without them and that Solharn would control their world. Despite this, they reluctantly obeyed her orders, for their faith in her words far outweighed their pride.

Their prediction held true. Without the Lealians Queen Elissa's armies were quickly dispersed, but before she was overtaken by the Dark Angel, she used the last of her powers to save what she could of Rhol. In doing so, she ordered the mighty Pegapires to retreat to Tamon where a second force field was created. The last and final field would protect a small portion of Solace and would become widely known as the Sacred Realm. It was a haven for any of the inhabitants of Rhol who could find their way to its doorsteps.

Without Queen Elissa, those who could not find shelter were helpless against Solharn's rage. They were ordered to follow him. Any who resisted had their villages burned and their lives terminated.

Many had refused and remained loyal to Queen Elissa, but this rebellion was short lived. Thousands were murdered in vicious attacks and thousands more suffered horrific deaths after falling ill from the black plague. The plague was a long, painful death. Anyone suffering from its ill effects was forced to endure endless days of crippling pain. The inflicted could be easily discerned for their skin would turn black and slowly wilt away from their body.

Eventually, after weeks of torment, they would meet a welcome death. The only one who could protect them against the plague was the very person who had created it. This alone persuaded many to join Solharn's ranks. Many were enslaved and compelled to serve him. Many others, less loyal to Queen Elissa, agreed to join his armies rather than become slaves in his quest to take over Rhol.

The Lealians had waited almost a decade for their chance to avenge Queen Elissa, but in that time they had become far too comfortable with their surroundings. Neither friend nor foe could penetrate the field that protected Leal and over time guard posts dwindled. Only a few remained, and they were housed only when the villagers entered the temple once a week to worship Rhol and Queen Elissa.

It was on this day of worship that Solharn had instructed the Kaltaures to attack. The Lealians were not yet aware that the force protecting their village was no longer. When the Kaltaures armies struck, the Lealians were unprepared. The few guards that had been posted in and around the temple were killed instantly by Kaltaures archers. The remainder of the village was trapped within the temple.

The Kaltaures army was relentless; they surrounded the temple and ran through the village burning down everything in sight.

Only Roland, an elder Lealian, had noticed the advance, which had allowed him the time to bar the temple door.

"Open the door Lealian or your whole town will burn to the ground," screamed Abednego, the feared leader of the Kaltaures army.

"We can see it is too late for that, Abednego," replied Roland. He would not get a response, and so he continued, attempting to delay the inevitable.

"What, surprised I know your name filth? I have fought many wars against you and your beloved Solharn. I would not soon forget the voice of the commander of the army that so cowardly follows the Dark Angel."

"Ah Roland, I thought you died bravely defending your Queen. It appears you survived after all and took refuge in Leal, leaving her to fight a losing battle. How does it feel to know the suffering others have endured, while for years you and your people have hidden safely away as if nothing is going on? And you call me a coward."

Roland did not reply. He had prepared himself for this day, the day Queen Elissa had foretold. He was quickly ushering his people to a gateway in the floor which led to an underground tunnel. Roland and a select few had dug the passageway over the many years of waiting. It would lead them to the Valley of Aura.

"Come to your senses, Roland. You will all die unless you and your people surrender. Solharn may show mercy and spare your pathetic lives. He still needs some slaves to complete his mission," Abednego gloated.

"The people of Leal would rather die than conform to the savage rule of Solharn."

"Then die you will." Abednego roared.

The Kaltaures began to ram the door and climb the walls of the temple. There would only be a few precious minutes to save as many of his people as he could.

"Quickly, quickly down the tunnel," Roland pleaded.

Roland knew that there was not enough time to get everyone to safety. The Kaltaures army had been quick in their attack and the door to the temple would soon be breached.

"Jayden, come quickly. You must go and lead our people to the Pegapires. The time which Queen Elissa foretold, has come."

"But father, what of you?"

"Jayden, I have taught you everything I know about Rhol. It is your time son. You must lead the Lealians. It is your destiny, not mine."

With that last bit of advice, Roland heard the temple door give way and quickly pushed his son down the tunnel.

"Father!" would be the last word he heard his son speak.

Roland quickly shut the gateway so the Kaltaures would not discover it.

The vicious assault on the remaining Lealians was relentless. The Lealians fought with all their strength, but with little weaponry, it only delayed the inevitable.

Roland deliberately positioned himself by the gateway so that when the tusks of the approaching Kaltaures soldier ripped through his body, he would fall in a forward motion covering the portal and blocking it from Kaltaures eyes.

He lay there for over an hour before he smiled and took his last breath. The gateway had not been detected, giving the Lealians a chance to live on.

"The Lealians are no more. Collect their valuables and report back to me!" Abednego screamed to his troops.

Ω

Abednego was pleased with himself at how easily he had exterminated the Lealians. It had taken less time to kill them than it had to collect their valued possessions. He smiled to himself, greedily looking at his new found riches, which his army had collected and piled before him.

His trance was broken as the ground beneath him trembled. Startled he looked up to find himself staring into the eyes of Phanthus.

"To what do I owe the pleasure, Phanthus?" Abednego snorted.

"Commander!" a Kaltaures soldier yelled.

A sly grin appeared upon the dragon. "So Abednego, you still waste time over the possessions and baubles of others, instead of concentrating on the task at hand."

"I was promised wealth and power when the Dark Angel requested my armies fight by his side and with my task completed, I will reap the benefits," Abednego chortled.

"Ah, yes your task to eliminate the Lealians. Successful I presume?"

"Commander!" a soldier panted while running up behind Abednego.

"Shut up fool; I am busy!"

"But Sir," the soldier stammered.

"Silence!" Abednego roared.

"Since you ask, Phanthus, yes very successful and with little effort, I might add," Abednego cockily retorted.

Phanthus was still holding his coy grin as he turned away to look at the ruins. "Am I to understand that you easily defeated the

Lealians, a proud race of ferocious warriors who have fought together for centuries?"

"We took them by surprise. They did not stand ….." Abednego did not finish his sentence.

"Sir, in the temple," the trembling soldier tried to explain.

"Spit it out you fool!"

"Sir, we found a tunnel. Their leader Roland fell on top of it when he died. Sir, we did not see it until we were searching him for valuables," the soldier stuttered while looking down at his feet.

Abednego screamed in anger lopping the soldier's head off with his sword.

"After them, you idiots! Send the Ralcriff down the tunnel!"

While the Kaltaures troops stumbled around trying to gather themselves, Abednego could hear Phanthus laughing.

"You are a fool Abednego. Did you even think to count the bodies before gathering their possessions? Perhaps you would have discovered that there were not enough to account for the entire village. You misjudged the Lealians. By now, if they have not already made it to wherever the tunnel leads, they will certainly be ready for any advance you make. They are masters of weaponry and warfare. You will not find them, and for that, you will answer to Solharn."

With that, Phanthus roared and flew off. He was quite pleased that he was not the only one who would have to face the wrath of the Dark Angel.

CHAPTER SEVEN

Jayden heard the slam of the door followed by the sound of a lock snapping shut. Now there was no way to help his father and the Lealians who had been left behind. The thought of how they would meet their end made him cringe. Many, who had chosen to stay back and fight, were his friends. With a heavy heart, he walked in silence, leading the survivors down the tunnel that he knew all too well. When the tunnel became damp, and drops of water began to fall from the ceiling like rain, he knew they were passing under the River of Juant.

When thick, twisting roots almost blocked their passageway he knew they were under the Forests of Selmont. He was aware of every landmark throughout the long narrow tunnel for over the years he had been down here many times. His father had insisted that every time they walked it, he call out where he was the moment he was asked. Back then, he had thought it just a game to pass the time of having to walk the tunnel which stretched well over fifty miles. He knew better now. It had been his father's plan all along to prepare him for this day when he would have to lead his people to the Valley of Aura.

Jayden was young for a Lealian, a mere ninety-eight years old and now he was the leader of these people whether he was ready or not. His family had ruled their small village for hundreds of years, and his father and fathers before him had taught their son's everything they needed to know about warfare, creatures both good and evil, different worlds and most importantly about Rhol itself.

He could not be sure how long they would have until the Kaltaures discovered the gateway. Jayden estimated they would need about a ten-hour head start to reach the first depot safely. They had food and weapons stored there in the event something like this happened. More importantly, once they reached the first depot, they could collapse the part of the tunnel in which they already travelled, making it impossible for anyone to pursue them further.

Many may have felt reassured at this prospect, but Jayden's father had taught him well. He knew that if the Kaltaures discovered the tunnel, they would surely send the Ralcriff after them. Ralcriff were particularly vile creatures. Their hair was black as were their eyes. Each Ralcriff had a full mane of poisonous quills capable of killing an inflicted individual within a day. Their teeth were razor sharp. Upper and lower fangs protruded from their steel trap like jaws, and when they penetrated a person's flesh, escape from their grasp was nearly impossible. Very few had ever escaped a Ralcriff attack and those who had; it was at the expense of a limb. They were killing machines bred for the sole purpose of tasting blood.

Ralcriff used fear as a tactic in their hunt, letting their victims know well in advance that they were coming. Their long ghostly howl was very effective for that. It would pierce your very soul and render the less trained, immobilized in terror. If that wasn't enough Ralcriff could travel five times faster than the Kaltaures.

Jayden hoped they wouldn't have to worry about the Ralcriff. He could smell the gas seeping through the soil and knew they were passing under the Mourning Sands. They were only about three hours from the depot. Nevertheless, Jayden summoned one of the Lealians to speak with him in private.

"Oisin, you are by far the fastest Lealian I know. I need you to take two men and get to the Depot. Collect as many weapons as you can carry and return as quickly as you can."

"Does it have to be men Jayden? Kaelyn is as fast as they come."

"Anybody, whom you choose Oisin, but make haste."

Without another word, Oisin collected Kaelyn and a young male named Palvoy and ran toward the depot.

Jayden could feel someone tugging on his shirt and looked down to see a small boy. "Sir, what is that awful smell? It is horrid."

Jayden grinned. "It is just the smell of Rhol letting off steam in the form of gas, lad. It will soon pass."

With that, the boy grimaced, pinched his nose and stormed back into the crowd of Lealians walking behind him.

Jayden had not told the boy everything, but then even he wasn't sure whether the smell was what he surmised it to be; rotting bodies.

Based on what his father had told him about the Mourning Sands, it was certainly possible. They were named for the lost souls that succumbed to its alluring setting. It was a pure spectacle of nature. Set in between hills of rock and swamps that were unfit for any living soul, the Mourning Sands provided the welcoming illusion of sandy beaches and fresh water along with a single tree for shade. But the beaches were alive. In fact, they were not beaches at all but the larvae of an insect known as a Mortynt. What looked like water was really a thick greenish-blue gas. What appeared to be waves rolling up onto the sands were merely thousands of Mortynts scurrying through the gas and back to their waiting place. A living creature entering the Mourning Sands was walking to its death. There was no escape. The Mortynt's larvae relied on living flesh for their metamorphosis and dead flesh for nourishment. Once you walked over them, they entered your body, unnoticed. The further you walked the more you ingested. By the time you made it to the tree, blisters would be forming on your skin, and each blister contained the Mortynt's pupae.

Unable to see or walk, the unfortunate victims would usually cling to the tree, screaming in agony, before the blisters would begin to burst, producing adult Mortynts. The victims would die shortly after only to have their dead flesh stripped from their bones by the remaining larvae.

It amazed Jayden how something could start life in such a grotesque way but then finish it in such splendor and beauty, for as adults the Mortynts were stunning to look at and quite harmless. They had six wings, three on either side of their small furry brown bodies. The female's wings were black with a chartreuse dot on the end of each. The males were covered in every color you could imagine, all in vivid stripes and circles.

Jayden's thoughts were interrupted by a faint sound in the distance. He immediately held his arm up signaling the rest of his people to be silent. There it was, a faint but clear ghostly howl coming from down the tunnel and they still had no weapons.

Jayden immediately began to organize the Lealian's. They did not have much time. The Ralcriff would be coming from the

32

rear, and so he placed the women and children at the front of the lines. All the Lealian men were trained warriors. Jayden put the youngest males in the middle, for they would have the stamina to fight a long battle should the Ralcriff make it past the rear of the lines. The back line would be where the eldest Lealians would be placed for they were experienced in all sorts of combat and would have the advantage in close quarters. He positioned himself in front of the elders because he had been taught to lead his people.

Jayden turned and spoke. "Lealians, hear me. The Ralcriff are upon us, pick up your pace and listen to my instructions. When I give the word, the elders will stop while the women, children and young warriors forge ahead. Young heroes of Leal, should the Ralcriff reach you, know that we did all we could to stop them. It will be up to you to fight for the lives of the women and children."

A young warrior named Talen interrupted "Jayden, please reconsider. You have no weapons; the Ralcriff will slaughter you. Let us all join and have the women and children forge on. There is strength in numbers."

"Very well spoken Talen; however every fight has a strategy, and this is our best given the circumstances. We must have as many survive as possible and if we must die to protect the lifeline of the Lealian's then so be it. Now let's move."

With that, the Lealians quickened their pace. They made it about another mile before Jayden heard the howling coming from just around the bend. It was time.

"Now!" Jayden yelled.

Alongside Jayden, the elders turned to face the Ralcriff. They knew they were simply barricades put in place to give the others a chance to make it to the Depot. With no weapons, they had no hope. They stood proudly, however, knowing the delay might give the young warriors a chance to retrieve arms and save the remaining Lealians.

The first two Ralcriff rounded the corner. Saliva dripped from their jowls at the sight of the Lealians. Their ghostly howl signaled to the Ralcriff advancing behind them that they had found their prey. Jayden immediately began to advance on them, but the first strike would not be his. Six of the elders jumped in front of him and tackled the Ralcriff. It was an honorable gesture that cost them their lives in a matter of seconds. The Ralcriff stood proudly over their kill, their thick fur matted with the blood of Jayden's brothers. They were joined by six more, and several others moved in behind them. They stood and stared at the Lealians as if looking for fear in their eyes. After finding none, they bound toward them snarling, with their chiseled teeth gleaming in the torch light of the tunnel.

Jayden heard a whistle of sorts and a slight breeze brushed by his ear. A Ralcriff was upon him causing them both to come crashing to the ground. Its foul breath turned his stomach. The weight of the beast made it hard to breathe. He instinctively lunged forward throwing the dead creature to the side. Blood was spurting everywhere. More Ralcriff began to let out high pitched whines before dropping dead to the ground, feet from where he lay. He could see that Orler arrows were what caused their demise. The whistle he had heard had been an arrow flying by in search of its target. It had found its mark with no time to spare.

Oisin's hand appeared in front of him, and as Jayden grabbed it, Oisin pulled him to his feet.

"Oisin, you have returned. Well done!"

Oisin passed Jayden a sword. "Jayden, we came with all we could carry. I left Kaelyn and Palvoy at the rear to shoot Orler Arrows for as long as they lasted. I am afraid there were less than sixty at the depot. We could carry only five swords each. The thirteen elders standing behind you now have one, along with you and me."

"Oisin, you have done us proud."

The Ralcriff continued to fall lifelessly to the ground as the Orler arrows twisted and turned around the Lealian warriors striking the beasts down. In the hands of a Lealian, the magic contained within the Orler tree came alive. A Lealian needed only to think of their intended target, and the Orler arrows would find their mark every time.

"Keep moving back toward the depot until the Orler arrows have run out. Once that time comes we will fight with our swords. If one man drops at the hands of a Ralcriff than the next will pick up his sword until victory is ours." Jayden instructed.

The Lealians' faces were beaded with sweat as they edged back toward the Depot. They all knew the Orler arrows would not last. It was not the sweat of fear but that of anticipation. They were born to fight, to protect their heritage.

Their gap to safety was closing. Palvoy and Kaelyn continued to fire their arrows at a rapid pace. The Ralcriff stood no chance while the arrows lasted.

Jayden was sure that the young warriors would have led the women and children to the safety of the Depot by now. They themselves had only a short distance to go. Jayden had carefully counted the Ralcriff that had dropped to their demise. It would soon be time to fight with swords. As quick as the thought had crossed his mind, he heard Kaelyn yelling from the rear.

"Shooting the last two arrows!"

Two Ralcriff dropped in front of Jayden, and the fighting tactics changed dramatically. Jayden took the head off the first one that neared his men. He was one of the most skilled swordsmen in Leal; his father had spent countless hours teaching him close quarter swordsmanship.

He had dropped another three by the time the Lealian Warriors suffered their first casualty. Many more would follow as the Ralcriff continued their relentless attack. It wouldn't stop the Lealians though. They continued to strike out at the Ralcriff. If one warrior got tired another took up his sword; if one fell, another would pick his sword up, seamlessly continuing the fight.

Jayden glanced at the walls of the tunnel. The sparkle of trite stone glimmered back at him. This told him they were less than one hundred yards away from safety. It was time to save as many of his people as he could, and with that in mind, he spoke.

"Anyone without a sword in hand, turn now and get to the depot! We will hold the Ralcriff off. Close the gate and collapse the tunnel if a Ralcriff comes within striking distance."

Lealians never backed away from a fight, but they did not question Jayden's authority. Knowing he had the Lealians' best interest at heart they reluctantly obeyed.

Fifteen warriors fought the never ending onslaught of Ralcriff as they backed their way to the depot. By the time the Depot was in sight only three of them had remained alive, Jayden, Oisin, and Aiden, who was one of the most respected of the elder warriors in Leal.

Jayden looked at them admiringly. Both were covered in blood and gore. Aiden had use of only one arm, and Oisin had several Ralcriff quills stuck into his side, no doubt from when he had tackled one to save Jayden.

Jayden himself had suffered the wrath of the Ralcriff quills and could feel them protruding from his neck. Jayden looked ahead to see more Ralcriff running toward them. With a heavy heart and a nod to both of them, he gave a final order.

"Collapse the tunnel!"

CHAPTER EIGHT

Deo led Deke deeper into the cavern; he gave off a glow which provided just enough light to see in the depths of the tunnel. Although Deke was still unsure of his surroundings and who Deo was, he followed him obediently. Deo was a welcome friend considering what he had gone through in the last few hours.

At Deo's insistence, they walked in silence. The cavern walls were laced in minerals of some sort that sparkled as they passed. After a prolonged period of walking in silence Deke's imagination began to take over. The crystals became thousands of eyes glaring at him as he passed. What were once stationary towering cones of molten rock hanging from the ceiling now appeared to come alive, jumping out in front of him.

It made Deke nervous, and he madly patted his pockets for any sign of the spearhead he had pulled from his cheek. For some reason, it gave him some comfort. When he felt a lump in his pocket, he sighed in relief. Although he didn't know exactly why the arrowhead was so important, he felt some sort of energy when he held it. Unfortunately, as he gazed at the object, it also reminded him of the gash in his cheek, which in turn reminded him of the searing pain emitting from it. Deke placed the arrowhead safely back in his pocket hoping this would relieve the pain. It didn't.

After several tense hours of walking through the winding corridors, they came to a dead end. Deo faced the wall and began to chant in a quiet sort of grumble "Solert a piony du sa trquil."

The wall in front of them became slightly transparent. Deo walked toward it motioning Deke to follow him. It was a strange sensation as he placed his hand through the wall. It felt like he had dipped it into a cold stream, sending a shivering sensation up his arm. When he sidled slowly through his body became relaxed and revived, so much, so he felt almost like he was floating. In mere seconds he was on the other side staring in disbelief at what surrounded him.

He was standing on the edge of a meadow of bright green grass that swayed slowly back and forth as if dancing for him in the wind. A lone tree, which Deke could not identify, stood in the middle of the meadow. The tree's trunk was at least fifty feet wide, and it stood hundreds of feet high. Its long branches reached out over the entire rock ceiling and draped down over its walls almost touching the ground again. The leaves were a brilliant red. He could see an abundance of black fruit, about the same size as apples slightly hidden behind almost every leaf.

A stream of water flowed steadily from a hole in the wall of the cavern and fell several feet into a flowing stream that cut its way through the grass and disappeared under the trunk of the tree.

On the far side of the cavern, beyond the creek, the grass appeared shorter and well groomed. A small village carved into the stone wall stood out to him only because he could see hundreds of holes, some with no windows and others with brilliant stained glass colored in red, yellow and blue. The windows glimmered in the light which came from thousands of creatures the size of hummingbirds that glowed, a brilliant blue. The creatures flew freely around the cavern, stopping periodically for what appeared to be a rest on the branches of the tree.

Deke looked at Deo noticing that he no longer had any cuts or scratches and that the large gash in his forehead had disappeared. Deke noticed his cheek had completely healed as well. He felt revived.

"Deo, what is happening, why…?"

"I have much to explain to you Deke, and I am sure you have many questions for me. Let's walk."

As he walked alongside Deo, his mind flooded with questions, but he had no time to ask them before Deo began to speak.

"You noticed that we no longer have any injuries. The Wall of Solace heals anyone or anything that passes through it. You are in Solace, a hidden realm of Rhol, one of only three that remain in this world. The amulet you pulled from your cheek, please take it from your pocket."

Deke stopped and looked at Deo suspiciously "How did you know what I pulled from my cheek and for that matter, how did you come to know it is in my pocket?" Deke asked abruptly.

"Because Deke, it was I who pushed you down onto it, watched you pull it from your cheek and then in the cave, place it in your pocket. I am sorry. It wasn't my intention to have it penetrate your cheek, but then it did work out quite nicely." Deo laughed.

"Quite nicely?" Deke shouted "I was chased and quite nearly killed by some vile creature that pursued me through the woods and onto the cornfield. The creature attacked me, and I ended up here, wherever here is. You were nowhere in sight."

"I was there Deke. It was I who guided you through the woods to the cornfield and then pushed you so you would land on the amulet and hopefully see it. It was your only chance of escaping the Kaltaures that pursued you."

"The Kaltaures, what on earth is that? And I think I might have seen you running beside me, don't you?" Deke exclaimed.

"No Deke, as I explained to you earlier, I am your Paladin. Just because you didn't see me does not mean I wasn't there."

"Oh yes," Deke said. "I remember, you are my guardian angel, you have been there since I was born. Then why can I see you now?"

"Please, Deke. Let me explain. Every human on earth has a Paladin. There are many names for us, but there is a simpler explanation. You do believe that you have a soul, yes?"

"Of course," Deke replied.

"Well, you are right. Every human has an inner soul but what you don't realize is that there is an outer soul that exists as well. Simply put, I am your external soul. I cannot exist without you, and without me, you would wander aimlessly throughout eternity."

"I may not know a lot of things, but a soul comes from within someone's body. You cannot see a soul, yet you appear as I do." Deke responded looking Deo over suspiciously.

"And how would you know what a soul looks like, Deke? Have you ever seen one? Did you even know for sure that you had one, let alone two?"

Deke thought about this momentarily. He had always assumed that a soul was not visible, but then again that is only what he had been taught.

Deo sighed "You see Deke this is where it gets a little confusing. Your beliefs were partially right. On earth, you are not meant to see me, but I am part of you, and I protect you. That is how it is designed. Souls are made up of energy. Your inner soul is protected by your body. The body materializes around your soul taking on its appearance. The outer soul is one with the Balance, the Universe. The external soul remains as such; it has no body. While you sleep, it comes alive within your dreams and helps you evolve by learning things beyond the comprehension of the inner soul. This will help you understand what lies ahead when your body dies, and our souls become one. You can see me now because when we left our world, my function changed. We're no longer guided by the laws of physics that encompass Earth. When we arrived here, I became embodied. That is why you can see me. Should, we ever return to earth, this body will die, and things will be as they once were. While we are here our souls will still function together, just in two different bodies."

"If what you say is true then where were you when I was being chased in the cave, and then trapped on the cliff with nowhere to go except to plummet to an untimely death! And where were you when a Falcon appeared out of nowhere and saved me from being burned to death by a rather large dragon!" Deke asked rather annoyed.

"Have you already forgotten the part about falling off that cliff with your father," Deo answered.

Deke was stunned. "What, how could you know that? I thought I had imagined …"

Deo smiled "Deke, please give me a moment to explain, I was there. As I said to you earlier, I am part of you. The amulet you hold, please take it from your pocket."

Deke hesitantly pulled the arrowhead from his pocket and looked at it.

"The amulet you hold is that of Queen Elissa, the ruler of this world and while you possess it, you will have abilities that no one else has, including the capacity to transform your Paladin. In essence, I will change into whatever you think of, as long as it is a real living being or creature and it is something you have seen with your own eyes. You must be aware though, that the larger you make the creature or, the longer I am in a transformation state, the greater the strain you will be placing upon yourself. It will drain your energy, making you weaker and weaker. I am sure you feel completely exhausted right now. That is because of the energy you used to transform me earlier. It takes time to master the art of turning me into another being at any given moment, but it will happen in extremely stressful situations."

Deke stared blankly at Deo as he continued "When you arrived in the cave, you were quite rightfully stressed after being chased by the Kaltaures. For whatever reason the cave made you think of bats, which in turn made me transform into one. I was trying to stop you from leaving the cave as I knew you were in grave danger. That is when, not knowing who or what I was, you struck me in the head causing me to lose consciousness momentarily. I could not stop you from running out of the cave directly into the path of Phanthus, the dragon you mentioned earlier. When I finally got to you, you were thinking of home, specifically of your father. I began to transform into him when you first saw me. As Phanthus' ball of fire was nearly upon you, there was no time to do anything but grab you and jump. It is why I told you to think of your Falcon, which you did. As the image of your Falcon filled your mind, I changed from your father to the Falcon and ultimately flew us from the Valley of Solace to here. When we passed through the falls, your anxiety level decreased, and I appeared as I normally would."

Deke stared at Deo in disbelief "Well, why did you not say something while we were in the cave? It might have made things easier," he exclaimed.

"And how would you have reacted Deke, talking to a giant bat?"

Deke thought for a second and agreed that might not have been the best strategy.

"I know it's not easy to comprehend Deke, but people believe in many things that cannot be seen. For instance, people believe in the Creator or as you know him, God. You must have read about or even seen people escape impossible situations without any other explanation other than a miracle, right?"

"Yes."

"Well, in those situations, is it so hard to believe that it was the person's Paladin that stepped in and helped save them? The outer soul is one with your inner soul; they're connected. It becomes simple for an individual's Paladin to change that person's path or thought process because essentially we are part of that person." Deo explained.

"Why couldn't my parents' Paladins have helped them, then? You must have been there if you're always with me. What happened?" Deke demanded. He was becoming visibly upset.

"Deke, not every situation is the same. If their Paladins could have helped, they would have; if I could have helped your parents, I would have. You cannot blame yourself for what happened. That was your parent's fate, and nobody can change that."

Deke could have continued asking questions, but he realized he would only become more upset and right now there more pressing issues. His parents were dead. Nothing could change that.

"How is it you know so much about this world?" Deke asked.

"The soul is a window to the universe, Deke. The outer soul has a greater understanding of what lies beyond than the inner soul. It is designed this way so that on the day a living being passes on and their souls become one they will have a full understanding of what life was and what it is going to be. This maintains a balance between life and the afterlife. I have travelled to this world many times while you slept. You are in a unique situation Deke. You will learn more about this world and others much before your time."

Deke thought he might know the answer, but he asked anyway "How and why am I here Deo and why are so many trying to harm me?"

"It's because you hold the amulet Deke. That makes you a very dangerous person to Solharn. I cannot give you all the answers you need, but once the Sacred Amulet of Rhol was taken from Queen Elissa, she became powerless against Solharn. The amulet must be returned to her. With that amulet Deke, you can save Rhol and help stop Solharn's depraved plan. It is the amulet that chose you and brought you to Rhol, and if Rhol has any chance of survival, it is now in your hands."

"But who is Solharn?" Deke asked.

"He is a Dark Angel, and he is pure evil. He and his armies quite nearly destroyed Rhol and enslaved the inhabitants but your questions are better answered by Kiran, Queen Elissa's closest confidant. We will go to her now."

42

By now they had crossed the river and were closing in on the small village. They were almost there when Deo turned abruptly and began to walk toward a rock wall.

"Where are we going?" Deke asked.

"To see Kiran, just follow me and don't worry," Deo said.

Deke followed Deo around a small tree that was growing from a cave that tunneled through the rock.

"That's an Orler tree, Deke. Remember it," Deo said.

Deke looked at the tree. It was a little unusual, and certainly not the most appealing thing he had ever seen. It grew straight up and down without a bend or branch on the trunk itself. The tree stood about seven feet high and was a foot around. It had no bark, and the dark grain of its wood glimmered as if coated in varnish. Straight spiraling black branches flowed from the top of the tree and were covered in purplish orange leaves which appeared much too large for such a small tree.

"I don't know how I could forget it," Deke whispered under his breath.

Deke could see the end of the tunnel almost as soon as he entered it. It opened up into a large cavern that appeared to be an extension of the hidden realm. The space was lit with lanterns, and in the middle of the cavern, something caught his eye, stopping him in his tracks. There was a building which looked like a modest log cottage. Long grass wrapped in bundles appeared to have been used to make the roof. Large rocks substituted for what might be called a fence and lined a flagstone walkway. The walkway stretched a few hundred feet or so, leading up to the door of the cottage. Smoke slowly billowed out of a stone chimney that jutted from the roof, but it was not the cottage that had him so awestruck; it was a magnificent creature, unlike anything he had ever seen before standing to the left of it.

Looking at Deke, Deo laughed "It is one of the most beautiful animals in Rhol, Deke Brolin, and perhaps one of the most dangerous. That is a Pegapire."

CHAPTER NINE

The last thing Jayden recalled was being struck in the head and Aiden yelling something to him before he lost consciousness. When he awoke, he was looking into the face of Oisin.

"Oisin, how did we come to be here?" Jayden asked while slowly sitting up.

"It was Aiden. Just before the Ralcriff reached us, he struck you in the head knocking you to the ground. He said it was not your time, and ordered me to drag you to the depot. Palvoy and Kaelyn saw what happened and ran out to assist me."

Oisin looked away from Jayden's eyes, and as tears slowly rolled down his cheeks, he continued, "I should have stayed with Aiden. If I had not seen it with my own eyes, I would not have believed it! With one arm he kept the Ralcriff from passing. Even with one tearing into his leg he still stood steady, slicing away at the hideous creatures. When he finally lost his balance and fell to his knees, he managed to swing his sword in an upward motion severing all four legs off a Ralcriff that attempted to leap over him. The Ralcriff fell within inches of you, unable to move. The last thing I heard him scream before the tunnel collapsed was "Rhol.""

Jayden placed his hand upon Oisin's shoulder, "My friend, I know how you must feel inside. It is not in a Lealian's heart to retreat or to leave another behind, but you must remember it was Aiden's wish. Aiden was a mighty warrior but a Lealian first. He has fought many battles to protect his people and Rhol. Aiden knew that we would never have left him there, and by knocking me unconscious, he gave you no choice. Aiden knew how important it was to save as many Lealians as possible, so in standing here, you have not disgraced him. You have honored him."

Jayden stood and raised his sword, "Let us honor Aiden and all the fallen Lealians who fought proudly for Rhol and whom we will never forget." Jayden was sure the cheer that followed must have been heard in the Valley of Aura itself.

"Our battle is just beginning. Tonight we will rest. Tomorrow we must forge on to the Valley of Aura and summon the Pegapires!"

Noticing the quills protruding from Jayden and Oisin, Kaelyn interrupted. "But Jayden, how long will it take to reach Aura from here?"

"We are about twenty miles in with another thirty or, so to go. I would say that it should take around fifteen hours," Jayden responded.

"But the quills, they are poisonous….." Kaelyn began.

Jayden cut her off. "Rest and fill your stomachs; we have a long journey."

Jayden found a place away from the others and sat down. He was exhausted but knew sleep would not quickly come for him. He looked up and saw Kaelyn walking towards him closely followed by Oisin. Jayden had expected Kaelyn to find him, but not this quickly. He knew what she was thinking before she spoke.

"Jayden, maybe some Lealians' are not aware that the quills are poisonous, but I know you are."

"Yes, I am well aware of the poison the quills inject their host with," Jayden said.

"Then you are aware that in a twenty-four hour period, twenty-three by now, you and Oisin will die a painful and horrible death. We must leave now and get to Aura to summon the Pegapires. They are your only hope. They can get you to the Wall of Solace in time!" Kaelyn exclaimed.

"What would you have me do, Kaelyn? The people are exhausted and hungry. Some have wounds to tend to, and others can hardly walk. Leaving now would inevitably result in some of their deaths, and I will not risk several lives for the sake of two."

Oisin, who had been listening intently stepped in, "He is right Kaelyn. It is not worth the risk."

"What is wrong with you two?" Kaelyn shouted. "You are every bit as important as anyone else. Oisin has shown his worth today, and the Lealians' need someone to lead them."

"Someone will take my place, perhaps you Kaelyn," Jayden retorted.

Kaelyn was now visibly angry, "The poison must already be taking effect, so you will just sit there and wait to die! You raise your sword in honor of Aiden who died to get us here, who died to save your lives. You give an eloquent speech to Oisin, who left Aiden so he could save you, but it means nothing! You don't honor Aiden; you dishonor him."

"Kaelyn!" Oisin shouted. "Mind who you are speaking to..."

"It is alright, Oisin. Kaelyn is right," said Jayden calmly.

"Kaelyn, take Oisin and Palvoy and leave. Bring food and water. You will need it if you are to make Aura by morning. You will know you are near Aura when you get to the next depot. It is one mile from the end of the tunnel. The depot contains additional weapons. Be sure to arm yourselves with as many Orler arrows as you can carry. I am not sure what will be waiting for you when you exit the tunnel and enter the Valley of Aura."

"You must come with us, Jayden. You will die otherwise," Kaelyn implored.

"Kaelyn, you challenged me! You said that Aiden need not have died to save Oisin and me if we were not willing to save ourselves, but you also pointed out that the Lealians need someone to lead them. I have heeded your words. Oisin will fight for his life, and I will lead the Lealians to Aura ensuring their safety."

"That is not what I meant Jayden...," Kaelyn stopped herself. There was no further point in arguing.

"Let's go. We have no time to waste," Kaelyn grumbled, and with that, she departed with Oisin and Palvoy.

Jayden leaned back against the cool dirt walls of the tunnel, closed his eyes and fell into a deep sleep. It seemed like it had been only five minutes, but it was more like two hours when Jayden awoke with a start. A young boy and his mother were urging Jayden to eat.

"Please Jayden. I have made you a plate of food. You must eat," requested the mother who Jayden knew as Cordelia.

Jayden took the plate thanking her as she sat down beside him. "Let me remove the quills from your neck," Cordelia said.

Before Jayden could answer, she was already digging away at them as her young son eagerly watched.

Cordelia grimaced, "The quills are embedded deep Jayden. This will take some time."

"I don't think your boy will mind Cordelia. He seems amused," laughed Jayden.

"Keagan, do not bother Jayden," his mother scorned.

"It is quite alright, Cordelia. I would not have been much different at his age; Keagan, that is a fine name!"

That acknowledgement was all the encouragement the boy needed to blurt out the questions he had so patiently waited to ask, "Sir, I heard Kaelyn mention that we must go to the Valley of Aura to summon the Pegapires. I have never seen one, but I have heard they are magnificent animals. Can they actually fly? How many are there? What...?"

Jayden laughed, "Well, so many questions and I can understand why. They are extraordinary animals. The Pegapires are a proud breed, and they are fiercely loyal to the Lealians, as we are to them. Would you like to hear about them, the way my father told me?"

Keagan nodded his head up and down several times.

"Very well, then." Jayden chuckled.

"In ancient Rhol, the Pegapires were worshipped by all inhabitants. They are elegant creatures, ivory white in color. They resemble a horse, but they have white wings spanning twelve feet on either side of their long muscular bodies. Their wings are so strong that they can fly great distances in a matter of moments.

"The only other colors visible on the Pegapires are their long graceful tails and their eyes. Their tails are jet black. Their eyes are a bright yellow. It is said that their eyes can hypnotize any creature that gazes into them. Their hypnotic power enables the Pegapires to attack their enemies effortlessly, and leave them standing, staring into emptiness for eternity.

"The, Pegapires lived in Tamon, which is a beautiful valley surrounded by mountains. No man or woman has ever stepped foot in Tamon, except for a very few Lealians of whom one was my father. Tamon cannot be accessed by foot, only by flight. Over the years, many have tried to enter the Valley of Tamon, but they met their deaths from the freezing cold temperatures and unpredictable weather high in the mountains.

"My father once described Tamon to me. He said that the valley was lush and green, with abundant streams of crystal clear water. The streams flowed freely over small pebbles and sand, which always kept the water pure. Many Orler trees grew there protected from the ravages of people who would destroy them all, just for the chance of using their magical powers. I don't know whether my father was exaggerating or not, but he claimed there was one Orler tree in Tamon that was over forty feet high. He said that tree kept the strain of the Orler trees alive. I have never seen an Orler Tree even a quarter of that size, but my father rarely joked about such things."

The conversation brought many memories of Jayden's father rushing back to him, and it made him pause momentarily before continuing to describe the Pegapires for the boy.

"The Pegapires are ferocious fighters who have sharp jagged teeth which they often use in battle, swooping down over their enemy biting down and carrying them high above the ground before releasing them to plummet to their death. They are loyal only to those of good nature. Pegapires used to roam throughout Rhol in abundance. They had no natural predators and rarely fell to enemies in battle.

"When Solharn started the Great War in an effort to take over Rhol and defeat Queen Elissa many years ago, he was surprised at the loyalty the Pegapires had to the Queen.

"He was even more surprised by their ferocity and stamina in battle. After two years of steadily losing men to the Pegapires, it was said that he created the black plague specifically to eliminate them. The epidemic took its toll, and the Pegapires along with many inhabitants of Rhol suffered great losses. The Pegapires numbers dwindled from thousands to a few hundred and it was widely thought that they would soon be extinct.

"It was my grandfather, Corceran, who managed to save the last few hundred Pegapires. In his day, Corceran was the most powerful warrior in Leal. He fought many brave battles and he was admired throughout Rhol. Corceran's bravery and skill soon came to the attention of Palto, who was one of the most respected warriors within the Pegapires ranks. Corceran and Palto were destined to fight together and soon became battle companions.

"It was in the Great War of Aura that the alliance between the Lealians and the Pegapires was forged. Corceran and Palto were engaged in a ferocious battle with Solharn. Together they had slaughtered hundreds of Solharn's army. They were mounting a second attack when Corceran looked behind him to see Palto lying motionless on the ground. Three Kaltaures were approaching Palto, and Corceran ran toward his friend. When he realized he wouldn't make it in time, Corceran took his last three Orler arrows from his satchel and placed them on his bowstring.

"Firing them in one shot, the arrows found their mark ripping through the heads of the three Kaltaures, killing them instantly. The lifeless bodies of the Kaltaures fell on top of Palto, and one of their tusks ripped into his side causing a deep gash. When Corceran reached Palto, he threw the Kaltaures bodies aside and began to tend to his wound."

Jayden paused and continued the story trying his best to mimic his grandfather's voice, along with Palto's.

'You will be fine my old friend,' Corceran assured Palto.

"Very weakly Palto responded. 'It is not the wound that ails me, Corceran, but the plague. I cannot move and I will die shortly where I lie.'

"Corceran would hear nothing of it, 'No, no. It is not the plague Palto; you are too strong. This will not be your last battle.'

"Palto laughed. 'My friend, you have been a loyal and faithful companion for many years, and we have fought many battles together. You have saved my life many times, and I yours, but you cannot save me now. We will see each other again Corceran, but you will have many more battles to fight in this world first.'

"With that, Palto stopped breathing and Corceran screamed. In anger, he began to punch at one of the Kaltaures soldiers, whose life he had just taken. In doing so, he fatally wounded himself by slicing his wrist. Blood spurted from him and covered Palto. In a matter of seconds, Palto arose from the ground having no ill effects of the plague.

"Turning to Corceran, Palto said, 'How did you…,' but abruptly stopped himself as he looked down upon him.

"Corceran grimaced and managed a smile. 'It is fate Palto. My blood…, Lealians are immune to the plague. When mine mixed with your wound, it cured you my old friend, and for that, I am honored. If one man must die to save an entire race, it is well worth it. Go and save the rest of your kind Palto.'

"Before Palto could respond, Corceran died. All Palto could do was to honor his friend's last request. He flew all over Rhol spreading word of the cure to the suffering Pegapires. Because of Corceran, the Lealians managed to save the remainder.

"The mixtures of blood would form an undying loyalty between the Pegapires and the Lealians. In battle, a Lealian is the only race that is allowed to ride on the back of a Pegapire. Before this, no creature had ever even imagined such a thing.

"Their union was a formidable one, making them the most valued and respected warriors Rhol had ever seen. Unfortunately, by this time Queen Elissa's armies had been decimated by Solharn and he was well on his way to destroying the empire.

"It was then that Queen Elissa used the last of her power to create the Sacred Realms of Solace, Leal, and Tamon in the hope that Rhol would live on.

"Queen Elissa told my father back then that we would know when it was time to leave the Sacred Realm of Leal. I believe it was no coincidence that the protective force field disappeared today. It was the sign my father was waiting for. It makes me think that the one surrounding Tamon, the home of the Pegapires, is also gone. We have waited a decade to avenge Queen Elissa and Rhol, and that is why we must reunite with the Pegapires."

Jayden looked down at the boy whose eyes were wide in anticipation for the next part of the story. Jayden did not get the chance. Cordelia was ushering the boy away saying something about rest, and Jayden's eyes suddenly felt too heavy to keep open. As they shut, he thought of what awaited Oisin, Palvoy, and Kaelyn in the Valley of Aura.

CHAPTER TEN

Deke could not take his eyes away from the Pegapire, and as they drew closer to the rustic cottage, he began to hear a voice in his head.

"The holder of the amulet, it is an honor. We have waited a long time for your arrival."

Deke looked at Deo somewhat confused. "Did you say something?"

"It's the Pegapire, Deke. She speaks to you. The Pegapires can communicate through telepathy or by spoken word."

Deke turned to the Pegapire. Although it was a beautiful animal, its jagged teeth were a little intimidating. The only thing he could think of saying was, "I'm Deke, Deke Brolin."

"And I am Lorca, Deke. I am Kiran's protector. She has been eagerly awaiting you." With that Lorca led them the remainder of the way to the cottage.

"Come." Lorca motioned to the door with her nose.

Deke nodded and both he and Deo entered the humble cottage.

The cottage itself was much bigger inside than he would have thought, and was very tidy but rustic. The inside was planked in a gorgeous wood much like pine. Pictures of great cities, beautiful rivers and waterfalls adorned the walls. A small kitchen had pots and pans hanging from the planks of wood. The furniture was sparse, all but a few wooden chairs surrounded a large stone fireplace. To the left of the fireplace, an older woman of around eighty sat staring at the roaring fire. She seemed mesmerized by the licks of orange and blue flames crackling away as they devoured the wood.

Deo was the first to speak, "Kiran, we're here."

The woman stood and without saying a word walked across the floor toward them and stopped. She had tears in her eyes as if she had just been weeping. Deke was a little surprised when she suddenly reached out and hugged him.

"I am glad you found your way here safely Dietrich Brolin. We did not know what Solharn would have in store for you, but it seems his plan of attack has failed for now."

She released Deke from her embrace and spoke once again, "Oh my, where are my manners. I am sorry Dietrich. My name is Kiran. Please, we have much to talk about. You and Deo come and sit with me by the fire."

Kiran walked toward her chair with Deke and Deo following. Deke was still mulling over how Kiran could have possibly known his birth name of Dietrich. He never used it, and nobody aside from his mother ever called him by that name. That was usually when he was in trouble "Dietrich Jonathan Brolin, come here!" she would yell. When they were all seated Deke decided to ask Kiran how she knew his real name.

She did not really answer the question when she spoke, "I am sure you have many questions, Dietrich, some of which Deo has answered for you, and others...well, I am here to help you with."

"First and foremost, let me explain who I am," and with that, she leaned back in her chair and began to speak. Only the crackling of the fire interrupted her soft voice.

"I grew up in Rhol in the small mountain town of Charn. The town itself was quite quaint and was located at the top of Mount Sibileo. This is the second largest mountain in Rhol of course, next to Mount Kartago where Queen Elissa lived," Kiran seemed to fall into a trance as if remembering happier childhood times before clearing her throat and continuing.

"Sorry, what I was saying? Oh yes, Charn was my home. It might best be described as a fishing village where modest wooden houses surrounded a small mountain lake which we called Shimmer Lake. It was abundant with fish, as well as two of the almost extinct Balane. Oh, the Balane were a magnificent animal who lived in the depths of the lake but could also fly very short distances. Unfortunately for them, the nearest lake was a long distance away which is why I am quite sure they never left," Kiran laughed. Deke giggled along with her, not at what she had said, but because of the way Kiran laughed at her own joke.

"I am kidding of course. The Balane were probably the only ones who loved the lake more than I. I can remember many mornings waking up to find the lake smooth as glass, so much so that the reflection of the trees in the water almost looked as if another forest had suddenly sprung up overnight in front of you. At the far end of the lake, you could barely see the shore for the light mist that floated in the cool air. On mornings like those, the Balane would eventually appear. You could see them slowly floating across the water side by side, diving every once in a while for a taste of fresh fish. It was a spectacular sight. They were enormous animals stretching at least seventy feet long. Their glimmering black skin was only outdone by their red bellies, which they showed every time they did a roll in the water. This in turn also exposed their long black wings that looked almost painted on their bodies, perhaps because of the lack of use. When they came back around for another breath of air, their long curved necks would arch out of the water as if trying to taste the sky. So gentle a creature they were that, if I had any fish to offer, they would slowly swim right up to me and gently snatch the treat from my small hands, grumbling a long soft moan to thank me. Personally, I thought they were more curious than hungry. They could have caught ten times the fish I offered them with a simple dive.

"Over several years the Balane came to know and trust me so much that they would allow me to ride them across the lake. I would sit in the notch where their necks joined their mammoth bodies. I never fell off because I held onto the bottom two spikes that jutted out either side of their long necks up to their head. If only I had known the fate that was to be bestowed upon them I would have…," said Kiran. She appeared sad, but caught herself and continued.

"Excuse me. I have gone a bit off track. Let me continue," Kiran said with her hand resting on her cheek.

"Oh yes, my home, well I led a pretty comfortable life you see. My parents were both servants for the royal family. This was a great honor in Rhol and my parents were quite proud when they were bestowed it. They began to plan a family shortly after they had saved up a little nest egg, and I was born a year later. The Queen took a shining to me from the very minute I was born. She told my mother I had a special heart and with that a particular purpose. I, of course always thought my mother made it up to make me feel special. She had a kind soul, my mother," Kiran said pausing again.

"Many of our days were spent at the castle on Mount Kartago. The castle was beautiful. Hundreds of people worked there and anyone with a caring soul was welcome. The Queen would throw lovely feasts at night on the top of the castle which was much like an outdoor ballroom. Everyone was welcome to join in the festivities. The Queen herself always attended the dinners sitting with her people, and even serving some of the less fortunate herself. What a remarkable women she was…is.

"Anyway, as I said before, the Queen had taken a special interest in me and often took me exploring through the castle, showing me hundreds of secret corridors. Some led to underground lakes deep in the mountains, and others led you to areas of Rhol such as the top of Mount Sibileo. Many others led to secret rooms. The castle was a magical place. Every room looked different from the rest, some strewn with art from centuries before, others with elegant furniture. Of course, they all housed books containing histories not only of Rhol but other worlds too. There were books about magic, books about war strategy, and books about magical creatures.

"By the time I was twenty I am quite sure that I knew the castle better than the Queen herself, and there was barely a book in the whole place I had not found and read. I loved reading. I would devour page after page, all while using my over zealous imagination to bring the characters to life, just as the author had described them. Even the sounds of their voices, or the expressions they used, would seem real to me."

The thought of this quite obviously made Kiran very happy and she smiled staring at the fire. At the same time, it made Deke feel a little sad for he could see that Kiran's eyesight had failed her some time ago, taking with it, her dream world which only a book could create.

"It was shortly after my twenty-first birthday that my parents retired and Queen Elissa asked me to stay on, not as her servant, but as her advisor and confidant. I could not believe the honor and gladly accepted. There were great times ahead. Rhol was at peace and very prosperous thanks mainly to Queen Elissa. She taught me many things over the years including the secrets of Rhol, and the secrets about herself that to this day few people know.

Unfortunately, with great times and peace, someone usually comes along that causes great sorrow and war...I don't know why that is," Kiran said with a tear in her eye.

"Perhaps greed or sheer arrogance, or maybe some are created who are just pure evil through and through. In any event, that person was Solharn."

For the first time, Deke saw this lovely old woman frown. Her voice changed from being a warm, gentle voice of reason, to being cold and full of disdain. It was as if telling the remainder of the story would leave a bad taste in her mouth for years to come.

"Solharn is a seraph and was a member of the Order of Six Angels. The Seraphim are what formed that Order. Now every living creature in every world describes divine beings, a creator of the universe if you will, as do many religions. There are many different names for the Creator; in your world, he is often referred to as God, Allah, or Buddha. The people of our world have many different names for him as well. To make things easier, I will refer to him simply as the Creator.

"Now, this universe is made up of hundreds of planets. Five of these planets or worlds sustain life enabled by the Creator. In order to maintain life on these five planets, the Creator designed it so each world would support the other, not only to maintain life but to evolve.

"This is why the Seraphim were created. The Seraphim consisted of six celestial beings and were dubbed the Order of Six Angels. They were the highest order of angels, and they served the Creator. Their primary purpose was to assist the five worlds in maintaining a stable environment, and ensuring that they evolved continuously together; if one world destroyed itself, or fell behind, the balance of all would be lost causing the imminent annihilation of all five worlds.

"The Seraphim would travel from world to world, and with them bring knowledge and technology from the other, allowing each world to balance itself in different ways. The Seraphim would appear at times in the form of angels when necessary, but for the most part, they blended in by assuming the form of the inhabitants.

"The worlds were created about two hundred years apart. Each was more advanced than the other, depending on when it had been created. Each contained within it the energy to enable the people of each world to possess a unique ability. Rhol was created first and was given the gift of knowledge. Beltic was created after Rhol. Their abilities were the honing of the five senses. Daikon followed and was given the capacity to evolve in the art of magic. Jinn, the second last world created, would eventually define the ability to self-transport. The last world created was Earth and it was given perhaps the greatest gift of all...balance."

"Balance?" Deke bashfully interrupted.

"Yes, Dietrich. Earth being the youngest of all the worlds would eventually bring balance to the other four allowing all five worlds to coexist as a harmonious whole. Can you imagine, Deitrich, the sheer exaltation of it all, the five worlds sharing what they learned, living and co-existing as one?

"This is why on Rhol, after many thousands of years and countless wars, we eventually through knowledge evolved into a peaceful world. A world that finally understood why we were created and what we had to lose if we continued to destroy it in our once barbaric ways. You see, Dietrich, Earth is still another eight hundred years behind Rhol. It will take many more centuries before your world reaches this realization, but through balance you will."

"But your world is at war now. In my short time here I have seen it firsthand." Deke interrupted.

"You are correct Dietrich, and this is because of Solharn. The Balance of Five has been altered. He has quite nearly defeated one of the five worlds, and because of that the others are barely sustaining themselves."

"But Kiran, why would a seraph such as Solharn being of the Order of Six, want to destroy the Balance of Five?" Deke asked.

"Ah, but I said Solharn was an angel of the Order, Dietrich not is. You see Solharn, by all accounts, was the most powerful angel in the Order of Six. It seems that the more power and knowledge he gained the more arrogant, and self-indulgent he became. He constantly challenged the Creator, and eventually began to dispense with anybody that did not do exactly what he instructed them to when he visited the five worlds. He carried this out in the most horrific of ways. This, of course, was not the purpose of the Seraphim. They were there to guide and help the inhabitants, not to harm them.

"The Creator grew tired of Solharn's ways; however he underestimated the extent of Solharn's power and prowess. You see Solharn had realized that the Creator was growing tired of his antics, but in his arrogance, he did not believe the Creator could do anything about it. He quite often imagined himself as the Creator and ruler of the five worlds. Even if, by some stretch of the imagination he was defeated, he knew that he, a Seraph could not be destroyed, not even by the Creator. The worst that could happen was that he be dispelled into the Black Abyss.

"As a safeguard, Solharn used black magic to create five Blackpools, one on each world. He hoped that, should he be dispelled to the abyss, these pools would act as a portal back.

"Finally, following one of Solharn's journeys to the five worlds, the Creator did confront him. He told Solharn that he must change his ways or forever be banished from the Order of Six. Solharn laughed, and gathering all the evil he could muster from inside himself, he lunged at the Creator and shot a torrent of black energy coursing with evil from his gaping mouth. Solharn hoped the energy would weaken the Creator allowing him the chance to overtake him and send the Creator himself into the abyss. The plan failed miserably as Solharn was no match for the Creator. The evil died slowly as the Creator sent stream after stream of light toward it. The light sliced through the blackness and enveloped what was left, leaving Solharn standing there in silence. He knew his arrogance had led him to failure, yet he still laughed as the Creator drained him of all his energy until there appeared to be none left. Solharn had been dispelled into the Black Abyss.

"However, Solharn's black magic worked. After being dispelled he returned years later to each of the five worlds through the pools, creating havoc, plagues, and wars. The more lives Solharn took, the more powerful he became. It was as if he used the life energy of those he killed to enhance his own. The abyss had made Solharn beyond evil, and he was hell bent on destroying the Balance of Five. If he succeeded, he would finally have his revenge on the Creator.

"In time the Creator realized that Solharn was slowly destroying the balance world by world, so he beckoned the remaining five Seraphim. He sent one to each of the five worlds in order to protect them from Solharn's wrath. Each was given an amulet which contained within it part of the Creator himself. This gave each of the seraphim one of the greatest powers one could possess, the power of life. For them, the amulet became a portal to the afterworld, in which the energy of one's soul could be released back onto the world or cast away to the Abyss depending on its essence. The amulets would help maintain the balance of the five worlds, but in turn would weaken the Creator. He knew that only by sacrificing himself could he protect the Balance of Five against Solharn.

"He sent Jobe to Beltic; his amulet was that of a gold moon which represented birth. Dierdra was sent to Daikon; her amulet was a wooden wand that represented growth. Trestin was sent to Jinn; his amulet was an emerald sun which represented light. Kraymona was sent to Earth, and her amulet was that of a ruby star which represented life. Lastly, the Creator sent Elissa to Rhol; her amulet was a trite stone arrowhead which represented evolution.

"Solharn learned of the amulets. He created armies by attracting creatures from the darkest corners of the five worlds. He used the promise of power and wealth if they supported his depraved plan to have all the amulets for himself. If he succeeded, the five Seraphim would be helpless against his powers. The energy of the souls would become trapped with no passageway to move on to their next phase of life. Evil would grow on each of the worlds because the negative energy would remain. It would not be dispersed to the abyss. The positive energy, the energy of the good, would not be reincarnated as it should be, and thereby would not sustain the balance of life. With this much power, he would easily defeat the Creator.

"Solharn set his sights on Rhol, and after many wars, he was able to defeat Elissa, the Queen of Rhol. There were faults in his plan, however. He was unable to control the amulet. The amulet became powerless in the hands of someone who stole it. For him to control it, the amulet would have to be given to him.

"Unable to use the amulet, Solharn decided he would destroy it so that nobody could ever have its powers. He became incensed after realizing that this plan would fail too. You see, much like a seraph could not be destroyed, the amulet contained the essence of the Creator making it indestructible.

"Solharn cursed and decided to send the amulet to Earth using the Blackpool. This would keep it far away from Elissa, and any of her supporters. He left his armies on Rhol to destroy whomever and whatever might be left, and moved onto Beltic. After many years he defeated Jobe. Solharn believed, and was at least partially right, that when the amulets were dispersed to other worlds, they would become obsolete. If anything or anyone found them, they would not work because they were not given to them, but Solharn was somewhat mistaken in his belief.

"You might be asking yourself why the amulet worked when it was retrieved by you. Why was a boy from earth entrusted with such a great responsibility? I can only answer that in part.

"Because you are from Earth, Deke, it makes you unique. Because Earth is the youngest planet, you and the other inhabitants of Earth have a paladin that exists as an outer soul, independent of you yet attached. It is not the same in the other worlds. Yes, they still have two souls, but they are more intertwined. Over the years the natural course of evolution has brought their souls together. They work more as one within the body."

Deke stood looking blankly at Kiran.

Kiran laughed, "I am confusing you. Let me put it this way. Have you ever heard it mentioned that humans utilize only part of their brain and that the rest lay dormant?"

"Yes, in school," Deke answered.

"Well, as people evolve their brains become more active, eventually functioning as a whole. This happens as your souls begin to fuse together over many years and many lives. Earth is the youngest planet, and as such the souls have not yet intertwined. So in essence, although everyone has two souls, yours can act independently of each other. It is why you can see your paladin, Deo for instance, but you cannot see mine. It makes the people of Earth unique from the rest of us. Do you remember when I explained to you that Earth was given the gift of balance?"

"Yes."

"Well, I believe that may be the reason the amulet works in your hands. You are from earth, and as such you have been given that gift."

"So anyone from Earth could have found it and come here to Rhol?"

"Yes, but its true powers will only work in the hands of one."

Deke's hand sweated as he gripped the arrowhead in his pocket. He knew before Kiran even said it, that he was holding the amulet of the seraph Elissa, and he had a feeling what was coming next.

"Dietrich, you are that person. You came into this world through the power of the amulet you are holding. I can feel that the protective forces surrounding both Leal and Tamon, places you will soon learn much more about, have been dispelled. The time is here, and the war is already waging against Solharn and his armies. You must find what Solharn has done with Queen Elissa, and return the amulet if there is to be any hope of restoring the balance."

CHAPTER ELEVEN

Kaelyn could see the dust floating in the beams of light that permeated the dark tunnel they had been walking through for hours. This meant they were near. They had made the journey in just less than fourteen hours. It would be impossible for Jayden to survive, for Oisin was already showing the effects of the poison he had been injected with by the quills. In ten hours he would be dead, and they were still a long way from Solace. She was not even sure if they could get Oisin there.

Oisin was walking beside Kaelyn holding onto her shoulder for support when Palvoy yelled from ahead. "Kaelyn, Oisin! The depot is just ahead. Come, there is food and water".

Kaelyn was glad to hear it. They had run out of water hours ago and were in need of rest even if it was only for a few minutes. Kaelyn rounded the corner with Oisin. She could see the depot and breathed a sigh of relief. Palvoy came to join them, bringing a cup of water. Oisin took a sip but could not hold it down.

"Kaelyn, he does not look well," Palvoy said taking Oisin's other arm and helping Kaelyn walk him to the depot.

They placed Oisin against the wall of the depot and lit a candle. It illuminated the effects the poison was having on him. Dark lines streaked his face running down his neck to the remainder of his body. He was sweating profusely, and his skin was almost gray in color.

Kaelyn held Oisin's head back and tried to give him more water. "Oisin you must try and keep some water down, you are feverish."

Oisin responded by taking a sip and then coughing the liquid back up all over her. She became concerned when she noticed it was fused with red.

"Palvoy, he is spitting up blood."

Oisin groaned and spoke, "You two must go on without me. I will be of no use to you in this condition, and I will only get worse. Perhaps Jayden knew of what was to come, and it is why he chose to stay behind with his people."

Without warning, Kaelyn slapped Oisin's face.

"Kaelyn!" Palvoy yelled.

"You fight Oisin! You are a fighter and I will hear nothing of leaving you behind, nor will I listen to such foolishness. We have come too far in such a short period. We came through this tunnel together and we will leave together. They are counting on us Oisin, and that includes you," she yelled.

Palvoy smiled, he did not know whether it was the three minutes rest that Oisin had or Kaelyn's persistence, but Oisin actually seemed to get some color back in his face.

Palvoy had grown up with Kaelyn. In the forty years, he had known her, she was always this way, never afraid to state her opinion, and never allowing herself to give up. Many joked that her persistence would eventually catch up with her. She never had an interest in boys except for competing with them, and quite often she would come out victorious.

Kaelyn had no idea that Palvoy was in love with her, and had been since they were young. He remembered the moment he fell for her as if it were yesterday. It was in the woods while playing war. She had snuck up behind him and tackled him to the ground causing them both to roll down a small hill and come to an abrupt stop against a log. Kaelyn had found herself on top of Palvoy. Her long brown hair was covered in leaves. They looked at each other and after a brief moment of awkward silence began to laugh. It was just a moment in time between friends, but Palvoy never got over it. For the first time, if only for that moment, he had felt her heart beating against his. He had looked not at, but into her deep brown eyes, seeing the beautiful person she was inside.

"Palvoy, stop daydreaming and gather some food and weapons. We have little time if we hope to make Solace within ten hours," Kaelyn shouted.

While Oisin rested, Palvoy and Kaelyn gathered as much food, water, and weapons as they could carry. There was plenty of everything. The depot had been well stocked. After Oisin had rested for an hour, the three set out on the last leg of the tunnel that would lead them to Aura.

It was early morning when they reached the valley and with just under eight hours to make it to Solace; they were disappointed to find that a thick fog covered the entire valley. As they exited the tunnel, they could barely see one another, let alone anything else.

"We must push on," Kaelyn whispered not knowing what lay ahead.

"Hold on," Palvoy said while rustling through the leather bag he had filled at the depot. When he pulled out a walking stick made from the Orler tree, Kaelyn could have hugged him right there and then, and might have had she not thought it would make her look weak. If there were a way out, the Orler trees' magic would guide them in the right direction.

"Palvoy, you are brilliant. I will help Oisin; you lead the way. Let's stay close, or we will have trouble finding each other in this fog."

They had walked about fifty yards from the tunnel when they heard the low howl of what was surely a Ralcriff, followed by a sharp slap and a whimper. "Shut up beast," a Kaltaures could be heard grumbling.

Kaelyn and Palvoy slowly put Oisin on the ground and looked at each other. Neither could see anything in front of them, but that voice had been no more than thirty feet away. Both instinctively grabbed their bows and placed an Orler arrow on their strings. They sat with their backs to each other with Oisin between them.

"We must wait till the fog lifts," Kaelyn whispered to Palvoy.

Palvoy only nodded his agreement. They could not fight without seeing their enemy, and they had no idea how many there were. After an hour passed without a break in the fog, Palvoy knew Oisin was running out of time.

While they waited in silence, Kaelyn began to reminisce. She was happy that Palvoy had come with her and Oisin to Aura. His presence always made her feel comfortable, content with who she was. He lived in the house right across from hers, so naturally, they had become friends from a very young age.

She fondly remembered how they used to imagine themselves as warriors fighting the evils of Rhol. They would disappear for the entire day on occasions, playing war throughout the forests of Leal. Kaelyn laughed inside remembering how Palvoy was always so protective of her. If anyone ever called her a name or acted inappropriately around her, he would jump to her defense. She could have handled herself, and she was sure that Palvoy realized it, but it was his way of showing her his affection.

Their friendship only grew closer the older they became. Unlike the other girls who were always telling each other their secrets, she trusted only Palvoy. It was not her nature to open up to anyone. She was a loner, but he meant something to her. He was someone she could always count on, someone who could make her laugh or console her when she was sad, somebody who would take long walks with her, and without saying a word, would know her very thoughts.

Palvoy was her very best friend. She could easily see herself growing old with him. She wasn't sure whether he felt the same way, but she was pretty certain he did. She was too stubborn or perhaps too insecure in herself when it came to romance to tell him that she loved him. But she knew in her heart it would happen one day.

Her warm thoughts were interrupted by Palvoy summoning her, "Kaelyn, the fog is beginning to lift."

It had taken two hours, and now they could see about four feet above the ground. Their hearts sank when they saw the rows and rows of tents that were set up around them, many with Ralcriff tied to a stake in front. Their only hope of getting through the field would be to slip through the camps unnoticed, and that would be nearly impossible.

"Oisin, are you able to crawl?" Kaelyn asked.

"I will follow you two. We can use the fog to our advantage now," Oisin whispered.

"Oisin cannot carry anything, and we can carry only the minimal weapons and water. We will have to leave the rest behind. If we are seen, we will not stand a chance Kaelyn."

Kaelyn glanced down at Oisin; his condition had deteriorated. "I agree Palvoy, but I do not see that we have any other way out of this."

Palvoy nodded and gathered as much water and weaponry as he could carry. Kaelyn did the same, and they set off through the field. Palvoy led the way, carefully crawling through the grass to the west of the camps.

Their plan was working, and they had gone several hundred feet avoiding any detection. Palvoy took turns with Kaelyn crawling up ahead to scout while the other stayed with Oisin, giving both a needed rest.

It had been Kaelyn who was sitting with Oisin when he became unresponsive. "Oisin! Oisin wake up!" Kaelyn pleaded as softly as she could, but no matter what she did he would not move. Kaelyn could not bear to leave him behind; he was still alive, but unable to move. She was beginning to panic waiting for Palvoy to return. What was taking him so long? It was long past their half hour limit of being gone from each other.

"Waiting for someone, Lealian?"

Kaelyn immediately went for her sword but was pulled by her hair to the ground before she could grasp it. As she was trying to focus on what had just happened, Palvoy came toppling down on top of her bleeding profusely from his nose and mouth.

Kaelyn frantically looked around. She could see only the legs of the creatures that were surrounding them. The fog was still too thick to make anything else out, but she did not need to see the heads of the beasts to know what they were.

"We figured you would come out somewhere around here Lealian. We were not sure exactly where, but we have been patiently waiting," Abednego snarled.

Kaelyn jumped at the Kaltaures leader only to be slapped to the ground again.

"Where are the other Lealians, girl?"

Kaelyn said nothing. Her left eye had swollen shut, yet she still glared up at Abednego.

"What of you, boy? Tell me where you crawled out from. Where does the tunnel come out?"

Palvoy turned to face Kaelyn and smiled at her. He knew they were about to die and wanted her to see into his eyes so she could feel what he had felt for years. When he was satisfied she had, he turned back to Abednego and spat. "You will get nothing from my lips other than my spit on the ground you filthy animal."

"Enough games," Abednego screamed "Take the girl back to my tent. She will talk eventually," he chortled. "Feed the other two to the Ralcriff."

One of the Kaltaures soldiers grabbed Kaelyn by the hair and began to drag her across the ground. Palvoy jumped to his feet and thrust a knife into the chest of the nearest soldier he could find. When he turned to run toward Kaelyn, he suddenly felt a warm sensation running through his stomach. He was confused; even though he was running, he was gaining no ground. He could hear the voice of Kaelyn screaming 'no, no' and repeating his name over and over; it was like a faint echo.

He looked down and fell to his knees. A long metal object protruded from his stomach. It was only then that he felt the pain. Not the pain of the sword that had been thrust through his body, but the pain of being unable to help Kaelyn as she was dragged away.

As his eyes began to close, he saw Kaelyn fall to the ground. The soldier dragging her had disappeared into thin air. Another soldier, apparently as confused as he moved in to take his place, but he too disappeared. Soldiers all around them seemed to be getting sucked into the fog. He thought he must be hallucinating.

Abednego was yelling in confusion to his troops trying to get them to retreat to the east. It was utter mayhem. Drops of blood fell through the fog like rain and covered the ground. Palvoy fell back onto the grass, and when he looked at the sky, he saw the wings of an angel breaking through the fog toward him. "This is it," he thought to himself.

Kaelyn ran through the fog toward Palvoy. She could see the Pegapire standing over him. There might still be hope she thought and hurried to his side.

"I am sorry child. We came too late for Palvoy."

Kaelyn grabbed her head as if to shake the words from it. She did not want to hear them.

"No, please, the Wall of Solace! We can get him there! He will heal! Please, it will bring him back! It is not his time; our time is yet to come," sobbed Kaelyn.

"Your time may come Kaelyn, but not in this world. You know as well as I do that the Wall of Solace only heals. It does restore life to the departed. I am sorry," said Palto.

"Where is Oisin?" cried Kaelyn.

"He is alive, but not well. How long ago was he infected with the Ralcriff quills?"

"Yesterday evening. He has but hours left before the poison takes him; and Jayden as well," Kaelyn answered.

Palto immediately hailed two other Pegapires. "Solko, Preta. Take Oisin and fly to Solace. There is no time to waste if he is to live. You must get him to the wall."

Kaelyn picked Oisin up from the ground and using all the strength she could muster, she pushed him onto Solko. They took flight immediately, vanishing in seconds.

"I will kill them for this!" Kaelyn yelled as she grabbed her sword from the ground. She was sobbing uncontrollably. Her chest was heaving, and she was struggling to catch another breath of air. She had just lost her only love, for a Lealian only finds love once. She did not know it yet, but this moment in time would change her life forever. Without love, her remaining emotions would push her to limits that she did not know she had. It would make her one of the most ferocious warriors in Rhol.

The fog had now lifted enough that she could see the battle that was raging on in the Valley. The Kaltaures army was massive. They used arrows and catapulted balls of fire at the Pegapires while they were in flight. They used their swords when the Pegapires swooped in to fight them on the ground. The Pegapires were extremely fast though, and were, for the most part, able to avoid injury.

Kaelyn had not noticed the Phits before, but they too had joined the fight with the Kaltaures and were having slightly better results against the Pegapires. They were flying in groups. When they got onto the back of a Pegapire, they had free reign to rip into its flesh with their teeth and razor sharp claws.

"Kaelyn, where is Jayden?" Palto asked.

Kaelyn turned and looked at Palto. "He remained in the tunnel. He refused to leave the other Lealians."

"What of Roland?" Palto asked.

"Roland was killed during the attack on Leal after saving us. Jayden leads the Lealians now. We forged ahead of them to bring help, but we have failed them."

"Kaelyn!" Palto snapped. "You have failed no one. You have travelled many miles and fought bravely. Do not dishonor the memory of Palvoy with regret. He would not want that. You found us, as we have found you. We must now join together if we are to win back Rhol."

Palto regretted the harshness of his tone, but it seemed to bring her back to reality.

Kaelyn realized that her anger would solve nothing at this moment. She had not understood her reaction at first. She had seen many deaths over her time, but never the death of someone she loved, someone to whom she would never get the chance to say those words, all because of her pride.

"You are right Palto, I am sorry. You were asking about the remainder of the Lealians. It is my guess that they would be three to four hours from the end of the tunnel, maybe further if Jayden is in the same condition as Oisin."

"Climb on my back, Kaelyn. We will go now to get Jayden and get him to the Wall of Solace if it is not already too late."

Kaelyn shook her head. "I belong here Palto. I would be of no use in the tunnel and would only slow you down."

Palto did not argue with her and summoned a Pegapire. "Very well Kaelyn. You are indeed a true Lealian. This is Issa; you shall fight with her and she with you."

Kaelyn felt an instant bond with Issa as she looked admiringly at her.

"I feel it, too, Kaelyn. The bond has existed for centuries between Lealians and Pegapires; ours will never be broken. Now let us join the battle."

Kaelyn did not need to be convinced and climbed onto Issa. Before they flew off into battle, Kaelyn looked at Palto, "He will not be easily swayed into leaving his people to save his own life. He is stubborn."

"Then I will just have to be convincing, won't I?" Palto said before flying toward the tunnel.

CHAPTER TWELVE

The night had fallen as Phanthus flew closer to his destination. He was in no hurry. He was not looking forward to meeting with Solharn, and quite enjoyed the freedom that only the night provided him. Phanthus had perfect vision at night, and with the cover of darkness, he could easily maneuver through the sky unseen.

Phanthus was well over two thousand years old and was the last remaining dragon in Rhol. His soul was filled with anger for many years ago he had watched as the people of Rhol needlessly hunted and killed all the dragons for mere sport and to garner prestigious titles, all except for him that is. Yes, of course, he had occasionally burned and destroyed their villages, but this was so that he could gather food to avoid starvation. He would have never thought to wipe out an entire race.

Phanthus hated them for it, and his hatred only grew more with every single year that passed. As far as anyone was concerned on Rhol, dragons no longer existed. Phanthus made sure their beliefs never wavered. He hid in his lair during the day and went out only at night. He would sporadically pick farm houses or very small villages to attack and would always make it look like an accidental fire caused by a villager.

That all changed when Solharn turned against the Creator; he became consumed with destroying the balance of the five worlds. Solharn came to Phanthus and promised him that if he fought with his armies, he would let him have Rhol to do with what he wanted, including what was left of any inhabitants. Solharn was confident that after Queen Elissa was defeated Rhol would be helpless, and Phanthus could get his revenge for the destruction of his kind. Phanthus liked the thought of this and reveled in the idea of becoming the ruler of Rhol. It was why he had agreed to join Solharn's armies.

As with everything, it was not as easy as it had sounded. Solharn had underestimated the inhabitants of Rhol, in particular, the Lealians and the Pegapires, not to mention Queen Elissa.

The first battle was the beginning of a war that would rage on for a decade. It was in this struggle that Solharn realized his plan would take much longer than he anticipated. The battle itself took place in the Valley of Solace, which was widely thought to be the most beautiful place in Rhol. With the Lealians and Pegapires on her side, Queen Elissa was winning the battle.

Phanthus laughed remembering the shock on the faces of her army when he flew at them from behind, reducing several hundred soldiers to ash with one breath of fire. They had thought he was extinct and were not prepared. Elissa had immediately used her powers to create a field of light that kept her armies temporarily safe from Phanthus. In doing so, she gave them a chance to regroup.

Solharn responded by using dark magic; he created black spheres which formed in midair between his hands, and he hurled them toward the light causing pockets of the shield to rupture. This allowed small contingencies of both armies to continue fighting. The conflict continued for days, during which Elissa and Solharn exhausted much of their powers over the prolonged period of battle, and it weakened both of them. In the end, many lives were lost, but neither side, thanks to Phanthus, had gained much ground.

Solharn who was surprised that Elissa's armies had held him at bay retreated to adjust his strategies and replenish his weakened powers. Solharn's new approach was slower and more methodical, taking years to execute. He created the plague to weaken his enemy, he fought smaller battles utilizing Phanthus, and he always attacked when Elissa was not around to defend them. He was also able to sway the Phits to join his armies.

The Phits were nasty beasts who were native to the swamps that surrounded a large portion of Rhol. A fully grown Phit ranged in size from four to six feet with arms and legs that were thin and wiry. They had flaps of skin that joined the arm and leg on each side of their scaled bodies making wings that allowed them to fly long distances. Their claws were sharp like the blade of a knife, and their teeth were long and pointed like needles. As if that wasn't enough, they could breathe both in and out of water.

It had not been difficult for Solharn to persuade them; their relationship with Elissa had always been rocky at best.

Decades ago after a prolonged war over territories, Queen Elissa convinced them to sign a treaty which handed over sole ownership of the swamps to them. In turn, they agreed not to harm or steal from any inhabitants of Rhol outside their boundaries, but over the years the Phits did not always abide by the treaty. This resulted in high tensions between the Phits and the other inhabitants of Rhol.

As time passed Solharn also learned that it was better to attack a person's soul, and so he sent many paladins to the abyss. It allowed him to use that energy for his purposes; what remained was a person with half a soul. They would become trapped in the world where their soul was taken. In time they turned completely mad, which only assisted Solharn's cause.

These unfortunate souls became widely known throughout Rhol as the Pintante. This derived from the ancient Lealian language meaning 'no core.' They had no allegiance to anyone; even Phanthus found them revolting, and whenever he had the chance he would disintegrate them. He was not very pleased when Solharn ordered him to stop.

To Solharn, the Pintante were his prized creations. In a short twenty-four months, they would turn into vile creatures devoid of any reasonable thought process. They would become pasty white, all of their hair would fall from their body, and their eyes would glaze over turning a purplish grey color. Their teeth would either turn black with rot or simply fall out, and their nails would grow thick and long. Their rancid smell was a blessing, as it was a warning that they approached. They thought nothing of maiming or killing anything that crossed their paths. Even after death, their soul was unable to join with its counterpart and move on to the eternal life. It simply lingered within the world it was lost in, causing mischief and havoc wherever it could.

The Pintante were indiscriminate in their attacks. There was no reasoning with them, and so they killed both Solharn's and Elissa's soldiers. However, Solharn knew that the Pintante had a far greater effect on Elissa's armies. The mere look of these creatures, and the thought that they could become one, spread fear among her soldiers.

Solharn's new strategy had worked. Over several years he had been able to reduce Elissa's armies drastically, and only then did he plan the attack on Mount Kartago.

Solharn had thought this would be the battle to end all battles and came well prepared. He strategically surrounded the mountain with thousands of Kaltaures and thousands more Ralcriff. Solharn used every creature in his army whether it had been forced or willingly fought for Solharn's cause. His military was given little resistance as it advanced destroying anything that stood in its way.

Phanthus was suspicious of how quickly their armies had infiltrated and believed they were walking into a trap. Under Solharn's orders, he flew around Mount Kartago looking for any signs of Elissa's armies. He found none, only Elissa sitting on top of her bastion surrounded by a small shield of light.

He returned to Solharn and reported his findings. He and Solharn agreed that her armies or traps lay within the castle itself. Solharn ordered the attack, and his soldiers converged on the castle. Phanthus breathed streams of fire toward the castle and used his tail to crumble its elegant brick. Kaltaures used ropes and grapples to scale the walls. Ralcriff upon Ralcriff charged through the smoldering wooden gates which Phanthus had burned, and the Phits flew in and around the castle at will. Still, they met little resistance.

Solharn cowardly watched from the shadows. When he had seen enough, he soared to the top of the castle followed by Phanthus. Elissa was waiting for him there, protected only by a small orb of light which surrounded her. She said nothing and simply stared at Solharn in disgust.

Solharn spoke to her in his drawl bleating voice, "It is fitting that you sit before me defeated, Elissa. Perhaps I overestimated you." Elissa continued to stare at Solharn; she remained silent. The contempt on her face said it all.

"Shall we end this quickly? Your armies have abandoned you, as I am sure the Creator has as well, after observing your pathetic plight. You know what I am here for, so hand over the amulet and bow to my rule. Perhaps I will let you suffer less than you have to."

Gazing at Elissa, Phanthus observed her smile and listened to her speak for the first time. She had such an alluring voice, so soft and enchanting. He was instantly drawn to her. "No one has abandoned me Solharn; they have simply retreated on my behest. You will find no fight here, no armies, only me."

Solharn's long black wings flared as he angrily glared at Elissa. "You are as pathetic as they are Elissa. You would sit here and lose everything for this world, a world infested with ignorance, one which is unworthy of the Seraphim. You, the next eldest to me, should know that the Balance of Five would have been lost long ago if not for us. They do not pay us the respect we deserve."

Phanthus looked toward Elissa. He yearned to hear her voice again. "Unworthy of the Seraphim, Solharn? It is only you who is unworthy. Your obsession with power has driven you mad. You have become an angel with no soul, and darkness fills that empty void. You are indeed tormented, fixated on leaving a trail of destruction and despair in your path instead of instilling principles and beliefs. You should be healing lost souls, not destroying them. These are the very foundations of what the Seraphim, stand for."

"Principles? Beliefs?" Solharn scoffed. "You are indeed a devoted pawn to the Order Elissa, and for all your efforts you will be destroyed along with the rest of them. You are the beginning of the end of the Seraphim and the end of the Balance of Five."

Although Phanthus could see a single tear flowing down Elissa's cheek as she spoke, her voice never wavered. "Your words illustrate your ignorance Solharn. All that you speak of are things that you don't understand; or refuse to understand. There is no single solution to the way things work or will work. It must be done as a whole. Only then will the balance become one."

Phanthus would hear her soothing voice only one more time before the orb of light surrounding her finally vanished. "You have only deceived yourself if you think this to be the end Solharn. It is only the beginning."

"Not for you Elissa," Solharn screeched, watching as the last of her powers dissipated.

A dark cloud streamed from his mouth and surrounded Elissa. Phanthus heard the screams from her angelic voice as the evil within the cloud consumed her. The cloud lifted her high in the air for several agonizing minutes before releasing her to fall to the ground writhing in pain and gasping for air.

Solharn approached her and wrenched the amulet from her neck. He leaned in close to her as if making sure she could hear, "That was but a taste of what is to come, Elissa; an eternity of darkness, an eternity of pain."

Elissa could say nothing as her body stretched and quivered in apparent agony. Phanthus never saw her again after Solharn carried her away that day in a cloud of darkness.

Solharn's pleasure at obtaining the amulet was short-lived. Try as he might, he could not use the amulet to his advantage because he had taken it. In his hands, it became a mere rock devoid of any powers. In frustration he tried to destroy it but could not, so he threw it in the Blackpool sending it to another world so that it would never be used against him.

Following this Solharn turned his mind to the Lealians and the Pegapires, but found that Elissa had used all of her remaining powers to create protective fields around their villages. Fields that could not be broken or undone by any powers he possessed.

Solharn was infuriated and took his frustrations out on the remaining inhabitants of Rhol, though many of them had already found refuge in Solace. Solharn knew now that Elissa had sacrificed herself by drawing his armies to the castle, and stalling him while as many of her people as possible could find refuge.

He knew that even though he had defeated Elissa, and was now in control, there were still unanswered questions. He kept his promise to Phanthus and left him in command, but he warned him that any changes to be acted upon were to be reported to him immediately. Phanthus was instructed by Solharn that he would contact him when required, and with that, he left.

Solharn communicated with Phanthus regularly in his dreams, or nightmares as he now thought of them. Solharn had done just that the night before last. He had informed Phanthus that a boy would appear near the Valley of Solace, a boy who was in possession of the Sacred Amulet of Rhol. This boy's appearance would cause the protective fields surrounding Leal and Tamon to be dispelled. Solharn had instructed Phanthus to send a Kaltaures army to Leal, as it would be the perfect opportunity to attack the Lealians. Solharn believed they would be oblivious to the fact that their protection was no longer in place and would be taken by surprise. Phanthus was to go to the Valley of Solace, destroy the boy at all costs and retrieve the amulet. He was then to report back to Solharn the following night at the Blackpool.

This was what Phanthus was doing as he reached Mount Sibileo and slowly glided over Charn landing at the base of what was once Shimmer Lake. Phanthus had come to this lake more times than he could remember over the past centuries to gorge on the abundance of fresh fish, or at times on the animals lingering around the water's edge quenching their thirst.

Those were distant memories now. The lake had been transformed by Solharn into the Blackpool. Anything that lived in the lake was now forced to filter pure evil through their system. The water, if you could call it that, was more like diluted oil festering and bubbling. The smell of it would keep any reasonable creature away; it smelt of death and decomposition.

Over a short period, the creatures that once relied on the lake to survive were consumed with hate as evil coursed through their blood streams. They all became unwilling participants in Solharn's bid to destroy the planet. They were devoid of any life worth living and would savagely tear apart and devour anything that dared enter the dark black waters. The creatures had insatiable appetites, and nothing they ate could satisfy their hunger. They became insane in their desperate search to find anything that would satisfy their appetite.

Phanthus was not fond of coming here and stayed well back from the water's edge. This was because of the Balane. They too had succumbed to the evil within the water and were especially dangerous as they had the ability to fly. Their sheer size and strength coupled with their constant desire to feed would be a match even for him.

As if thinking about them had jinxed him, Phanthus saw what he had been hoping he wouldn't. Directly in front of him was the telltale head of a Balane emerging from the water. The creature was swimming steadily toward him. Its crazed blue eyes were as big as saucers and circled in a crimson red. The Balane screeched and bawled as it stared at him, apparently crazed with hunger.

Phanthus let a burst of fire out over the lake in the hopes of discouraging the Balane, but the animal in his state continued swimming right through it. He was about to try a second time when he saw the one for whom he had been waiting. Solharn emerged from the Blackpool riding the back of the beast. As they approached Phanthus switched his focus to Solharn. He could see that the evil inside Solharn had grown. His body was much larger, and his face was now black and scarred. He was almost unrecognizable.

When the Balane neared the shore, Solharn jumped from its back high into the dark sky. His wings expanded in midair as he ascended toward Phanthus. As he closed in on the dragon, he arched his wings to slow his speed and landed with a thud in front of him.

"I trust everything went as planned, Phanthus?"

"It was as you foretold, Solharn. The boy appeared and the protective fields dispelled. The Kaltaures did as they were instructed and attacked while the Lealians were in the temple. However, it was only moderately successful. The Kaltaures, being as stupid and greedy as they are, began to collect baubles before discovering that several hundred Lealians had escaped through an underground tunnel."

"Idiots!" Solharn screamed. "What of the boy? I trust you retrieved the amulet Phanthus."

"There were unexpected obstacles," Phanthus started to say before he was cut off.

Solharn became enraged, "Obstacles! What obstacles you fool? You were entrusted with these simple tasks, and I can see it in your eyes. You have failed me!"

"There was a creature with him," Phanthus explained. "It was different than anything I had ever seen. It morphed into some bird and flew the boy to the Sacred Realm. I gave chase but was unable to catch him. If I had known about this creature, I would have been better prepared to deal with the situation. Is there a reason you didn't tell me of this most unfortunate surprise, Solharn? Could it be that you did not know?" Phanthus angrily smirked.

Solharn raised his wings, and torrential winds came out of nowhere. The Blackpool formed a giant wave behind him that towered over both him and Phanthus. It did not come crashing down but stopped in midair as if standing there waiting for a command.

"Do not tempt me dragon; you are here to do my bidding. You may think you are too valuable for me to destroy, but you would be wrong," Solharn slowly spoke.

Phanthus forgetting in his anger who he was speaking to, aggressively moved toward him. "I have done your bidding and done it well. It is not my fault that you were unprepared for Elissa's plan. I told you at the time that it was too easy."

Phanthus did not have a chance to react before he was struck by the wave. He tried to fly up, but his wings were pinned below the putrid water now swirling around his body dragging him back toward its evil depths. Phanthus clamped his mouth shut so as not to swallow the water, and dug his claws into the rock and dirt in a feeble attempt to withstand the wave that was sucking him to his demise. He could feel the black liquid enveloping his body as he sank deeper and deeper into the pool. Phanthus stuck his neck out in a final effort to keep his head above water. He could see Solharn hovering above him waiting for the inevitable to happen.

"Solharn, you can't do this! I will do what you ask!" Phanthus pleaded.

Solharn laughed. "Yes, you will, Phanthus. Yes, you will."

In his panicked state Phanthus opened his mouth to spew a torrent of fire toward Solharn. He was surprised when nothing came out except the black water that had already filled his lungs. Phanthus felt numb as his memories and thoughts slowly faded away. Whatever good he once had was replaced by evil.

Only after Phanthus was completely submerged within the Blackpool did Solharn use his powers to raise him from its murky depths. Phanthus had turned completely black in color, unable to think or speak for himself.

Solharn ordered him to bow to him and laughed when the dragon complied. Phanthus was no longer what he had been. He was now just a pawn to the evil that coursed through his veins. He belonged entirely to Solharn now.

"Come dragon. We will go to Solace and finish what was started decades ago."

CHAPTER THIRTEEN

Deke stared in disbelief at Kiran and Deo. "Maybe there's been a mistake of some sort, Kiran. Maybe someone else was meant to find the amulet! I am sure Queen Elissa didn't mean for the fate of Rhol to lie in my hands."

"You are the person that was intended to find the amulet Dietrich, of that I am sure. The Queen was very specific when she entrusted me with when to avenge Rhol. She told me that a boy from the world Earth would come and that he would have the Sacred Amulet of Rhol with him. She said that the boy who possessed it would have an extraordinary power, a gift that nobody else possessed, not even her. She said the arrival of this boy would cause the protective fields around Leal and Tamon to dispel and the last fight for Rhol would begin.

We thought that time had come about three years ago when a girl came to us from your world carrying the amulet. I thought that I was mistaken in the fact that Queen Elissa had foretold of a boy arriving. I was aware that the protective fields surrounding Leal and Tamon had not dispelled at her arrival, but I foolishly didn't take heed of it, thinking that they would in time. I should have been more cautious, but with Solharn and his armies destroying Rhol, I was not thinking as I should have. The girl left here in search of Queen Elissa. She was strong and determined. She and her paladin, Delca, proved to be very worthy and soon found themselves near Mount Sibileo. That was as far as they would go. The fields had not dispelled, and without the help of the Lealians and the Pegapires, she was doomed to fail. Solharn learned of her plight and was moving in on her quickly. Realizing this, I sent my protector Lorca to find them and bring them back, but it was too late. Solharn sensed they were near and sent a Balane down from the Blackpool. Not the ones I described to you earlier, but one possessed by evil. Seeing the

Balane the girl ran to the base of the mountain and changed her paladin into a Kruntulla, which she and Delca had seen on her journey, and narrowly escaped."

"A Kruntulla?" Deke asked.

"They are powerful beasts, native to Rhol. They walk on two legs but have four arms which enable them to climb or dig at a breakneck pace. Their size varies depending on how old they are. A hundred-year-old Kruntulla can be sixty feet tall, and as strong as any creature that exists in this world. They live deep within the many mountain ranges of Rhol, but after Phanthus was left in charge by Solharn, he convinced them that they should not hide in the mountains. He told them they should venture out and take what was rightfully theirs. Most Kruntulla were happy with their surroundings and paid no attention to Phanthus, but others agreed with him and forged their way out into Rhol inflicting pain and misery on anyone not loyal to Solharn.

Delca put up a good fight against the Balane, but the girl was not ready to transform her paladin into such a massive beast. The harder Delca fought, the more energy it drained from her. I suspect she was eventually drained completely. Lorca found the girl lying by the Blackpool unconscious. Her Paladin was nowhere to be found, and the Sacred Amulet of Rhol had vanished. Lorca returned to Solace with her, and eventually, she awoke. She had no memory of what happened to her paladin or the amulet. We thought Solharn had been successful in stealing it back and had left the girl to suffer the fate of a Pintante after destroying her paladin.

I believed that any hope of saving Rhol was over. It was not until we learned from a spy within Solharn's armies, that he too, was concerned about the whereabouts of the amulet. Eventually, he surmised that the girl must have thrown it into the Blackpool, and so he sent a Kaltaures soldier to earth in search of it. Thankfully you found it before the Kaltaures did, and when its powers brought you here to Rhol the protective fields around Leal and Tamon were dispelled.

Solharn predicted this would happen after the Kaltaures soldier reported back to him about you, and he was able to plan an attack on Leal before anyone was aware of what was transpiring. Phanthus was sent to destroy you, and luckily he failed. Since your arrival, everything that Queen Elissa foretold has occurred. It is how I know that you, Dietrich, were meant to find the amulet."

Deke's mind was in overdrive. Could it be a coincidence that a girl from earth arrived three years ago, the same time his friend Mary went missing? Before he could ask the question, Kiran answered it for him.

"Yes, Dietrich. You know the girl of which I speak."

"Hello, Deke," a familiar voice came from behind him.

Deke turned quickly. He smiled when he saw his long lost friend and ran to embrace her. Mary was alive. Tears rolled down Mary's cheeks as she hugged Deke. She did not want to let him go.

"Deke, I had hoped this day would come," Mary said choking back her tears. "How have you been? It must have been horrible for you when I suddenly disappeared. You must have felt...," Mary could not speak anymore as she began to sob uncontrollably.

With all that was going on Deke had forgotten the anguish he had felt when Mary had gone missing, and the pain he had suffered when the searches for her had come up empty.

"I gave up hope that you were alive. I wasn't myself for years," Deke said looking at Deo, "but someone...something convinced me to return to the place I'd lost myself. Now that I've found you we can return together, Mary." Deke said trying to boost Mary's morale.

Mary began to cry even harder, and Deke continued to try to console her, "Mary, all that matters now is that we have found each other again. We will find our way back."

"I can never return Deke," Mary sobbed.

Deke could not stand the thought of his friend's heart breaking. "Of course you will Mary. We'll go now if you want. Kiran, we must get her back. I'll return if that's what's meant to be, but there must be a way to help Mary."

Kiran looked at Mary. She could not speak. Deke's arrival had brought back too many emotions that she had kept bottled up inside for years. Kiran decided to tell Deke what Mary couldn't.

"Dietrich, Mary can never leave. When one's paladin is destroyed that person can never move on from the world where it happened; they are trapped."

Deke could not believe what he was hearing, and could not stand seeing Mary in such distress. "It's ok, Mary. I will stay here with you. You'll always have a friend close by."

Kiran continued, "Dietrich, that is not all that happens when a person loses their paladin."

Mary pulled herself together momentarily and gave Kiran a sharp look before cutting into the conversation. "It will be great to have a friend close by. I've longed for the day we would see each other again. You're a true friend Deke."

Kiran let it go. Mary knew Deke better than she did, and she would tell him the fate that was to bestow her in her own time.

"Then there's nothing more to worry about except the task at hand," said Deke.

Mary smiled, "And I promise you this, Deke, I will be by your side no matter what we encounter."

Kiran felt that Mary might regret deceiving Deke by not telling him what would become of her in the next few months, but she also knew that if she did it would not help him in his quest to restore the Balance of Five. If Mary told him of her fate now, he would become obsessed with trying to save her from becoming a Pintante. Mary was thinking of Rhol, and since there was nothing Deke would be able to do anyway, there was no point in divulging her secret. She would tell him when she had to for his own safety.

"Mary will help you on your quest to find Elissa. The amulet itself will guide you as it did her. She has already travelled through many parts of Rhol and knows of the dangers that lie ahead. I have been able to spend the past several months with Mary, giving me time to explain some of the secrets of Rhol that you will need to assist you if you are to find Elissa. I was not foretold what was to happen after you got here Dietrich, but I do know that you, Mary and Deo will be in grave danger on your journey to save this world. Protect each other at all costs. Solharn will be focused on destroying all of you and retrieving the amulet. Oh, yes, one other thing, take this chain. It will carry the amulet for you and protect it from becoming lost. It is important that you never let it leave the confines of this chain. Do you understand Dietrich?"

"Yes, Kiran," answered Deke.

Lorca suddenly entered the cottage. "I am sorry for interrupting Kiran, but Solko has just entered the Wall of Solace. He comes with Preta and carries a young Lealian with him. They have news and request your presence."

Kiran climbed on top of Lorca and instructed Deke, Mary, and Deo to follow her. In moments they were at the very spot where Deke had first observed the Sacred Realm of Solace.

"Welcome Solko, Preta. It 's nice to see the Lealians and the Pegapires have joined once again. What news do you bring?"

Solko bowed to Kiran, "Thank you Kiran, but the news is more dismal than it appears. This is Oisin. We brought him to the wall as quickly as possible to heal the wounds inflicted upon him by the Ralcriff. He had few hours to spare."

"So you have joined with the Lealians then Solko?" Kiran enquired.

"Not quite Kiran. Once the fields dispelled around Tamon, we knew it was the time Queen Elissa had told us to wait for. We immediately raced to Leal to join with them in the fight for Rhol. When we arrived there, we found no one. The village had been destroyed, burned to the ground. We found several of the Lealian's lifeless bodies strewn about the village, and several more within the temple, but most were burned beyond recognition. We also found the bodies of several Kaltaures soldiers among them. Fearing the worst, we began to search for any survivors. We found a tunnel leading from the temple going underground and had renewed hope that some had survived. But when we began to follow it we discovered that it had collapsed.

Palto ordered that we follow him. He told us that just after the Queen had ordered us to retreat to Leal and Tamon, Roland had told him of his plan to dig a tunnel which would lead to the Valley of Aura as a safeguard. We flew as fast as the wind would carry us. When we arrived, we could see hundreds upon hundreds of Solharn's armies gathered in the fields surrounding the valley. It was Palto who saw the Lealians first, three of them surrounded by Kaltaures soldiers. Knowing that this could be the last three alive, Palto immediately ordered the attack. We took the Kaltaures by surprise due to a thick fog which concealed us. We were able to save two of the three Lealians; a girl named Kaelyn, and Oisin who stands before you."

Oisin had not been told the news. "Palvoy is dead?" he asked staring blankly at Solko.

"I am sorry, Oisin. He died trying to save Kaelyn and you. If not for him you two may well have been killed. His actions provided us with enough time and distraction to save you both."

Kiran looked deeply concerned. "Is it what you surmised then? Only two Lealians have survived?"

"No. According to Kaelyn, several hundred remain in the tunnel about three to four hours outside of Aura. Their leader, Roland, is dead. His son Jayden, the last remaining blood line to that family, is gravely injured. He was infected with the poison of the Ralcriff quills at the same time as Oisin."

"Then Jayden will succumb to the poison in how many hours?" Kiran asked now very concerned.

"About three," Oisin interrupted looking down toward the ground.

"Palto is racing through the tunnel to Jayden as we speak. He hopes to bring Jayden to the wall before it is too late. We are hoping the Lealians arrive in Aura soon to join us in the fight. Without them, we will take on too many casualties. The girl Kaelyn, at her insistence, is in battle with Issa as we speak," Solko advised.

"Very well, we will wait for Palto to decide what our next move will be. He will be able to inform us on the progress of the Lealian warriors," Kiran said.

"That is yet another problem," Solko indicated. "When we flew here with Oisin we were able to arrive at the entrance to the mountain just ahead of an army of Phits and a rather large Kruntulla. I fear by the time Palto gets here they will be lying in wait for him."

Kiran thought for a moment contemplating the next move. "Lorca, gather all the people we can. The armies of Solharn are upon us."

"How will we know when Palto arrives, Kiran? He is too far away to communicate with, and I am sure by now Solharn's army stands between him and us," Lorca asked.

"Deo and I can help!" Deke said. "I can change Deo into a small bird, and he can fly past the armies undetected to inform us of Palto's arrival. It is the only way we will know when to advance."

Kiran was concerned. "Dietrich, you have more to learn before you transform Deo at will. You are not entirely aware of all the tribulations you will have to face when attempting this."

Deo, who had been listening intently, finally spoke. "I agree with Deke, Kiran. Although I am sure we have much to learn from you, there is no time. Solharn's armies are already advancing on Solace, and the Pegapires are in battle at Aura. We must move now. Palto and Jayden are the leaders of the Pegapires and the Lealians. Their leadership will be essential in coming out of this war victorious. I am confident Deke can do this, and by transforming me into something so small he will still maintain much of his strength."

"I am afraid I have to agree Kiran. I can think of no other way," Solko added.

Kiran was silent for several minutes. Deke suspected she was contemplating whether she was making another mistake, as she had with Mary.

"Kiran, what is your decision?" Solko impatiently asked.

Kiran turned to Deke. "You have transformed your paladin before Dietrich, but that was only in a very stressful situation. This will be different. You must clear your mind if it is to work and imagine only what Deo is to transform into. After he is transformed comes the difficult part. Keeping Deo in that state will not be easy, especially if you are distracted. Over time it will become much easier. You must learn to separate the parts of the mind that you use for imagination and reality to be able to function fully."

Deke closed his eyes and began to imagine a hummingbird. It was the smallest and fastest bird he knew. In a few minutes, he opened his eyes and found Deo hovering directly above his shoulder. It had worked. With a slight nod, Deo disappeared through the Wall of Solace. Kiran took Deke's hand and sat him down in a quiet place away from everyone else and beckoned Mary over. "Keep a close eye, Mary. He must not be distracted. The fate of Deo and perhaps all of Rhol depends on it."

CHAPTER FOURTEEN

As Palto raced toward the tunnel, he thought of Roland. He had been a close friend; he had looked forward to fighting alongside him once again. Jayden was now the last in the bloodline of the family that had ruled the Lealians for centuries. Without him, they would lose considerable knowledge of their history that only he possessed, but more so they would lose a great leader. In these dismal times, a strong leader was essential for their survival.

He had fought alongside this family for decades. He would not be standing where he was today if not for Jayden's grandfather Corceran. In fact, the Pegapires would have been extinct long ago.

He was deeply saddened when Corceran died. He had not even had time to thank him before he succumbed to his wounds, but he would repay him in his own way. He vowed to himself that he would always protect his family. He became fast friends with Roland after returning Corceran's body to Leal and paying his respects. He had met Roland's son Jayden at that time. After that he visited Leal frequently, making sure they were okay. Quite often he and Roland would take long rides discussing their families or various strategies of war. Roland turned out to be just as ferocious as his father in battle, and even savvier with a sword enabling him to gain respect throughout the battlefields of Rhol quickly.

Palto had not seen them now for over ten years, just before the Queen had ordered them to retreat to their homelands. It was too late for Roland, but he was not going to let Jayden die.

Palto worried as he approached the tunnel. He knew that his speed would be drastically reduced when he entered. He was capable of travelling great speeds while in flight, but on the ground, he could move only as fast as his legs would carry him. He landed and began racing through the tunnel knowing that Jayden's time was running out.

Palto had travelled an hour into the tunnel when he finally saw torch lights flickering on the walls. It was a welcome sight when he saw Jayden still walking on his own accord. He was standing in front of his warriors, all of whom had their bow and arrows at the ready. As Palto drew near, he could hear Jayden ordering them to stand down.

"Palto, I was expecting far worse than you when I felt the vibrations of something moving quickly toward us. I am relieved to see you!"

"And I you Jayden. You appear to be faring better than Oisin, although the streaks in your face show me that the poison has taken its toll on you as well."

Jayden ignored the observation. "You have seen Oisin? What of Kaelyn and Palvoy? Are they alright?"

"I am sorry Jayden. By the time we arrived in Aura, Palvoy had succumbed to an injury he had sustained in battle. Kaelyn was unharmed, and Oisin was alive, but unconscious due to the effects of the poison. Solko is taking him to the Wall of Solace in hopes that he will make a full recovery and I have come to retrieve you to do the same."

"What battle awaited them when they exited the tunnel?" Jayden asked, regretting the decision to let them forge ahead of the rest.

"The battle that goes on as we speak, Solharn's armies were waiting for you in Aura. When we saw Leal had been burned and found no survivors we flew directly to Aura where we knew the tunnel led. When we got there, the Kaltaures were already questioning Kaelyn and Palvoy. We had no choice but to attack and try to save them, but in doing so, we lost any time we might have had to strategize our attack along with you. The Pegapires are holding their own, but without the Lealians help, they are suffering casualties. We must hurry if the battle is going to be ours."

"How far are we from Aura, Palto?"

"It took an hour for me to reach you, so it is at least three for you at a fast pace."

Jayden turned to his warriors, "The war against Solharn's army has already begun! As we speak, the Pegapires are fighting the battle alone. We should be fighting alongside them as it was meant to be. Our brothers are suffering at the hands of this evil, and without

86

us, they will suffer more losses than need be! We are still several hours from Aura, and I ask you, my fellow Lealians, to follow me there as fast as our feet can carry us. Are you with me?" Jayden yelled.

The cheer that followed thundered down the tunnel. "Let's go, Palto. Aura awaits us."

Palto did not move. "Aura awaits these fine warriors Jayden; Solace awaits you."

"Surely you do not expect me to abandon my people Palto? You know that is not my way, nor is it the nature of any Lealian."

"Is it in the nature of a Lealian to senselessly die, because that is what your fate will be if you decide not to come with me."

"I am fine Palto. Now, we are wasting time!" yelled Jayden.

"You are strong Jayden; I can see that by the mere fact that you are standing in front of me, but in a few hours' time the poison coursing through your veins will overcome you. Who will lead your people then? Do you think this is what your father would choose for you? Is this what he died for?"

"My father died for the Lealians, for Elissa and for his love of Rhol!" Jayden responded angrily.

"Exactly Jayden and that is why you must come with me. They don't need you to lead them down a tunnel. They need you to lead them in battle. You must teach them the values that your father taught you. Kaelyn already fights the battle with Issa. She will await the arrival of her fellow Lealians, and you will join them after you have healed."

Jayden looked back at his people; many that had survived were young. When Cordelia, the woman who had mended his wounds, looked at him and told him not to be a fool he realized Palto was right.

"Kaelyn and the Pegapires await you in Aura, make haste and be safe. I will return to join you in battle. That is my word!"

The Lealians gave yet another cheer as Jayden and Palto disappeared down the tunnel. Palto had been right; by the time they reached the depot, Jayden felt very weak. He had to use all the strength he could muster to hold on when Palto sprang from the ground and took flight. Jayden looked down and saw the battle of Aura raging on. Bodies were strewn throughout the fields, and smoke filled the air making it difficult to breathe. He was sad to see that at least three Pegapires had fallen victim to Solharn's army.

"Jayden, are you able to fight?" Palto asked. "I see Issa and Kaelyn are in need of help."

Jayden looked up to see Kaelyn swinging her sword at attacking Phits, while Issa maneuvered strategically around large arrows coming toward them from the ground. When the headless bodies of three Phits fell aimlessly through the sky, he smiled. His father had always liked Kaelyn and had taught her swordsmanship from an early age. She was one of his best students, and Jayden realized why as he watched her master the sword even while swinging her body down and around Issa. The Phits must have realized these two warriors were a dangerous combination as well, for they were swarming them from every direction.

Palto flew within range of them while Jayden drew arrows from the satchel that Palto carried to his left side and retrieved a bow from the right. They weren't Orler arrows, but to Jayden, it didn't really make a difference. He was a master archer and could easily shoot three arrows at a time, never missing the target. He was able to drop six Phits in two shots. Kaelyn was surprised when she looked over to see Palto and Jayden, and it allowed her some welcome time to take care of the other two Phits that had been pursuing them. Palto tuned to fly west to Solace. Kaelyn raised her sword to him in thanks, and Jayden gestured back raising his closed fist high in the air.

Jayden had used his last bit of strength in that fight, and as Palto soared through the sky toward the entrance to the Sacred Realm, he began to feel dizzy. Palto was telling Jayden to hang on, but his voice became blurred in his head, and gradually he lost consciousness. This slowed Palto down considerably. He was forced to maintain a steady flight pattern so Jayden would not fall off from any sudden movements. Palto estimated he was a mere fifteen minutes from the tunnel entrance, but he would have to get him through the tunnel to the actual Wall of Solace. It would be close. Jayden was succumbing to the poison.

When Palto flew over the mountain range that surrounded the Valley of Solace he paused and then dove as quickly as he could toward the abundant vegetation surrounding the lake. When he was safely hidden, he looked in disbelief as a Kruntulla blocked the torrents of water that cascaded down the mountain which had once provided a natural camouflage to the entrance. To make matters worse there were now hundreds of Phits flying into the passageway.

He knew it was going to be impossible to save Jayden. There was no other way that he knew of to get to the realm and an entire army of Phits now stood between him and the wall. He was contemplating what his next move could be when he heard a loud buzzing around his ear. He turned to face what was causing the annoying sound and gazed upon a bird the likes of which he had never seen before. The bird darted around his head stopping in mid-air as if to tell him something but he could not understand what message it brought if any. Palto hoped it was some sort of sign. This creature was quite obviously not from this world. There wasn't a living thing on Rhol that he had not seen at one time or another. The bird moved in close to Palto's ear, but still, all he could hear was a high pitched whine of some sort. After several minutes of listening to the same sound over and over Palto thought he heard the words "remain here" but it was still unclear.

Ω

Deo hoped that Palto understood him. He had no time to waste. At least when he left him, Palto had not moved. It was to Deo's advantage that he had been transformed into a bird that could fly at such speeds and maneuver through small places, but it made speech almost unrecognizable. Deo quickly flew by the Kruntulla unnoticed and silently flew over the Phits. He headed through the tunnel toward the Sacred Realm. He was relieved when he saw they had only progressed about a quarter of the way in. It made flying much more enjoyable not having to worry about being detected.

When Deke saw Deo come through the wall, he was so excited he forgot to keep his concentration which made Deo change back into himself in midair and come crashing to the ground. He came to a stop near Kiran after rolling over several times.

"Sorry about that," Deke said, smiling a little when he realized Deo was unharmed.

89

"Don't worry. You're learning," Deo replied just a little annoyed. "Palto has arrived with Jayden. He hides in the trees to the east of the lake. Jayden's not well. I fear time is running out for him. We must come up with a plan and quickly."

"What does Palto think?" Kiran asked.

"I could not communicate very well with him. I am not even sure if he knew what I was, but I think I convinced him to stay hidden until my return."

"Have Solharn's armies entered the tunnel yet Deo?" Deke asked.

"The Phits are about a quarter of the way to the Wall of Solace, and the beast still waits at the entrance way."

"We cannot fight them all, and we have no one to assist Palto at his end. This is not an ideal situation," Kiran thought out loud.

"We can create a channel through them!" Deo excitedly shouted. "I have an idea."

Ω

Palto was convincing himself that he had imagined what the bird had said and Jayden was not far from death. He would charge the entranceway and hope for the best. They would only have a slim chance of survival, but he decided it would be the only way.

He was just about to execute his plan when he saw the bird hovering in front of him once again. He was looking intently at this strange creature waiting for a sign when it started to distort and change shape right before his eyes. Palto stepped back on his hind legs causing Jayden to fall to the ground. It could not be helped Palto thought. He had to get into a position to strike out at this creature. He was convinced now that he had been tricked by Solharn's black magic.

Palto stood poised to attack, watching as the bird changed into a small boy. Deo realized the danger right away and immediately dropped to one knee all the while bowing his head toward the ground. He had no desire to be either hypnotized or ripped limb from limb by this mighty warrior.

"Palto, please don't be alarmed. I've come to help you get Jayden to the Wall of Solace. I'm not what you think. My name is Deodatus. I'm a Paladin of the boy from the world Earth. The one Queen Elissa foresaw would come and start the chain of events that are happening as we speak. "

Although Palto now stood on his four legs, he was still wary of the boy. The Queen only told three people of this. Roland was dead, and the other two were Kiran and himself.

"How do you know of this Deodatus, if that is your real name?"

"Kiran, she has been preparing me for this day for over a year now," Deo said while continuing to stare at the ground.

"And how is it that a Paladin can shape shift into another being?"

Deo realized it was not going as well as he had hoped. The plan was precisely timed. If he did not convince Palto soon, he would shape shift again, and it would fail. He had to get Palto to trust him. He decided to take what could be a much more hazardous approach and stood up to face the mighty Pegapire.

"There is no time to explain the ways in which all things were designed, but in short the amulet the boy holds has many powers which enable him to do many things! Now if Jayden is to live and Rhol is to be saved you must throw caution to the wind and trust what I am telling you! There is no time for any more questions."

Deo stood there aggressively staring at Palto. He thought that since he was still alive, it was a good sign. Only after several seconds of staring at each other did Palto respond.

"What is the plan then, boy?"

"Alright then," Deo said still a little shaken.

Deo quickly explained the plan. After Deo had finished, Palto looked at him skeptically.

"If I am to understand what you have just told me, then I tend to agree with Kiran. What if Deke cannot hold the transformation of this massive beast for such a prolonged period?"

Deo looked at Palto. "Then we will be left with the two of us to fight the army of Phits, and we will most likely die along with Jayden."

CHAPTER FIFTEEN

Kaelyn was exhausted. Her arms ached from the constant swinging of her sword and the pounding her body was taking as Issa led her into attack after attack. Both were covered in both blue and red blood splatters. The blue came from the countless Phits they had slaughtered and the red from the Kaltaures and Ralcriff that lay dead as a result of their collaboration.

Over the last several hours Kaelyn had come to know her companion quite well. Issa was a true warrior. She could fly at the speed of lightning and if need be, stop in midair at any fleeting moment. In Kaelyn's mind, Issa was the reason that they still had an advantage in this battle.

Issa was a hundred years old, sixty more than Kaelyn. She had been trained to fight by Palto himself. The fact that their leaders had personally taken on the challenge of training them both was a huge statement in itself. She did wonder why Palto had decided that Issa would fight alongside her though. Usually, a Lealian and a Pegapire that were chosen to fight together were roughly the same age and had the same experience; it made them a more lethal combination.

Issa had fought in several battles already and was very experienced. Kaelyn had fought in only one battle if you could call it that. It had been just prior to Queen Elissa ordering the Lealians to retreat. Roland had not allowed Kaelyn to fight in the wars before that, saying she was not ready. She, being stubborn and foolhardy, had not agreed and unbeknownst to him, had slipped out of the village one night to find a battle of her own.

As she crept through the forest several miles from Leal, she found a group of Kaltaures sharpening their blades for what was to be a feast on a prisoner they had captured. Kaelyn had taken out three of the soldiers with her sword before the other five even realized what was happening. She had begun to advance on the remainder of them when a Ralcriff jumped in her way. It's snarling teeth just missed her face when the chain it had been tied to came to an abrupt end and jerked the beast back. Kaelyn cursed herself.

When she picked herself up from the ground, the Kaltaures soldiers had surrounded her. As they stared at her, looking her up and down, she thrust her sword forward slicing open the stomach of the nearest one. When she turned around to swing at the soldier advancing on her from behind, she was hit in the head and fell unconscious to the ground.

Kaelyn awoke to find herself shackled to a tree. The beasts were feeding on the prisoner she had failed to save. The grotesque snakes that formed their hair stabbed out at scraps as they shoveled meat into their mouths. Knowing that nobody had any idea where she was, she remembered what Roland had said and knew he had been right. She had made a terrible mistake and was going to pay for it. They would either enslave her or eat her; neither was a particularly pleasant way to go but if given a choice she would take death. She had heard far too many stories about the way enslaved women were treated by the Kaltaures.

When they finished their meal, they unshackled her from the tree, bound her hands with rope and tied it to one of the Kaltaures horses. She screamed and cried for them to kill her. They had chosen to enslave her.

The soldiers rode through the woods dragging her behind. She had tried everything she could to taunt them into killing her, but they only laughed. She finally gave up, slowly becoming immune to their constant beratement. When they had stopped for the night, they shackled her to a tree again and contemplated who would have her first. She had slowly fallen asleep from exhaustion.

She awoke to her shackles once again being removed. With her last bit of strength, she yelled, turned and struck her enemy in the face with her forehead breaking the nose of a Lealian elder. She stood there in shock until seconds later she heard a familiar voice within the ranks. It was Roland ensuring her she would be alright. She had burst into tears. The Kaltaures soldiers lay dead on the ground surrounding their makeshift campground, the victims of Orler arrows and swords. They had also lost one Lealian warrior in the fight. She had known Salden since she was a small child.

Kaelyn began to apologize profusely to Roland, but he would hear none of it. He never spoke of the incident again. Perhaps he thought she had learned a valuable lesson. None the less she never forgave herself for being the reason behind Salden's death.

Roland gently guided her through the camp in silence. Eventually, they came to a stop beside a Pegapire. It was the first one she had ever seen, and as Roland helped her onto the magnificent animal, he introduced him to her as Palto. She learned later that Palto had been the one to find her after Roland had asked him to help in the search. Perhaps Palto had seen something in her that he liked that day, Kaelyn thought, realizing that Palto had now saved her life on two occasions.

The voice of Issa beckoning to her brought Kaelyn's mind back to the battle she had been fighting for the past several hours.

"Kruntulla have joined the Kaltaures," she yelled.

Kaelyn looked down to see three of the enormous beasts swiping at Pegapires whenever they charged at the Kaltaures soldiers. It made ground fighting almost impossible, and the Pegapires casualties were climbing. This was an unexpected turn which gave the enemy the advantage. It left the Pegapires to fight mainly with the Phits thereby allowing the Kaltaures soldiers to fire their weapons at will from the ground, with little resistance. Neither Kaelyn nor Issa could think of a feasible strategy. If they retreated, the Lealians would exit the tunnel and eventually be slaughtered without the Pegapires help, but if they continued to fight the Pegapires might well be wiped out. They could not afford any more casualties.

After watching two more Pegapires fall victim to the battle, Issa told Kaelyn to remove a wooden horn from her side and to blow it as hard as she could. Kaelyn lost all hope knowing that this would sound the retreat of the Pegapires.

"Issa, if I blow this horn my people will be doomed!" Kaelyn screamed through the wind.

"And if you don't mine will, and yours will follow. We must regroup, Kaelyn. We have lost too many already. Without the Lealians, we stand no chance. It is not what either of us wants, but we both know it is what we have to do."

Kaelyn could not argue and sadly put the horn to her lips. She was about to sound the retreat when she noticed a significant portion of the Kaltaures army beginning to run south toward the tunnel. She looked over to see her people, hundreds of them, storming onto the fields of Aura toward the Kaltaures.

"Issa, they have arrived!"

"Then we have hope," Issa said while re-engaging the battle with renewed faith.

The Lealians who were well adapted for ground fighting had quickly formed two platoons. The front platoon clashed with the Kaltaures soldiers using swords while the second fired hundreds of Orler arrows toward their enemy.

The climate in the battle changed within minutes. Most Kaltaures soldiers were no match for the Lealians who were masters in swordsmanship, and the Kaltaures army who had been taken by surprise were losing soldiers by the dozens after falling victim to the Lealian archers.

Kaelyn could hear Issa communicating with the other Pegapires telling them to join with a Lealian when they had the chance. It was not an easy task though as the Phits continued to attack relentlessly and the Kruntulla had now moved over toward the Lealian ground troops. This was balancing things out again. The Kruntulla, although not very smart, had skin as thick as a tree making it difficult to cause damage with any weapon.

Several Pegapires had seized the chance and were able to join with Lealian archers who still remained a safe distance from the Kruntulla. This allowed the archers to fire on the Kruntulla at short distances causing at least some damage. But it was not enough. The majority of their arrows simply bounced off the Kruntulla's skin. It was hardly even slowing the beasts down, and the ground troops were suffering because of it.

"Kaelyn, we must deal with the Kruntulla. The only way to kill it is to penetrate the skin and sink arrows deep into its brain. We must make an outlet for the archers to fire at," Issa said as she circled high above one of them.

"What do you have in mind?" Kaelyn screamed back.

"A sword will cut through the layers of skin. We have to create a hole, take a patch of skin off its head and then penetrate it with as many arrows as we can."

Kaelyn knew what that meant. Issa could not fly close enough for her to use the sword on the Kruntulla. It meant she was getting off.

"Okay, get me as close as you can," Kaelyn said without hesitating.

Issa was not surprised to hear Kaelyn's response. She was impressed with the young warrior. Kaelyn reminded her of another Lealian she had fought with in several battles leading up to the retreat, named Hallin. He was three times Kaelyn's age and could handle any weapon that was put in his hands.

She remembered the last time they had fought together; it was outside Aura. They had been walking along a pathway toward the stronghold near the base of Mount Sibileo. There were nine of them, eight Lealians and her when they were attacked by Ralcriff and a troop of twenty or so Kaltaures.

Hallin had heard the Ralcriff coming out of the forest and alerted the rest, thus giving their small contingent the chance to prepare and find cover. As the Ralcriff leapt from the forest and down a dirt bank toward them, they were met with arrows. The Ralcriff had not stood a chance with the seven Lealians on the ground along with Issa and Hallin in the sky piercing their wretched bodies with arrows.

It had also allowed Hallin and her to spot the Kaltaures soldiers following behind them. Hallin instructed the Lealian warriors on the ground to circle back around the Kaltaures and attack them from all sides using their swords. The forest was too dense to use bows. It was a short battle that the Kaltaures lost. Hallin was a brilliant strategist, and he had taught her this skill over their time together.

Issa remembered what happened next all too well. She and Hallin had met back up with the Lealians on the ground. Everyone's spirits were high after coming out of the fight victorious. A young warrior was re-enacting how he was able to take out two Kaltaures soldiers on his own when he suddenly evaporated in a stream of flames. Phanthus had planned his assault well; everyone was now scattered, and in the melee that followed, Issa could not find Hallin.

She flew through the sky and was able to spot and safely remove two of the Lealians from danger. She returned to save more only to find four of them burned to death. Still, she could not find

96

Hallin and did not know yet whether he had survived or not. She flew in mad circles around the burning forest looking for any sign of him. So intent was her vigil on the ground that she did not see the Phit coming up behind her. She had no time to react before her wing had been broken causing her to crash to the ground breaking her legs.

She lay there helplessly and watched as two more Phits flew down to finish her off. When they drew close, one suddenly dropped from the sky, an arrow embedded in its gruesome head. She had looked over to see a badly burned Hallin running toward her. He had discarded his bow after using his last arrow and had no other weapons. She tried to lift her head in an effort to fend off the remaining Phit, but she could not move for the pain. She could see her time was near, the Phit was going straight for her neck, its gaping mouth was dripping saliva, anticipating the taste of blood. She closed her eyes waiting for its teeth to penetrate her exposed skin but it never came.

When she opened them again, she saw Hallin hanging from the jaws of the Phit in mid-air wildly punching at the beast. He had managed to get in between her and the Phit. It was over in moments for him, and she screamed when the Phit dropped his lifeless body to the ground and circled back toward her.

It was not her time though. The Lealians she had saved had managed to alert other troops, and they arrived in force, killing the Phit before it came within reach of her. Phanthus had long since disappeared. She was taken back to Tamon. Her broken bones mended quickly, but she could never erase the memory of Hallin dying such a horrible death to save her.

Kaelyn was now standing on Issa with her sword at the ready. "Issa move closer!"

She did, narrowly missing two Phits that had approached them from the side while her mind had been elsewhere. When Issa saw them both fall to Kaelyn's sword, she refocused herself. "Kaelyn, once you have opened the wound on the Kruntulla, jump and I will be there to catch you. I will not let you down."

"I have no doubt, Issa."

They were nearing the giant. Kaelyn could see seven Pegapires all with Lealian archers that Issa had summoned. They were forming what looked like a V in the sky above them. This formation would allow them all to fire a clean shot at their target. It was up to her now. Issa flew over the head of the Kruntulla and Kaelyn jumped. When she landed, she thrust her sword into the beasts head and held on tight so as not to slide back off.

She was having difficulty pulling herself to her feet as the Kruntulla madly flailed about, but after several seconds she managed to, pulling the sword from its head. She drew her sword back behind her shoulder and began to swing it forward in an attempt to scalp a portion of its thick skin off and complete the target, but when the Kruntulla grabbed at whatever was causing his head to hurt, she was forced to duck. Kaelyn lost her footing and started sliding off.

Issa looked from the sky, and knowing that their plan was about to fail, quickly flew downward to catch Kaelyn before she fell, but she didn't. Issa could not believe her eyes while watching Kaelyn roll over twice with her sword held high above her head. On the second turn, she jumped to her knees and swung her sword with all her might cutting a small piece of skin from the Kruntulla's head. Completing her goal she jumped to her feet and kicked herself off its head, flipping into a free-fall. Issa was there to catch her, but when Kaelyn landed, she could not hold on and bounced backward. Gravity was causing her to fall from Issa's back. She toppled off but managed to grab onto her tail and hang on. Issa maneuvered around the Kruntulla who was madly trying to crush them with his hands.

She was flying around the front of the Kruntulla when it suddenly seemed to freeze and come crashing toward the ground. Issa flew as fast as her wings would carry her to avoid being crushed by the toppling body of the beast.

Issa came around the right side of the Kruntulla flying directly upward between its two arms just before its body hit the ground. Following this, she managed to flip Kaelyn around onto her back before stopping in midair. They could hear the cheers from both the ground and sky. The archers had found their mark, and the plan had succeeded. The Kruntulla lay dead on the ground.

The death of the Kruntulla forced Solharn's army to rethink their strategy. They retreated to the east side of Aura to gather themselves. It was a welcome break and allowed the Lealians and Pegapires to join for a well-needed rest finally.

By the time they had landed on the ground, Kaelyn had realized that it was around the same time yesterday that Jayden and

Oisin had been inflicted with the Ralcriff quills. She climbed off Issa wondering if they still lived.

CHAPTER SIXTEEN

Palto didn't take long to agree to the plan. It was much the same as his except now he would have a little more help. They would wait until Deo transformed back into the bird and then it would be time.

In the meantime, Deo got Jayden back on Palto and secured him so that he would not fall. Deo could feel by a touch of Jayden's cold and clammy skin that he was not far from death. Once he was secured, they waited.

Ω

Kiran had gone to great lengths to make sure that Deke was relaxed and would not be distracted. Mary still stood by him making sure he was alright. Many of the Rholians had now gathered near the wall, wearing makeshift armor and carrying weapons, should they need to enter the tunnel to fight. Kiran looked them over seeing that many were younger. It made sense. Their age was probably a huge factor in being able to get to the Realm when Solharn finally defeated Elissa. She could see it in their faces that some were scared, but many had a look of determination etched in their faces. Their pain for the loved ones they had lost, at the hands of Solharn, would certainly help them on the battlefield.

"It is time Dietrich," Kiran said walking over to him. "Let us pray we are successful."

Ω

Palto watched in amazement when Deo transformed back into the bird and flew toward the Kruntulla.

In minutes, he could see the Kruntulla madly swatting at something around his head. That was his cue. He wasted no time, flying rapidly toward the entrance to the tunnel. He flew low to the lake until he reached the base of the mountain and then shot straight up through the water that had escaped the Kruntulla's blockade. The Kruntulla was none the wiser, and Palto quickly slipped unnoticed into the passageway leading to the sacred realm. Unfortunately, the Phits that had been left behind to guard the entranceway to the Realm were still there. One flew down the tunnel to alert the others, while the rest instantly flew toward Palto as he landed.

Palto took out the first two Phits with his powerful jaws and discarded them in a lump against the wall of the tunnel. Another that came from his rear was met with his hoof and fell helplessly to the lake below. Two others made the mistake of looking into his eyes and were instantly paralyzed. The last one managed to bite into his side ripping a deep gash into his body. He knew it would go for his neck next, so he crushed it into the wall using the weight of his body before it had the chance.

There was no point in going after the last Phit that had flown off to warn the others. The Phits could easily maneuver through this tunnel using their wings. Palto's wing span was too broad, and it would not be possible to catch it on foot. He looked at his side. The wound was deep and oozing blood, but at least Jayden was unscathed. He hoped Deo would arrive quickly. Now, he too was in dire need of the Wall of Solace.

Ω

Deke continued to concentrate. He could barely process Mary's voice whispering to him. Her voice was soothing, which was probably why Kiran had chosen her for this task. Yet as she began to tell him that the next stage of the plan was here, it sounded strange.

This was the part of the scheme which Deke feared the most. There were so many unanswered questions. If Deo was still in the process of flying around the Kruntulla, the transformation would

101

cause him to fall to his death. If by chance they still had not left the woods by the lake he would be unable to fly, which would cause the plan to fail. Finally, even if everything had worked as they hoped, how long would he be able to keep the transformation of such a large animal alive before his energy was completely drained?

These were questions that he would have to wait for. As he began the transformation, he hoped he would not be disappointed in the answers.

Ω

Palto was relieved to see Deo fly up to his side. Deo looked around at the dead bodies of the fallen Phits, strewn about the cave. Looking at Palto, he noticed the wound he had acquired in the battle and was concerned. However, there was nothing he could do for him in this state other than take his place at the front as planned and wait.

"I hope this doesn't take much longer Deo. One of the Phits was able to escape me, and I am sure it has informed the others by now. We will not stand a chance against a battalion of them. If the transformation has not happened before they arrive, you must leave me behind and fly to the wall. It makes no sense for all three of us to die here."

Deo hoped it would not come to that but knew if it did, Palto was right. They could both hear the Phits coming closer. The telltale whine of their wings easily gave them away. They would be there in minutes.

"Go now Deo, before it is too late!"

Deo knew Palto couldn't hear him, but when he didn't move, he suspected Palto would get the idea that he was not going anywhere until he absolutely had to.

The Phits were now within sight, hundreds of them. Some walked while others flew, moving swiftly toward them. It was now or never. Deo was beginning to lose hope, but fate was with them. He started to feel that familiar sensation. It was the sensation of his body melting away as new hunks of flesh replaced what was left of his once familiar shape. The Phits stopped advancing. They didn't know what they were looking at, as his body slowly twisted and contorted into an animal which they had never seen the likes of.

Palto too looked on in wonderment at the animal which now stood before him. The beast was enormous and must have weighed two tons. It's horns wrapped over its head providing invaluable protection for anything that might try and strike it and then continued nearly three feet from either side. The creature's black skin appeared thick and leathery making it hard to penetrate.

"What animal is this, Deo?" Palto asked as he prepared himself.

"It is one of the most dangerous animals on Earth, Palto. It is a Cape Buffalo."

At that, Deo began to run toward the Phits, closely followed by Palto. The plan was working. The Phits that didn't get out of the way, or couldn't, were launched through the air or bludgeoned with the beast's horns. They had no time to react and scrambled to get out of the way. The first hundred or so Phits were of no consequence, and Palto met no resistance as he followed the path Deo created. When they cut through several hundred more with relative ease, they became even more confident. They had broken through their lines and now had nothing between them and the Wall of Solace other than distance. Their only problem was that the Phits could move much faster than them in the tunnel and after reorganizing themselves, they were quickly coming up from behind.

"We are close Deo, I can feel it," Palto panted as he ran.

"I do not feel well Palto, I …."

Ω

Kiran ran toward Deke after Mary beckoned her. He was sweating profusely lying in the prone position unconscious.

"It is what I feared," Kiran said. "He has exhausted his body. He was not ready for a burden such as this. We must snap him out of his unconscious state, or he will die. We can wait no longer."

Mary held Deke up while Kiran began slapping his face "Talk to him, Mary! Bring him back to reality!" Kiran screamed.

Deke could not move and was having trouble breathing, yet he forced himself to keep concentrating. He was lost in his consciousness, unaware of his surroundings. He could hear something in his head, a distant moan but he kept fighting it off. He could not lose his concentration or all would be lost.

"It is not working Mary. He is not coming out of it!" Kiran said as she ordered her awaiting militia to proceed through the wall to find Deo and Palto.

"Run as fast as you possibly can. Their lives may depend on it!" she yelled as they streamed through the wall.

"Oisin and I are going after them as well Kiran," Lorca said. Oisin was already on her back. "Solko and his sister will remain here, should they be needed."

Kiran looked at Lorca and just nodded as the two turned and rode into the tunnel.
Solko looked at Deke and noticed that his face was turning a bluish grey. "Kiran, Deke is not breathing!"

Kiran leapt toward him and grabbed the amulet hanging from his neck.

"Ko liak somu, ko liak somu, ko liak somu," a light burst out from her hand and shot her several feet through the air. She landed with a thud in the grass.

Deke coughed and gasped for air. "Mary…what happened?"

Ω

Palto ground to a halt as the mighty beast that was collapsed and rolled through the dirt. The dust cleared, and the buffalo was gone, leaving Deo standing there in his true form.

"Deo, take Jayden and get him to the Wall of Solace, I will hold them off."

"No Palto, we can all make it if we run!" Deo begged.

"No, we cannot. Now go!" Palto yelled.

Deo pulled Jayden from Palto and slung him around his shoulders and neck. He began to run taking one last glance back. Palto was standing on his hind legs preparing for battle, ready to die for Jayden and his beloved world.

104

Deo had run maybe fifteen minutes down the tunnel when Lorca came around the bend with Oisin. They were followed by a small army of Rholians.

Oisin jumped off Lorca and ran over to Deo. "You have Jayden, Deo! Does he still live?"

"I am not sure but thanks to Palto he has a slim chance. You must hurry. Palto is fighting the entire army of Phits on his own."

Lorca was gone before the words left Deo's mouth. Oisin who she had left behind in her haste organized the Rholians and followed at a distance, unable to keep up with her speed.

It was not long before Lorca could hear the fight just ahead. She was almost there. When she rounded the last bend, she stopped and stared in disbelief at what she was witnessing. She became consumed with anger. Palto lay on the ground unable to move while Phits fed on his flesh and blood. Lorca was disgusted. Her leader was slowly being eaten alive. Rage took over her anger and her eyes filled with hatred. The Phit's did not know what hit them as she ripped and tore into every one of them that dared to disrespect Palto. Covered in blood, she stood over him waiting for the next group to arrive. They came, but none could get past Lorca who was being driven by pure insanity.

The Rholians finally arrived behind her, staring in astonishment at her valor as she continued to tear apart anything that came, within reach. When nothing else came she continued to stare down the tunnel. Oisin finally approached her.

"Are you alright Lorca?"

"Get Palto to the Wall of Solace; I will stay here in case more come."

"I will stay with you, then," Oisin said.

"Leave five soldiers with me; I will be okay. I would like Palto to have a Lealian….you with him, should he succumb to his injuries before he reaches the wall and I am absolutely certain you would like to see Jayden. I will wait here for a half hour, and then return to Realm."

Oisin obeyed Lorca. He and the other soldiers quickly loaded Palto onto a makeshift stretcher and began carrying him to the wall.

Ω

Deke was awake but was still having trouble breathing. Mary had gone to check on Kiran. When she got there she found Kiran unable to move, she could hardly talk and seemed to have trouble catching her breath.

She asked Mary if Deke had survived. Mary assured her he had but that his breathing was raspy, making him too weak to move. Kiran smiled and said that he would get better soon.

Kiran weakly asked if their plan had been successful, but before Mary could respond, she had at least part of her question answered as Deo walked through the wall carrying Jayden. In minutes, Jayden was standing and appeared to have suffered no ill effects from the poison. Jayden immediately noticed Palto was not with him.

"Where is Palto?"

"He remained in the tunnel to hold off the Phits. It was the only way he could save you...us," Deo responded.

Upon hearing this, Jayden immediately grabbed a sword from a nearby soldier and headed back toward the tunnel. He did not make it outside the Realm before Oisin, and the Rholian soldiers rushed through the wall carrying Palto.

"Palto are you alright?" Jayden asked looking him over.

"I am now Jayden," Palto said as he stood up and looked over at Deo crouching beside a sickly looking boy. "It seems our plan may have worked. Would I be correct in assuming this to be Deke?" Palto asked Deo.

"It is but he is not well. He can hardly breathe."

"He will live," sounded Kiran's weakened, crackling voice.

Palto turned to see Kiran laying on the ground in obvious distress. He ran to her side.

"Kiran, are you alright, what has happened...?"

"All in good time Palto. Where is Lorca?" Kiran whispered as she gasped for air.

"She is here with you, is she not?" Palto said looking around.

"She will be here shortly. She stayed behind to make sure you got back to the wall safely," Oisin informed him.

"She is supposed to be by Kiran's side; perhaps she would not be in this state if....."

Oisin interrupted. "If not for her you would be dead, Palto. She risked her life to save yours."

Ω

A half hour had passed, and with no sign of the enemy, Lorca was satisfied that the remaining Phits must have retreated. She instructed the soldiers to head back to Solace with her. She strolled slowly behind the Rholians tired from the battle she had just fought. She had no idea that she possessed that kind of resilience until then.

She was glad to see the last leg of the tunnel, the wall was finally in sight, and she was due for a welcome rest. She heard the soldier say the words that were so familiar to her. "Solert a piony du sa trquil." She loved the ancient language which meant. "Open to a world of tranquility." The wall turned from rock to clear welcoming warmth. She could see Palto was alive and well, waiting for her on the other side. She would probably be in a little trouble for leaving Kiran, but it would be worth it.

She quickened her pace, but upon approaching the wall, she noticed a strange orange glow reflecting off it. Some sort of light she thought. Lorca turned in curiosity, to see what caused the reflection. It was the last thing she would ever see as flames enveloped her and continued racing down the tunnel toward the Wall of Solace.

Palto saw it coming and threw Oisin out of the way as the fire tore through the wall causing him to fall backward.

"It is Phanthus! Solharn is near," Kiran weakly whispered to Mary. "The wall must be closed before he gets here....Pert ne sacco."

Mary jumped up and ran for the wall screaming, "Pert ni sico, Pert ni sico!" she repeated the words again and again, but still nothing happened.

Palto hearing Mary realized what was happening. "Pert ne sacco!" he yelled.

Solharn would not make it there in time as the wall once again turned to stone. He was incensed and used all the dark magic he could summon upon the wall. But nothing worked.

107

"You cannot hide in there forever Kiran. I do not know why the Realm of Solace remains protected, but Elissa's spell will not last forever!" he screamed in a rage.

Deke seemed to get much worse when Kiran spoke. "Your days on Rhol are coming to an end Solharn. You underestimate the power Elissa holds over you."

Solharn laughed. "Elissa holds nothing, Kiran. All of her power lies within the amulet the boy holds. I know you are too stubborn of an old lady to simply hand him over to me but you will in time. And rest assured, the longer it takes to get him the more I will make him suffer. Do you hear that boy?"

The words echoed through Deke's head as he lay on the ground gasping for air.

"There is only one way out Kiran. The dragon will remain at the tunnel entrance should you think of trying to find refuge elsewhere. When the wall finally fails you, I will be there, and I will watch you all suffer the most painful deaths you can imagine. Until that time I will finish what I started in Rhol," and as quickly as he had arrived Solharn was gone.

At her bidding, Mary bent down closer to Kiran. "I am sorry Kiran, I spoke the wrong words," Mary said quite upset with herself.

"There is nothing to be sorry about child; we are safe for now. You must guide him, Mary, go now. There is no time to waste, show him the way," Kiran said with her last breath.

Palto walked over and looked mournfully down at the lifeless body of Kiran. He was joined by Jayden, Oisin, Deo and Deke who by now had fully recovered.

After a prolonged period of silence Palto finally asked again how she came to be like this. Mary explained through her tears what Kiran had done when Deke had stopped breathing. That she had put her hand on the amulet and repeated words that she did not understand. Following this, a bright light had shot from the amulet hurtling her back to where she lies now.

"What words were they?" Jayden asked.

Mary repeated the words to the best of her memory. "Ko liak somu."

Jayden translated. "Take my breath."

PART II

THE BEGINNING OF THE END

CHAPTER SEVENTEEN

Deke stared sadly at Kiran. She had given her life for him. He continued to gaze at her remorsefully, unaware of anything around him. It was only the gentle voice of Mary that broke his trance.

"Deke," was all she said as she gently grabbed his arm and pulled him away.

Hundreds of the blue creatures that he had first witnessed when he walked through the Wall of Solace suddenly swept down and surrounded her. A light blue glow began to emanate from Kiran's body until it too formed what appeared to be one of the glowing creatures. In an instant, the creatures dissipated and flew to the top of the cavern surrounding the tree; all except one. It remained hovering in front of Deke. He wondered if it was somehow trying to communicate with him. He could not understand what if anything the creature was trying to convey, but he did feel a sense of calm before it slowly floated away to join the others.

"They are called Chilings," Deo said looking into Deke's eyes. "Do not be sad Deke. Kiran would have died for anyone, or anything had she thought its purpose was good. Her souls have joined now, ready to experience the next phase of life. She is complete, a Chiling."

"A Chiling is a higher form of life Deke, like an energy life force. The word is derived from the ancient language meaning Divine Spirit. It is the last journey one makes before entering the eternal life," Jayden continued.

"Is this where it starts then, the eternal life? There are so many that remain here," Deke said looking up at the thousands of Chiling.

Mary was quick to respond. "No we, or at least Kiran, did not know why the spirits remain in this world. Only the Seraphim would have been able to communicate with them. Kiran believed however that they are only trapped here, as a result of Solharn's evil. She believed that it signals the beginning of the end of the Balance of Five and his plan coming to fruition."

Mary paused before continuing, "if he should succeed in destroying the balance there will be nothing, no worlds, and no eternal life…just blackness, nothingness."

"Whatever the reason, the number of Chiling shows how many lives have been lost as a result of Solharn's malicious intent, and they just keep coming, entering from where the river runs into the Realm," said Palto.

Even now, Deke could see a Chiling enter Solace as he glanced upon the river surging through the wall of the cavern.

"Why do they gather here?" Deke asked.

"We do not know the answer to that question either. It is possible that they are simply finding refuge here. At least Kiran finally knows the answer," Palto said turning slowly and walking away.

"Deke, it is time for us to go. The last words Kiran spoke to me were to get you and Deo out of here," blurted Mary remembering Kiran's dying words.

Palto stopped and looked at Mary. "You heard Solharn, Mary. Phanthus lies in wait, at the entrance to the tunnel. It would be suicide for anyone even to attempt to leave the Realm."

"There is another way," Mary asserted.

Palto was surprised, but more so concerned with what Mary had just communicated to him. He knew what she was to become eventually.

"Do not seem so surprised Palto. When I first arrived in Rhol, I spent several months here with Kiran before continuing on my journey to find Queen Elissa and nearly another two years after Lorca saved me and brought me back here. Kiran shared many secrets of this world with me during that time in hopes that Deke would finally arrive and that I might help him."

"That is not what concerns me, Mary. The concern I have is what you will do with your knowledge when the inevitable comes," Palto said glaring at her.

"What do you mean inevitable? How dare you accuse Mary of anything less than her good intentions," yelled Deke turning to face Palto.

"I will excuse your tone because you do not understand what I speak of. It is something I would have thought you had already been told, but obviously, you have not. It is only a matter of....."

"Enough!" screamed Mary cutting Palto off. "There is no time for idle bantering. We must go now before Solharn destroys everything that remains in Rhol."

"I agree," Jayden said. "Palto, we must warn our people that Solharn has returned and is planning attacks as we speak."

"Very well," Palto said still looking at Mary.

Mary sadly shook her head, "you will not be able to accompany us Palto, nor will your two warriors. You would not survive."

Jayden looked at Mary, as did Palto. The rest stood still in their place, their expressions blank, not saying a word.

"Mary, I have just met you today. I do not know the extent of your knowledge of this world. Perhaps you don't understand, but Palto is the leader of the Pegapires and is the most feared warrior in all of Rhol. Do not question his chances of survival," Jayden sternly said.

"I do not question that, nor was any disrespect intended, Palto," Mary said pointing to the tree in the meadow. "That is the way out, beneath the tree in which the water flows. Once you enter the water, it sucks you under, and there you will stay swirling around through the narrow cavern with no air to breathe until eventually, it spits you out into the Swamps of Tiqor. I had done it once before and barely survived. The legs of a Pegapire would surely be crippled. Your size is too great."

Palto thought momentarily before responding. "She is right. Jayden, you must warn our people that Solharn comes. You and

Oisin go with them; it is your safest route. We will take our chances with Phanthus."

"That as you said earlier, would be suicide Palto. Wait until I return. The Swamps of Tiqor are a little over a one day journey from the Valley of Aura. Once I reach our people, I will have them branch off to fight Phanthus. It may give you the time you need to escape the tunnel. You must give me at least that much time before you begin to move."

Palto said nothing. Jayden knew that he was as stubborn as he and wouldn't agree; before he could respond Jayden continued. "You convinced me in the tunnel to come with you and to save myself for my people. You said they needed a leader, that there was no need to die aimlessly. You saved my life; at least let me have the honor of repaying you. Your people also need a leader Palto."

Palto smiled to himself. Jayden was a worthy ally. He was already a respected leader among his people, and soon his enemies would come to fear his presence in the ranks. He was also wise beyond his years. He knew that his request would not be denied.

"Agreed then, a day, but it will not be wasted. People of Rhol, gather around me. You have much to learn about your enemy if you hope to save your world!"

Palto turned and looked at Mary, Deo, and Deke. "You three must find Elissa before it is too late. Without her, Solharn will have his way with the Balance of Five. Now go!"

"Quickly, follow me," Mary said to the others as she began to walk swiftly across the meadow toward the tree.

Mary stopped just before the surging water that disappeared under the tree's massive roots.

"Once you enter the water you will be unable to return through this passage. It will seem like an hour, but you will be able to breathe again in about three minutes."

Jayden jumped followed by Oisin, and in seconds they had disappeared without a sound. Mary, Deo, and Deke jumped in unison. Their breath was instantly taken away as the currents hidden within the water sucked them into its depths.

Deke did not know how long he had been underwater. He struggled to breathe; his lungs were running out of air, slowly being replaced by water. Relief finally came when he began to cough uncontrollably. He spewed the water from his lungs as he fell through the air toward some particularly vile smelling water.

He landed with a large splash and began to trudge through the shallow water causing the deep mud below its surface to release pungent gases that had probably lain dormant for years. The smell was almost unbearable; looking around he could see no signs of anyone else and worried what had become of them. He could see some scrub brush in the distance giving him hope that dry land lay ahead. The mud was now well past his waist making it harder to move his legs through the thick sludge. As he neared the embankment, he heard a scream coming from the other side. He knew that scream; it was Mary.

Covered in mud from head to toe Deke climbed up the small hill using a nearby root as a rope and began to run toward her screams. He strategized how to deal with whatever was causing her strife while he ran. Where were the others? Where was Deo?

He grabbed a stick hoping he could use it as a makeshift weapon while continuing to run blindly through the thick brush toward the screams. When he rounded the bend, he realized he was standing on an island. He could see Deo on dry land across from him. He too must have heard Mary's pleas for help.

Deke could see Mary swaying back and forth in the water, her arms helplessly flaying away while she was swung to and fro in the murky swamp. Her eyes were as wide as saucers, and her face was distorted by pain. He could not see what was causing her distress but knew he had to act quickly. He began to concentrate, to clear his mind. Deo's body transformed and then immersed itself into the water disappearing into its depths.

After several seconds the water erupted. Deo had obviously sunk his teeth into the creature, which had now emerged from the water screaming in a high pitched wail. Its grasp on Mary gave way, and she flew through the air landing in the water just short of where Deo had been standing. She was not moving, but at least she was a safe distance from the creature's grasp.

Deke remembered this creature from the walls of the cave when he first landed in this strange world. The creature's attention was now focused on him, and as it began to move closer, it screamed once again in pain. Deo had obviously clamped down again on its grotesque body.

114

Its mouth reminded Deke of a lamprey eel, round and full of teeth that were designed to clamp on to its victim and suck it dry of blood. One of the four tentacles which protruded from its smooth blubbery body struck out at him, narrowly missing, as it crashed into the ground knocking him over.

Looking back up Deke could see a crocodile wrapped up in another of its twelve foot long tentacles. Deke quickly thought of a dragonfly and watched as the creature, somewhat confused, lost its second meal of the day after the crocodile simply disappeared.

Deke was exhausted; he had over exerted himself and fell to the ground. The creature's tentacles were reaching out for him again, wrapping themselves around his legs. He kicked wildly in the air fighting to avoid the inevitable.

He could hear yelling and looked over to see that Deo was once again himself. He was madly trying to distract the creature, trying to draw it away. But it paid no heed to him and lifted Deke high in the air by his feet. He was upside down, dangling helplessly in the air. Slowly the creature was lowering him down toward its revolting mouth. The creature's eyes were bulging from the side of its massive head in anticipation of its pending meal.

Deke's face was mere feet from its putrid mouth. The smell was almost enough to make him pass out. There was nothing more he could do. He had completely exhausted himself. He had left the safety of Solace only to fail in his journey minutes after. With his last bit of strength, he reached for the amulet in an attempt to throw it to Mary and Deo. Maybe there was hope that they would find Elissa. Maybe it was his destiny to save them so they could return the amulet to its rightful owner.

As he clutched it in his hand, he was instantly blinded by a bright light. A horrific pain, unlike anything he had ever experienced before, coursed through his body before complete darkness overtook him.

CHAPTER EIGHTEEN

"Jayden are you alright?"

Jayden coughed and spat water from his mouth. "I am fine Oisin. Where are the others?"

"I don't know. It seems we have been separated. I see no sign of them anywhere."

Jayden looked around. The smell was unmistakable. They were in the Swamps of Tiqor. He looked up to see where they had exited. Water continued to pour out of the crevice in the side of the cliff, which he knew surrounded the swamp. His father had taught him much about the swamps, and Jayden knew the cliffs were a telltale sign that they were on the outer edge. The trees were much fuller where they sat, not at all like the brush that grew deep within it, deprived of proper air and sunlight. The lynch grass that grew for miles in front of them also marked the edge of the swamp's boundaries. They would not have to worry about running into Phits here, only getting through the grass whose purple blades were as sharp as razors.

"The underground creek must have more than one exit," Jayden said seeing no sign of the others. "It would only have been mere seconds that separated us exiting the underground waterway. Mary must have been unaware of this. After all, she had only travelled through it once before."

"Where will we find them then, Jayden?"

"We won't," he responded.

Oisin looked at Jayden somewhat surprised. "We must try Jayden. They are not from this world and have no idea what they will encounter. Their chances of survival in this swamp are slim."

Jayden looked at Oisin hating his words as they came out of his mouth. "I am aware of that Oisin, but if we do not reach Aura in time to warn our people of Solharn's return, they will be slaughtered.

Deke and Deo have Mary. She has been through the swamps before, and Kiran, I am sure, has prepared her for this journey. It could take days to find them or for them to find us, and I pray they have made the same decision as I."

Jayden knew Oisin would follow him whether he agreed with his decision or not, but he hoped he understood the basis for it. He would need Oisin's help and his trust; not that he would ever question it. He and Oisin had been friends ever since he could remember. Jayden's father had taken him under his wing. They were relatively the same age, and their friendship had only grown stronger with time.

Oisin was always a tall, lanky boy, but with striking features. He could stand up for himself in any given situation. The odd thing about Oisin was that he did not have any parents, or relatives to speak of. Obviously, he had at one time, but if you asked him, he could not tell you a thing for he had no memory of them. It was strange, given that Lealians were so close with one another. It bothered Jayden, and eventually, he had gone to his father for answers on Oisin's behalf. His father had told them that he too had no knowledge of who Oisin's parents or relatives were. Oisin had simply walked into Leal one day confused and unaware of whom he was. He was obviously Lealian, but no matter how hard they searched, they were unable to find any family origin for him. After a few months, they had named him Oisin and put him up in a small humble house near Jayden's. Oisin never really seemed bothered about his family ties but did tend to worry about others. He was very caring, and Jayden believed it was because of his past. He did not want anyone else to go through what he had.

Jayden was not much different; he too worried a great deal about others and Mary, Deke and Deo were no exception. His father had once told him that the most important trait a leader should have was decisiveness. Make a decision and follow it through. Although not every decision will be the right one, if you believe in it enough and more importantly, if your people believe in you enough it will work out. You will succeed not because the decision you made is always the right one but because the people you lead make it right.

"Which way is it to Aura then?" Oisin asked without hesitation.

Jayden never doubted Oisin's trust in him, but he was glad to hear it just the same. "We are lucky enough to be on the outer edge of the swamps. Unfortunately, we cannot climb the cliffs. It would take too much time and use too much energy. We must head north through the lynch grass. It will lead us to the village of the Kilto. From there it is only another half-day's journey to Aura."

"Very well, let's waste no more time," Oisin said as he walked over to the water's edge and began to rub mud all over his exposed skin. Jayden followed suit. It was the only way to get through the lynch grass without being sliced to pieces. Once the mud dried and caked to their bodies, it would act as a natural shield and protect them from the grass that had killed many less learned travelers.

After several hours, they were safely out of the swamp and happy to be breathing clean air.

"The village is just around the bend. I have not seen it for over a decade, and I fear now it will not be what it once was," Jayden said to Oisin.

"I remember hearing stories about its people, extraordinary and mysterious; although I am ashamed to admit that, even after hearing so many interesting things about them, I never bothered to journey here," Oisin responded.

"Mysterious but vulnerable is how I would describe them. The Kilto were faithful to Elissa, but I am sure Solharn would have had no difficulty destroying their village and enslaving their people if they were there. There would have been no point in him killing them; they were no threat to him, or for that matter, anybody. They don't believe in harming others even in self-defense which makes them easy targets. They live entirely off the land and only eat what they grow. Their homes are elegant, all made out of trite stone, the same as the sacred Amulet of Rhol. At night when the fires are lit from within, their homes glow a bright orange. Unless of course, it was the fires are fueled by the wood of a Korten Tree which burns blue, making their homes look like great glowing ice sculptures.

They are very spiritual, which is why they built their homes from trite stone, for it is believed by many on Rhol to contain great energy. During the Dragon Wars centuries ago they disappeared and were thought to have died out completely. Out of respect, Queen Elissa ensured their village was kept in a pristine condition, should they ever return. Many decades passed without any word of them and then one night, perhaps a few years before Queen Elissa ordering our retreat, their homes lit up again. They had returned. They would not enlighten anyone as to where they had been, nor divulge the reason for their return. They would remain in their village for six months of the year and then disappear again. As far as I know, nobody has ever laid eyes on the mysterious place. Even my father was unable to pinpoint a location. Many have tried following them but have always returned without even remembering the purpose of their journey. It is only a myth of course, but many believe that it is some sort of Divine place."

"Maybe they returned to help in the battle against Solharn's armies?"

"Of that, I have no doubt, Oisin. Their appearance came shortly after Solharn began to gain an advantage in the war, which came mainly because of Phanthus. Nobody had ever expected to see a dragon again on Rhol, but there he was."

"Perhaps when we retreated to Leal and the Pegapires to Tamon they left too, and are safe from Solharn's wrath."

"Perhaps Oisin, we can always hope...," Jayden stopped and stared at the village as it came into view. Oisin stopped beside him.

"What is it Jayden. Is it what you feared?"

"The village has not changed a bit," Jayden whispered. "Quickly, we must find some cover."

When they were safely hidden within the forest, Jayden crouched down staring at the village toward what he thought he had seen. His hand remained on his sword, so it was at the ready should he need it in a hurry. It was gone, vanished. Had he imagined seeing the figure standing just before the village? His eyes scoured the area looking for any sign of activity, but he saw none. Perhaps he was making too much of the sign that had made him so cautious, but he was not one to take a chance. He felt something was wrong, and he had to trust his instincts. The village appeared to be abandoned, untouched by time. Perhaps the Kilto were not here when Solharn's army arrived making it pointless for them to waste any more time here. Furthermore, because the entire village was built with trite stone, it was impossible to burn or destroy.

His thoughts were broken by Oisin whispering into his ear. "Jayden what is it? I see nothing more than an abandoned village."

"As we walked toward it a figure appeared to me just ahead of us. It was a Kilto elder, of that I am sure. But not in the form I would expect; it was more like an apparition. It was waving us away, and then it simply disappeared."

"I did not see anything, how do you know it was a Kilto elder?" Oisin asked.

"They cannot be mistaken. Elders are tall, thin people, with pasty white skin only enhanced by the black robes they wear. They have long ivory white beards which almost part at the end and they all bear the Sign of Life, a quarter moon. It is etched into their foreheads from the time they are born."

"What does it mean Jayden?"

"A warning I presume although, with the armies in Aura, I cannot imagine Solharn wasting time here; what would be the point! There is nobody here," Jayden paused in thought.

"...Unless they knew we were coming."

Oisin looked at Jayden bewildered. "That is impossible Jayden. How could they possibly know such a thing! We did not even know where we would end up when we entered the river that led us here."

"No, we did not, but perhaps someone else did. Move cautiously Oisin; we will stay in the forest out of sight. Perhaps I am overly cautious, but better that than oblivious."

Oisin did not doubt Jayden's foresight and followed closely behind in silence while they slowly advanced around the village through the forest. They had made it to the far west side without any signs of trouble when Jayden stopped and lay on his stomach motioning Oisin to approach. Oisin was by his side in seconds peering over the small embankment that overlooked the last stretch of buildings that marked the end of the village.

He could see what concerned Jayden. The remains of a Garin which had recently been butchered lay just outside one of Kilto houses. The Kilto did not eat meat and Garin were used only for producing milk - unless you were a Kaltaures or a Phit.

They did not have to wait long for their answer as a Kaltaures soldier was thrown out of the nearby building.

"You idiot, clean it up. You were told explicitly not to leave signs of our presence outside the buildings," a Kaltaures voice bellowed from inside the cabin.

"Ahh, I am sick of it. Perhaps Solharn's source was wrong, an entire battalion of us locked up in these shacks for two days when we could be fighting and feasting, for what? Two measly Lealians? They will not even cure the hunger of two of us."

"Just clean it up, or Solharn will have all of our heads."

Jayden and Oisin looked at each other astonished at what they had overheard. There was a traitor amongst them. They had not arrived in the swamp until this morning yet two days ago Solharn knew they would end up here in Kilto. How was it possible? And more importantly, who was it that could have possessed such knowledge.

After the Kaltaures had cleaned up his mess and returned to the cabin, Jayden and Oisin slid back down the embankment. "We will wait until nightfall. I see no other choice. There are five dwellings that I count before we are past the village. We have been lucky so far, but in darkness, we will have more of an advantage to approach the last house and capture one of those soldiers."

"Capture?" Oisin whispered loudly.

"We must find out who betrays us Oisin."

CHAPTER NINETEEN

Deke sat up and noticed that he was no longer in the swamps. The air was crisp, and a light breeze made him shiver as he rose to his feet. He was standing on a beach of white sand that surrounded a small crystal clear lake. The lake was perfectly round and its waters, so calm it appeared to be made of glass.

A large range of mountains surrounded the lake. Their slender snow-covered peaks jutted high into the sky creating what appeared to be a natural fortress. He could see wisps of snow blowing gently from the tops of the mountains which shimmered briefly in the sunlight before coming to rest once again.

There was no way in or out from where he stood. Further down the shoreline a large piece of land, rich with vegetation, was nestled into a section of woods that began where the beach ended. He could just make out the top of a building towering above the trees.

Even though it was midday, he could see a quarter moon outlined in the bright blue sky.

He felt at peace here; he felt no fear. There was no sign of Mary or Deo. Deke wondered if this was the afterlife; perhaps it was a waiting place for one's soul to await the other. The last thing he remembered was trying to throw the amulet to Mary and Deo; grasping his chest, he was disappointed to find the amulet still hanging from his neck. He had failed to get it off in time. There was no way Elissa could be saved now. He was starting to feel dejected again.

"Do not carry your burdens so heavily, Deke Brolin."

Deke stopped walking and quickly looked up to see an elderly man with a silvery white beard that dangled far below his waist. A quarter-moon was etched into his forehead.

"You have great responsibilities, but success will come only if you trust that the people around you will carry some of those responsibilities for you."

"Who are you?" Deke asked.

"It matters not who I am Deke, but who you believe yourself to be. When you come to that realization you will succeed because then you will believe in yourself. Only you can define who you are. No one else can."

"Are you the Creator then?" Deke asked.

The elder laughed. "I am no more the Creator than anyone else is in the five worlds. We all have the Creator within us, some more and some less than others."

Deke considered this answer. Was this a riddle of some sort? "How did I get here?"

"You are full of questions that you already know the answers to Deke Brolin. Trust your instincts for you will need them very soon. You wield more power than you know, but when one carries such power, betrayal always follows closely behind. Weigh your choices and consider the people around you carefully."

"But..."

"There is one other thing you must remember Deke. It will be essential if your quest is to succeed. The purpose of your journey is to prevent the extinction of a world, but do not forget that the extinction of any single living thing can bring an end to what we fight for. To renew a life that can be saved is a step forward in completing the quest you were sent on."

"What does that mean?" Deke asked.

"I cannot answer that for you Deke, but remember this: whatever action you decide to take at any given moment will always cause a reaction. Trust your instincts…"

"Deke!" Mary yelled.

"…Trust your instincts."

"Deke, snap out of it," he could hear Deo saying.

"Trust your..."

Deke sat straight up nearly knocking over Mary and Deo who had been trying everything they could to get him to regain consciousness.

Mary hugged Deke. "Are you okay?"

"I feel fine. What happened? Where was I?" Deke asked.

"You have been here unconscious for over an hour. When you touched the amulet it caused the creature that held you captive to implode, and in turn, it sent you flying several hundred meters through the air," Deo responded.

"But it was so real, so vivid …"

"What?" Deo asked.

Deke described the elder that who had spoken to him and what he had said.

"It sounds much like a Kilto elder," Mary said, "Kiran told me much about them. They are a very mysterious race and very spiritual. Perhaps, you were visited by one to give you some sort of warning?"

"It is possible Deke. I, too, have learned that the Kilto have many spiritual powers that most cannot comprehend," Deo added.

"Well, if it is true then we must be wary of what is to come," Deke said still pondering the elder's advice.

"That would be wise indeed," a scratchy broken voice came from behind them.

All three looked over to see who was there. It was not pretty. It was hard to tell, but the figure appeared to be that of a female. Her small body was mainly skin and bones. Her face was long and drawn, wrinkled as if time had taken its toll on her very being. She wore ripped filthy clothes making her unhealthy appearance even more unappealing. Her greasy unkempt hair dangled down obscuring half of her face. She crouched to the ground just staring at them as she drew circles in the dirt with her long filthy nails.

Deke began to walk toward the creature, but Deo grabbed his arm holding him back.

"Be careful Deke. This person is not what they used to be. She is almost Pintante."

Deke had heard this word before when Kiran had told him why she thought Solharn had left Mary alive. He had been so excited to see Mary he had not thought to ask what it meant.

He looked over at Mary. She was crying, holding her hands to her face. "Mary, what is this about?"

"Deke, I did not want to tell you yet. I feared that once you found out my fate, you would not concentrate on the greater good. I feared you would spend too much time trying to save me."

"To save you, what are you talking about? I have told you I will stay with you. Everything will be okay Mary."

"Deke, I am sorry I did not tell you sooner. When someone loses their Paladin, this is what they become, a crazed animal, not to be trusted, a Pintante. They take no sides and will attack anything that comes in contact with them," Mary cried.

"But you look nothing like this creature. You are fine Mary," Deke responded.

"It is only a matter of time Deke, a matter of days by now before I'll start to change and there will be nothing you can do to prevent it," sobbed Mary

"Deo?" Deke said looking over at him.

Deo did not take his eyes from the creature when he responded, "It is true, Deke."

"You knew as well and did not tell me?" Deke said glaring at Deo.

"It wasn't my place Deke. Mary wanted to tell you herself. If she did not, I would've told you before we were in any danger."

"Danger, are you serious? Do you think that is what I am concerned about? If you two had told me sooner, perhaps I could have done something. Perhaps we could have formulated a plan to save Mary. I cannot let her turn into this," Deke said pointing back toward the creature.

"You are aware that I can hear you," the creature responded.

"I'm sorry," Deke said looking empathetically at the creature, "but she means far too much to me to lose her again."

"Well, I'm not sorry Deke. Your mind set has already changed. You're already thinking about me instead of thinking about finding Elissa. I haven't gone through all of this and nor should you, just to fail, for it to be all for nothing."

"But Mary…."

"No Deke. This is my choice, not yours," Mary yelled back.

"She is right Deke, and I can help you," the creature said.

"I mean no disrespect, but if you are almost what they call a Pintante, I don't think it would be in any of our interests to trust in your help, particularly in light of the fact that a Kilto elder just warned me to be wary of a betrayal. We don't even know who you are…or were."

"The elder also told you to trust your instincts Deke. The words he spoke of betrayal and instinct don't necessarily intertwine. Besides, how could I have betrayed you when this is the first time we have met?"

"Deke, you must be wary of this creature. Pintante are mad and treacherous. Do not let her confuse you. Whether she has betrayed us or will betray us is the same thing," Deo said.

"You are right. I will soon become what you describe, but I am not there yet. Solharn stole my paladin from me, and it is why I have become...well...this. I want him destroyed as much as you three do. My name is Torrell. I, too, have been in search of Queen Elissa. I was very near to what I thought would be the end of my quest when I was attacked by Solharn himself. He laughed at me after taking my energy, my spirit. He told me to enjoy my new life to come. I have nothing but disdain for him. I have hidden in these swamps for almost two years. I know them better than anyone, and I can lead you out. I can also lead you to where I believe Elissa is," Torrell explained.

"How do you even know of our quest?" Deke asked.

"I have been listening to you talk, and I certainly recognize the Amulet of Rhol which you wear around your neck. The creature that attacked you was a Sloto. They are abundant in these swamps, but they are not the most horrific creatures that live here. Please, let me guide you. The direction you are heading is not the right path."

"Excuse me," Mary said, "but I was here before, not that long ago, and I don't like your inference."

"There was no inference intended miss. I'm sure you once knew this swamp, but it's grown and changed drastically since you were last here."

Deke was searching his feelings deep into his soul. He thought about the elder's warning to him but also his advice, to trust the people around him to take some of the responsibilities. Perhaps this is what he was referring to. After all, Torrell made sense, and she was not a Pintante yet. They could make faster time with someone who knew the swamps as well as she claimed she did. He also secretly thought that it might give him the extra time he would need to save Mary if he could.

"Okay Torrell, I am still wary of how you come to be here and of your motives, but I have no reason not to trust you, so I will agree to let you travel with us."

"You have no reason to trust her either, Deke!" Deo said.

"Deke, this could be a terrible mistake," Mary chimed in.

"I trust my instincts," Deke lied. He did not trust Torrell completely, but he needed to take the chance if he would have any hope of saving Mary.

CHAPTER TWENTY

The night had come. It was not as dark as Jayden had hoped. The moon was full and cast a dim light on the ground making it far too easy to see. This would have been a good thing if he did not have to worry about attracting attention while he and Oisin tried to weave their way through the woods unnoticed. Now, it would be much more challenging. It would also take more time.

He and Oisin set out toward the last Kilto home hoping to find the answers they sought. It was slow going as Jayden had decided to stay in the cover of the trees far past the house and then backtrack. After leaving the cover of the forest they crawled, staying as low to the ground as possible. Small sporadic bushes provided some relief and a place to rest and stretch their aching knees. It took about two hours before they finally reached the outside of the building that they had their sights on.

They did not speak. They had formulated their plan well before they started. Jayden would gaze through the window and determine if any Kaltaures were there and if so, how many. If there were two or more, they would both enter. If there was only one, Jayden would enter while Oisin kept watch outside. The latter was what Jayden was hoping for, and as he gazed through the window, he smiled when he observed only one Kaltaures sitting down on a chair with his feet resting on a table. It was more than he could have hoped for; the soldier was sleeping. His sword was leaning against the fireplace mantle several feet away from him. Jayden could see that the fire had recently gone out, leaving several embers still glowing within the hearth of the large stone fireplace.

Jayden signaled Oisin to let him know that there was only one soldier inside. Oisin gave him a nod and readied his sword. Jayden inched his way to the front of the dwelling holding a knife which his father had given him as a boy. In his other hand, he carried some vine that they had gathered while waiting for nightfall to come.

The door was unlocked which did not surprise Jayden. It would be rare for any Kilto even to possess a lock. They were too trusting. The door squeaked somewhat as he slowly pushed it open. The soldier moved slightly, but not enough to cause Jayden to rush in.

Jayden was well trained in stealth and combat fighting. He controlled his breathing and walked across the floor without a sound. He was now just feet away from the back of the soldier. He placed his knife in his mouth and readied the vine by twisting it around one of his hands and then the other. Jayden was wearing leather gloves to prevent the snakes which adorned the soldier's massive head from digging their fangs into his exposed skin. He left about four feet of the vine in between each hand. He would need it to keep his body well away from the snakes reach.

When Jayden was a mere foot away, he quietly sat on the floor. Once he had placed his feet securely on the back of the chair, he swung the vine up and over the soldier's head, while at the same time pushing his feet into the chair and falling back.

The chair creaked slightly as the weight on it shifted from four legs to two. The soldier tried to scream, but no sound came. The vine was digging into his neck cutting off his airway. Snakes hissed and lunged out at Jayden, but they were unable to reach any part of him aside from his well-protected hands.

Jayden held his position. He was surprised how long the snakes held on deprived of the air and the blood that they relied upon from the soldier. If it took much longer, the soldier would die, and they needed him alive. Finally, the snakes succumbed dangling limply from his head.

Oisin did not miss a beat and instantly activated the second phase of the plan. Upon entering the dwelling, he placed a bag over the soldier's head and tied it tightly with a vine just at the point where the bodies of the snakes joined the base of the soldier's skull.

"Hurry, Oisin! We need him alive. I don't know how much longer he will last. The snakes took far longer to succumb than I would have thought," Jayden whispered.

Oisin continued to bind the soldier to the chair working as quickly as he could. With no time to spare, he finally tied the last knot around the soldier's feet.

"Okay," Oisin said.

Jayden immediately released the vine. The chair rocked forward making a loud bang as the front two legs once again resumed their normal position. The soldier's head fell lifelessly forward. He was not breathing.

Jayden quickly got to his feet. Cursing, he started slapping the soldier's face, making sure to avoid the long jagged tusks.

"Breathe you, filthy creature, breathe!" Jayden said as he began to pound on the soldier's chest.

Oisin began to think that their plan had failed. This soldier would not be giving them any information. Just as they both had given up hope, the soldier's body convulsed, and he gasped for air. The chair came crashing to the floor from the sudden movement.

"Quickly, Oisin, check outside in case anyone heard anything."

As Oisin ran out of the building, Jayden looked down at the creature who surprisingly looked rather scared.

"How did you know we would be coming through here?" Jayden asked glaring at the soldier.

"How did you know we were waiting for you?" the soldier laughed in response.

Jayden had run out of patience. He grabbed his knife off the floor and rested the blade on the soldier's left cheek.

"You think your race is the only one capable of committing horrific acts, beast? I will do anything to save Rhol. You would be wise to listen. Perhaps I should start by cutting off the pets that grow from your head, one by one?"

Jayden knew this would cause excruciating pain to the Kaltaures. Jayden could see in his eyes that the threat had him thinking.

"But that won't kill you right away, will it Kaltaures? So I will finish by gouging your eyes out, so you will never see again, and then your tongue so you will never be able to say what happened to you. And you know as well as I do that the Kaltaures will not want you around. They will be embarrassed at your weakness. They will kill you and feed you to the Ralcriff. Won't they?"

The soldier just stared at Jayden still not saying a word. "Perhaps you don't believe me," Jayden said covering the Kaltaures' mouth and slicing off one of the snakes. The soldier's eyes opened wide with pain. Oisin was becoming worried. Although the soldier's screams were muffled, he could still clearly hear them.

"Still not talking? Well, you have no need for your tongue then, do you?" Jayden asked thrusting his knife through the soldier's cheek.

The soldier frantically mumbled something under Jayden's hand. Jayden left his knife in place as he lifted his hand from the soldier's mouth.

"Abednego sent us. He said that two Lealians would come through here."

"What else did he say?" Jayden sternly asked.

"We were to capture the one named Jayden and kill the other. Solharn wanted the one called Jayden alive so he could control him or something. His plan was to place him back in the Lealian army."

"You lie! Solharn would know better than to think a Lealian would ever betray another, let alone Rhol," Jayden responded twisting the knife.

"It is true," the soldier said panicking, "I have seen it."

"Seen what?"

"He forces them to swallow some black liquid that comes from inside him. It is horrible to witness. If they live through the pain, they are completely in his control. It is how he builds his armies."

Jayden pulled the knife away from the soldier's cheek. "You have still not answered my original question. How did Abednego know to send you here for us?"

"I am not sure exactly, but there has been someone working against you for a long time. It is someone of Solace who betrays you. That is all I know."

Jayden's mind fought to comprehend this information. Who could it be? He was only a little further ahead than he was before, but he believed the soldier knew nothing more.

"I will keep my word. I will spare your life Kaltaures. That is what separates us," Jayden said walking away.

"You might as well kill me if you are going to leave me here like this! When they find me in the morning, they will kill me themselves and brand me a coward for being captured."

"Perhaps, or you can spend the night thinking of a story to tell them. Either way, your death will not be by my hands."

After placing a gag on the Kaltaures soldier, Jayden exited the house and was met by Oisin who had been waiting for him. Neither said a word as they quietly escaped the Kilto village.

They had travelled for several hours before Oisin finally spoke. "Jayden, I overheard the soldier. What do you make of it? Do you have any idea who betrays us?"

"I have been giving it a great of thought Oisin, and still I do not know. The soldier specifically said the traitor is of Solace. This means Palto and the inhabitants of the Sacred Realm are in grave danger. It gives Solharn an advantage; he may already know where Deke, Deo, and Mary are. This information drastically changes our tactics. We must find our armies before it is too late."

"How much further to Aura?"

"We should be there just before sunrise, but it will take time once we get there. When Palto flew me to Solace, I could see that Solharn's camp was positioned to the east of Aura. That is where we will come out when we arrive. Hopefully, we will still have some cover of darkness because we will have to travel north through the woods to maneuver around his troops; once we have done that we will have to find our armies. We can only hope that they are still where I saw them last. Our only advantage is that Solharn will not think we are coming. He will not hear about the Kaltaures failure to capture us until we are long past his camps."

Oisin did not respond as he and Jayden continued toward Aura. He, too, had thought deeply about who could have betrayed, them, and whoever it was, did they do so of their choosing or were they under Solharn's control? He had become more powerful, more evil. Jayden was right. Solharn had a huge advantage over them now. They were without Elissa, the boy from Earth who held the amulet was in the middle of the Tiqor Swamps, and they had a long way to go to finally reach their destination and hopefully find their armies intact. To top it all off, their side had been compromised by a traitor.

Oisin greatly admired Jayden but realized even he could not have predicted this. Oisin hoped Jayden had some sort of plan because he was beginning to feel as if the survival of Rhol was slipping away. In any event, he would fight alongside Jayden until he could do no more. They were nearing Aura and were both exhausted, but rest would have to come later, much later.

Oisin stopped when he saw Jayden's hand suddenly signal him. They were still under cover of woods but Oisin, not wanting to take any chance of being seen, fell to the ground and sidled up beside him. He could see what had caused Jayden to stop suddenly. Solharn's camps were visible now. He could see hundreds of smoldering fires and makeshift tents. They were still a good mile away, a safe distance except for the troop of Kaltaures soldiers who were being led across a field to the north of the camp. They were a mere hundred yards from them. Jayden and Oisin looked on as the sixty or so soldiers hid amongst the grass and boulders that surrounded the area and disappeared from sight. Following this, he could see a single Kaltaures soldier leave the others and run back toward the main camp.

"What are they doing Jayden?" Oisin asked.

"It looks like they are preparing for a surprise attack," Jayden said looking on intently.

"Do you think our armies are coming then?" Oisin asked enthusiastically.

"No, our armies would not attack from the north. The wind would not be in their favor, and the Kaltaures army would be much larger if they anticipated an attack of that nature. It is troubling though. They are blocking the way we must go to get around the camp."

"Perhaps they have already heard the news of our escape from Kilto and lay in wait for us," Oisin said not wanting to believe their bad luck.

Jayden was still staring intently at the field thinking. All of the sudden it came to him, "Oisin, we must move!"

"What is it?"

"The Nightstalkers, they have been discovered! It is the only explanation. They would enter the camp from the south and leave from the north. The enemy is setting a trap for them. It explains the small number of Kaltaures soldiers and the time of night they set their position up, which means they will be prepared for them inside the camps as well. They are walking to their demise. We must stop them before they enter the camps." Jayden quickly started running through the forest to the south

It took longer than they would have anticipated, but finally, they came around the back of the camps to the south side.

"Oisin, we must split up in order to find them. Return to this spot in an hour if…"

Jayden was interrupted by a dark figure that jumped down upon him from a nearby tree knocking him to the ground. Oisin ran to his aid but made it only a few feet before he too was struck down. Oisin rolled and jumped back to his feet holding his knife in a combat position. Jayden, unable to get to his feet, was still struggling with three of the assailants.

They were surrounded by dark figures dressed completely in black. Only their silhouette made them stand out against the backdrop of the moon.

The circle surrounding Oisin was beginning to close in slowly. He was positioning himself for the attack when a voice boomed out from behind him, "Toltad, it is Jayden, these are Lealians."

Without another word the Nightstalkers, lowered their weapons and looked toward Jayden.

"You're alive, Jayden! We had begun to lose hope. It is an honor to be the first to welcome you back."

"I wish my return came with better news Toltad, but at least we arrived in time to stop your men from entering the Kaltaures camp."

Jayden knew something was wrong by Toltad's silence.

"Toltad? We have arrived in time, haven't we?"

"The first half entered the camp a half an hour ago, Jayden. What is wrong?"

Jayden cursed. "They are walking into a trap."

Toltad immediately signaled to the remaining Nightstalkers readying them for battle, but Jayden stopped him.

"Your men are not going in Toltad," Jayden said.

"What do mean Jayden? We must save them."

"If I thought there was a chance we could, I would lead the remaining Nightstalkers into the camps myself. You are probably not aware of this, but Solharn has returned and has already joined his armies. To make matters worse, there is a traitor amongst us. Solharn will have ensured that the Kaltaures were well prepared for the Nightstalkers' return. Your men are some of the top warriors in the Lealian ranks, but they will not expect what is to come. They will not stand a chance, and I will not allow another Lealian to die here tonight if nothing good can come from it."

"I respectfully disagree, Jayden. I will not leave them to walk into a trap that will cost them their lives," Toltad said staring at Jayden.

"They have already walked into the trap Toltad, and fifty more Lealians will be of no use in fighting against thousands. You will have your revenge, but not tonight," Jayden responded sternly.

Toltad knew Jayden made sense, but in his heart, he would rather die than stand back and do nothing. As if reading his mind Jayden began to speak, this time to everyone.

"I know this goes against everything we believe in, but these are different times. We have lost too many already, and our armies are dwindling more every day. I am not saying that we must stand idly by and do nothing. I will stay back here to gather whatever intelligence I can from the camps and try to find out what has become of our fellow Lealians. The remainder of you will go with Oisin. Sixty Kaltaures are lying in wait on the north side of the camp for any of the Nightstalkers that have avoided capture. Oisin will point their exact location out to you. Stealth will be the key. You must kill them in silence so as not to alert reinforcements. That will give us an escape route and is the only chance we have of saving any of the Nightstalkers who evade capture. If I have not joined you within an hour before sunrise, then leave to find our armies and give them the news of what I have told you."

Toltad and Oisin nodded in agreement. Within seconds Jayden stood alone in the dark forest.

CHAPTER TWENTY-ONE

Palto looked proudly at his two warriors. Solko and Preta had been working with the Rholians, teaching them basic combat skills for hours upon hours. When the Rholians took brief breaks to rest their aching muscles, Palto would tell them whatever he knew about the Dark Angel and his armies so as to prepare them when they finally faced the scourges of battle.

They were as ready as they would ever be, given the short amount of time he had to train them. The majority would last only minutes when facing Kaltaures soldiers or Phits for that matter, but he did see resilience in them, and their hearts were big. That would go a long way when fighting for a cause that meant so much to them. They fought for their country, their world. Their enemies fought only for power and riches. They would prevail because their cause was the just one.

"Solko, Preta," Palto said getting their attention. The Rholians did not hear Palto. He did not use spoken words, but telepathy. He did not want them to hear.

"We can wait no longer. Jayden has had his day. We do not even know whether he survives or not. We must leave Solace and join the battle."

"I do not have to tell you Palto that the Rholians are far from being prepared for what they are about to face, even if we make it by Phanthus," Preta responded.

"I know," said Palto, "but would a day make much of a difference, or a week for that matter?"

"No," Preta retorted still looking into the Rholian's eyes.

"Then prepare them for our journey. Have them sleep for the next few hours. They are exhausted. We will leave shortly after sunrise."

"Very well," Preta said signaling the Rholians to stop what they were doing.

Palto slowly walked away. He had to come up with a plan to get out of the tunnel without being burned to death by the dragon's fiery breath. Furthermore, even if the plan (which he had yet to think of) was successful, they would still have to slip by Phanthus undetected. They were no match for him without reinforcements.

He spent the remainder of the night trying to time the fire the dragon spewed down the tunnel, but there was no real pattern. The longest break had been almost two hours and the shortest, just under an hour. Given that it would take them at least a few hours to get to the entranceway, there was no possible way they could make it.

There was nothing he could think of that would withstand the heat of the fire and allow them to continue safely on. Palto was perplexed and stared into the Wall of Solace, straining to come up with an idea.

"There is a way," a gruff sounding voice spoke out from behind him. "Of course your timing would have to be impeccable."

Palto turned to see the source of this information. Standing behind him was a Brawltug. The Brawltug were shorter than most and generally kept to themselves. They were from the northern reaches of Rhol and were quite friendly, but as stubborn as Girons. If they ever drank spirits of any sort they turned into quite vile creatures. Spitting, cursing and fighting seemed to be the only thing that pleased them in that state. You could always tell if they had dabbled though, as their eyes turned a deep red and their cheeks became lined with veins.

They were very loyal to the Queen, and even though they would never admit it, they did like to help people in need (and brag about it later). As Palto looked at the Brawltug, he couldn't help but notice the left side of his face was missing an ear and scarred down to the bone. A scruffy brown beard hid whatever other damage he had suffered.

"And you are, sir?" Palto asked curiously.

"I am Alaster O'Dufaigh of course, but most people just call me Duffy," the Brawltug responded, almost insulted that Palto did not know his name.

Palto thought for a moment before politely responding. "What has brought you to the Sacred Realm Duffy? If my memory serves me correctly, your people refused to go to any of the realms. In fact, my understanding was that they decided to spread themselves all over the vast lands of Rhol to exact revenge upon Solharn, all the while keeping watch over the less fortunate."

"And that we did Palto sir. As you have probably heard, we were almost successful in destroying the sod. My family, the O'Dufaighs, were an integral part of that. In fact, we believe that is why he left Rhol. He knew what was coming. You're sure you have not heard of me, eh? Strange indeed."

Palto tried to keep a straight face. He knew the Brawltug were proud and in fact very useful warriors. They did tend to stretch the truth a little and quite fancied themselves. Some say they may have even been the original settlers of Rhol, but Palto was sure that had come from the Brawltug themselves. In any event, he knew they responded to compliments.

"Well, now that you mention your name again, perhaps I do remember hearing something about the O'Dufaighs," Palto fibbed chuckling on the inside.

"Ha! I knew it. Well, let's see, yes. How did I come to be here, you ask? Well, it is kind of interesting you see. My family and I were returning from a serious battle with several Kaltaures soldiers. I guess that was, well, between ten and eleven years ago now. We had to take on at least four of the beasts each! Of course, we were quite successful in winning the battle, and in a short period of time I should add," Duffy said very pleased with himself.

"Anyway, we were in search of a place to rest. We had not slept in at least four days and five nights. We found what we thought would be a safe place to lie down for the evening, on top of this mountain range, in fact. Well, I kept watch for the first two hours while everyone slept. Then my brother took his turn. That's when it happened. I remember waking up to a shooting pain running through my body and looking up to see a Cawlaway flying away. The cowardly creature must have attacked us in our sleep, I guess for a good reason. It would not have stood a chance had I been awake, and it probably knew it."

Palto listened intently, a Cawlaway? He had not seen one for years, but could never forget them. They were a monstrous bird, black with aqua highlights. They had pearl eyes much like a Kaltaures and were a most dangerous creature that fed solely on a meat diet. They were made for killing. Once you were in their grasp, there was no escape. Their feathers were long, slender and as sharp as lynch grass. If their wing came in contact with their prey, it would slice them to pieces.

"I stood up to give chase, looking around for the rest of my clan. I saw none of them. I circled the area in a mad attempt to find them, but there was nothing, not even a trace of blood or a footprint to track. I began retracing my steps thinking I must have missed something. I had only walked a few feet when the ground beneath me crumbled and I fell for what seemed to be forever. Luckily, I landed on some thick moss inside a long tunnel. I followed it blindly until I finally saw some light in the distance, and I walked into this place. I did not even know where I was. Delirious from exhaustion and pain I crawled through the field to the river and collapsed. When I awoke my face had been bandaged and a lady was tending to my wounds. Kiran was that woman. She told me I had been sleeping for six days in and out of fever. I immediately got to my feet still worried about my clan, but collapsed again. It would be another two months until I was well enough to go in search of my family, but it was not to be. On the very day that I was leaving Queen Elissa cast the spell that would keep me in here for the next ten years. Kiran convinced me that it was fate that brought me here. She explained that many lost travelers and people in need would be coming to the Realm and they would need our help. She convinced me that my place was here and that only in time would my destiny take me outside these walls again. Of course she would never have stopped me from leaving, but she was a very convincing woman. She promised that my fight against Solharn would come, but only when the protective fields around Tamon and Leal no longer existed. I wasn't overly enthused with the idea of staying here, but I owed her my life, so I agreed." Duffy looked around admiring the Realm. "It was with my help that much of the shelters within here were built."

"That is quite a story, Duffy. The other way out that you speak of, it is where you fell into this tunnel?"

"Precisely, it took me just under two hours to walk to this place in the dark, while injured. So I figure we can make it in just over an hour without those obstacles."

"And by taking this way we can avoid Phanthus at the other end of the tunnel," Palto said, already formulating a plan.

Duffy looked confused. "Well, if you want to I suppose. I was thinking more of a surprise attack."

Palto laughed. "I have no doubt that's what you were thinking Duffy, but Phanthus I think, will have to wait for another day."

Duffy looked disappointed but didn't argue with Palto. "Are you sure of the amount of time it took you to get here Duffy?"

"Well, I was not myself, that is for sure, but it will be close to that time frame."

"Very well, I will go down the tunnel to see if I can find what you speak of," Palto said walking closer to the wall to await the next ball of flames.

"If you find my hatchet then you will locate the tunnel. It will be stuck into the wall directly below it. I marked it of course, in case that was the only way out," Duffy boasted.

"You are indeed the Brawltug I heard of Alaster O'Dufaigh. Who else could have fought through so many tribulations and still kept his head? You are a true warrior."

Duffy stood proudly; he would tell many people this story. Palto, the leader of the Pegapires, considered him the greatest warrior of all time.

As the flames in the tunnel disappeared, Palto nodded a goodbye to Duffy as he ran through the Wall of Solace and down the tunnel, hoping to avoid the next fiery breath of Phanthus.

CHAPTER TWENTY-TWO

Mary and Deo were not at all impressed with their new companion, but Deke simply would not listen to reason, so the four set off through the swamps. Mary insisted on leading the way, and Deke did not argue. He knew Mary did not trust Torrell, and he himself had his doubts.

They had been walking for about two hours and had managed to cover significant ground when Mary turned to the north and began to lead them down the bank of a creek. Torrell, who had walked in silence for the majority of the journey, suddenly stopped.

"This creek will only lead us further into the swamp and further into danger. If we head to the west, we can reach the outer edge of the swamp and avoid, for the most part, any of the creatures that live within it."

Mary turned to Torrell. "Oh, you would like that, wouldn't you? If we head west, we will have to walk right through the core of the Phit territory. The bushes and trees may have changed in my absence but I remember this creek, and it leads us out of the swamps."

"Any direction will eventually take us out of the swamps, but the faster, the better, and your way is the longest and most dangerous," Torrell said looking toward Mary.

"My way," Mary yelled, "does not include getting attacked by thousands of Phits. You speak of all these creatures that lie within the swamps. I have seen none of them. I have seen where the Phit camps lie and I do not wish to come even close to them. That is why I am taking the long route."

"Just because you have not seen something does not mean it doesn't exist. You need to trust me. If we encounter a Tetagorous, who live in the very heart of this swamp, you will wish you were fighting an entire battalion of Phits instead. And that is where this creek is leading us."

"Okay you two, enough. Deo, have you heard of this creature that Torrell speaks of?"

"I cannot say that I have."

"And is it true Torrell, what Mary says in regards to walking into the very heart of Phit territory should we walk to the west?" Deke asked.

"It is, but I know many ways around and through their camps that will allow us to pass without being detected."

"And what is this Tetagorous you speak of?"

"Well to start with they will eat only that which is dead, so rest assured when it sees you it will try to kill you, and it has two ways of doing that. The Tetagorous has a unique way of controlling air. It will suck it right from your lungs and slowly suffocate you, which would be the best way to go, or it will enjoy watching you suffer a slow death by playing on your fears. The latter method is its favorite. You see, the Tetagorous can use air currents to entrap you, making escape impossible. It will then play on your worst fears by controlling your mind. It makes you relive over and over what you fear the most. Every time you relive your fear, it will only get worse. It may last days or even a week, but it will continue until eventually, your heart explodes with fear. Then it will feast on your flesh and build its home with your bones."

"It sounds perfectly awful!" Deke said looking around to make sure the beast was nowhere in the vicinity.

"Do not fear Deke. It rarely leaves the heart of the swamp, but even when it does, you would not see it before it was too late. When it moves at its fastest, it cannot be seen with the naked eye. Once it ensnares you, it will reveal itself as whatever you fear the most. If the mere sight of that doesn't stop your heart, well then, I have already explained what will happen."

"And how would you know this, if you cannot see it until you are captured. Have you escaped a Tetagorous attack?" Deo questioned.

"Not quite, but nearly. It was almost a year ago when I stumbled across a horrible smell while walking through this very swamp. At the time I had no idea where I was. As I came over the crest of a hill, I saw a building that I would later come to know as

142

the home of a Tetagorous. Bones with rotting meat stood in the form of its rustic house."

"Outside of the house a Brawltug was trapped inside a swirling shaft of air. It almost looked as if a mini twister had landed over the top of him. I was moving in to help when the Tetagorous appeared out of nowhere. It appeared as a Cawlaway. I was barely able to contain my own fears. The Brawltug began to scream and cry. With each hour that passed the screaming became louder and louder. At first the Brawltug was screaming at the mere sight of the Cawlaway, which is a most dreadful bird, thought to be extinct on Rhol. Then out of nowhere other people started appearing around the Cawlaway. The beast was projecting images of a most horrific attack on what appeared to be the Brawltug's family. Their bodies were being ripped to shreds at the hands of this beast. The Brawltug was screaming about his brother and sister and other family members as they appeared in front of the Cawlaway just to be torn apart over and over again. I could see that it was clearly an illusion that the Tetagorous was projecting, but the Brawltug did not know the difference. The screaming stopped after the third rendition of the attack. The Brawltug`s body went stiff and he just fell with a thud to the ground. I won't repeat what happened next, but based on what I have just told you, you can imagine."

"And what did the actual beast look like?" Deke asked.

"That's just it. It looked like a Cawlaway, but the Tetagorous can look like anything."

"What does that mean?" Deo asked.

Mary, unable to contain herself, interrupted before Torrell could speak. "Oh come now, this is just a legend. I have heard of something similar, but with a different name from Kiran and not even she believed it to be true. What she means, is that it can look like anything and that it will appear before you as what you fear the most. But nobody knows what the Tetagorous actually looks like. Right, Torrell?"

"Right!"

"She is beginning to lose herself, Deke, believing in myths. I have been here, and I can tell you first hand that we will not make it through the Phit camps. It will take a little longer this way but it will be much safer and in that respect faster because we won't have to fight any Phits," Mary pleaded.

"Torrell, how did you know it was not an actual Cawlaway?" Deke asked.

"Well first off, a Cawlaway, even if they still existed, could not project illusions of actual events, but that is not the only reason. Just for a second it looked toward me, and it changed, it changed into what I fear the most. I have no idea why it didn't give chase when I ran. I would learn much later on, as I got to know these swamps more and more, what in fact I had just witnessed."

"And what is it you fear the most Torrell?" Mary asked while glaring deeply into her eyes.

Torrell hesitated and slightly stuttered as she spoke. "It does not m-m-matter what I fear the most. What matters is getting out of these swamps."

Mary just smiled back at her.

Deke was sure of it now. Torrell was losing her mind. It was too much. "We will follow the creek," Deke said.

Torrell became enraged at hearing this and began to fidget. "You are making a mistake. You will listen to me, Deke Brolin," she shrieked.

"Calm down Torrell; it will be alright."

"It is not alright, you, you, you are g-g-going to die, d-die, all of y-you," Torrell screamed.

Deke could see Torrell was becoming unglued and knew that Mary and Deo had made the same observations as he watched them slowly moving in behind her.

"Torrell, just relax," Deke begged as she moved slowly toward him. She was giggling while she sang what sounded almost like a broken poem in a high uneven voice.

"How many tears have people shed?
When their souls break
When their thoughts turn dead
I guess it's no one's fault
Evil is strong
No wonder faith goes wrong

Down by the Blackpool
Where evil rules
Don't ever go swimming

144

By the Blackpool."

Deke slowly backed away as she moved closer to him. He should have never allowed her to come with them. He was a fool. He fell backward, losing his footing and Torrell lunged at him.

He tried fighting her off, but she was mad with anger and as strong as an ox. Deo and Mary grabbed her and pulled her off, throwing her to the ground. Deke quickly got up, and while Mary and Deo held her down, he bound her arms and legs with a nearby vine. She just laughed hysterically, her eyes bulging from her head as she continued to sing.

> "Every now and then
> Your souls become one
> You're on top of life
> There is no need to run
> It can last for years
> Or it can turn in a day
> But the dark will come
> No matter how much you pray."

"She's mad; she has become a Pintante. I've never seen one so close. What a horrible way to go, and it will soon be my fate," Mary cried.

Deke put his arm around Mary's shoulder and tried to comfort her. "We'll find a way to help you, Mary."

"Shut her up! I can't stand that rhyme. Make her quiet," Mary cried aloud.

> "Down by the Blackpool
> Where evil rules
> Don't ever go swimming
> By the Blackpool"

"Torrell, please calm down, or we will be forced to leave you here," Deke begged.

"What? You're actually thinking of bringing her with us!" Mary yelled.

"Mary, we can't just leave her tied up here with no way to fend for herself," Deke said.

"It will never happen
Everybody tells themselves
But it will
Faith, no dark will always rule."

"Shut her up! Shut her up! I can't take it!" Mary screamed uncontrollably.

"With hate and rage, your soul will fill
If only you had listened
When I told you, you fool
Don't ever go swimming
By the Blackpool."

'Torrell, please!" Deke yelled.

At this, she suddenly stopped and looked at Mary smiling. Her teeth were beginning to turn black which made her smile appear all the more evil. Perhaps realizing this, she closed her mouth and turned to Deke.

"I am sorry, my mind ....I can't think...I can't.... don't leave me here. Help me, please. Give me a hand," Torrell begged.

"Deo, what should we do?" Deke asked.

"There is nothing we can do for her Deke. If she is not already Pintante, she will be soon. For now, let us leave her where she is and get some sleep. It has been a long day."

Deke felt sorry for Torrell, but Deo was right, and so was Mary for that matter. Torrell could no longer be trusted. Too exhausted to think anymore he sat down on a grassy patch of ground and was soon fast asleep.

CHAPTER TWENTY-THREE

Jayden had made it to the edge of Solharn's camp well before sunrise. He could move much faster on his own. He climbed a tree to get a view of the inside of the camps and saw what he had feared. He watched with an aching heart, as one by one, his warriors succumbed to Solharn, just as the Kaltaures soldier had described.

His eyes filled with tears as he watched the Nightstalkers standing tall, knowing what was to become of them at the hands of this monster. Out of respect, he did not leave until the last of them had gone through the evil ritual.

It was not hard to figure out Solharn's plan. He would send these soldiers back to the Lealian camps and then control them from within, just as he had planned to do with him. Hundreds would die at the hands of their own people; the Nightstalkers were perhaps the most dangerous of all Lealian warriors. Jayden knew he had no time to waste and scaled down the tree. They would have to find a way to beat them back to the Lealian camps. He ran back toward Oisin and the others knowing it would be nearly impossible.

Ω

Oisin watched in admiration as the Nightstalkers ran through the woods in silence. He was right behind them, yet he could not hear a sound. When they finally reached their destination, Oisin pointed out the location where he and Jayden had seen the Kaltaures positioning themselves. Toltad only nodded and motioned for Oisin to stay where he was. When Oisin began to protest, Toltad gave him a stern look as if to say there was no time for this. Oisin knew better than to say another word as he watched Toltad using only hand signals to command his troops.

The last of the Nightstalkers disappeared a mere ten feet in front of him. Less than an hour had gone by when a hand grabbed him from behind and covered his mouth. He looked up to see Toltad; his face was splattered with blood. They were soon joined by the others.

Oisin wondered why he was still being silenced until Toltad motioned for him to look to his left. He could see a lone Kaltaures soldier exploring the area where his soldiers must surely be lying dead. After a few moments, the soldier turned and rode back toward the camps. When he was out of sight, Toltad released his grip.

"We could not have timed it better Oisin. Jayden was right. After we disposed of the Kaltaures soldiers, we could see people starting to emerge from their camps. We thought at first it was more soldiers approaching and braced ourselves for another attack, but as they got closer we could see that they were our own, and we were able to save another eighteen of the missing Nightstalkers.

Unfortunately, we arrived back here only to see a Kaltaures soldier riding from the camp. We could not move fast enough to stop him. It means that we can wait no longer. That soldier will be alerting the camps, and these woods will soon be swarming with enemies. We must move now," Toltad said grimly.

"But what of Jayden? We cannot just leave him here," objected Oisin.

"Jayden would expect no less Oisin. You heard him back there. He knew the risks, and told us to leave without him if he wasn't here an hour before sunrise."

"That is another half hour away, Toltad."

"Yes, but he gave that time for a reason. He knew if he was any later there would be a greater chance of being discovered. A chance he would not take. We will soon be discovered, and he would want us to move. That is what we are going to do."

"Then I will stay, so he knows what has happened. At least he will know he was not abandoned," Oisin said.

"That is honorable Oisin but foolhardy. Jayden will figure out what has happened in mere minutes. He does not need you to risk your life for something that would make no difference in his strategy."

"Just the same Toltad, we have made it this far together, and I will not leave his side."

"Very well, Oisin. I wish you well and hope that you find safe haven soon."

With a few hand signals from Toltad, the Nightstalkers disappeared into the night air leaving Oisin standing in the dark forest alone.

Oisin had waited just under an hour. The sun was rising over the fields, and still, he had not seen Jayden. He was contemplating walking back toward where they had separated when he heard a noise coming toward him from a distance. Oisin readied his sword from his perch in the tree he had climbed for cover.

He was pleased to see he would not need his sword when he saw Jayden running through the forest toward him. Oisin was impressed at his speed; he was wasting no time.

Oisin began to scale down the tree but stopped when he heard a sound resembling a loud buzzing noise. There was no mistaking that sound, Phits. Oisin turned to see that Jayden was being chased by a troop of them. He stopped half way down the tree ready to move. His best chance was to attack from above and take them by surprise. Jayden was still running straight for him. He could count at least six Phits converging on him.

When Jayden ran beneath the tree, Oisin gave a yell and jumped doing a flip and a somersault all while swinging his sword up and around. He beheaded two of the unsuspecting pursuers.

The other four turned on him instantly. He was able to wound one by slicing into its wing which caused it to come crashing to the ground. He lost the grip on his sword when another took him from the side biting into his arm. In a single motion, he grasped for his knife with his free arm and came around to attack. He jumped back when he saw only the head of the Phit attached to his arm, its lifeless eyes staring back into his and its teeth deeply embedded into his flesh.

Jayden had heard him yell and had ended the Phit's life before it could do any more damage. He was now rolling on the ground and coming up at the remaining two Phits. It seemed almost like it was in slow motion as Jayden's sword sliced into one of them and its head rolled slowly through the air toward him. Oisin ducked as the head spun by him and rolled across the ground. The last Phit was flying down toward Jayden. Oisin threw his knife, striking it through the heart. It landed at Jayden's feet; in its last throws of life, its nerves caused its wings to flap widely to and fro for several seconds until finally, it relented to its fate.

Jayden turned to Oisin; he couldn't help but smile while containing his laughter. Oisin still had the Phit's head attached to his arm.

Even Jayden was surprised at the grip this Phit had on Oisin. After several minutes of trying to pry its jaws open without success, they finally opted to break its teeth and pull them out one by one. It was a long, painful process, but in the end, they managed to free Oisin's arm and bandage it.

"I owe you, my friend. I was in such a hurry to get back I failed to see the Phits patrolling the outer edge of the camps. There were too many of them to fight, so I ran in hopes the Nightstalkers would still be here."

"They left Jayden. Their attack was a success; they were able to save eighteen of the missing Nightstalkers as they slipped out of the camps. Unfortunately, when they returned a Kaltaures soldier discovered the mission and was able to make it back to the camp; the Nightstalkers left knowing that reinforcements would soon come. I stayed to advise you of the situation."

"They made the right decision. You should have gone with them Oisin, but I am glad you stayed. I would never have survived without you."

"The strange thing of it was that no troops ever came. It was as if the Kaltaures soldier did not alert anyone."

"That is strange, but even if he failed to alert reinforcements, I am sure the seventh Phit that was chasing me did. He veered off toward the camp less than half way back."

"Did you find what became of the other Nightstalkers, the remainder of them?" Oisin asked.

"The good news is they are still alive; the bad is that they have been possessed with the essence of Solharn, which for now makes them our enemies. He has sent them back to our camps. They will be at least an hour ahead of Toltad and the remaining warriors. Kaelyn and Issa will have no idea what has hit them, and unfortunately, we have no way to warn them in time."

"What are we to do then, Jayden?"

"The only thing we can. We must get back to our camps. It will not be easy for daylight has come and Solharn's army will be starting to move. We will go now and hope for the best. We have no other choice."

Oisin and Jayden left the safety of the woods and began to move across the fields using the cover of whatever they could find. Jayden knew it would not be long before they were discovered but he was counting on having some time. They had gone less than half a mile when they heard the rumble of thousands of their enemies behind them. They would not make it. Even if they could out run the Kaltaures, they would be overtaken in no time by the Ralcriff and the Phits.

Jayden was sure that Oisin would be wondering why he had decided to leave now instead of awaiting the cover of darkness. There was only one reason. He knew Kaelyn was taught many of the same battle strategies that he was. After all, his father had taught them both. He was hoping she would have sent a scout over Solharn's camp in the morning as he would have done. Jayden knew the only chance such a scout would have of seeing them would be in the open. It was a gamble he wished he had not taken, at least not with Oisin's life.

They had run maybe another quarter mile when Oisin stopped and grasped his sword with the only arm he would be able to use in a battle.

"Oisin?" Jayden said turning briefly to look at the droves of Kaltaures and Phits that were quickly closing in on them.

"I will run no longer Jayden. We will be overrun any minute now and if I am to die it will be fighting, not running away."

Jayden smiled while pulling his sword from his side and his father's knife from his boot. "I am sorry that we will die so soon in this quest Oisin, but I am honored to die with you."

Both turned and ran toward their enemies. It would be their final battle, but one fought for the pride of Leal and the love of Rhol. They screamed their allegiance to Rhol and engaged their enemies who had already taken too much from them. They fought with unsurpassed valiance. Fourteen Kaltaures, two Ralcriff and four Phits lay dead on the ground before Oisin received a blow to his leg causing him to fall to the ground. Jayden stopped and stood over him swinging his sword in full circles.

Oisin could see the blade glimmering with blood in the sunlight as it sliced through the bodies of anyone who dared get near. Oisin had never seen anything like it, and as Jayden fell beside him; a sword impaled in his side, Oisin rose to his knees and continued where Jayden had left off.

He was exhausted, his arm burned trying to tell him that enough was enough, but he continued to swing. He was amazed that the thrusts of his sword were causing so many of his enemies to fly through the air away from them. One by one they disappeared. When he looked down to see that his arm had given out, he could not understand. He was no longer swinging, but it didn't matter; neither Phits nor Kaltaures nor Ralcriff could get within ten feet of them.

All at once he felt a tug on his shirt and found himself staring down at his enemies from high in the air. He was riding on the back of a Pegapire. They had come, they had found them. He looked around for Jayden to give a victory yell, but no matter how hard he looked he could not see him. He was not there. Jayden was gone.

CHAPTER TWENTY-FOUR

Issa and Kaelyn flew around the outskirts of Aura in search of a place where they could safely rest and build a home base. They had located a small ridge in the mountains just west of Aura. The caves located around it would provide shelter for the wounded and tired warriors. There was no way to access it on foot, which allowed them some peace of mind that they would not be surprised by an attack.

After several hours, all of their warriors had reached the safety of their base with the exception of the Lealian Nightstalkers. The Nightstalkers consisted of one hundred soldiers that were highly trained in stealth fighting tactics. When night fell, they would slip into their enemies' camps undetected and slit their throats while they slept. Each warrior would return to a designated meeting spot after completing one kill. If every warrior returned safely, they knew they had not yet been discovered, and after a brief rest they would return to the enemy camp and repeat the same process all over again. If at any time one of the warriors failed to return, the mission would be discontinued out of an abundance of caution that they had been compromised. It was quite a brilliant war tactic, and over time it drastically reduced their enemies' numbers, while they suffered very few casualties.

Issa had sent Yita, an eager young Pegapire, to remain at the Nightstalkers base and report back frequently on their progress. She had already returned twice to advise they had successfully entered the camp, returning unscathed and were in the progress of mounting a third and final attack.

Things seemed to be going as planned. After a brief rest, Kaelyn and Issa began to strategize and pair off the Lealian warriors with their Pegapire counterparts. They would be prepared with a plan the next time they met Solharn's armies.

It had also given them a chance to replenish their arrows which had been depleted during battle. Kaelyn had sent several Lealians to places in and around Rhol to retrieve wood from Orler trees. Jayden's father had once shown her a map detailing the location of several hundred of the well-hidden trees. Her hope that her memory served her well was answered when she saw two of the three Lealians return with large amounts of wood tied to their Pegapire counterparts.

Kaelyn smiled as several warriors immediately retrieved the wood and began to form the wiry branches into arrows. Even the wounded, some of whom could not even walk, were handed wood which they instantly began to forge into the long slender arrows. It made her proud to be a Lealian. They never tired of making a wrong into a right. They would not stop until Rhol was saved, or until they could no longer fight.

Kaelyn's thoughts were interrupted by Yita who landed too quickly and skidded across the ground, narrowly missing her before coming to a stop. Issa ran to her side.

"Yita, what is wrong?" she asked.

"The Nightstalkers! Only twenty-eight returned, and they just sit on the ground staring into space. They will not talk or move. Daylight is almost upon them, and they just sit there. They will be slaughtered when the Kaltaures discover them," Yita panted.

Issa wasted no time gathering twenty-eight Pegapires and flying off with Yita to retrieve them. She took ten Lealian warriors along with her in case the Nightstalkers were unable to move themselves.

Kaelyn watched as the last Pegapire launched into flight and hoped they would return safely. The Lealians could not afford to lose any more of their dwindling army.

Ω

"Excuse me, sir," Abednego stammered. "Several of our soldiers did not report to their post. When we went in search of them we found they had been murdered; their throats slit while they slept."

"How many?" Solharn's voice boomed.

"Two hundred, sir."

"Nightstalkers."

"Nightstalkers?"

"For someone who claims to be a skilled warrior Abednego, you woefully lack the most important skill; knowing your enemy. Your ignorance makes you weak. Nightstalkers are skilled Lealian warriors who work during the night to reduce the numbers of their enemies. They use only edged weapons and work in silence. They will keep returning until they lose one of their own. How many did you say have been killed?"

"Two hundred."

Solharn sneered. "Then prepare your warriors. They will be back for another strike. Depending on whether you allowed them to sneak into the camp unnoticed once or twice will determine how many there are. In case you don't understand the reasoning Abednego, that means there will be either one hundred of them or two hundred. It will not be an easy task as they will travel on their own once they near the camp. Capture them alive if you can and bring them to me. We will use them to our advantage. Now go! They could return at any moment."

Abednego ran off ensuring that his warriors were ready. Solharn had been right. Within an hour they had captured twenty-eight Lealian warriors, five more had been killed, but the remainder were nowhere to be found.

Abednego was confused. They could not have escaped. He had sent an army of Kaltaures soldiers to lie in wait just outside the camp for any that tried to flee. Frustrated, Abednego rode out to where he had positioned his men. They would pay for letting them slip by. When he got there, he found there would be no need for punishment. They were all dead.

How was it possible that they were discovered, and furthermore that no one heard the battle? Out of an entire troop of Kaltaures warriors surely one would have been able to provide a warning. He cursed and turned back toward the camp. It seemed unlikely, but the Lealians must have left some warriors back that had discovered his trap.

Solharn would not be pleased, and this worried Abednego enough that he decided to tell Solharn that the rest had been killed in battle. Who would know? In the end, at least they had captured

155

several alive he thought. Abednego ordered his men to bring the captured Nightstalkers to Solharn.

The Lealians stood in line with their hands and feet so tightly bound that the ropes cut into their skin. A Kaltaures soldier stood behind each one to ensure they did not escape. Abednego was taking no chances.

Solharn approached them hovering just above the ground, gliding slowly up and down the line.

"Who would like to tell me where your armies hide and save themselves from what will come?"

Although the mere sight of Solharn would make most answer his question, the line remained silent. They knew they would soon meet their end, but there was not a Lealian alive who would not die for the other. To betray their fellow man was far worse than death.

"Ahhh," Solharn gurgled. "You would all bravely die for each other, is that it? You are all so very loyal to a cause which is destined to fail. Very well, but before you make your hasty decision, I should warn you it is not death you should prepare yourself for but much worse. Commander bring one forward." Solharn bellowed.

Abednego quickly grabbed one of the Nightstalkers out of the line and threw him at Solharn's feet.

"It just would not be fair," Solharn laughed. "If I did not at least demonstrate what is to become of you, should you keep up your brave front," Solharn said as he moved closer to the prisoner.

The Lealian looked to the ground but showed no fear of what was to come. Solharn motioned to Abednego instructing him to force the Lealian to gaze at him. Abednego grabbed the soldier by the chin forcefully pulling his face up toward Solharn's gaze.

Solharn reached out placing his hand over the soldier's head and moved it around in a circular motion; blood began to ooze from his ears and nose. When the soldier began to scream, Solharn's lower jaw dropped down and just hung there, waving in the wind. A steady stream of a black fluid poured from his mouth into the soldier's, which caused the screaming to change to a disturbing gurgling sound.

The sight of it caused the remaining Lealians, and even some of the Kaltaures, to look away in horror. With the transfer of fluid complete, the soldier fell to the ground. His body was convulsing, and his face was contorting in ways that made him unrecognizable. It took several minutes for his body to stop moving and go limp. The Lealians looking on breathed a sigh of relief thinking the soldier had finally passed on relieving him of this horrific pain, but it was not over. Solharn, who had backed away slowly, floated over to him again.

Thrusting his hand out, he began to smile as he motioned the soldier to stand. He immediately did. Solharn ordered him to bring another Lealian forward, and he complied without hesitation. As if the pain had not been enough, Solharn had now taken the soldier's very soul forcing him to do what no Lealian would ever do, betray a fellow Lealian. The others did not blame him. They could see he was no longer who he used to be. His eyes were black, and his face was blank, devoid of any expression. Solharn was in complete control of him, and they knew they would all suffer the same fate in a matter of time.

"Do you still wish to remain silent? Come now, who among you wants to avoid this most unpleasant experience?" Solharn smirked.

Solharn was surprised by the silence that his question was met with. Even after witnessing the same thing twenty-seven more times, no Lealian came forward. Nevertheless, Solharn enjoyed the pain he was able to inflict upon each of them.

He also liked the results. He now controlled the twenty-eight Nightstalkers, and they would lead him to their camps whether they wanted to or not.

Solharn addressed the Lealians who were now simply standing there staring into space. They were devoid of any real thought process of their own.

"You will return to your meeting place, and wait there until you are rescued by your fellow Lealians. Once you are back in their place of refuge, you will await my instructions."

The Lealians walked off in silence through the dark. Solharn could now see and control everything they did. Now he had a powerful army ready to attack from inside his enemies own ranks.

Ω

"Are they alright Issa?" Kaelyn asked when she saw the first few soldiers arrive.

"I do not know. They seem to be in shock; it is strange. They just stare into space refusing, or at least unable to speak."

Kaelyn looked sadly at the soldiers as one by one they were carried from the back of the Pegapires to a nearby cave. Their bodies appeared limp and lifeless, as they dangled from the shoulders of the warriors that were carrying them.

What could have possibly caused them to return in this state? These warriors were fearless and what of the rest of them? Were they dead or merely held captive?

"Kaelyn, we must prepare for battle. The sun will rise in less than an hour; we have little time."

"Very well, can you send a scout over the enemy camps at first light Issa, to see if there are any signs of the missing stalkers?"

"I would be happy to Issa," Yita, overhearing the conversation, chimed in.

"Good," responded Issa. "I can't think of a better choice."

Kaelyn just nodded and began to assemble the Lealians. They were going to need some help. She wished Jayden were here. Perhaps he would know what had become of the Nightstalkers; maybe he would know what they might face when first light came.

CHAPTER TWENTY-FIVE

Palto had been looking at the cave walls for well over an hour now. He could not see the passage, or the hatchet Duffy had described, even though he was sure that he was in the right area. He was running out of time.

He knew that the hatchet would not be easy to find after ten years of weathering, but he was hoping he would see the opening Duffy described. Palto was thinking of heading back to Solace when he felt it; the air was becoming warmer.

He quickened his pace looking frantically up and down the walls, when right in front of him a thick branch appeared, poking out of the wall. It was tucked back into a crevice in the cave, which aside from ending in ten feet seemed almost like another tunnel. Slightly wilted vines adorned the wall disguising what Palto hoped would be the hatchet. It would explain why he had passed it so many times.

Palto nuzzled at the vines pushing them aside and found what he had been looking for. He could not believe his luck. The small crevice within the tunnel had protected the vines and the hatchet from the burning flames of the dragon. The fact the vines even grew here was a good sign as they needed sunlight and water to grow.

He looked up to the ceiling of the cave but could see nothing aside from the massive leaves covering whatever was behind them. Palto suspected their roots started at the top of the mountain where Duffy had tumbled through ten years ago. Over time they must have grown to cover Duffy's escape route.

Palto ran and jumped into the air. He could feel the searing heat of the flames passing by him as he pushed off the side of the wall. He hoped that the alternate exit would be big enough for him to maneuver through. Breaking through the vines, he was relieved to find it was larger than he had expected. It twisted through the walls of the cavern like a winding road allowing him to use his legs periodically to gain more momentum. In less time than he thought it would have taken, he broke through the ground which had hidden the entrance over the last decade.

Palto walked around breathing in the fresh air that his lungs had craved over the last couple of days. He listened intently for a sign of anyone, but the sound of the falls gushing down the side of the mountain was all he could hear. He was a mere six hundred yards or so from where Phanthus was lying in wait. Palto knew his initial plan of avoiding Phanthus would not be possible. There was no way the people of Solace would make it up the tunnel. Even if they could climb the vines, it would take hours. They would remain trapped in the realm unless he was able to, at the very least, distract Phanthus. He would need Solko and Preta before he even thought of trying it and would have to return to get them.

As he made his way back to the Sacred Realm, he noticed that the ground was covered in skeletal bones that gleamed almost disturbingly in the sunlight. It had to be the remains of Duffy's family. He thought about removing them so Duffy would not have to bear the pain of realizing they were no longer alive, but then Palto realized it would be worse for Duffy to continue searching endlessly for loved ones that no longer existed in our form. He was not looking forward to giving him the news.

When Palto walked through the Wall of Solace Solko, Preta and Duffy along with hundreds of Rholians stared at him in silence. Duffy had obviously told everyone within the realm about the passageway, and they were eagerly waiting to hear if it existed.

"I have found the way out," Palto said calmly.

A loud cheer rang out. "We have Duffy to thank, but I am afraid it is not all good news. It will take hours for you to climb your way out and time will not allow us that luxury. The route that Mary took the others down will not help us either. It only leads to the Swamps of Tiqor."

"What are you saying, Palto? Are we stuck here? I must leave to find what has become of my family and fight for Rhol," Duffy said walking toward Palto.

"I understand Duffy. We will not leave you or anyone else stranded here. You will all get the chance to defend Rhol. Solko, Preta and I will exit through the passageway and engage Phanthus. I hope this will provide a long enough distraction for one of us to return and lead you out of the tunnel to safety."

"If you are to engage that monster then I will be coming with you. You cannot deny me the chance to fight alongside you. It was me, after all, who told you of the tunnel. My family can wait till this battle is over," Duffy insisted.

Palto addressed the Rholians, "if you have not prepared yourself to leave already then do so now. When we come back to retrieve you, there will be no time to waste."

They began to slowly disperse, all except Duffy who remained poised, refusing to back down.

"We must speak, Duffy," Palto calmly said.

"Very well, Palto, but you will not change my mind."

"We can speak of that later. There are more important matters to deal with."

"What is it then?" Duffy enquired.

"It is about the story you told me, Duffy. How you came to be here."

"It is the truth, I swear it," Duffy responded curtly.

"Even if I had doubted it, I wouldn't now."

"I do not understand, Palto."

"You see Duffy. You were obviously dazed when the Cawlaway attacked. You did not see your family, but they were there."

Duffy just stared at Palto in silence as he continued. "I believe I found them or at least their remains. Their bones lay scattered over the ground. I am sorry to have to tell you such news."

Palto could see Duffy's knees starting to shake before they buckled beneath him. He knelt upon the ground burying his face in his small hands and wept, then yelled and then wept again.

After several minutes Duffy rose to his feet. His sorrow had turned to anger.

"It is his doing, Solharn's. He and his loathsome followers will pay for all the grief they have caused. Now, more than ever Palto, you cannot deny me the chance to battle beside you against Phanthus."

"No, I cannot," Palto answered. "You may come if you wish, but I can only take you to the opening. The passageway is not big enough for you to ride with me. There are vines there, sufficient to hold your weight, but it will take you several hours to climb."

"It will take less than you think, Palto."

161

"Very well, let us summon Preta and Solko. When the next burst of flames dies in the tunnel, we will ride."

It wasn't long before they reached the passageway leading to the top of the mountain. Duffy hopped off Palto saying only that he would see them soon. As the three Pegapires disappeared through the passageway, Duffy grabbed his hatchet from the wall and began to climb.

When Palto emerged from the ground, followed by Preta and Solko, he had not anticipated that Phanthus would be flying directly toward them. He cursed to himself at their timing. Phanthus could not have expected them. He must have been taking a brief flight before returning to his perch. The reason did not matter though; they were now in his line of vision.

"Preta, flank right, Solko left! Do not try to be heroes, let us draw him away. Our only advantage against Phanthus is that there are three of us and only one of him. Do not communicate vocally. The dragon can hear for miles, and it will not help our strategies if he knows them in advance."

Preta and Solko reacted immediately. Palto flew toward the dragon. He saw the first stream of flames spew from Phanthus's jaws and only then did he react and change direction, flying straight up toward the sky and over the dragon. When the fire dissipated, Preta caught the dragon's attention by flying in front of him from the east. When Phanthus turned toward her, Solko crossed in front from the opposite direction causing the dragon once more to change his attack.

The Pegapires were trained in every form of warfare, and this was merely a distraction tactic meant to confuse the enemy. This technique caused the enemy to change focus several times, making any attack they had planned less effective. It was all they could do for now. They knew they would stand no chance of defeating Phanthus without help. Their strategy was simple. They would try to slowly move the dragon away from the mountain range to allow a safe escape for the Rholians that remained in the Realm.

Palto turned to come at Phanthus from above. When he looked down, he could not believe his eyes. It was Jayden riding on the back of the dragon. Perhaps this was why the dragon had left his perch. Jayden had somehow attacked the dragon from above and now clung to his back. It also meant that the rest of the army was on its way. Palto had a renewed hope.

"Preta, Jayden is fighting the dragon while he clings to its back. He will not be able to hold on forever. We must help him. I will swing in front of Phanthus and distract him. You fly from behind and try to retrieve Jayden."

"Just say the word Palto. I am in position."

"Now!" Palto yelled.

Palto flew close to the dragon's snout, missing it by mere feet, and began flying downward. Phanthus fell for Palto's trick and followed, allowing Preta to move up from behind without Phanthus detecting her.

She could see Jayden stand in anticipation of the rescue. She slowed herself as she neared him, but then she became confused. Jayden was removing his sword from its sheath and was swinging it in her direction. Preta moved quickly to avoid the blade but was not fast enough. It cut into her front leg and sliced through her wing.

"Nooo," Solko screamed while watching his sister fall helplessly to the ground.

"What is it Solko?" Palto asked.

"Jayden, he fights with Phanthus, not against him. When Preta neared him, he swung his sword at her. She is wounded or worse I fear."

"That cannot be! Are you sure it was Jayden and not Phanthus himself that caused your sister to fall?"

"I saw it with my own eyes. I must go check on her Palto."

"Do not land Solko or Phanthus will have both your lives. The best we can do for now is to keep his attention drawn away from her in the event he wants to finish her off. Do not attract attention to her."

"As you say, Palto, but I will have Jayden's head," Solko yelled while diving toward Phanthus.

"No, Solko. Do not engage them."

"I am sorry Palto, but Jayden must die for his treachery," Solko screamed as he veered toward the dragon.

"Solko, listen to me…," but it was too late. Solko had only revenge on his mind and flew as fast as he could toward Jayden. Palto quickly positioned himself between the two.

"Solko, do not make me fight one of my own. Now back away."

Solko did not slow down and continued to fly toward Palto. "Get out of the way, Palto."

Palto would not allow Solko to attack Jayden. Something was not right; he had seconds to think as Solko drew closer. It would be his sister that snapped him out of his tirade.

"Solko, look below. Your sister lives! She is moving across the top of the mountain."

Solko looked to see his sister limping across the grass with her wing hanging abnormally by her side. Phanthus had seen her too and moved in to finish her off.

"Quickly, Solko! We must distract him so she can get to safety."

Solko immediately flew to the front of the dragon and past. Palto did the same from the opposite direction. It did not even faze the dragon this time. He continued to fly toward Preta.

The pair tried several other maneuvers, all with little or no effect. There was nothing they could do. The dragon was too powerful for them to bring down. He was being guided by Jayden who could clearly see the advantage in removing one of the three of them. Preta would soon be nothing more than ashes blowing in the wind.

CHAPTER TWENTY-SIX

"Did you see Jayden?" Oisin yelled to Orulla, the Pegapire that had just saved his life.

"I grabbed you when I saw the chance. Jayden was beneath you. That was the last I saw of him. I am sorry, I could only grab one of you."

Oisin's heart sank. There was still hope that another Pegapire might have swooped in to save him. Either way, Jayden would want him to deliver the message of Solharn's return to the rest of the camp. But first, he had to warn them of the soldiers that Solharn now controlled.

"How far are we from our camps?" Oisin yelled through the wind.

"A half an hour. They are organizing themselves for an attack as we speak."

Oisin began to panic. They would not make it to their camps in time. Suddenly he had an idea. "Orulla, can you get a message to them using your telepathy?" Oisin asked.

"I must be able to see them to communicate in that manner, Oisin. Do not worry; we will be there shortly. If Jayden is there, you will find him."

"That is not my concern right now Orulla. The Nightstalkers, have they returned to the camps?"

"Yes. What was left of them."

"They are not as they seem. They are controlled by Solharn. He has returned and leads their armies now. The Nightstalkers have to be held at bay or we will suffer significant losses."

Orulla looked back at Oisin with concern in her eyes. "But we have no way of telling them that. Are you sure? They seemed harmless when they returned, almost as if they lost their lust for life."

"They have, and when Solharn demands it, they will attack. They no longer are in control of their actions."

Orulla picked up her speed and communicated this information to the other Pegapires that flew beside them, about twenty in all.

It seemed like the minutes had turned to hours by the time Orulla spoke again. "We are close, Oisin."

Now Oisin could see the camp nestled into a high ridge on one of the mountains. When he looked down, it was mass confusion. Lealians were fighting amongst themselves, and the Pegapires were hesitant to engage in the fight.

"You must hypnotize them Orulla," Oisin said.

"That is dangerous Oisin. Only Palto can reverse the effects of that, and he has yet to return."

"I know," said Oisin "but we have no other choice at this point. Look, the Pegapires are no longer sitting back; they are engaging the Nightstalkers."

"Quickly Orulla, let them know ahead. It looks as if the Pegapires have been told to engage. They are attacking and will likely slaughter them all without understanding their affliction. Kaelyn must know what has happened so she can judge it accordingly. Better they are hypnotized than slaughtered."

"Very well," Orulla said.

Ω

Kaelyn was screaming at the Lealians. She did not understand what was happening. She had left momentarily with Issa to scout around the camp and returned to this, her people fighting each other. The Pegapires had flown to safety obviously confused themselves, and unable to decide what to do.

"What are you doing?" she yelled as she approached the back lines with her sword drawn.

"The Nightstalkers, Kaelyn! They just got up and attacked us without warning. We have been using defensive tactics on them, but we cannot keep it up. We have lost five Lealians already!"

"What?" Kaelyn shouted.

She did not understand. Had she failed them as a leader? Why were the Nightstalkers suddenly fighting against their own people! What had happened in the enemy camps? She knew one thing, she had to make a decision and make it fast, and with a heavy heart, she did.

"Issa, Lealians. We can afford no more losses! Switch your tactics and engage them! I do not know why the Nightstalkers have changed their allegiance, but we can afford no more deaths at their hands."

Kaelyn wept as her sword sliced into one of the Nightstalkers causing him to fall lifelessly to the ground. She watched two others being ripped apart by Pegapires before Issa got to her with the message of Solharn's treachery.

Immediately Kaelyn yelled to the Lealians. "Defense! Return to defensive tactics!"

There was no hesitation. It made the Lealians sick to think they could be responsible for the death of another.

"Issa please let the Pegapi……."

"They have already been instructed," Issa said watching the Pegapires swoop in leaving in their wake one Lealian after another standing there as if frozen in time. In just over an hour the Nightstalkers all stood there, silent.

Kaelyn looked at them with tears welling up in her eyes. They were slowly losing this battle. Solharn had returned, and she was now at a loss for what to do.

"Palto can restore them Kaelyn. It was the only way to contain the Nightstalkers without killing them. You made the right decision," Issa reassured her.

"Yes, but where is Palto? Where are Oisin and Jayden?"

"I am right here Kaelyn."

Kaelyn turned to see Oisin standing behind her. "Oisin, you live! You are here. Where did you come from?"

"Jayden and I were caught in a fight with Solharn's camp while making our way here. Orulla was able to pull me to safety just in time. I had her get a message to Issa about the Nightstalkers."

"But how did you know?"

"It is a long story, but basically I knew through Jayden."

"Jayden is with you? Where is he Oisin?" Kaelyn asked excitedly. She suddenly felt a weight being lifted from her.

Oisin looked toward Orulla whom he had sent to see if Jayden had somehow made it back to the camp. Orulla just shook her head telling him that he had not.

"He was lost in battle."

Hearing this, Kaelyn turned and slowly walked away, dragging her sword behind her. Oisin followed.

"Kaelyn!" he shouted. "He was my leader too, and more importantly he was my friend. He once said that you might be the one to replace him should he die. Well, that time has come! Do not walk away defeated."

"We need him, Oisin. I am not a leader."

"Jayden thought you were and that is good enough for me."

"But not for me," Kaelyn responded.

"Then for who, Kaelyn? You have been leading our people since you left Jayden in the tunnel. We have not lost yet!" Oisin yelled.

"I cannot make life and death decisions any longer Oisin. It is not in me!" Kaelyn shouted.

"There cannot be life without death, Kaelyn and it is not you who decides either. You are a leader. These people follow you because they want to because they want to fight for their world. It is they who choose the path of their life, and they already know that death will eventually come to them no matter what path they take. They are simply looking for you to guide them down the best one."

"He is right, Kaelyn. We must lead like we have been doing. Palto chose us to be together for a reason. He knew we were capable of succeeding even if we had to do so without him and Jayden," Issa said.

Kaelyn knew they were right. She could not come this far just to abandon the cause because of her insecurities.

"Enough!" Oisin shouted. "Solharn's armies move toward us as I speak and there is much you need to know before you decide on what strategy we will take."

Oisin's outburst brought everybody back to the reality they currently faced. The three walked to the edge of the cliff, out of earshot of anyone else. Oisin told them everything he knew about Solace, the death of Kiran, Solharn's camp, about Deke, Deo, Mary and finally about Palto and Phanthus. He saved the knowledge that there was a traitor amongst them for last, and knew instantly it was neither Issa nor Kaelyn. The anger on their faces told him all he needed to know.

The remaining Nightstalkers had finally found their way back to the camps. Kaelyn was elated to see that they were safe. Toltad was happy to see her as well but had mixed feelings when he found his men, the unfortunate warriors that had not escaped Solharn's camp, were mere statues under a Pegapire's trance. Kaelyn explained to him the circumstances behind her order, but he did not want to believe that his men would ever turn against their own. After a lengthy standoff between the two, Oisin intervened and became the voice of reason. He explained to Toltad what Jayden had seen.

Toltad insisted that the hypnotized warriors be treated with the utmost respect and that they be safeguarded at all times. However, there was no need for him to assert this; Kaelyn had already made these arrangements. Two Pegapires and two Lealians would stay with them at all times.

Toltad was a little embarrassed when he realized that Kaelyn now led the Lealians. He was unaware that Jayden had not escaped Solharn's armies. He apologized for his tone with her, but there was no need. Kaelyn understood his loyalty toward his men.

"Warriors of Rhol, Lealians and Pegapires alike, we are going to move on Solace. Phanthus holds our people captive inside the Sacred Realm by blockading the entrance and breathing fire down the tunnel. Phanthus is perhaps our most fearsome enemy aside from Solharn. This will not be an easy battle, but it is one we must win if our quest is to be successful. Join together and gather as many weapons as you can carry. We fight Phanthus today, and if it goes as I expect, Solharn will meet our blades and arrows tomorrow."

Oisin was pleased to see that Kaelyn had her confidence back. She had just ignited the entire brigade with a twenty-second speech while sitting poised on top of Issa. Although he could not hear Issa, he did not doubt that she, too, was driving home the importance of this battle to the Pegapires.

CHAPTER TWENTY-SEVEN

Duffy could see the light beaming into the tunnel from above. He was almost there. His arms were so tired from the climb it felt like they could fall off at any moment. He had not taken a break for nearly two hours. Nothing could stop him now. Several minutes later his hand reached out of the tunnel, followed by the other. He had made it. Using his last bit of strength, he hoisted his body up and over the crest of the opening.

Only his legs remained in the passageway when the ground shook beneath him, causing him to lose his grip, and slide helplessly back into the hole that had defeated him ten years ago. Not this time, Duffy thought, as he grasped at vine after vine. He finally managed to grab onto one and slow his descent. Duffy tightened his grip. The leaves slapped his face as they were torn from the vine. Finally, he came to a stop. His hands were bleeding from where the vine had sliced into them, but that would not deter him. He began to climb back up the vine which now resembled a rope. He had more strength than ever now. Nothing would deny him the chance to avenge his family.

Moments later he stood on the mountain looking at what was transpiring in the sky, but more importantly, what was lying on the ground just feet from him. It must have been what had caused the ground to shake. It was Preta, lying motionless on the grass and bleeding profusely from her wing. Duffy ran toward her hoping he was not too late to help.

When he got to her side, she was conscious but in a daze. "Preta, get up! You must move," Duffy screamed as he shook her.

Preta managed to get to her feet but was too shaky to make it any distance. Duffy could only think of one way to get her to safety. He would have to get her to the passage which they had just struggled to get out of. It would not be easy for her to maneuver down the hole, but he had survived the fall ten years ago, so she stood a fighting chance. It was her only hope.

He walked alongside Preta and guided her toward the hole. They were halfway there when he realized they would not make it. Phanthus had seen the movement and was advancing on them. Palto and Solko were doing everything they could to change the dragon's course, but it was not working.

If he only had his Cortuc, he would be able to do something. He struggled to remember that fateful night ten years ago. What had he done with it when he woke up and ran to find his family? He hadn't had it when he fell into the hole; leaving Preta, he ran toward the area where the Cawlaway had attacked him and his family. He soon saw the bones Palto had described scattered over the ground. He struggled to control the pain that he felt coursing through his body as his eyes scoured the ground for the Cortuc.

The Cortuc was the Brawltug's most cherished possession. There were so few remaining that only one was entrusted to each Brawltug family. The Cortuc was given to the eldest male in each clan. It was a formidable weapon used for both attack and defence. It resembled a staff of sorts, measuring about one inch in diameter and six feet in length, and was said to have been forged from stone obtained from the very core of Rhol. A square piece of metal that resembled pewter adorned one end of the staff, and a round metal piece the other. The round end was used to attack, the square to defend.

The Cortuc used the energy of Rhol as its primary source of power which came from the ground itself. When the square end was placed on the ground, the round end would shoot currents of electricity, much like a miniature lightning bolt, in the direction in which it was pointed. When the round end was placed on the ground, the square end would produce an electrical shield that was nearly impossible to penetrate. The Cortuc was useless in the hands of anyone other than the Brawltug who possessed it.

If it were taken or stolen from a Brawltug, it would become nothing more than a fancy walking stick. This was one of the reasons the Cortuc had become so rare an item. Greed had often led to the Cortuc being obtained in devious ways which would quite literally destroy its powers. The second reason for its rarity was that only the Brawltug that possessed the Cortuc could pass it on. The passing of the Cortuc involved a simple ritual, but if it were not followed precisely, the Cortuc would not retain its powers. In the ritual passing, both Brawltug would hold the Cortuc while its owner gave one simple chant "haf broinko pe broinko" which simply meant "from brother to brother." Many Brawltug died in the wars of Rhol before they could perform the ritual. As a result, many more Cortuc's became obsolete.

No one really knows how the Brawltug obtained the stone from the core of Rhol, nor how they came to develop it into such a useful weapon. If they did, they weren't saying. Either way, Duffy was one of the few Brawltug that still possessed a Cortuc or at least he had a decade ago.

Duffy stopped suddenly in his tracks. He became overwhelmed with a feeling of guilt and regret. Tears rolled down his weathered cheeks leaving a noticeable line as they rinsed away the grime that covered his face, before disappearing into his tangled beard. He was staring at a large rock. It was the rock he had used to keep watch over his family that fateful night. Over the past ten years, he'd convinced himself that the story he had told Palto was the truth, but it wasn't. Not completely. The rock reminded him of the one little piece of the story that his mind had slightly changed to protect him from the guilt and torment of the actual event. But the rock, the rock brought the actual memory flooding back to him.

He had not switched watches with his brother that night. He had fallen asleep on top of that very rock, and his family had been killed because of him because he fell asleep when he should have been keeping a close vigil.

He was awakened by the screams of his family as the Cawlaway attacked them. The memory haunted him as he recalled the horrific event.

He had run toward them in a panic. He was the eldest in the family, and he alone possessed the Cortuc that could have saved them from the vicious attack, but in his haste, he had forgotten it atop the rock. He had stood there helplessly watching his family being ripped to shreds.

Grabbing his hatchet, he ran toward them. In a desperate bid to save them, he lunged at the Cawlaway, but he missed his mark and stumbled to the ground. The Cawlaway turned on him digging one of its claws into the side of his face. The weight of the

Cawlaway on top of him must have caused the ground underneath him to crumble. The Cawlaway flew up and away as Duffy fell through the hole. Perhaps it was fate. Had everything not transpired exactly the way it had, he would have died along with his family. Right now, at this moment he wished he had.

"Duffy. Are you there?"

He looked back to see Preta wobbling around aimlessly, still dazed from the fall she took. Phanthus was almost upon her. Duffy ran to the rock. He had not saved his family, but he could save Preta. He climbed to the top of the boulder as if it was a mere pebble in his way, and found what he had been searching for. Lying on top of the rock, exactly where he had left it ten years ago, was the Cortuc. Grabbing it, he leapt down and ran toward Preta.

Ω

Solko realized now that his sister was going to die. He told her one last time that he loved her while watching the flames exiting the dragon's mouth. He hoped she was close enough that she would receive his message and his apology for not protecting her as he should have.

Seconds later he could no longer see her for the inferno that surrounded her. He watched the grass turn from green to black as the blaze lit the ground on fire for hundreds of yards around where he had last seen her.

He could see Palto come through the smoke toward him. It was so thick by now that he could barely breathe.

"I am sorry, Solko," was all Palto could muster.

Solko could not respond. He still did not want to come to terms with it.

"It is just us now, Solko. Let us do what we can to avenge your sister and all of the souls that have been lost due to Phanthus."

"And what of Jayden?" Solko responded with hate in his eyes.

"I cannot believe that Jayden is acting on his own accord, but we are left with only each other to fight Phanthus now. We do not have the luxury of trying to protect him, and I am sure he would rather be dead than assisting Solharn," Palto said.

Solko nodded, and both flew through the smoke to find Phanthus. They knew their chances of victory were slim.

When there was no more grass left to burn, the fire slowly died, and the smoke began to clear enough for them to see the destruction the blast had caused below. Everything was burned aside from one patch of green grass. Solko wept as he looked down upon it.

Ω

Duffy could see the inferno of fire shooting from the dragon's mouth as he approached Preta's side. With the square end pointed straight toward the sky, he drove the round end into the dirt. The shield spanned around them blocking the flames. From inside it looked as if they were trapped in the center of a large sphere of fire. The flames roared out and over the walls of energy surrounding them.

When the flames died, Duffy flipped the staff in the opposite direction sending orbs of electric currents into the sky toward Phanthus, as he flew over and away from them. Several hit the dragon but did little to slow him down. As Phanthus glided across the ground toward the cliffs, Duffy took one more shot in desperation. The wave of electricity missed the dragon but struck its passenger. Duffy could see the person fall and hit the ground several hundred yards from him.

Phanthus did not seem to notice and disappeared into the clouds flying at a high rate of speed. Duffy wondered if he had wounded the beast; he seemed to be retreating.

Ω

"Palto, do you….."

"I see Solko, I see. It seems we are indebted to Duffy. Let's get them out of harm's way," Palto responded happily.

"And look Palto, behind us, our armies have arrived."

Palto turned to see Issa and Kaelyn leading the charge with Oisin flying close beside her. Hundreds of Lealian warriors followed them on the backs of the Pegapires. That would explain why Phanthus had retreated.

"The fight is our's Solko. Go to your sister!"

Palto looked toward the approaching armies. It was indeed an impressive sight. He was flying toward Oisin and Kaelyn when he saw Oisin break off and fly quickly toward the ground. He looked down to see a lone figure waving frantically at him. It was Jayden. Palto raced toward him. It seemed Jayden was luring Oisin in, just as he had Preta. Oisin too was obviously unaware of Jayden's sudden change in sides.

Ω

Oisin could not believe his eyes when he saw him. "Orulla, it is Jayden!" He had somehow made it out alive. Perhaps Palto had saved him. It did not matter. His friend was waving for help, and he would get those answers soon enough.

Orulla dropped down from the ranks and flew toward him. "It is a miracle Oisin. How could he have survived?"

"We will find out soon enough!" Oisin responded.

Orulla was coming in for a landing when she suddenly stopped several yards from Jayden.

"Orulla, what are you doing? He is over there. He could be hurt."

Oisin did not wait for an answer. He jumped off Orulla and began to run toward Jayden.

"Oisin do not go any closer. Palto communicated with me. He believes Jayden no longer fights for Rhol."

"Don't be ridiculous," Oisin said ignoring Orulla.

"Oisin!" Orulla shouted.

Oisin turned to face her. "You can stand back there if you wish. I will not leave Jayden. He needs our help!"

Oisin did not see Jayden coming up behind him with his sword drawn ready to strike.

"Oisin, behind you!" Orulla yelled.

When Oisin turned, he could see the glare of steel coming down upon him. He reacted immediately by rolling away to the left. The blade struck the ground beside him. He looked up to see Jayden. His eyes were black as coal. Oisin had not even brought a weapon. He was helpless as Jayden lifted his sword above his head and turned the blade in a downward direction.

Oisin knew the person that was about to end his life was no longer his friend. His eyes had the same hollow emptiness that the Nightstalkers had when they too turned on their own. Oisin knew he was not looking into the eyes of Jayden but those of Solharn.

"I have no regrets and no ill will my friend," Oisin said as the blade moved down toward him.

Oisin was sure he saw Jayden pause if only for a second, before the blade once again resumed its path toward his chest. It was not Oisin's time though. Orulla had moved up behind Jayden and grabbed him within her jaws, flinging him to the side. Even that would not stop him. He got up from the ground and ran toward Orulla in a fury.

"Jayden, no!" Oisin yelled.

Jayden would not advance any further. Palto appeared between them, and Jayden froze as he gazed into his eyes. He was no longer what he once was. The mighty warrior was now just a feeble reflection in Solharn's evil game. It was a dark day, one of many more to come.

CHAPTER TWENTY-EIGHT

Deke shivered as he awoke. He had needed the rest, but the cold dampness of the ground had not provided him with the most memorable sleep he could remember. He stretched as he crawled to his feet and looked down at Mary. She was still fast asleep. Deo rumbled and slowly rose rubbing his eyes, trying to focus in on Deke.

"We have to save her Deo. I cannot bear to think of her turning into something like Torrell."

"I know, but it is not like there is a cure. Half her soul is missing Deke, and I don't think there is any way to stop it. If we cannot find her paladin, then that will be her fate."

Deke glanced over toward Torrell. His face had a blank expression as he stared in the direction of where she had slept. Observing his face, Deo turned to see what had caused him to go silent. Torrell was gone. Only the vines that had once held her captive remained on the ground along with a small chain and locket that hung from a branch underneath where she once was.

Deke walked over and grasped the chain from the branch. "It is Mary's, Deo. I gave it to her one year after we met as a symbol of our friendship."

"How did Torrell get it?" Deo asked.

"I don't know," Deke said running toward Mary. "Mary, wake up Mary!" Deke shouted as he shook her.

"Is she alright, Deke?"

"She is not waking up. I will never forgive myself if Torrell has done something to her."

"What is all the fuss?" Mary asked suddenly sitting up from her deep sleep.

Deke felt an instant relief at the sound of her voice. "Are you alright?"

"I'm fine. What's wrong?" She responded still drowsy from her deep sleep.

Deke held up the locket. "What is it?" Mary asked.

"What is it? It is the friendship locket I gave you the year we became friends."

"Oh, yes. I am sorry. I am still half asleep. Why do you have it?"

"Torrell left it behind," Deo said.

"Left it behind? What do you mean, left it behind?" Mary asked.

"She is gone, Mary. She escaped her bonds. We have no idea where she is. When I saw your locket I thought she might have harmed you in some way," Deke responded.

"Strange, she must have taken it from me while I slept. What do you think it means?" Mary asked.

"A sign of some sort, I don't think she liked you very much. It could mean she plans to bring you harm. We will have to be extra cautious from here on out," Deke said.

"If that was her plan then why wouldn't she have done that while we slept?" Deo suspiciously asked.

"She was probably afraid that I would awaken and scream to alert you two and did not want to take that chance. Who knows, she is crazy," Mary answered.

Deo was troubled by this turn of events. There were lots of ways to kill someone silently in their sleep, but she hadn't, she had just left. Why?

Deke handed Mary back her necklace. "Well, whatever the reason, we will have to be careful. She knows the way we are heading and knows the swamps better than us."

"We should start moving. How long will it take to get out of this swamp, Mary?" Deo asked looking around expecting Torrell to jump out any moment.

"I would say less than a day if we hurry," Mary answered.

They did not have much to pack, and in a matter of minutes, they had started on their journey. Although the night had been relatively cool, as the day wore on, it became sweltering hot. The stench of the swamp did not help, nor did the insects that nibbled away at their faces and arms. They walked without a break for several miles until finally stopping to douse themselves with cool water from the creek.

"This will be our last chance for water. We must veer off from the creek. We are almost out of this swamp," Mary said. "The water is not fit to drink, just dab some on your lips and wet your clothes. We will have fresh water once we are outside the boundaries of Tiqor. Then we will make our way to the Blackpool. I believe that is where Solharn hides Elissa."

"I cannot wait to put this swamp behind us," Deke said.

"I too, am looking forward to leaving this tangled, smelly mess. Perhaps it will diminish the distinct feeling I have that we are being followed," added Deo.

Mary walked further ahead. "Well, let's go then."

It was slow walking as the three made their way through the thick scrub brush. Mary seemed to know where she was going as she pushed the overgrown vegetation aside and continued to follow a very narrow path.

After several hours, the bushes seemed to become less dense. Deke wondered if they were finally out of the swamps.

"What is that smell?" Deo asked gagging as he spoke.

Deke pulled his shirt up over his nose. "I smelled it earlier, but it seems to be getting more and more rancid."

Mary chuckled to herself. "Come on boys; it isn't that bad. We will be out of here soon."

"We have been walking through this swamp forever with no end in sight. Deke, why don't you change me into something that can fly and I will scout ahead? I might even be able to fly you two out, one at a time," Deo suggested.

Deke thought about it for a moment. It would tire him out, but at the same time, he wanted out of the swamp. He could rest when the swamp was behind them, and flying out would save them valuable time. It was not the first time he had thought about it, but Mary had said it was too risky as any movement in the sky over the swamp would attract Phits, and that was the last thing they needed. Maybe if it was a short distance though, it might be worth the risk.

Mary stopped and looked toward Deke. "We have gone over this before Deke. Did you not hear Kiran when she said you had to use your powers sparingly? It could kill you if you exert yourself too much. You do remember what happened in the Realm of Solace, don't you?"

"I have grown stronger since then. Don't you want to get out of here?"

"Of course I do but not at the expense of your safety or ours. The Phits do regular patrols of this swamp, and if they see any one of us, it will be the end of our journey. Besides, we are almost out of here. Why risk it now?"

"Let's just keep moving Deke. Mary is right. It is not worth it. I am sorry I suggested it."

A small knoll appeared before them in the distance. Mary stopped and looked back at Deo and Deke. "That hill marks the beginning of the end of this swamp. In another hour or so it will be behind us."

They were both thrilled to hear it. The smell had become so rancid Deke didn't think he'd ever be able to wash the stench from his skin. They began their climb, and in a short amount of time, they'd reached the crest of the knoll. There, they found the source of the smell that had plagued them for the last several hours. Thousands of bones had been piled into a large mound; bits of flesh still clung to many of them. This was the source of the smell. Flesh decomposing in the hot sun.

Mary urged them on. "Quickly, we're almost there."

"Mary, this looks a lot like the place Torrell described," Deke said cautiously looking around.

"Nonsense, I know exactly where we are. Besides, there is no such creature," Mary said while hiding her smirk.

They had only walked a few more steps when Torrell jumped out from behind the pile of bones. She was still a ways off from them, but there was no mistaking who it was.

"Be careful, it's Torrell," Deke whispered running for the cover of a nearby bush. Mary and Deo followed closely behind him.

"What is she doing?" Deo asked.

"I don't know, but I don't think she saw us," Deke said glancing over at Mary. She looked enraged.

"What is it, Mary?" Deke asked.

"Nothing, I just knew she would try to ruin things."

"Ruin what?" Deo asked.

As the words left his mouth, a loud screeching noise caught their attention. All three glanced over to see Torrell surrounded by a small twister. She screamed aloud at a lone evil looking figure that stood less than ten feet away from her.

"That is Solharn," Deo said.

"Solharn! What would he possibly want with Torrell?" Deke asked.

"It is a good question Deke, and one that I think we will soon have the answer to," Deo said, repositioning himself.

Out of nowhere, two more figures appeared. Deke could clearly see one was Mary, and the other must've been her paladin, Delca.

Deke turned to Mary to find she was no longer beside him. "Is she crazy? What is she doing down there?" Deke said as he stood to go after her.

Deo pulled him back down. "It's not Mary, Deke. It's Torrell's memory of Mary and her paladin, Delca. The story she told of the Tetagorous, it was true. Torrell's been caught and is living out her worst nightmare. It's the only thing that makes sense," Deo explained.

"But how would Torrell even know Mary's paladin?"

"I don't know, but look," Deo said pointing toward Torrell.

Torrell's screams grew louder as the Tetagorous, who quite convincingly looked as if it was Solharn, projected the illusion of him grabbing Delca by the throat. Delca cried helplessly. Mary, who appeared to be lying on the ground writhing in pain, was begging him to stop. Her screams fell on deaf ears as Solharn extended two of his fingers on either side of Delca's cheeks, and forced her mouth open. Deke felt sick as he watched Solharn's lower jaw drop, and begin to fill Delca's mouth with a thick oozing black fluid. She gurgled helplessly trying to spit the liquid out, but eventually, she succumbed, swallowing it. Afterward, he laughed and threw her to the ground, watching as her body convulsed. Only after her body lay stiff on the ground did he turn and gaze at Mary with a sickening grin.

Deke could hear Torrell's screams become louder and louder.

"I own half of your soul now earth child. Did you ever really think you could defeat me?" Solharn drooled. "Do not worry. Soon you will not remember who you once were anyway. Soon you will be Pintante," he laughed.

Solharn and Delca slowly evaporated, leaving only the apparition of Mary lying on the ground weeping. Deke and Deo watched in shock as she slowly changed into Torrell.

Torrell's screams became deafening. She was now sitting on the ground with her hands to her ears while the whole scenario started again.

"Deo, I cannot believe what...Torrell...Torrell is Mary."

"And Mary, or whoever she is, has led us into a trap," Deo said finishing Deke's thought.

Deke shook his head. "She left the locket as a clue. I should've known when Mary...or whoever she is, didn't recognize it. Torrell, or I mean Mary, was trying to help us all along. She has sacrificed herself for us so that we could see the truth through her nightmare. We have to save her Deo."

"But how do we fight a myth? We don't even know what the creature actually looks like," Deo responded.

Mary's screams were continuing without a break. It wouldn't be much longer before her heart succumbed to her fears.

"If only I could change you into the creature itself, then you could trap it in its own snare," Deke said.

"You cannot change me into something that you have no knowledge of, but perhaps we can confuse the creature. Quickly, change me into Torrell."

"But even if that works, you will just take her place."

"Yes, but you can change me again. Deke, it is her only hope."

There was no time to debate. Deke began to concentrate on Torrell. In seconds Deo's transformation was complete. Deo ran down the bank toward the Tetagorous who still appeared as Solharn. He stopped just behind it waiting for Deke to make his way around the creature's rotting house.

Once Deke rounded the first bend leading to the house, Deo began to scream as loud as he could. The Tetagorous spun around looking at Deo in confusion. Deo began to feel wind at his feet. Before he knew it, he could not move. He was trapped inside a pocket of air. The plan had worked. It had confused the creature enough that it had dropped its hold on Mary, perhaps thinking that she had somehow escaped.

When Mary fell to the ground, Deke ran to her aid, pulling her in behind the mass of bones and up over a large bank. Leaving her there, he moved back to help Deo. A strange sensation came over him when he saw the Tetagorous. It was still disguised as Solharn, but a new figure had appeared. It was him. Five miniature worlds revolved around in front of them. Deke was sure they represented the Balance of Five. One by one each world began to turn black until all five were in darkness. Solharn and he looked at the worlds and laughed. Was Deo's worst fear that he would help Solharn in his bid to destroy the Balance of Five? It made no sense. Deke was confused while watching the scene play out. Deo's screams finally brought him back.

He quickly changed his mind set and watched as Deo disappeared from the air trap the Tetagorous had captured him in. The air currents did not dissipate though. Obviously confused, the creature moved closer to get a better look. It would never see the beetle swirling madly around in the wind.

Finally, after a prolonged stare, the Tetagorous growled and turned. Deke watched the air swirling around Deo slowly stop spinning, eventually disappearing altogether.

Deke would be the first person to see this mystical creature in its true form. He shuddered at the sight of it. He wanted to scream. He wanted to turn and run as fast as his legs would carry him. He held his breath fearing that the creature might hear him. His muscles went tense, perhaps as a defensive mechanism brought on by pure fright. The Tetagorous was a gruesome monster. It walked on four legs that covered in a yellowish fur. Its massive head appeared far too heavy for its body to sustain its weight. Its ears were simply large empty holes in the side of its head. Several eyes, too many to count, popped out everywhere, allowing it see in virtually any direction. Their bright blue color stood out against its brown leathery skin. Its mouth appeared almost like an amphibian's, designed to swallow its victim's whole, and then later regurgitate their bones. Its body, however, was by far, the most revolting. Big and bulky, it had transparent skin that allowed Deke to see its intestines and internal organs. He was sure he could see the form of what was some unfortunate creature that had succumbed to the fears brought on by this monster.

Deke stayed as low to the ground as he could. He wished he could dig a hole and hide as he watched the Tetagorous amble back toward its makeshift home. He watched it stop and look around as if unsatisfied with what it had accomplished so far today. Then it slowly transformed into a magnificent bird. A bird, he had heard described before by Torrell, a Cawlaway. As it flew away, Deke's body finally began to relax. As if remembering that he had to breathe, he gasped and rolled over trying to fill his lungs with the air, of which they had been deprived.

Deke waited several minutes before concentrating on Deo. There was no telling where he could have ended up. The wind could have blown him anywhere. When he finally appeared as himself a few feet from where the Tetagorous had imprisoned him, Deke could not help but quietly laugh to himself. It took Deo several attempts to stand before his body reacquainted itself to being grounded.

Deke walked over to help him.

Their plan had worked, but they still needed to be wary of Mary's imposter and the Tetagorous, should it return. Deke quickly described it to Deo, and both agreed that they had to make it out of the swamps in a hurry. They quickly ran toward the small knoll where Deke had left Mary. She wasn't hard to find, and neither was the imposter. She had her arm tightly wrapped around Mary's neck, allowing her just enough air to breathe.

"Who are you?" Deke demanded.

"I am who you fight against, Deke Brolin."

It was no longer the sweet voice of Mary, but rather a low, raspy and sinister voice that sounded slightly familiar to Deke. The imposter's head cocked to one side, its twisted smile and bulging eyes sent a shiver down Deke's spine as it stared at him waiting for a response.

"You are Solharn? Not quite how I pictured you."

"I am a form of Solharn. I come in many forms, and right now I choose to use this body. She is not really worthy of me. She is weak and easy to control. Then again, she played her part," he snickered.

Deke glared at the person he once believed to be his best friend.

"You dare to talk of weakness? Only a coward would choose to take advantage of those who are less powerful than they. You, Solharn, are a coward and that is the weakest form of life. You believe yourself to be the almighty, but you are nothing compared to Queen Elissa. She rules with her heart; her people follow her because they love her. You rule with nothing but scare tactics and promises that you cannot or will not deliver upon. Your people follow you because they are spineless cowards. You're a picture of everything that's wrong, and nothing that is right. Now, let Mary go!"

"Or what?" Solharn said laughing through his clenched teeth. "You will give me another speech on moral principles?" Solharn laughed again before continuing. "Why continue on this petulant quest? You have two choices as I see it. The world you fight for is weak and you, Deke Brolin, are weak, but given a chance to learn the power you hold, you could become strong. I can help you realize your true capabilities. I alone can make you unstoppable and I will if you join me. Or you can take the second choice. Just hand me the amulet, take your friends, and live the less than perfect life you have led up to this point."

"I don't know why I was chosen for this quest. I do know that I have done everything I can to complete it successfully. I may not have a perfect life, but I do have integrity and loyalty which are qualities of strength not of weakness. I will never join with you; nor will I walk away," Deke responded.

"You talk of doing everything you can, of integrity and loyalty. It is those two traits that have made you weak. Those qualities have landed you here. You have blind loyalty and blind faith. That is why you will fail. Think about it boy; you could not even detect that I was not your long lost friend, Mary."

Deke stood in silence thinking about what Solharn had just said. He was right. He never suspected Mary was anyone aside from herself, but then again, why would he?

Solharn continued. "Oh come now, boy. Don't stand there thinking there were no signs, no way that you could have known. You ignored the signs. You chose to ignore them."

"I didn't choose to ignore anything!" Deke yelled back at Solharn in disgust.

"Really? Do you expect your friends, do you expect anyone to believe that you did not suspect Mary was not really who she said? After all, she was your best friend. You, more than anyone should know her."

"I would never...."

"Never have led your friends down the wrong path?" Solharn laughed. "If you believe that, you are not the person you think yourself to be. Let us look at what you chose to ignore, shall we? You could not remember or chose not to remember that it was Mary that caused your stress, which caused you to fall into a deep coma that would have eventually cost you your life. What about when you stopped breathing? Did you not find it strange when you learned it was Solko that alerted Kiran, and not her? Nobody could have predicted that Kiran would give her life for you, but even when she did, you chose not to notice that Mary instantly ran to her aid, and left you alone to suffer. Did it even cross your mind that Mary was doing everything she could to save Kiran so you would die? So you would never get that last breath. Then, once again, you chose to ignore when she purposefully spoke the wrong passage in an attempt to give me more time to enter the Sacred Realm. Perhaps you will stand there, and tell us that you had no idea that Mary was leading you straight into danger, despite warnings from Torrell which you chose not to consider. She even left you Mary's chain as a sign. The chain you gave her. When a Kilto elder appeared before you, warning that someone would betray you, you chose not to heed that warning. If all of this is not enough to convince you then how about you choosing to allow Mary to talk you out of simply flying from the swamps to safety? You may not realize you are working with me Deke Brolin, but you have done nothing but help me. Why change the path you have already chosen? Join me."

"Don't listen to his treacherous lies, Deke. He tries to blame you for something you could not have known," Deo said.

Deke looked dejected. "But should've known."

Deke knew what Solharn was doing, and it was working. His words got to him. He was responsible for not noticing Mary was an imposter, and that did make him weak. Solharn was trying to break him, weaken his mind, to make him more vulnerable and thereby more accessible to him. But it wouldn't work. He'd listened to the

Kilto elder who had told him to believe in himself, to define himself. He wouldn't allow Solharn to define who he was.

"Perhaps I should've been more suspicious of Mary, Solharn, but even if that's true, they were mistakes and nothing more. You're wrong if you think it was anything else. I think that answers your question, doesn't it?"

A sarcastic grin appeared on Solharn. "Let me put it this way then. Hand the amulet to me, or I will snap the neck of your friend whom you so valiantly saved from the Tetagorous."

Solharn knew this was Deke's weakness. He would never let any harm come to Mary. Deke reached for the amulet.

"Deke, don't give the amulet to this...this thing. It won't save Mary's life," Deo begged.

"And if it doesn't, at least I won't have to live with the burden that I could've done something to save her," Deke retorted.

But Deke was not ready to hand the amulet over yet. While talking to Solharn, he had recalled the Kilto elder telling him that he possessed more power than he knew. He remembered the creature he had defeated earlier in the swamps, and what Kiran had done to save his life. It all revolved around the power of the amulet. Every time the amulet had helped him in his cause it had done so at his bidding when he held it. He grasped the amulet and held out his other hand in one motion, pointing it directly at Mary's captor. He thought of the power within the amulet, the power of the light and imagined it flowing through his body and exiting his hand.

Deo watched in amazement as a stream of light shot from Deke's hand and struck the imposter, whose body Solharn had consumed. It caused her to fall backward, leaving Mary to fall to the ground. Deo quickly grabbed her and pulled her away.

"Don't kill her, Deke! She is Delca, my paladin. It is Solharn that controls her. She doesn't know what she's doing!" Mary yelled.

Deo doubted that Deke could hear her. He seemed to be transfixed. He stared blankly ahead as the light continued to flow from his hand into Delca's body. He began to moan as the core of the light he transmitted turned black. Delca gradually started to change from Mary's form, to what Deo knew to be her own. Finally, the light detached itself from Delca and shot back into Deke's hand. Deke fell to his knees. His body felt different. He bent over and began to vomit.

"Are you alright Deke?" Deo asked.

Deke rapidly turned his head toward Deo in anger and looked at him. For a moment Deo thought his eyes looked black. "Of course I am alright!" Deke screamed angrily causing Deo to back away.

"Deke, your eyes," Deo said.

"What's wrong with them?" Deke calmly asked.

Deo looked, but they were normal again. "Ah, nothing, nothing," Deo answered wondering if he'd just seen what he thought he had.

Deke looked over Deo's shoulder in disbelief. "Mary? Is that you, Mary?"

Mary smiled. She was what she had been before she came to this world. She was standing beside a stranger whom Deke had never seen before.

"Deke, I'd like to introduce you to Delca, my paladin."

PART THREE

THE FINAL BATTLE

CHAPTER TWENTY-NINE

The time had come. All light eventually succumbs to darkness. He controlled the darkness and therefore, he could extinguish the light. With no more light there could only be darkness, and with only darkness, he would command the Balance of Five. Without light, there would be no growth. This would allow for a new species, a species that would feed off the dark. A species he would create. With him in command, he could give life or take life away, as he saw fit. He, in essence, would be the almighty, the Creator himself, as he should have been all along.

Through the life energy of the thousands he had slain, Solharn had finally reached the level of power he needed, to bring Rhol to its untimely end, should he have to use it. Solharn had convinced himself that this was his destiny, and it was time to fulfill that destiny. In his mind, the Creator was a fool. He had created the five worlds to evolve together, to balance each other out, thereby creating the Balance of Five. Each planet needed the other to thrive, in order to sustain the balance. When one was destroyed, it would weaken the others making them more susceptible to him. In time, he would easily kill them all. There would be no more balance. The Creator had designed the Balance of Five so that eventually, over time, everyone would live together as equals. Only then would his creation succeed in the way it was meant, and Solharn would not let that happen.

Solharn would create worlds where only the strong survived. A supreme race where there was no room for the feeble minded or the kind of heart. The inhabitants of Solharn's worlds would not make their own decisions in order to survive, in order to evolve. He would make those decisions for them. It was the way it should be. It was he who allowed them to live so he would control how they led their lives. This was what Solharn intended, and it was time to start the chain of events that would lead to his supremacy.

It was true that things hadn't gone quite as he had planned. First, he lost his eyes within the Lealian army when the Nightstalkers had been discovered. He had regained the advantage however when his soldiers captured Jayden. Jayden had been harder to convert than he would've believed. Only after he'd forced Jayden to swallow the dark liquid on two occasions, did he finally become his pawn. That was short lived, however; he was discovered quickly by Palto.

Solharn had been surprised when he looked through Phanthus's eyes and saw Palto outside the secret Realm of Solace. He had reacted too quickly when he sent Phanthus and Jayden to destroy him. It had been his plan to have Jayden lead his armies into oblivion by having Phanthus drop him at the tunnel to Solace. There he would have returned to the Sacred Realm to reunite with Palto. With Jayden in this position, he would have been privy to every move the Lealians, and the Pegapires made. He would have trounced them. It was an unfortunate event that Jayden was discovered before Solharn had the chance to use him to his advantage.

Perhaps his biggest disappointment had led to an unanticipated advantage he could never have expected. He'd discovered Mary and Delca near Mount Sibileo when they attempted to return the amulet to Elissa, and he had defeated them with ease. He had been furious when he found Mary had somehow sent the Amulet of Rhol back to Earth, but it had given him another idea.

He'd forced the girl's paladin Delca, to swallow his essence and thereby controlled everything she did. Because she was a paladin, he could easily manipulate her body into a replica of Mary. When Lorca returned to find her, she had unwittingly returned his pawn to the Realm of Solace. Mary was left deep in the swamps and would soon suffer the fate of a Pintante. This had allowed him the

190

time to gain invaluable information from Kiran. Solharn gained an unexpected further advantage when he learned that Mary was the friend of the boy who would eventually bring the amulet back to Rhol.

Everything was going as planned as his pawn led both the boy and his paladin to their deaths in the Swamps of Tiqor. When the real Mary eventually found them, Solharn had cursed himself for not destroying her when he had the chance, but he had so loved the idea of her suffering the agony of becoming a Pintante.

He had been able to manipulate her through her own paladin and to turn Deke and Deo against her. However, Mary was far more persistent than he'd realized. She was able to regain their trust by using the very beast that was meant to kill them. Solharn was beyond contempt when Deke was able to return Mary and her paladin back to their former selves.

Despite these setbacks, he still had one thing working in his favor. Whenever the boy used the amulet's power, Solharn could feel him. He was not in control of the boy, but rather he was joined to him in some unusual way. At first, Solharn didn't understand the implications of his connection with the boy, but then it came to him. When the boy used the amulet to save Delca, he had absorbed Solharn's essence from her. Solharn was excited at this revelation. If Deke continued to use his powers without fully understanding them, he would become consumed with darkness. Then Solharn and the boy would be one. Solharn would prefer to see the boy destroyed along with the cursed Amulet of Rhol, but if the boy lived then, their union could be a formidable one. Solharn thought it was unlikely that the boy would survive his next plan of attack, but if he did Solharn would savor the power of their union.

Solharn's ruse with Delca had failed to destroy Mary, Deke, and Deo but at least he knew where they were. He'd already summoned Phanthus and an army of Phits to seek them out and destroy them. The remainder of his army would be advancing on Solace.

He could wait no longer. It was time for him to prepare what would be the end of Rhol. It would take days to perfect his plan, and he would have to focus all of his energy. He doubted it would come to this, but if his armies failed, and if the boy succeeded in finding Elissa, then he would have no choice. When Solharn was finished, this world would be forever night, forever black. The sun, the moon, and the stars would forever be gone from sight. The light they shone to sustain life would be unable to penetrate the darkness. Rhol would be barren and cold. Eventually, it would be lifeless. Only then would he let it grow again the way it should be, the way he wanted it to be.

Solharn walked slowly back to the camps. He had left its confines to gather his thoughts in the woods west of where they were positioned. "Get Abednego, now!" Solharn yelled at the first soldier he saw. The soldier had jumped back in fear at the sudden appearance of Solharn, but he quickly gathered himself and ran away as fast as he could in search of Abednego.

Abednego arrived just as Solharn strolled into the camps. "You summoned me Solharn?"

Solharn looked down upon Abednego with contempt. "Yes. The time has come for Rhol to feel our wrath. I have matters to attend to which will inevitably assist your armies in the defeat of anyone who dares to fight against me…us. You will take the armies to Solace, and there you will engage the Lealians and the Pegapires, and you will defeat them, Abednego. I have wasted too much energy already relying on your word only to be disappointed in the results. Do not fail me this time."

"I will not fail you, Solharn. Our army more than triples theirs. They will not stand a chance…Of course, any help you might give us would be greatly appreciated." Abednego groveled looking to the ground.

Solharn would give them the help they needed; whether they died as a result of it did not matter to him. He had wished to destroy this world without having to use his most powerful weapon. It would weaken him, and it would require almost all of his energy, energy he wished to conserve for the other worlds. He had hoped he could take Rhol without it, by using minimal dark magic. The boy had been right, by utilizing the promise of power and riches to those who would be easily swayed, Solharn had hoped victory would be his against those who had fought alongside Elissa for the freedom of Rhol.

But the unexpected arrival of the boy from Earth who possessed the Amulet of Rhol led to unfortunate predicaments for Solharn. The boy's presence filled the surviving warriors of Rhol with renewed hope; it gave them spirit. Moreover, the boy was much more intelligent than Solharn had expected. Already he had learned in some respects how to manage the amulet, and that was dangerous for Solharn.

The boy was too close to finding Elissa. Of course, he had many obstacles still standing in his way, one of which was Phanthus, but he had outmaneuvered the dragon once before. The second obstacle to the boy's success would be the Phits; they were seeking him out at this very moment. Still, this did not completely put Solharn's mind at ease. There was something about this boy that was different. Solharn did not know what it was that separated him from others and for that reason, he could not take any more chances on the boy's resilience. He would not be able to go after the boy himself because it would leave him no time to prepare for what would become of Rhol should his armies fail. But if the worst came to fruition he would have to be prepared.

His other armies had already succeeded in taking over Beltic. It was nearly at its end. Perhaps he would not need all of his energy to defeat the other worlds. In any event that power would come back in time. No, he had made his decision. He would leave now and prepare for the Darkness, something that would destroy every living thing on the planet.

With a grin, he answered Abednego. "Of course you will have my help, Abednego, but from afar. Rhol will be defeated no matter what happens."

"What form of help should we expect Solharn?" Abednego excitedly asked.

"Do not worry. You will see it coming, and when it comes you will know what I speak of, now go! Gather the armies! You must ride and strike out at the very heart of Solace."

Solharn rose up into the sky, spinning as he ascended. Abednego breathed a sigh of relief. No longer would he have to look at Solharn. Solharn had become more monstrous with each passing day. He smelled of death. He exuded death. He was beyond evil, beyond compassion, he no longer lived. As Solharn disappeared from Abednego's sight, Abednego had a sudden realization. Solharn was death, resurrected in the form of a malevolent, dark energy.

CHAPTER THIRTY

Deke ran past Deo and embraced Mary with all the strength he could muster.

"I'm sorry Mary. I should've known when you left the necklace, but I was too determined to save Delca...er..you...or I should say the imposter."

Delca hadn't moved. She stood staring at Mary and Deke. "Mary? Where are we? Deke, you can see me?" Delca stammered.

"It's a long story, Delca. One I'm sure you'll be in no hurry to hear. We are in the Swamps of Tiqor, and yes, Deke can see you, just as he can see Deo," said Mary looking around frantically. "We are still in danger here and are in desperate need of some food and a little rest. We can all talk later, but first, we have to find refuge from the Tetagorous. Please, follow me and be quiet about it."

As the three slowly ambled behind Mary in silence, Deke could barely contain himself. He had so many questions, and he was sure Delca, who seemed to have no memory of what had transpired, would need some answers, but it would have to wait. Mary was insistent that they walk with as little noise as possible. Who was he to argue? After several hours they crossed a small creek which, unlike the water in the swamps, appeared to be crystal clear.

The ground that surrounded the creek was dirt rather than mud, and the trees growing around the area were mature unlike the scrub brush in the swamps. Deke began to hear birds chirping as if they were welcoming spring. Little animals jumped from one tree to another, looking down upon them, wary of those whom they thought were invaders to their small forest.

From a distance, the animals appeared to be squirrels, but on closer inspection, he could see they weren't. Most were black, but the odd one was a bright yellow. Their tails were much like a rats, and they used it to fling themselves from tree to tree by wrapping it around a branch and then flipping themselves, somersaulting through the air, to reach another one. After they felt they were close enough to get a view of the intruders, they would hang upside down cackling away with their fur standing straight out. Deke was sure this was their way of trying to be intimidating, but it only made them look cuter, like cuddly big balls of fur hanging from a tree. That was until a rather large object bounced off his head.

"Hey, you little buggers!" he yelled.

"Quickly! We are upsetting the Chumpralas," Mary said as she waved the others over to a hole leading into the ground.

Mary climbed in first followed by Delca, Deke, and Deo. No more than a few minutes later they found themselves in a surprisingly large, comfortable home outfitted with all the basic amenities one would require to survive. Mary covered the hole leading in, by draping some canvas over it. She then lit a small lantern and placed it on the table.

"The Chumpralas," Mary explained, "are used to me, but they are not particularly fond of anyone else coming into their territory. It took a month before they stopped chirping and throwing nuts at me, but they have served their purpose. You will know in an instant if anyone comes near this place," Mary explained, half smiling.

"Are we out of the swamps then Mary?" Deo asked.

"Not quite, we are on the very outskirts. This has been my home for almost two years now. Ever since Solharn captured and possessed Delca."

"Since Solharn did what?" Delca asked with surprise.

"It's good that you have no memory of it Delca. It was awful. How should I put this? You've been me for the last two years. Do you remember the battle we had to undertake when we reached the bottom of Mount Sibileo?" Mary asked.

"Yes, we came across a Balane, and to equal its strength you changed me into a Kruntulla. I remember being surprised that you would be able to maintain enough energy to keep me in that form, but you did. I remember going head to head with the beast, but it must've gotten the better of me. I recall plummeting to the ground and then...and then, strange, that is all I can remember," Delca responded.

"Yes, I don't doubt it. You see, you were right. I should've have thought that I was ready to transform you into such a powerful beast, and at the same time remain conscious. I collapsed from exhaustion, and that caused you to transform back into your own body. That was why you fell from the air. I tried to run to you, but my legs would not move. I was too weak. Out of nowhere Solharn appeared before me and demanded the amulet. I told him it was gone; little did he know it was hidden less than two feet from where I lay. He was furious. He must've seen me look at you and thought you had it. It was demoralizing when he cackled at me and shook his head before walking over to you. I screamed for you to run, but you were dazed, and my cries fell on deaf ears. Solharn grabbed you by the neck and lifted you high in the air. I was sure he was going to break your neck, but that was not his plan. He forced your mouth open and spewed some sort of black liquid down your throat. After that, I watched as he slowly transformed you into me. I was horrified; you were no longer yourself. He carried you over to where I lay and threw you down, ordering you to remain where you were. Then he snatched me off the ground. His fingers felt like icicles, sending shivers up and down my spine, as he lifted me off the ground and gravitated up into the sky. I was terrified, but more so because I thought he would find the amulet which I had now retrieved again. As he pulled me through the air, to what I thought would be my death, I knew I had to give someone else the chance to find it. Kiran had told me how Solharn had dispelled of the amulet originally, so when I spotted Shimmer Lake, or the Blackpool, as we have come to know it now, I tossed it in. I hoped it would find its way to you Deke, as it should have in the first place.

He brought me here to this swamp, threw me to the ground and laughed. I thought this was it. He would bury me here so nobody would ever find me, and Delca would go undetected while she posed as me, but I was wrong. He told me that ending my life would be too good for me, that Delca was his now and that she had crossed over to the dark side. He grabbed me by the collar of my shirt and lifted me toward his rotting, decomposing face until it was just inches from mine. His breath smelled of death. No, it was worse than death. It smelled like...like he was death. He told me that Delca was lucky and that I would suffer a far worse fate, that I would suffer the fate of a Pintante.

I had no idea what this meant until much later, but I knew it certainly couldn't be good. I stared at him waiting for something to happen, but nothing did. He just stared back at me with his hollow black eyes. After a minute or so I could see his lips curl into a cruel smirk, and then he just disappeared leaving me in the middle of what I would soon learn to be the Swamps of Tiqor."

"And what became of me?" Delca asked.

"That question would be better answered by Deke and Deo, for I didn't see you again until I tracked you three down in these very swamps."

Delca sat staring in disbelief as they told her what she had done while she was in the form of Mary. Deke described what he believed was her sole purpose, to obtain the amulet and to destroy him in the process. Delca was shocked to learn that she had almost succeeded, but she was grateful that Mary had intervened enabling Deke to save her from Solharn's grasp.

Delca was crying as she spoke. "I am so sorry...it feels as if somehow I have betrayed all of you, yet I can't remember anything."

"There's no need for you to be sorry, Delca," Deke explained trying to console her. "It wasn't you. You were under Solharn's control. There was nothing you could have done to prevent it."

"Well, just the same, I feel awful. I feel used. I'm grateful that you were able to bring me back Deke. Thank you."

Deke blushed as Delca hugged him, and then kissed him on the cheek. After clearing his throat, he turned to Mary. "Mary, I've been waiting for ages to ask you. How did you ever come to be here, in Rhol?"

"The same way you did. That morning I waited for you on the bridge; it was a beautiful morning. After a short time, I figured you must be running late. I was excited to get to the fort and thought, what would be the harm? You would be along soon enough. So I headed to the fort, but I never made it. While I was walking through the cornfield, I could see something sparkle as the light of the morning sun glanced off it. I immediately walked over to where it was laying and picked it up. Suddenly, I felt dizzy, and I fell to the ground, slicing my ankle open on a rock. I sat down and shook my head trying to rid myself of the peculiar feeling I had. I took my shoe off to check out the damage I had done to my foot. Then I simply blacked out. I have no idea how long I was out, but when I opened my eyes, I found myself in a cave. I had no idea what had happened, or how I got there. My stomach churned as I walked toward the only light I could see. It led me to a cliff where a young girl stood. She was beautiful with skin like ivory, her eyes a deep blue and she looked to be about the same age as me. The wind was gusting causing her long black hair to whisk across her face, but it couldn't disguise the smile she had. I asked her who she was and where we were. She told me that she would answer all my questions in time, but first, we would have to find shelter, because a storm was coming in fast. She told me that someone was going to come and get us, someone, that I would be shocked to see. She asked me to trust her when that someone arrived and to just follow her lead. She would answer any questions I had later.

I was shocked when I saw what looked like a horse flying at great speed through the air toward us. As it got closer, I saw its fangs or teeth and became slightly more unraveled. But, for whatever reason, I trusted this woman that I had just met, so I did as she asked. She was, of course, Delca, my paladin and she took me to the Sacred Realm of Solace where I met Kiran. Kiran would spend the next several months preparing us for what was to come, well most of it. That reminds me, Deke. How is Kiran? I miss her terribly."

Deke looked over at Deo. He knew this question would come eventually. "I'm sorry Mary, she has passed on."

"What? How?" Mary asked becoming visibly upset.

Deo could see Deke was choked up at the very thought of it, so he answered for him. "It's a long story Mary, but in the end, she died saving Deke's life."

Mary was distraught, but she knew Deke would be far worse. She knew her friend better than anyone except perhaps Deo, and she knew how he would feel if someone had died to save him. She didn't have to hear the intricate details. She knew Kiran. She knew them both.

Pulling herself together, Mary walked over to Deke and hugged him so tightly he could hardly breathe. "I have missed you Deke, don't let Kiran's death burden you. She had her reasons for everything. She loved Rhol more than life itself. If she died for you, it was because she knew you were worthy of it, and you are. I'm just glad we found each other."

Her words reminded Deke of another question. "How did you find us Mary, and why didn't you just say who you were?"

"The last part of that question is easy; I was almost Pintante. You would've thought I was completely out of my mind if I told you who I was. Since Solharn was controlling Delca, who knows how she would have reacted? I told you I was Torrell in hopes that I could convince you to follow me in the direction you should have been heading, to the camps of the Phits. I would've tried to tell you the truth before we got there, but it wasn't possible. I was slowly losing my mind and struggled to stay focused long enough to convince you. Instead, my actions scared you away. Luckily, I knew exactly what Solharn had planned simply by the direction that he had Delca leading you. I thought of another plan of attack, allowing myself to get captured by the Tetagorous. I followed you all day and timed my capture to coincide with your arrival. It was risky, but it was the only chance I had left to try and save you. It was either die at the hands of the Tetagorous or die as a Pintante. Either way, death was coming. My plan was simply to make you aware of Solharn's plan. It turned out much better than I anticipated," Mary explained.

"How I found you is a little more complicated. First of all, these swamps have been my home for over two years now. There's little I don't know of them. I'm sure you're wondering why I would've chosen to stay in these swamps instead of trying to find my way back to Solace. That's where it becomes complicated. After Solharn had abandoned me, I did try to find my way out. For weeks I wandered aimlessly around in circles. To survive, I ate bugs along with things that I don't care to recall or repeat. Creatures, which I'd only heard about through Kiran, continually tried to attack and devour me. I'd finally given up. I sat down not far from where we sit now. As I listened to the Chumpralas berating me while I sat there alone, I finally made up my mind. I would sit here and wait until death found me, but death never came, just quietness. All at once there was no noise. The Chumpralas just disappeared, the birds stopped chirping and then right before my eyes, an elderly man appeared."

"Why do you give up child, when you are so close to finding a home?" he asked me.

"I didn't know what to say, so I said nothing. He didn't seem to mind though. He just came closer, eventually sitting down beside me while continuing to talk."

"A person who takes it upon themselves to do something right, to do good in these times of strife, cannot be measured by their success or failure. They can only be measured by how they will live with that success or failure."

"I told him I didn't understand."

He continued. "If someone succeeds initially, it doesn't mean that eventually, they won't fail, and if someone fails initially, it is not to say that eventually, they won't succeed. You see child, success, and failure are words that mean nothing. Their meanings can be changed in a way that cancels the other one out."

Then he looked at me and put his long bony hand on my shoulder.

"If you do something for a good reason, it is simply that. And if you do something for a wrong reason, it too is simply that. You should not measure yourself by your success or failure, but by whether you did it for good or bad. Those words are much different. Their meanings cannot cancel each other out. The journey you undertook was for a good intention. Nothing can change that. You believe that you have failed. If you have heard me, you know that the meaning of failure is quite inconsequential. Have you ever considered that perhaps, you have just not completed your journey?

After he spoke those words, he simply disappeared. I thought he must have been a hallucination brought on by fatigue and hunger, but his words rang over and over again in my head. I stood up and slowly walked, trying to make sense of it all. I hadn't gone far when I stumbled across this hole in the ground. I could see a light coming from deep within it, and decided to investigate. When I reached the end, I found a home, this home. I assumed it was someone's place, but nobody ever returned, so I made it my own. Then it struck me. The elderly man had spoken quite literally when he, said I was close to home. After that, his words made more sense to me. I was meant to be here, in the swamps. It was the next part of my journey. So for the next two years, I learned everything I could about them."

"I was also visited by an elderly man. He was skinny and had a long white beard. I believe he was a Kilto elder," Deke exclaimed.

201

"Based on what Kiran taught me, I think you are right. He was a Kilto elder," Mary said.

"Did he ever revisit you?" Delca asked.

"Only once, on the day before I found you. I was heading to explore the east side of the swamps when he appeared. He pointed west and said simply, "Just because things are lost, does not mean they cannot be found." I assumed he was referring to the amulet, and immediately made my way west. Eventually, I found you three. I watched you for several hours until I realized what Delca was doing. That's when I made an appearance, hoping that I could change your path. The rest you know."

"I do have to ask you about the poem or rhyme you repeated to us. What did it mean?" Deke asked.

"The poem? I don't remember any poem."

"You were a little crazed at the time, but you refused to stop. The more you said, the angrier Delca, or I should say Solharn, became."

"Strange, I have no memory of this. Do you remember how it went?" Mary asked.

Deke thought about it for a minute and then repeated the strange rhyme back to her.

"How many tears have people shed?
When their souls break
When their thoughts turn dead
I guess it's no one's fault
Evil is strong
No wonder faith goes wrong

Down by the Blackpool
Where evil rules
Don't ever go swimming
By the Blackpool

Every now and then
Your souls become one
You're on top of life
There is no need to run

It can last for years
Or it can turn in a day
But the dark will come
No matter how much you pray

Down by the Blackpool
Where evil rules
Don't ever go swimming
By the Blackpool

It will never happen
Everybody tells themselves
But it will
Faith, no dark, will always rule
With hate and rage, your soul will fill
If only you had listened,
When I told you, you fool
Don't ever go swimming
Down by the Blackpool…"

"I haven't any recollection of it. It seems like a very disturbing passage. Perhaps I was warning you of something, or maybe I was just crazy? I was almost a full Pintante at the time. We should try to decipher it though. It could be helpful. It certainly can't hurt."

"I guess I have only one more question, Mary. You know the swamps inside and out. Why did you want us to head into Phits territory when you could have directed us here to safety?" Deke asked.

"I have been waiting for that question, Deke. It was for one reason and one reason only: to help you on your quest."

"How so?" Deke asked.

Mary turned her head and looked at them. "That's where Solharn keeps Queen Elissa. He has her wrapped in a cloak of darkness and heavily guarded by the Phits."

CHAPTER THIRTY-ONE

It would be a day of reckoning, Palto thought while standing on the edge of the cliffs looking down upon Solace. It was to him, the most beautiful place on Rhol. The rivers that wound through the many mountains surrounding Solace were a spectacular sight. Gravity pulled them steadily downward, eventually coming to an end where they leapt from the ridges of rock and fell through the air to form much larger river. This river was called Jiulta, meaning "Life."

Ancient Rholians so named it because of all the little rivers that came together to create it. The large river twisted through the mountain he was now standing upon, and eventually cascaded over the edge, creating the largest most spectacular waterfall he had ever witnessed. The water fell thousands of feet eventually flowing into Solemn Lake, the largest lake on Rhol. The river was the lake's life force, and was thereby named "The River of Jiulta."

Looking in the other direction was Solace, fields of beauty, surrounded by gigantic rock formations that seemed to move if you stared at them too long. Huge trees dotted the landscape for miles upon miles, providing shelter and food to the animals and birds that burrowed into their comforting branches, and ate their bountiful nuts and seeds.

He wondered whether this serene beauty would survive the battle that would soon take place upon its hallowed ground. The Pegapires had long since delivered the Lealian ground fighters along with the Rholians from the Realm of Solace, to the fields below. They were severely outnumbered. They lined up across the fields in rows of two ready to fight for their world, the world that had been snatched from under them, one which they would try to win back. Behind these rows, several Lealian archers readied themselves to hold off Solharn's armies as long as they could.

Palto stared proudly down at them from above, flanked by his army of Pegapires, who were each accompanied by a Lealian warrior. Orulla stood to his left as Oisin slung provisions over her. Kaelyn, on his right, prepared Issa for the battle. Preta had volunteered to stay with Jayden as he was still unable to move or speak. Solko walked toward his sister with Duffy by his side. He had insisted that Duffy ride on his back in the coming fight. It was unheard of among Pegapires to have anyone but a Lealian ride them into battle, but Solko felt indebted to Duffy for saving his sister. Besides, Solko was impressed by Duffy's ferocious fighting abilities.

Palto had agreed to this, but only under the condition that before either entered the battle, they would scour Rhol for any inhabitants that were willing to fight for their freedom. He instructed Duffy to find all of the Brawltug he could and to tell them that Solharn had returned. Duffy was to tell them of the impending battle in Solace, and that the Pegapires and the Lealians would be privileged and honored to fight alongside them. They mildly protested, but it was not hard for Palto to convince them that what they were doing would be essential to the success of the battle. It was why Solko was saying his farewells to Preta.

"Once you go through the Wall of Solace Preta, you will be healed, but you must return here and stay with Jayden. It will be hard not to engage in the battle, but you will have to resist for his sake. If the armies are not held back, take Jayden back to Tamon. I will look for you there."

"Is Palto sure that Jayden cannot be healed by the Wall of Solace?"

"He is wise, but does not know enough about the hold Solharn has on Jayden. Nor does he know if the wall will reverse his hypnotic state, as nobody has ever breached the wall under a Pegapire's trance. He cannot take the chance. If it cures him of only his trance, then he will be a dangerous opponent. Do not forget the news Oisin brought to us that there is a traitor amongst us. That traitor was from Solace. It is possible that they are also under Solharn's spell, and if they passed through the Wall, its magic did not work on them."

"I understand, brother. I only wish I could be of more use."

"Do not belittle the importance of your assignment, sister. Protecting Jayden will not be easy, and it is essential that he survive.

205

He is the last in the line of the Lealian Ancients. They...we need him."

Preta nodded. "Travel safely brother, and Duffy, keep safe. I have yet to repay you for saving my life. I would like very much the opportunity to do so in the future."

Duffy blushed slightly. "You are too kind Preta, but you would have done the same for me. There is nothing to repay. The honor of fighting alongside you is quite enough."

"Take care, sister," Solko yelled as he took flight.

Still miles away, but approaching fast, Palto could see dark clouds forming in the sky, and great clouds of dust rising from the ground. The clouds would soon turn into battalions of Phits flying in the air, and the dust into the Kaltaures army. There was not much time, but they were as ready as they could be.

Solharn's armies were bigger than he had expected. They were outnumbered tenfold, if not more. He had already prepared for this by assigning ten Pegapires, along with their Lealian counterparts, to retrieve wounded warriors and bring them back and forth from the Wall of Solace. That was the only way they would keep their numbers up. It was a great advantage to them. Perhaps Queen Elissa had somehow known that the final battle would take place near Solace and had created the Wall of Solace to even out the playing field. Perhaps, that was why this was the only field that remained intact. This was the field she had created to renew life, not just to protect it, as in the cases of Leal and Tamon. Whatever the reason, he knew it would be imperative that they not lose it to Solharn's armies. If they lost their access to the Wall of Solace, it would prevent them from using its healing powers. Gradually, their armies would be depleted until eventually the battle would be lost.

Palto beckoned Oisin, Kaelyn, Issa and Orulla over as he stepped away from the line.

"It will be a matter of hours before we have to engage Solharn's army. Oisin, I want you and Orulla to lead the ground troops. Kaelyn is more used to fighting on the back of a Pegapire and you, Oisin, are an experienced warrior on the ground. Orulla, you can engage the enemy in the air, but do not stray too far from Oisin. He will need your eyes to tell him what to expect as the armies approach."

"I will go now and make sure they are organized, Palto," Oisin said while mounting Orulla.

"Kaelyn and Issa, you will be in charge of the right flank, and I will lead the left. We cannot lose the tunnel that leads to the Realm of Solace under any circumstances. I fear our fight will be over if we do. Make sure you take precautions to ensure it never happens."

"Understood Palto," both of them said in unison.

"You two were evidently meant to ride together," Palto laughed as he turned and walked toward his troops to instruct them on the impending battle.

"He does not seem himself, Issa."

"A lot rides on his shoulders, Kaelyn. He has seen many wars and has lost none, aside from when Elissa ordered their retreat. He knows if this battle is lost, then so too will Rhol. On top of this, I am sure that Jayden's fate weighs heavily upon him. He is burdened with the fact that it was he who immobilized Jayden."

"But he had no choice," Kaelyn insisted.

"No, but I know Palto, and in his mind he regrets giving Jayden the day he requested that he stay in the Realm. He blames himself for not acting right away, and being unable to save Jayden from Solharn. I am sure that after hearing the story from Oisin of what transpired, he believes that it is his fault Jayden was captured. He knows Jayden far too well, and in his mind Jayden would never have taken the chance of crossing that field in daylight, unless it was, in at least some regard, to get back to Solace to save him."

"That is absurd. There were many reasons he made that choice."

"Perhaps, but you will never convince Palto of that."

Kaelyn and Issa walked over to their half of the army, and explained to them what their strategy was for the battle to come. There was a disturbing silence in the air as they talked. The only other sound they heard came from Palto, who was ensuring his fighters were aware of what was to come, how proud they would be when the battle was theirs. How they were all heroes. How strong they were. How their heart would guide them to rise above and defeat Solharn's armies. Palto was a true leader, unlike no other. He was a leader whom even other leaders followed. After hearing his speech, Palto's troops were confident. They all believed that this battle was theirs to win, even though Kaelyn was sure Palto knew how slight the chance of victory was. And so Kaelyn followed suit and gave a similar speech to her warriors until they too held their heads high. In their minds, nothing could defeat them.

After everyone had finished the last meal that they would have for a very long time, they lined up along the edge of the cliff looking down upon Solace. Six hundred strong paired up Lealians upon Pegapires, a formidable alliance. The weight of each Lealian must have been tremendous on the back of each Pegapire. Each Lealian was adorned in brilliant armor, and each carried long gleaming swords. Orler arrows and bows were strapped within their reach, on the side of every Pegapire. They stood strong, steady as if frozen in time awaiting Palto to give the final order to attack.

Palto looked down to the ground. He could see Oisin and Orulla were also ready and waiting. They had done well to organize the troops in a short span of time. Oisin had used an older strategy that only Roland or Jayden, on his behest, must have shown him. It was a good strategy to use, given that their numbers were so small. Instead of the warriors lining up in one straight line they lined up in a V pattern. The archers remained well behind them. Their position wouldn't change; they remained in a line.

The advantage to the V pattern was that when the enemy army observed them from a distance, it would appear as if their army was much larger than it actually was. It was a strategic illusion, which if it worked, would change how their enemy would fight. Not only would it work for reasons of intimidation and fear, but it would draw a larger portion of the army toward them leaving the lesser portion far more vulnerable. Palto was impressed. Oisin and Orulla were drawing attention to themselves so that Palto could drastically diminish the portion of Solharn's army that was left behind as reinforcements.

When Solharn's army approached, Oisin would order the V formation to slowly fall back into a straight line. This would appear to the enemy that they were retreating, giving them a false sense of confidence. It would also allow time for Palto and his armies to return and attack from behind. It was a strategy that came with a lot of risk, particularly with timing. Once Oisin's troops had formed the line it would mark the signal for the archers to release their arrows at the enemy. Once the first set of arrows flew through the air, Oisin's army would advance on them hoping that Palto had already defeated the reinforcements and swung in behind the attacking army. This would essentially trap the enemy. It required a great deal of trust to believe in this strategy. A trust that Palto was glad Oisin had in him.

Palto beamed confidence, at least to his troops. He had to; if he did not show them that he had confidence, then they would not hold onto theirs. Solharn's army was now in sight, although still a few miles away. You could hear the distant sounds of drums, or perhaps it was the sound of the Kruntullas feet as they slammed into the ground with each step they took. Another mile and it would be time. He could not believe the endless streams of soldiers walking in groups of one hundred, nor the number of Phits that flew directly over the Kaltaures soldiers.

But that wasn't what suddenly caused Palto to lose his poise. He had not expected to see what abruptly approached him from the rear. It was not something he was unfamiliar with. In fact, it was something he had seen quite recently. He should have been prepared, but he wasn't, and as Phanthus descended down upon them, he suddenly lost his confidence.

CHAPTER THIRTY-TWO

Silence surrounded the humble home buried deep within the soil of Rhol. Everyone's eyes were glued to Mary with this sudden revelation.

Before anyone could ask any more questions she continued.

"You see, the Kilto elder was right. I hadn't failed my quest. It just wasn't completed. My quest was to find the Queen, and then lead you to her. It wasn't easy. It took me a full year to finally realize what I suspected; there were far too many Phits skulking around the swamp. It didn't make any sense to me that Solharn wouldn't use them for some other purpose. They wouldn't be of any help to his cause just idling away in the swamp, besides, what better place would there be to stash her away? The Tiqor Swamps are full of vile creatures, and they have no redeeming qualities. Nobody ever enters them.

I set my sights on their camps, their home territory. It had to be where Elissa was imprisoned. It took several months of hiding away, watching the Phit patterns, their security patrols and where they gathered in larger concentrations. Each time I returned to their territories, I moved in closer and closer. I always followed the same route until I felt uncomfortable. Then I would change it slightly. Within half a year I could move with ease, in and out of their camps with confidence. As a precaution, I had escape routes planned should I be detected, but I never needed them. I had adapted well to the swamps and after learning the topography, I simply blended in.

I was focused on one particular section. It was almost impossible to get there due to the sheer number of Phits that congregated there morning, noon and night. It was about a week before I found you that I was able to use the cover of the night to slip my way in. The fact that there were hundreds of Phits within this area actually helped me, as the buzzing of their wings provided the perfect mask for any noise I might have made.

I neared a heavily guarded cavern. Two torches blazed away on either side of the opening providing all the light I needed to see. Seven Phits milled about making sure nobody came close. Several others flew in circles above the cavern, but never far enough to lose sight of the entrance. I realized there was no way I could make it without being detected. I would have to come up with another plan to deal with the Phits that guarded the makeshift jail, one that could be executed quietly. So, I returned here. I made poison darts from the Derinto plant that grows in abundance in these swamps. A mere drop from the nectar of these plants is enough to paralyze a full grown man for a week. I crafted a blow gun from some hollowed wood. I was intending to return to the cavern on the very day the Kilto elder appeared and told me to go west. I heeded his words. I knew I was running out of time, but I thought there must've been a good reason for his advice. Perhaps he knew I wouldn't have been able to save the Queen on my own, or that my mind would soon be too crazed to help the Queen, even if I had found her. Whatever the reason, he once again steered me down the right path."

"So, you never actually saw the Queen there?" Deke asked.

"I didn't have to. I know that's where she's being held. It all makes sense."

"It's certainly a possibility," Deo said.

"I know she's there. I can't explain it, but on top of everything I've just told you, I just feel it. You don't have to be as convinced as I am, but where else do we start? We can't just ignore it."

"Mary is right," Delca added. "We owe her our trust considering what she has just gone through to bring us all together."

"Okay," Deke answered. "What is the plan?"

"My plan is the same, only now I have all of you to help me. We must immobilize the Phits guarding the cavern, and rescue the Queen. I have enough wood left to make a blow gun for each of us."

They wasted no time and immediately fetched the hollow sticks that Mary had piled in the corner. Deke and Deo began to cut the pieces to length, while Delca carefully dipped shards of wood into the poison that Mary had placed into a clay bowl.

Mary left the house to gather some food. She had agreed to prepare a dinner for them while they worked. She went by herself on purpose. She didn't think any of them would want to see what they would be dining on. Torslendas were one of the few things within the swamps that one could eat without becoming violently ill. They tasted fine when boiled for a few hours. However, the outward appearance of a Torslenda would cause most people's stomach to turn, particularly if they imagined having to eat it. They looked much like the slugs one would find on Earth except, on Rhol they each weighed about twenty pounds.

Mary walked slowly through the woods in search of Korten trees; that was where she would find the Torslendas. They fed on its sap. It was also why the Korten tree wood burned blue. The Torslendas left buckets of blue mucus behind. They were covered in it which was part of the reason they looked so hideous. The wood of a Korten Tree was a soft wood with thin bark. The wood absorbed the mucus deep into its pores. When the wood was subjected to extreme heat, the mucus turned into a fuel that burned blue.

As she walked she could see the Chumpralas following her from tree to tree. They were in a playful mood, occasionally throwing large nuts at her feet, hoping that she would react, but she wasn't in the mood. There was too much on her mind. Disappointed, the Chumpralas gave up. They were curious animals though and continued to follow her, wondering what she was doing.

She hadn't walked far when she spotted a Torslenda half way up the trunk of a large Korten tree. She carefully aimed the homemade spear she had brought along with her, and thrust it toward the unsuspecting creature. It fell and hit the ground with a thud.

All at once the Chumpralas started cackling. Mary immediately ran for cover. The Chumpralas had seen her hunt Torslenda on countless occasions. There was no reason for them to start chirping unless something else had entered what they deemed to be their territory.

Her instincts proved to be right. Something was casting a large shadow across the ground toward her from well above the trees. She didn't move a muscle; only her eyes glanced upward in an attempt to see what was angering the Chumpralas. The creature finally came into view. She had heard many stories and seen many pictures of it, but this was the first time Mary had ever seen the creature in the flesh. Its enormous size made it seem so close. Her body was frozen. She held her breath not wanting to make the slightest of sounds. Several seconds passed before its massive body finally disappeared. Mary breathed in and slowly rose to her feet. Her body still shook from what she had just witnessed. She would have to warn the others. Grabbing the Torslenda, she ran as fast as she could toward her underground shelter. She reached the entrance without incident and slid the remainder of the way through the hole, bowling over Deke as she emerged at the other end.

"Are you alright, Mary?"

Mary ran to the small stove. "I'm fine," she said as she poured water onto the fire she had lit before leaving that morning.

"What's wrong? Mary, you are as white as a ghost," Delca added.

Mary threw supplies into a bag as she spoke. "Our plans have changed. I think we're going to need some help."

"Ok, Mary. Calm down. We'll figure something out," Deke said.

"We will have to because Phanthus is now scouring the swamps. I can only assume that he's looking for us, which means the Phits are sure to be on high alert," Mary casually said.

The room went silent for a brief moment as everyone took this information in. "I'd heard of the dragon but never actually laid eyes on him. He is a massive beast," Mary continued.

"Did he see you?" Deo asked.

"No. He flew right over me. The Chumpralas began to cackle allowing me the time I needed to hide, but he flew directly over this place. I'm sure he would've seen the smoke from the stove. Even though the smokestack comes out of the ground a few hundred yards from here, it will only be a matter of time before he figures out that the stack leads back to here. We have to leave now and fast."

The other three moved all at once, grabbing whatever they could. Within minutes, Mary was beckoning them over to the hole.

"Follow me and stay close. I can still hear the Chumpralas which means danger is still near."

Mary began climbing up through the hole followed by Deke. Delca and Deo followed behind him. When Deke's head poked up through the ground he could see Mary standing just in front of him. Her eyes were transfixed directly to the front of her. He could see her legs slightly shaking as she stood there staring straight ahead. He didn't have any trouble seeing what made her so petrified. Phanthus was hard to miss.

Before climbing out to join her, he waited until he could feel the top of Deo's head with his foot and then kicked him, sending both he and Delca tumbling back down the hole.

With that part of his makeshift plan completed, he climbed out and stood beside Mary, holding her hand.

"And so we meet again, young human," Solharn's voice boomed from the mouth of Phanthus.

"I'm looking at Phanthus, yet you sound much more like Solharn?" Deke questioned.

"Then once again you can see the power I hold. Phanthus was, how should I say...hmm, too outspoken? Yes, those were the words I was looking for. So, much like your friend, I decided to, well ...embody him," Solharn began to laugh loudly at his play on words.

"Did you really think I could not smell you, girl? I simply needed you to lead me back to where this boy was. Now, where are your two soul mates?" Solharn laughed again.

"Laugh all you want, Solharn. You may have found us, but you haven't defeated us," Deke shot back. "Our soul mates, as you put it, are not here."

"It matters not. All I really need is to destroy you, boy. With you gone, my plan will fall back into place. I will not have to waste all the energy I have gained to finally destroy this world. I must say, you had me wondering, but in the end you never stood a chance against my power."

Deke still grasped Mary's hand tightly. His other hand slowly inched toward the amulet.

"Please boy, do not insult me. I have seen you use what little power you have before. You will die before that prized amulet of yours can do you any good. It is over, boy. Your quest to save Elissa has failed."

"Perhaps," Deke said grabbing the amulet.

Smoke began to bellow from Phanthus's mouth as Solharn prepared to reduce both Deke and Mary to ashes. But as he slowly moved his head toward the pair he received an unexpected blow from behind.

Solharn turned in surprise and jumped back. He was looking into the eyes of a dragon and behind that dragon stood a Kruntulla. It took Solharn a few seconds to comprehend what was happening but all at once it came to him. The boy had managed to transform his paladin into a mirror image of Phanthus, and somehow was providing the girl with enough energy to transform her paladin into a Kruntulla.

"You are not strong enough to command your paladin as a beast this size, human," Solharn screamed as he flew along the ground crashing into Deo. The two dragons rolled through the forest taking out several hundred trees.

Solharn ended up on top of Deo, but was quickly flung to the side by the Kruntulla that had come to Deo's aid.

"Delca, how did you transform?" Deo asked.

"Deke must've figured it out. By physically touching Mary, he enables her to feed off the power of the amul…" She had no time to finish her sentence as Solharn grabbed her with his massive claws and hurtled her several feet through the air.

Deo immediately took flight all the while breathing a ball of fire toward Solharn. It was a direct strike, but it was ineffective against the other dragon. The flames simply bounced off his scales causing everything around him to combust.

Solharn flew toward him in a rage. Their wings entwined as their claws ripped and tore at each other's bellies. Their fierce jaws snapped to and fro, but both were too fast to cause any real damage.

Deke and Mary had made it back to her underground house. They were safe from the carnage around them, but Deke was already feeling weak and he knew Mary could not be much better. Her breathing was already raspy. He would have to let go of her hand. It would be over for Deo if he did. He could not take Solharn by himself.

Delca looked up from the ground. Using all of the strength she could muster, she uprooted a burning tree in an effort to throw it at Solharn, but she was unable to determine which dragon was which. She stared at them rolling and fighting in the sky trying to get some sense as to which one was Deo. She knew time was of the essence. In a matter of moments both she and Deo would become their regular selves.

All at once she saw it, the weaker of the two. One of the dragons was drastically losing its strength. Its wings had failed it twice. It had to be Deo. Deke must be losing his strength. She would have to take the chance. She sent the tree hurtling through the air. Solharn didn't know what hit him and plummeted to the ground. The mighty dragon possessed by Solharn was defeated.

Deo immediately landed. By now Deke had long since relinquished Mary's hand and climbed up through the hole. Delca ran to his side. "Is Mary alright Deke?"

"Yes, she is resting."

Delca ran to look after Mary as Deke looked over toward the dragon. Deo, now himself again, was standing over the dragon's head with a sword pointed directly at its eye. This was the only part of the dragon that was not protected by armored scales. Solharn was taunting him.

"You have only delayed the inevitable. Deke will die. So will you along with everything else in this world. It is the way it is. There is nothing you can do," he laughed.

"I know one thing, Solharn. This dreaded beast won't be helping you any longer," Deo yelled as he raised the sword high above his head.

"Deo stop!" Deke yelled.

Deo paused, looking over at Deke. "It's not Phanthus, Deo. It's Solharn who possesses him!"

"What does it matter Deke? Don't you remember? Phanthus has been trying to kill us since we arrived in Rhol?"

"I remember, Deo. But this is the last living dragon on Rhol. We won't be responsible for their extinction."

"Deke, this dragon, by all accounts, assisted Solharn in capturing Queen Elissa! He is far too powerful a foe to just leave out here!"

"Perhaps, but when the Kilto elder visited me, he said something that I could not quite figure out until now. He said, 'Your journey is to prevent the extinction of a world, but do not forget that the extinction of any single living thing can bring an end to what we fight for. To renew a life that can be saved is a step forward in completing the quest you were sent on.'

"Deke, I don't think he was referring to Phanthus. He is as much an enemy to us as Solharn is!" Deo shot back.

"I can't think of any other creature in that predicament, Deo. I believe he was speaking of this moment and he's yet to be wrong on any advice he has given." Deke reached for his amulet and motioned his hand toward Phanthus.

"Deke, stop! There is something I didn't tell you. When you tried this with Delc..."

But it was too late. A thick blue stream of light flew from Deke's hand and attached itself to Phanthus. Almost immediately the core of the blue light turned black, slowly draining the essence of Solharn from the great dragon. It took much longer than it had with Delca. Phanthus was enormous in comparison. Deo had seen how it had affected Deke the first time with a much smaller subject. He was unsure if Deke would be able to withstand the power of Solharn this time, but he could do nothing about it, aside from watch and pray.

Ω

Deke's mind was wandering off to a dark, lonely place. His body was slowly being filled with blackness. He no longer had any comprehension of where he was or, for that matter, who he was.

A low raspy voice boomed out from within his head. "Join me, Deke Brolin. It is your legacy. You are me, and I am you. Together we can rule the worlds as one...join me."

Deke was not afraid of the voice. In fact, the clearer the voice became, the better he felt. He could now see a dark form standing alongside a large lake. He could not recognize what it was. It was simply the silhouette of a shadowy figure. As its hands moved up and down, so too did the waves of water within the lake, sometimes reaching hundreds of feet high.

"Come, Deke. Together we can create our dynasty. A dynasty that will last forever, one that you and I control, a new existence, a new way, a better way."

Deke moved closer to the strange form. He could see it quite clearly now, but it still had not turned to face him. He felt more at ease than he could ever remember being. A feeling of power coursed through his veins. Deke slowly stretched out his hand. The figure turned in response and reached out to him. Solharn grinned as his long bony fingers slowly extended toward Dekes. At last the boy had realized his true destiny.

Ω

Deo tried everything he could to snap Deke out of it, to no avail. Deke's eyes were completely black, and he continually moaned a strange language that seemed to be based somewhat on ancient Lealian. Deo could only make out some of the words that flowed from his mouth in a monotone.

He talked about souls becoming one, of a black pool of darkness and power, the power of evil. Many of the words rang back to him, words vaguely familiar to him. All at once it came to him ....the rhyme that Mary in her crazed state had repeated to them. The poem was about Deke...And Solharn...The power of evil...Souls becoming one, intertwined together, through the power of darkness. The poem was about what could happen should Solharn persuade Deke to join him.

In desperation, Deo ran at Deke tackling him to the ground. The stream of light connecting him and Phanthus broke at last. The dragon rose to his feet and stared down at Deo who was now lying across Deke. Deo covered as much of Deke's body as he could and turned his face toward the ground in anticipation of the flames that would soon envelop them.

Ω

Deke tried to run toward Solharn, but the faster his feet moved, the farther away he got. Every second that passed created a greater distance between them until eventually, Solharn was a mere speck in the distance. All at once Deke found himself face down in the dirt. He screamed with rage and flung Deo through the air as he sat up, crazed with anger.

Ever so slowly, things began to focus again. The memory of where he had just been disappeared as the memory of where and

218

who he was returned. He had still not noticed the dragon. He was too concerned about Deo who was lying motionless on the ground a few feet from where he was sitting. Deke crawled quickly over to his friend.

"Deo! Deo are you alright?"

Deo's eyes fluttered slightly. "Deke, behind you…!"

Deke turned quickly to see Phanthus staring down intently at them. Several moments passed until the dragon finally broke the silence. It was not the voice of Solharn that they heard, but that of Phanthus.

"The last thing I remember is Solharn betraying my confidence, and now I stand here before you human, the one thing that Solharn fears the most. I do not remember how I came to be here. Perhaps you could enlighten me," he snarled.

Deke mustered up all the courage he could as he spoke to the mighty dragon. "Solharn took over your body, just as he had done to my friend, Delca. I don't know how, nor do I know when. Solharn spoke to me through you and then tried to destroy me. Delca and Deo fought you to protect me and my friend Mary. You lost the fight and fell from the sky. I had learned, quite by accident that I had the power to reverse Solharn's possession of people, and I decided to free you from his hold. That is all I know," Deke explained.

"And why would you bother to save me, human? It is me who has been trying to kill you since you arrived here."

Deke answered the dragon in a loud, steady voice. "For a couple of reasons, firstly, I have heard many stories about the dragons of Rhol. I know you are the last one that lives. Dragons must have been put on Rhol for a reason. To kill you, the last of your kind would be a travesty. And that leads me to the second reason. I believe you have something to give this world, to help it survive."

"And what might that be?" Phanthus asked.

"I don't know, Phanthus. What do you want out of this world, your world?"

"Redemption!" the dragon bellowed.

"Then maybe that is your answer. Perhaps you haven't found it because you've been searching for it from the wrong side. Fight with us Phanthus, with the people of Rhol, and you will find your redemption."

Phanthus did not say anything for several moments. "I have never had any reason to trust anyone in Rhol, but you put your beliefs before all else. You believe in preserving life, not destroying it. You trusted that I would understand what you were doing and in turn, help you in your quest to save Rhol."

Phanthus stopped speaking for a moment and looked around as if considering what he had just said. "And you were right to trust in me, so for now, I will trust in you. Now, apparently, I have missed out on quite a bit. Please tell me what my mind has chosen to forget over these past few days, and let us determine what our next move will be."

Deo could not believe his ears. Deke had been right, and now they would have one of the most powerful assets in Rhol fighting with them. Their odds of succeeding had drastically improved. Any fear that Deo once had was gone, aside from the screams that came from behind him causing him to jump momentarily. He didn't need to investigate. Delca and Mary had quite obviously made an appearance.

Deke and Deo immediately calmed their friends' nerves explaining what had just occurred. When they had calmed down Phanthus began to tell them how he had come to fight for Solharn. He told them of the wars that followed their pact. Deke could see the sadness in the mighty dragon's eyes as he recounted the story of Elissa's capture. Phanthus told them that he had felt a strange connection to the Queen. He believed that Solharn had sensed that connection as well and that was why he insisted that Phanthus stayed behind when he flew off to imprison Elissa. It was because of that regard that Phanthus would eventually become enraged with Solharn's ways.

Once Phanthus was finished speaking, Deke explained what they had been through. He finished with Mary's explanation of why she believed Elissa was being held by the Phits. Phanthus concurred with Mary's logic.

"Then, that is where we must go…," Deke began to say.

"Ugh, those Chumpralas, I thought they had become accustomed to you after they calmed down, but there they go chirping again," Mary said to Phanthus in frustration.

It wasn't Phanthus however that had the Chumpralas so upset. It was the thousands of Phits that swarmed down upon them.

They were everywhere and were attacking Phanthus in particular. They tried their best to gouge at his eyes. He let out a stream of fire disintegrating several of them, but they came far too quickly, one after another. Phanthus was unable to gather enough breath to cast more flames in their direction. He attacked many Phits with his powerful jaws, but it did little to prevent them from continuing their offensive. He would soon be overtaken.

"Phanthus, go! Leave us and find Palto! We will need his help!" Deke yelled.

Phanthus looked down upon them. His tail was waving frantically in the air at the Phits. "I cannot leave you here. You will die at the hands of this filth. You do not have the energy to transform again."

"Don't worry, Phanthus. Mary knows these swamps. She'll be able to find us refuge. Go! Before it's too late! Solace is where the battle will be. It won't be easy to convince Palto of your change of allegiance, but you must!" Deke yelled.

With a heavy heart, Phanthus flew up into the sky. He owed the boy his life, yet he was leaving him here in the midst of the swamps. It wasn't much of a thank you. If the Phits found them, they would stand no chance in their weakened states, but he also knew the boy was right. They'd need help if they were to save Elissa, and he was the only one that was in a position to get it.

Once Phanthus found himself in the open air he had no trouble escaping the Phits. He could fly much faster than them, and in time they were left behind as the wind carried him to Solace. The boy had made a valid point. Palto would be next to impossible to convince. They'd been enemies for many years, and there was no love lost between them. All he could do was to try. If he failed, he would return to fight and most likely die, alongside the boy.

CHAPTER THIRTY-THREE

Solharn stood looking out over the Blackpool. He was still reeling from losing the connection with the boy. A few more seconds and they would have been joined. His power along with the boy's control over the Amulet of Rhol would have made things much simpler. They...he would have been unstoppable. The boy was still not out of his reach. Solharn was confident that he was getting to the boy. He was slowly making him realize what his true purpose was, but he did not have the luxury of time.

The boy was a far more vehement opponent than he had realized. Avoiding his armies and the many traps he had set for him was one thing, but what bothered Solharn the most was how quickly the boy had mastered the amulet. Solharn never expected that the boy would figure out that he could use both his and the girl's paladin together by letting her feed off the amulet too. The sheer arrogance of the boy enraged him. Even while engaged in a conversation, he was able to change their paladins into small enough creatures that they were able to slip behind him unnoticed. The fact that he then changed them into two of the largest creatures in Rhol was also quite astonishing, but to hold their form for that long was extraordinary.

No, he could wait no longer. The boy was more powerful than he would like to admit. If the boy were able to save Elissa, it would not bode well for Solharn, but he had not used his greatest power yet. It was a far greater power than Elissa could ever command. Elissa would never be as strong as him, mainly because she felt such a need to protect the ungrateful degenerates that inhabited the five worlds.

He had to agree that those degenerates had their uses. Without them, he would never have gained the energy he needed to exact his revenge. He laughed remembering how they begged for their lives. They did not even understand that it was not their lives he was after, nor their broken bodies. They were so beneath him. They didn't even comprehend the energy of their outer souls; they didn't even know they had one. It was their external souls who gave him the energy he needed, not their flesh and blood. So he took their souls from them and left them to wander aimlessly as their bodies stopped growing and slowly decayed. Eventually, they became Pintante. They had begged for their pathetic lives, and he had given them that, temporarily. Without their outer soul, they became devoid of energy, devoid of their aura. Elissa could never do such a thing, nor would any other in the Order. That was why he was superior.

The souls he devoured on Rhol had given him the energy he needed to bring the people of Beltic to their knees. He had quickly regained his power by feeding on the souls of the weak, hapless people of Beltic in the aftermath of that war. When he returned to Rhol, he continued with his wicked ways, soon gathering more power than he had ever experienced before.

Elissa's power was all but gone. The power she used to protect the inhabitants of Rhol over the last ten years had dissipated, thanks to the boy's appearance. Because of this, Solharn believed he could conserve the power he had gained to conquer the remaining worlds. The destruction of Rhol should have only required a little cleanup. It was unfortunate that he had underestimated them, especially the boy. No, it had not been his plan to have to use so much of his power to destroy Rhol, but he would regain it all. He had already conquered Beltic, but there were still three worlds remaining with thousands upon thousands of souls waiting for him to feed on.

Rhol would soon be his. He could feel the currents of power begin to course through his body as he began to conjure up the life energy of the souls he had appropriated. With his arms outstretched, his soulless figure began to slowly rise from the ground until stopping high above the Blackpool. Slowly he began to turn in circles. The Blackpool began to bubble and froth as hundreds of small funnels of the dark liquid began to rise.

In minutes they were the size of twisters swirling around him, waiting to be released onto Rhol. It was not time though. Lightning struck out against the dark skies, torrents of rain poured down feeding the Blackpool. No, the twisters would not be released until they had formed significant tornados, swirling masses of wind and energy that would leave a path of destruction in their wake, taking everything with them into the dark depths of the Black Abyss.

They would all feel what Solharn had when he was banished into its depths, the feeling of nothingness, of helplessness all while surrounded in an eternity of darkness. They would not escape it as he did. They would be under his command; slaves forced to do his bidding whenever he chose to call upon the energy of the souls. It would be a fitting end to Rhol, one that all of the Balance of Five would eventually face.

Solharn's eyes burned like fire as the wind and rain whirled around him. Soon the transfer of energy would be complete. One by one the tornados would leave the Blackpool and surge out over Rhol consuming everything in their path as if they had a never-ending appetite for destruction. They would feed off the terrain of Rhol and take any life that walked upon it. It would help them grow. It was almost ironic, Solharn thought. In a matter of days, the energy of the very souls that had at one time fought so hard to save their precious world, would be responsible for destroying it. It was an irony Solharn relished in an irony that would bring darkness to the entire planet.

CHAPTER THIRTY-FOUR

"To arms!" Palto screamed at his troops.

Without a second of hesitation, the mighty Pegapires flew from their perch. They did not know why Palto had suddenly decided to call them to battle, but it did not matter. They trusted him. Only when they turned in the skies did they understand the urgency of his tone. Phanthus had somehow managed to fly in behind them unnoticed.

But even as they flew from the cliffs, Phanthus had not reacted as they might have expected. In fact, he still had not moved, seemingly content with simply staring down Palto.

"I do not come to fight, Palto."

Palto did not seem convinced by the dragon's statement. "Then why have you come at all Phanthus?"

"In hope, that we could wage war as allies, not opponents."

Palto did not believe a word he heard from the dragon. No more than a day ago he was willing to kill anyone that stood for Rhol.

"You must take me for a fool, Phanthus. You were an integral part of defeating Queen Elissa, and you are responsible for the deaths of hundreds of my people, innocent people."

"Innocent, Palto? Come now. You have been around almost as long as I. Do you remember nothing of the way my kind, were quite literally slaughtered by your people?"

"Neither the Pegapires nor the Lealians had anything to do with the massacre of the dragons. It was you who attacked the innocent inhabitants of Rhol!"

"Then perhaps your memory does fail you Palto. The dragon attacks were only a reaction to the people of Rhol hunting us down and killing us for fame. We reacted to save our species. It was a war of survival. One that regretfully, became bitter when the dragons came closer to extinction, eventually leaving only me."

"That is not the way I remember it, Phanthus, but I have been around long enough to know that there are two sides to every story. Even still, you have been an enemy of Rhol for centuries. As recently as yesterday you attacked my people and me. I have no reason to trust you."

"Nor I you Palto, yet here we stand. It is true that I have been your enemy for what seems to be an eternity. As far as the last few days, I have no recollection of what I did. I was under Solharn's spell until a boy saved me. I would never have thought there would be a day when we could become allies, but then I never had any faith in the inhabitants of Rhol, or for that matter, anyone but my kind. Then I saw an unexpected side of a boy who was brought here to save Rhol, a side that showed compassion for another kind that was quite unlike himself. If he is, in fact, the prodigy who will save Rhol, then I will fight alongside him because he has a unique view of life. To him, every life is precious, and everyone is equal. The boy put his life at risk to convince me of this. He knew that your chances of defeating Solharn would be far greater if I fought alongside you. He counted on his faith that I would believe in what he had to say, and he is relying on your faith to believe in me."

"The boy you speak of. What is his name?" Palto asked.

"His name is Deke. He is in the Tiqor Swamps, and he and his friends desperately await our help to free Elissa."

"They have found Elissa?" Palto exclaimed.

"The girl, Mary, claims to know where she is. They make their way to her through the swamps as we speak."

"I would like to believe you Phanthus, but what you say could be nothing more than another trap. I cannot trust you."

"Yet you still have not given the order to attack. Why?"

"I don't know," Palto answered.

"Perhaps it is because you know I could have wiped out your entire army within seconds. Yet even as they flew from the cliffs, they remained unscathed. Maybe it is because you would like so very much to be able to trust me, for I would be a valuable ally to you Palto, as you would be to me."

"If what you say is true then why did the boy or one of his friends not come with you?"

"Because time is running out for Elissa and as we speak they are converging on her location, all while fighting the Phits. They need your help. I can help more here in the open fields. My switching of sides will take Solharn's armies by surprise, but if you cannot find a way to believe what I tell you, then let us go our own ways. I will return to the boy and do what I can to help save Elissa. It is your decision to make but decide now."

Palto continued to stare at Phanthus. He was having a hard time believing what Phanthus said. For all he knew, Phanthus had killed the boy, and this was a convenient trick. On the other hand, if Phanthus was being honest and truly wished to fight alongside them, it would certainly improve the odds of victory. It was a hard decision for Palto to weigh in his mind.

His troops eagerly awaited his next words. Palto looked over at Jayden. If he had been possessed by Solharn, it was certainly possible that Phanthus had also been. The dragon could most certainly be lying, but it was also true that Phanthus could have wiped out a significant portion of their army without difficulty had he wanted to. His story was certainly plausible, but this was Phanthus. He had never doubted one of his decisions before, nor had he taken so long to make one. He knew if he did not make it soon it would show doubt and weakness. He hoped he would not regret the decision he had just made.

"Stand down!" Palto yelled to his troops.

He noticed some hesitated, but eventually, they too fell back into line amongst their fellow warriors.

"I will go to the boy and his friends Phanthus. Which part of the Tiqor Swamps will I be headed toward?"

"The Phits home territory is where we believe Elissa is being held. That is also where you will find Deke, Deo, Mary, and Delca. At least that is where they were headed when I left them."

"And what am I up against?" Palto asked.

"More Phits than you can imagine. Even I could not hold them at bay in such close quarters."

"Kaelyn! Issa!" Palto yelled.

Issa walked toward Palto. Kaelyn sat tall and proud upon her as they approached. "Yes, Palto?"

"You will lead our troops here on the battleground of Solace. I will take a small contingency of the army and head to the Tiqor Swamps where we believe Elissa is being held."

Kaelyn did not ask any questions nor did Issa. Both just nodded a response with their heads indicating that they understood.

"And Phanthus, what should I expect your role to be?" Palto asked.

"I think my capabilities can best be put to use here in Solace, in the open air. I am more than willing to sit and discuss strategy with these two young warriors that you placed in charge," Phanthus said staring down at Issa and Kaelyn.

"Very well, if I might ask one more question Phanthus? You said the boy saved you when you were possessed by Solharn. Can he save others in the same way?" Palto asked looking over toward Jayden.

"I do not know, Palto. He did mention saving a friend of his from the same fate, so I can only assume he can."

That was all Palto needed to hear; he had Jayden placed onto his back and secured. He would carry him to the swamps in hopes that Deke could save him. It would be the second time Jayden's fate would rest with Palto.

Palto selected twenty-five Pegapires and their Lealian warriors to accompany him to the swamps. It was time, a decade in the making. These would be the final battles which would determine whether Rhol lived or died.

He briefed his small army, and without another word, they took flight toward the Tiqor Swamps. He could see abnormally dark clouds coming in over the mountains from the west. Rolling waves of lightning appeared to light them up from within before they spat out branches of atmospheric electricity that crackled loudly before crashing to the ground.

It seemed to him that the unstable weather which suddenly appeared might just be nature's nervous reaction to what was about to take place.

CHAPTER THIRTY-FIVE

Everyone was making sure they kept up with Mary. They'd been walking, running and crawling through winding trails, underground tunnels and deep scrub so thick you couldn't see more than a foot in front of you. She wasn't lying when she'd said she knew these swamps inside and out. If any of them had become separated from her, they would never find their way out. That worked to Mary's advantage because on top of knowing where she was going; she was determined to forge on without rest. She hadn't taken a single break in the last five hours.

They'd been lucky when the Phits initially attacked. The Phits had concentrated on the larger target, Phanthus, which had allowed Mary to lead everyone away with relative ease. Since then, they'd run into very few Phits. So few, that she alone had taken care of them with the blow gun she kept wrapped around her back. Deke was amazed as he watched her maneuver through these swamps. She knew every twist and turn and made no sound at all. He wasn't as stealthy and quite often got a little look from Mary, silently telling him to be quiet.

Finally, Mary allowed them to take a break. "We we'll rest here for the next hour. We're almost upon the Phit camps and will have to gather as much strength as we can," Mary said to the relief of the others.

Deke, Deo, and Delca sat down almost in unison and began to rub their aching feet. Mary was rustling through her bag.

"Unfortunately, I had no time to skin and cook our dinner for today. I tried to avoid you having to see what you were eating, but we've no time for luxuries," Mary said throwing what appeared to be a big blob of skin to the ground.

"It smells awful," Delca said turning up her nose.

"It tastes better cooked, but we can't start a fire either, so dig in," Mary said throwing three knives to the ground.

Deke cut into the side of the blob only to have a blue liquid squirt all over his face. "Ahh, this is disgusting! What is it, anyway?"

"It's a Torslenda. Pretty much all you can eat in these swamps. So eat! All of you need your energy. Just close your eyes and hold your breath if you can't stomach it."

The three found that was good advice as they dug away at the Torslenda. Its flesh was soft and squishy and felt much like warm ice cream sliding down your throat when you swallowed it. Other than nourishment, it really had no redeeming qualities at all. It smelled foul and left your teeth and lips blue. They finished their meal as quickly as they could to avoid any prolonged suffering.

Mary smiled briefly, looking at their blue lips and teeth before readying them for the next part of their journey. "We'll be in the Phits' prime territory within the hour. Hopefully, many of them will be looking for us throughout the swamp, but even if that's the case, there will be more than enough for us to deal with. I'm going to take you to specific spots surrounding the area where Elissa is being held. Use all of the darts you have. You'll be well hidden, and if you don't move, they won't detect you. We can only hope that Phanthus has convinced Palto to send help, but we can't count on it. So, once the Phits surrounding the cavern have fallen, we'll move in immediately."

They all rested a little longer before heading out on the last leg of their journey. It didn't seem long before Mary started placing them in their designated spots, warning them not to move before continuing. They were to give her a half an hour before they took out a Phit. She wanted all four of them to attack at one time. It certainly wasn't easy; there were Phits all over the place. They sometimes appeared as if they were looking right at you. It made Deke's skin crawl.

Deke had counted at least seven while he waited. It had become surprisingly cold in the short time that he had sat there. He chalked it up to the fact that it had started raining, and his body was slowly cooling off from sitting still. It was also getting much darker, earlier than usual, he thought. He'd done the best he could to count down a half an hour in his head. He didn't want to strike early but was sure it was time. He looked up hoping to see Pegapires flying through the air but saw nothing aside from a Phit plummeting down from the sky toward him. He readied his blow gun but didn't have to use it as the hideous creature crashed to the ground mere feet from him. He could see a dart protruding from its side. If he previously had any doubts that it was time, there was none now.

It wasn't much longer before Deke downed his first one and then his second. He was getting used to hearing their wings, and that gave him the advantage. Several minutes had passed without any sign of the Phits. Then he heard the signal Mary had told them all to listen for. It was a low growl followed by a popping noise. It was apparently the mating sound of some sort of giant toad. In any event, it meant that the time to advance was near. Deke figured it was really more of a warning not to shoot Mary in a panic when she came to get them.

Within minutes after the signal, Mary appeared before Deke followed by Delca and Deo. She used a hand signal telling them to be quiet as they moved in on the cavern. Phits were lying everywhere. Mary quickly grabbed the first one they came to by the feet and dragged it out of sight. The other three followed suit, hiding the motionless bodies of the Phits as they walked along, until finally reaching the entrance to the cavern.

Mary squeezed through the small passageway first, followed by the rest. Steps led them down a dimly lit corridor. Mary made sure they stayed a distance back. She wanted complete silence while she maneuvered each step slowly making sure to peer around every corner they came to. Occasionally, her hand would come up motioning them to stop. Then in one movement she would reach for her blowgun, pull it up to her mouth and sling it back around her back. That motion was followed by a scraping noise as the paralyzed victim slowly fell against the wall and slid to the ground. By the time they had reached the bottom of the stairs, Deke had walked past the bodies of at least four Phits who had succumbed to the darts laced with poison.

The stairs led them to a large room. They frantically searched it for any sign of Elissa. Their search did not end in the celebration they had hoped for. Elissa was nowhere to be found amongst the gold urns and trinkets that adorned the room. Mary kicked out in anger at the coins which lay strewn all over the floor. It was a dead end; the only way out was the way they came in. There wasn't any sign of Elissa. It was simply the Phit's treasure trove.

Mary was devastated. "I don't believe it. I've put all of our lives in danger for what, trinkets?"

"Mary, you couldn't have known. It was the most logical place to look. If we'd ignored it, we would just be wondering," Delca said comforting her.

"Or perhaps we'd be closer to finding Elissa. Because of me, we've wasted two days here. I should've considered the fact that the area was guarded to protect their treasures," Mary responded. She was clearly frustrated.

"We all made the decision to come, Mary," Deke pointed out.

"I convinced you to come, and you trusted me. Even Phanthus trusted my instincts. I failed you, and I have failed myself."

"Stop, Mary. There is no time for this. We will find Elissa, maybe not today, but we will find her. Right now we have to get out of here before we are discovered."

Mary just shook her head, dejected. "I'll lead you out of here Deke, but that will be the end of my journey. I have spent the better part of two years living in this swamp, mapping and making plans to break into...into this."

"Mary...," Deke began.

"Never mind, follow me," Mary said in frustration walking toward the stairs.

Deke knew there was no point in talking to her now. He would try to comfort her later. He could not blame her for being upset. He probably would have felt the same way.

The other two had already begun to follow Mary up the stairs. Deke followed behind feeling a little dejected himself. They were running out of time. He reached the bottom of the steps and began to climb. He wasn't sure why but every step he took became harder as if something was weighing him down. His neck felt tight, and it was becoming harder to breathe. He wondered if his body had finally given up.

He grabbed for the amulet that hung on his chest. It was gone. Deke became frantic. How could I have lost it, he thought? He turned around quickly to look for it and there, in front of his eyes, was the Amulet of Rhol. It was floating in midair still attached to the chain around his neck which was ever so slightly pulling him forward in the direction in which it was pointed.

"Mary! Deo! Come back!" Deke yelled up the stairs.

He could hear them running back down toward him.

"What is it, Deke?" Deo asked with his sword at the ready.

But they did not need an answer. The amulet was glowing. A brilliant blue color surrounded it and got brighter with every step Deke took.

"What do you think is happening, Deke?" Mary asked.

"I think the amulet is telling you that you were right, Mary. I believe it is leading us to Queen Elissa," Deke responded in excitement.

"But we checked everywhere, we…"

Everyone stood in silence staring at the amulet. It had led Deke to one of the rock walls. The point of the arrowhead was just touching it. Slowly the wall began to crumble into small pebbles that fell to the floor of the cavern, eventually revealing the outline of a door. There were several locks around the outer edges which melted away one by one as the amulet moved to touch each of them. When the last of the locks had disappeared, the amulet fell back onto Deke's chest, its blue light extinguished.

Deke reached out and grabbed the handle. The door creaked loudly as if moaning in protest at being disturbed as he pulled it open. Mary hugged Deke. It looked like a crypt large enough for one person. There was no coffin though. Instead, there was a dark force, a shroud, surrounding the figure of a woman, a Queen. It was Elissa.

"We've done it! We have found her Deke!" Mary exclaimed.

"Deke, can you release her from her bonds?" Delca asked.

"There's only one way to find out," Deke answered grabbing the amulet. He could feel the power begin to surge through his body. He reached out toward the shroud that encased Elissa, not knowing, but hoping that something would happen. Blue streaks of light shot from his extended hand and attached to the shroud of darkness. Deo watched expecting to see the core of light turn black, to see Deke slowly absorb it and free Elissa, but that did not happen. Instead, the shroud began to absorb the blue light. The more it absorbed, the closer Deke was pulled toward it.

Unlike the other two times, Deke had used the amulet's powers, Deo could feel something within himself, an overwhelming feeling of distance, of loneliness. He felt almost disembodied, and he suddenly realized why.

"Deke, let go of the amulet! The shroud is absorbing the amulet's energy. It is absorbing your energy!" Deo yelled.

His pleas fell on deaf ears. Deke was becoming far weaker than he had ever felt before. He could not hear, nor could he feel anything, as the shroud pulled him closer and closer, slowly sucking away at his very essence.

"Mary! Delca! Quickly, we must pull him away!" Deo yelled.

All three grabbed Deke trying to slow his advance. Almost instantly Mary began to scream and convulse uncontrollably. Her mind suddenly became filled with death, with the image of rotting bodies strewn over the ground. She could not escape the faces of the dead. Their eyes were white, and blood oozed out of every orifice. In her nightmare, she frantically ran, but there was nowhere to go. At every turn, she ended up tripping over another rotting corpse.

"Mary, what is it?" Delca yelled.

She did not answer, she couldn't answer. She was too frightened, unable to move. In her dream, she had fallen again, fallen over yet another corpse. But this one was much different than the others; this face she knew all too well. It was the face she had seen countless times in the form of her own reflection. She screamed in horror as it laughed back at her.

"It's the shroud!" Deo yelled. "It must not affect us as it does them. Their souls control emotion. The shroud has taken them both to a dark place! Quickly! We have to find a way to break the link!"

Deke was staring at himself in a mirror. His eyes were black; his face was expressionless. A tall looming figure stood behind him. It was Solharn. His hand was resting on Deke's shoulder; his finger stretched out toward the mirror pointing seemingly at him. Deke looked harder at his image. He looked inside himself, and he found himself wanting, lusting for power. It was an uncontrollable urge; he needed it. A smile formed on his face as he began to realize what could be his. He wanted it and reached out for it. It was almost in his grasp when the mirror shattered. Shards of glass flew through the air toward him in slow motion. He tried to grab the pieces one by one as his body jettisoned back through the air.

He awoke to see his friends by his side. For several minutes their hollow voices echoed in his ears, but he couldn't understand what they were saying. As seconds turned into minutes, he began to understand their reassuring words and sitting up; he looked toward the shroud. It remained undisturbed with Elissa still entombed within it.

"Deke, are you ok?" Deo asked.

"What happened?"

"The shroud began to pull you into it, draining you of your energy. It had the same effect on Mary. Delca found a mirror amongst the Phits' treasures and placed it between you and the shroud. It redirected the light that the amulet emitted and broke the hold that the shroud held over you and Mary."

Deke stood up. He could see that the other three were feeling as dejected as he was. They all realized that they did not possess the power, or the knowledge to free the person that they were meant to save.

"If the amulet won't free her, then what will? Have we come all this way only to find that we can't break the curse that holds Elissa hostage?" Deke screamed in anger.

"There must be another way, Deke," Deo reasoned.

"What other way, Deo? Mary, Delca, have you any ideas?" he asked.

"Deke, did Kiran say anything to you before she..."

"Before she died to save me, Mary? Isn't that what you wanted to say?" Deke harshly snapped at her before continuing. "No, she didn't. We didn't have the luxury of spending too much time together. She told you everything, but then it wasn't you, was it? It was Delca or Solharn or whatever! It makes no difference! We don't know if she had the answers and she's not here to help us, is she?"

Deke stared at his three friends. Delca was hugging Mary who was sobbing. Deo just turned and walked away without saying a word. Deke had no idea where his anger had come from. What was happening to him, he asked himself. This step back was not their fault, and they certainly did not deserve the brunt of his sudden anger.

"I'm sorry. I don't know what came over me," Deke said. "I know you're as frustrated as I am. I just wish that she was here, Kiran, I mean. Anyway, there is no excuse. Please accept..."

Deo cut Deke off. "There is no need for a second apology. We are all friends, here to accomplish the same thing. We just have to put our heads together and figure it out. If..."

"Quiet," Mary loudly whispered interrupting Deo.

Heeding Mary's warning, the four instantly paused, listening intently. A low whistling noise could be heard, not unlike a light gust of wind. It was steadily becoming louder. They looked toward the stairs, readying themselves for whatever was coming. A small dim light that cascaded a blue glow on the walls of the cavern grew ever so slightly. They stood in silence in the middle of the room. There was nowhere else for them to go while they waited and wondered if this would finally be the end of their quest.

CHAPTER THIRTY-SIX

The wind howled, and dark clouds moved in extinguishing what was left of the sunlight. It made the afternoon hours appear as if they had been vanquished by the dusk.

Now and then brief flashes of light broke through the darkness as great branches of lightning boomed down from the clouds. The bolts appeared to strike the top of the mountains as the storm slowly crept over them.

Phanthus saw it first. Solharn's army had chosen that moment to attack. Ralcriff charged from below followed by troops of Kaltaures. Legions of Phits flew in the sky above them, supporting them as they converged on the ground forces with impunity. Their army was overwhelmingly huge in comparison.

Phanthus took to the skies immediately and came in behind the Phits. News of Phanthus's sudden change of allegiance had obviously not made it back to them, for when they saw the dragon they rejoiced in the thought that they had just gained a huge advantage.

With Phanthus at their side, they were inspired. Inspired that they, the Phits, could end the battle quickly and revel in the glory of it all. With their renewed confidence and a little encouragement from Phanthus, they veered from their original path and headed straight for the cliffs where the Pegapires and the Lealians still stood watching down upon the ground troops.

Excitement took over their common sense as they came within striking distance of the seemingly unaware Pegapires. They dropped their guard in their feeble effort to become heroes. They were sure they would soon bathe in Solharn's rewards once they delivered the blow that would end Queen Elissa's empire forever.

The Phits were so consumed with the desire for glory they failed to think it strange that the Pegapires had still not moved, even as they began to descend toward them from above. They neglected to comprehend, as one normally would, that this was just far too easy.

The Phits were almost upon them. Their thirst for power and riches had blinded them. It was a blindness that would ever so slowly dissipate though, one that would allow them to see again and see they did. They watched as the Pegapires split their ranks, not flying but running, half to the east and the other half to the west. They were not engaging them but running away. It was only then that they saw again and with their new found sight came logic and reasoning. There was something wrong. Even they knew that Pegapires and Lealians would never run from a fight. Even when facing death, they would take it in stride.

The Phits were right in their reasoning, but it was too late to avoid the trap in which they found themselves. They could see the ground below them suddenly light up as the air around them became warmer. It was as if the sun was rising in the morning, casting its glow and warmth upon them. But it was not sunlight that was rapidly enveloping them. Their bodies ignited and fell upon the cliffs smoldering away. They'd been outmaneuvered by Phanthus.

It had been Phanthus' idea to use the Pegapire and Lealian army as bait to lure the Phits out over the cliffs and dispose of them there. He knew the Phit's arrogance would take over whatever strategy they might have had. From the ground it appeared as if Phanthus had attacked the Pegapires; nobody could see the lifeless bodies of the Phits lying upon the cliffs. This would allow him to mount a second surprise attack on Solharn's ground troops, lessening their enemies' numbers even more.

Phanthus turned in the sky looking down upon Kaelyn and Issa. It was time, and he quickly descended the cliffs toward the front of Solharn's battalion. The next phase of the plan was to take out as many Ralcriff as he could before they closed in on the ground troops.

Issa and Kaelyn took flight, followed by the rest of their army. "Stay to the edge of the cliffs. We do not want to be seen until we come up from behind them!" Kaelyn shouted.

This was it, the last battle for Rhol. They had come far and fought hard to come to this point. They could not afford to make any mistakes.

Ω

"I am surprised they don't give up," Abednego laughed when he saw Phanthus arrive. He was sure that the dragon was the help Solharn had told him to expect.

Abednego turned to his troops. He was already savoring the victory. His soldiers were feeling it too. He could see it in their eyes which were glowing a brilliant pearl with the impending excitement. The snakes that adorned every one of their massive heads swayed to and fro. Their forked tongues burst from their mouths every few seconds, reaching out into the air to taste what would soon be theirs.

Abednego rode upon his horse, up and down the line of soldiers who obediently stood awaiting his instructions as the rain poured down upon them. The rain made the ground muddy and hard to walk on. They did not care. They had a taste in their mouth, a taste for blood. They would soon be able to gorge on the rotting bodies of the Rholians. The ones who were unlucky enough to survive would serve them their food. Serve them their own friends whom they had fought beside. They would have to watch as their comrades were devoured. Rhol would be theirs and the feeble creatures that inhabited it would be their slaves. They relished in the glory of what was to come.

"Once the Ralcriff descend upon these pathetic fools, we will follow, and when we converge on what is left of their dwindling masses, we will show no mercy! We will strike out at them and force them to lie at our feet and beg for their lives. Spare nobody until that moment," Abednego growled down to his troops.

They stood ready for his next command, drooling at the anticipation of the impending bloodshed, of anarchy. It was what they reveled in, what they lusted for. The promises that Solharn had filled their heads with. The promises of control, power, and wealth had long since taken over their minds and their souls. They thought of nothing else.

Abednego turned to look at the Ralcriff fighting to break loose of the thick chains that held them back. Their lips were curled revealing their snarling ivory teeth, teeth that would soon be stained with the blood of battle. Their coarse poison filled manes stood at attention quivering slightly in anticipation. Saliva dripped from their jowls. Their hunger would no longer be hindered as Abednego released them upon Rhol.

Ω

Oisin and Orulla stood out front of their troops waiting. Their plan had worked, but not quite as they had envisioned it. The V formation was meant to draw a significant portion of Solharn's army, not the army in its entirety.

It forced them to make slight changes to their strategy. Kaelyn and Issa had long since left after discussing the new plan with them. They had both been shocked, and both were somewhat suspicious when it was revealed that Phanthus now fought for their side. They feared that it was some sort of trap, but it had been Palto's decision.

That was all they needed to know. Even if they had their doubts, they trusted Palto for he was the most highly regarded warrior in all of Rhol. Their warriors had long since fallen back from the V formation and had been carefully instructed on when to act. Everything was in place, and that was why they were waiting, looking up at the cliffs.

"There he is," Orulla said calmly to Oisin.

Oisin could see him now. Phanthus was descending from the cliffs toward the front of Solharn's battalion. His massive wings cut through the rain and with the wind at his back he moved at a rapid pace. It would not take him long to reach his destination. Orulla must have come to the same conclusion for when Oisin turned to speak with her; she was already gone. He could see her at a distance briefing the archers, ensuring they knew when to strike the army with their arrows.

"When the fire bursts across the fields let your bows guide your arrows. The Kaltaures army will be trapped behind the fire. The other half of our army will be coming in behind them. When your arrows are gone, then and only then will we move up to the wall of fire."

Oisin joined Orulla, once again taking his place upon her back. She walked toward the front lines while Oisin gave his last orders to the Rholians.

"The time is near. Rhol will once again be ours to live as we should live and to be as we should be. When the fire strikes the fields of Solace follow me, Rholians, and prepare yourself for the battle that will define your future."

Ω

Phanthus could see that the Ralcriff had already been released. He would not be able to take them all out. The ground troops would have to deal with the stragglers.

Abednego was waving to him, signalling him to join him on the ground. Phanthus thought it a shame that he could not just extinguish Abednego's life right then and there, but unlike most leaders, his death would not do much to discourage his troops. The Kaltaures would replace him in an instant. They had no respect for anyone, including their own kind. Abednego would have to wait for another time. For now, the look of surprise on his face would have to suffice.

Phanthus flew at ground level toward the Ralcriff which had only managed to gain about fifty meters from where they had been released. Abednego suddenly stopped waving his hand, yet his arm remained frozen in the air. He was obviously confused, wondering why Phanthus was taking the path he was on.

Minutes later, Abednego found himself crawling back to his feet after being knocked to the ground by the waves of heat that had suddenly filled the air. He looked in disbelief at the wall of fire that stretched out along the plains in front of him. Burning balls of fire were running all over the place growling and snarling. Blinded by the fire that consumed them, the Ralcriff lost all sense of direction. Some were lucky and quickly ended their suffering as they ran into the Kaltaures' ranks and were met with swords.

"Traitor!" Abednego yelled into the sky.

His words were cut short by his warriors suddenly dropping to the ground. Everywhere he looked, they fell. Hundreds of them splayed out upon the ground with arrows protruding from their lifeless bodies. He was incensed. The rest of his troops just milled about unorganized and in shock.

He screamed at his men. "Gather yourselves, you idiots! Attack! Attack!" he shrieked over and over again, but he too had lost control of his senses. There was nobody to attack. They could only see the fire that burned in front of them.

Realizing this, he yelled back again. "Prepare your shields, you fools! Return to your lines!" His men were scrambling. They tripped over their fellow warriors lying dead on the ground and fell into the mud in the panic of it all. His troops were in disarray. Abednego cursed looking at the fire burning in front of him. It was slowly dissipating. It was slowly revealing what was to come next as shadows suddenly became silhouettes, hundreds of them standing just to the other side of the flames.

He realized at that moment what was happening. "Ready yourselves!" he screamed, and cowardly maneuvered his horse to the rear of his men. In the distance, he could see a Kruntulla madly swiping in the air at the very back of his battalion. He squinted in an effort to see what caused its strife. Pegapires and Lealians were attacking from the rear. They were surrounded. They had been betrayed by Phanthus and outsmarted by the armies of Rhol.

Ω

The Rholians were still outnumbered, but the odds had become drastically better. So far their strategy had worked. The ground troops could not have timed it better. Trapped with nowhere to go; hundreds of Kaltaures succumbed to the Orler arrows being shot in their direction.

The ground troops had lost several of their warriors to the hundred or so Ralcriff that had escaped Phanthus, but not one of them made it past the front line to the archers. Eventually, all of the Ralcriff had succumbed to the swords of the skilled warriors that fought them. When their arrows were depleted the Rholians moved in unison, and quickly realigned themselves in front of the wall of fire.

Once Issa's scout had returned with the news that the ground troops were advancing, she and Kaelyn wasted no time. They led their warriors into the fight, attacking from the rear. Although they surprised Solharn's forces, they too were met with an unexpected turn. A second battalion of Phits had been held back, and they now took to the air charging after Kaelyn's warriors.

This posed a problem as they could not assist the ground troops. Even Phanthus was growing tired from fighting the Phits off. In addition, two Kruntulla were advancing, and they were not an easy foe to stop.

On the ground, even though the Kaltaures were disorganized, they still posed a significant threat. While their swordsmanship paled in comparison to the Lealians', their size and strength were much greater. Another unanticipated problem came from the Kaltaures' soldiers who lay on the ground merely wounded. If their heart still beat, then so too did the snakes that grew from their heads. When a Lealian stepped too close to a wounded Kaltaures soldier, they were bitten and injected with venom. Because of this, many Lealians were becoming ill and weak. In time they would succumb to the poison and die.

In the air, the Phits were slowly losing the battle, but it was far from over. The ground troops would not get their help anytime soon. Becoming concerned, Oisin and Orulla took to the air to survey the ongoing battle. It did not look promising. The Kaltaures' numbers were still far greater than the Lealian's.

"Orulla, we are losing this battle. There are too many. We need help!" Oisin yelled.

"They had another battalion of Phits hidden in the ranks. The Pegapires have their hands full," Orulla answered.

"What of Phanthus?"

"I don't know. We will try to find him."

Orulla flew as fast as her wings could carry her. The weather did not help. She was blinded by the pelting rain, and the wind currents made navigating next to impossible.

"Look out!" Oisin yelled.

Orulla swerved, narrowly missing a tree flying through the air toward them. "Where did that come from?" Oisin asked.

"The Kruntulla, more than likely."

"There!" Oisin yelled.

243

In the distance, they could see the mighty dragon. He was swarmed by Phits. Orulla moved in. As they drew near, they could see the Phits had been successful in severely damaging one of the dragon's eyes, and were working on the other. Phanthus was struggling to escape them.

The Pegapires that had been assigned to fly alongside him following his second attack were no longer there.

"We have to help him, Orulla."

Orulla swept by the nose of Phanthus drawing the attention of the Phits'. Oisin was able to drop two of them as they flew by. They converged on Orulla and Oisin which gave Phanthus the chance he needed. He gathered his strength, and in one breath they were burned to ashes.

Orulla moved over to flank Phanthus. "What happened, Phanthus? What happened to the Pegapires that rode with you?"

"They fought valiantly, but three fell to the Phits and one to a Kruntulla. I am sorry."

"We need help on the ground. The Kaltaures still outnumber us," Orulla exclaimed.

Phanthus just nodded and veered toward the ground followed by Orulla and Oisin. Suddenly he turned back and took to the sky.

"What is it Phanthus?" Orulla asked.

"The Lealians and the Kaltaures, they are entwined together in battle! If I attack with fire, I will kill just as many of us. The best I can hope for is to back them off," he answered discouragingly.

With that, he flew to the ground and landed in the heart of the battle. Phanthus stood on his hind legs with his wings pinned back and sent a stream of fire over the heads of the warriors. It worked for a moment, but only briefly. A Kruntulla came out of nowhere, throwing a large boulder at the dragon. Phanthus reacted instantly jumping to the side. The rock missed its mark and flew by him crushing several warriors. In a fury, Phanthus charged at the Kruntulla.

Orulla was amazed that Phanthus was able to withstand the blows of the Kruntulla as the two massive beasts savagely fought. They grappled with each other in a fight that few, if any, would ever see again. Claws and teeth fought against raw strength and size. It was hard to tell which creature, if either, had the advantage. Tense minutes lingered on into what seemed like an eternity and then, all at once, Phanthus dug his claws into the chest of his opponent and used his wings to drive the beast backward. The Kruntulla was unable to keep his balance and toppled backward crashing to the ground. That was all Phanthus needed. In seconds the Kruntulla's head was transformed into a burning inferno. Its screams were not what one would expect, more like a long moan which Phanthus ended quickly by killing the beast with his massive jaws. It was the mark of a warrior; one never rejoiced in the suffering of a fallen enemy.

"What is that?" Oisin asked in curiosity.

Orulla looked toward the blue flash that appeared from the mountain ridge behind Phanthus.

"I don't kno...oh no, Phanthus look out!"

Phanthus heard her, but it was too late to react to the three bolts of blue electricity that shot through the air striking his body. He fell to the ground stunned. The electricity coursed through him refusing to let go. It would eventually weaken him to the point of no return.

"It is the Brawltug! Duffy has returned. Quickly, Orulla! They do not know Phanthus fights with us and not against! We must apprise them before it is too late!"

Without hesitation, Orulla began to fly toward the mountain ridge. "Wait Orulla! The Kaltaures, they are advancing on Phanthus. We must protect him! Take me to him; I will stay here!" Oisin yelled.

Orulla flew to the ground. Oisin quickly dismounted and ran to Phanthus' side. The Kaltaures were already closing in on the ailing dragon that still lay there, unable to move.

"Quickly!" Oisin yelled to other warriors fighting nearby. "Surround the dragon and protect him at all costs! We owe him that!"

Phanthus was dazed and losing energy quickly. He could still see, and what he saw filled him with profound respect for the side he now fought for. He understood now that they, the Lealians, would give their life for anyone who fought beside them. It did not matter to them that he had been their enemy at one time. It was the present that mattered.

They could well have left him to suffer the fate of death, but they rallied around him. He was surprised at Oisin's power. His size was small and skinny, yet his heart must have been enormous. Three

Kaltaures had already fallen by his sword. His speed, determination, and swordsmanship were his strengths. He never wavered, and his sword never slowed, as he fought to keep the ever advancing Kaltaures away from the dragon's head. He was nearly decapitated on more than one occasion by the sickles that the Kaltaures swung toward him. It was a favorite and an effective weapon for them. Fortunately, it proved to be ineffective on Oisin as he rolled and ducked, slicing through the wooden handles, leaving nothing more than a stick in the hands of his enemy.

Phanthus watched in admiration as one Lealian warrior worked off the other. They were masters at it. Someone was always watching the other's back. There was complete trust between them which meant they never had to worry what was coming from behind them. If one Lealian was forced to duck, he somehow signaled the warrior behind him. There was no hesitation. The person at the back would roll away instantly and come up around the front, quite often disposing of the enemy. Then they would switch places and continue.

It was sheer determination that allowed them to keep fighting with such aggression, but Phanthus knew determination would only sustain them for so long. Over time their strength would dwindle and they, along with him, would be pawns in the hands of the Kaltaures. They knew it too, yet they continued to utilize everything they had left to save him.

"Phanthus, Orulla must have reached the Brawltug! Their weapons no longer impede you! Can you move?" Oisin screamed while still fighting the onslaught of Kaltaures.

Phanthus tried but could not. "You have done what you could young Lealian. Leave me to die at the hands of these cowards. My death will not be in vain for I have seen you fight for my life, and that is something I could never have imagined. In the end, I will die honorably fighting for a worthy cause and with admirable warriors. That makes it a good day to die."

Oisin broke away from the fight for a mere second and stared deep into the dragon's eye.

"It may be a good day to die Phanthus, but it is a much better day to live. We will not leave a fellow warrior wounded at the mercy of our enemy. Only the end of this battle will determine which day that it is to be, but it will not be your day, it will be ours."

Without another word Oisin turned and continued fighting. Phanthus knew better than to argue, it would be futile. He was proud to die amongst them, and as the Lealian warriors began to fall at the hands of the Kaltaures army, he knew that the time to die was not far off. They still had their hearts, but they were losing their strength.

It did not appear to him to be something to rejoice about, yet unless his ears were failing him, Phanthus could hear the sound of cheering in the distance. He was confused and wondered why. He was too weak to lift his head. His line of vision allowed him to see only brief glimpses of some sort of blue flash.

Oisin still fought to the front of him. He was the only warrior whom Phanthus could see was still alive, but the battle had taken its toll. He was exhausted and barely able to stand. Phanthus noticed him glancing away occasionally, in the vicinity of the flashes. There was a look of anxiousness chiseled on his face, a look of hope.

But whatever he hoped for would be too late in coming. Phanthus felt powerless and overwhelmed by a sense of helplessness as he watched Oisin's arms give way to the weight of the sword he had so valiantly swung to save him.

Oisin had nothing left in him; he was on his knees. His arms lay limp at his sides, his hand barely clinging onto the sword which had served him so well. He turned to look at Phanthus and smiled. Phanthus could see two Kaltaures running up behind him; mere yards separated them. Phanthus fought to get up, struggling as the Kaltaures closed in on Oisin. He had to do something. It could not end this way.

"Oisin!" Phanthus yelled in vain.

Oisin just continued to look deeply into his eye, smiling. "It appears the end of the battle has determined our fate, my friend."

Phanthus yelled again in desperation, still unable to move. "Oisin, behind you, Oisin!"

Oisin could hear the soldiers behind him. He could hear the sword being pulled from its sheath, but he merely continued where he had left off.

"In the end, it is a good day for me to die and a good day for you to live. Be well Phanthus."

Phanthus roared, but Oisin would not hear the dragons anguish. The Kaltaures showed Oisin no mercy.

Seconds later, Phanthus watched as a sword which was destined for him suddenly came to a stop in midair. The Kaltaures soldier who was wielding it bounced back and fell with an expression of confusion on his face.

Phanthus could see three Brawltug standing in front of him. Each one held a Cortuc. The round ends of each instrument were pointed to the ground creating a shield that surrounded him.

The Brawltug had arrived by the hundreds. Their Cortucs proved to be invaluable for both the Lealians and the Pegapires alike, acting as both a weapon and a source of protection against the Kaltaures attacks.

In time, the Kaltaures numbers dwindled. They scattered and fled with the cowardly Abednego leading the way. The Phits had also felt the pains of battle and scampered back to the swamps to find refuge. The fields of Solace were suddenly barren. One lone Kruntulla stood in the middle. The daft creature was confused. It did not understand what it was supposed to do. It was not advancing, or becoming violent, so it was not met with any attack. After several awkward minutes of contemplation, it only turned and disappeared into the backdrop of the landscape.

By now the torrential rain, wind, and thunder had moved in from the mountains. It was deafening. It was the worst storm Phanthus could remember seeing, but despite the weather, Phanthus could still hear the cheers from the warriors of Rhol celebrating their victory.

Normally it would have been cause for Phanthus to celebrate amongst them but he could not celebrate, he could only mourn. He would never forget Oisin's sacrifice for him. He wished he could have saved him or, at the very least, done something to help him. He looked down upon the fallen warrior, the proud Lealian...A friend...His friend. A tear gently rolled down his cheek and fell upon Oisin.

Phanthus patiently waited, hoping...but nothing happened. The mighty dragon turned and walked away feeling dejected.

The Ancients had been wrong. It was just folklore, a mere myth in which a dragon possessed a magic of sorts, a magic that could only be used once. One the dragon would never part with unless he felt the deepest respect and admiration for an individual. It was a magic that they kept bottled up and hidden away inside of them, and it came hand in hand with extreme emotions. It was the magic contained within a single drop of water; the magic of life that was contained within a dragon's tear.

CHAPTER THIRTY-SEVEN

The sacred baubles and treasures of the Phits' contained within the cavern began to vibrate. Whatever was behind the blue light that slowly inched toward them was emitting some sort of invisible energy. It caused Mary's hair to stand on end. She was holding Deke's hand, and her eyes were glued to the stairwell.

Delca and Deo stood on either side of the wall at the bottom of the stairs hoping that their counterparts would have the time to change them into something that would be able to combat whatever crept toward them. There would not be much time to determine what exactly that would be, but they had little choice in the matter.

Deke was the first to spot what caused their anxiety as it floated down the last two stairs and made its way toward them. It was followed by hundreds of others.

"Chilings!" Deke exclaimed.

The Chiling that led the way stopped in front of Deke's face while the others encircled the small room. Its blue light pulsed in front of him as if it was trying once again to communicate.

"Kiran, is that you?" Deke asked.

He thought he could hear some sort of muffled response and strained his ears in an attempt to decipher it, but the sound slowly faded away and disappeared.

"Why do you believe this Chiling to be Kiran?" Mary asked a little bewildered.

"I can't be sure, but when she died, I watched her transform into one and join the others. When they felt it was time, they all flew away, except one that remained hovering in front of my face, much like this one. I believed it was Kiran. Something inside of me felt it, as I do now," he answered.

"The important question is why they are here?" Deo asked.

"Because you asked for her, Deke!" answered Delca before anyone else could respond.

"Don't you remember? In your apology, you wished for her to be here!"

The words came flooding back to them. "Then perhaps they're here to help free Elissa," Mary eagerly said.

"I think you're right, Mary," Deo said looking toward the Queen.

They'd been too busy staring at the Chiling hovering in front of them to notice that the others had surrounded Queen Elissa. They watched as the final Chiling took its place amongst the others. With the last one in place, they began to pulse around her, with their blue light fading in and out. It was not noticeable at first, but in time they could see that a black spot was slowly growing in the core of each one. Each time the light grew brighter the dark spot would grow larger.

"What do you suppose is happening?" Mary asked with curiosity.

"I don't know," answered Deke looking at the strange growth within them.

Their black core had almost entirely consumed them. The light that once shone from the Chiling was no longer a calming blue glow.

"I know," answered Deo.

"What is it then?" Deke asked.

"They are consuming the darkness that holds her hostage. I have seen it before."

"What? When have you seen it?" asked Deke.

"When I watched you do the same thing to free Delca and then Phanthus."

"I remember freeing them. I don't remember becoming consumed with anything."

"I know you don't," Deo answered. "But every time you did it, you were drawn closer and closer to the dark side. I could see it in your eyes. I could feel it taking control of you."

"That's absurd, Deo. Then why couldn't I free Elissa's binds when I tried?"

"I can only guess that this is a much more powerful force, a dark evil force that Solharn concocted to prevent any one person from being able to penetrate it; to keep you from penetrating it. It would have never entered his mind that so many would give up their very souls to save one."

"But if what you say is true then the souls, the Chiling, will not die. They will be consumed with darkness, with evil?"

"Yes."

"And they will be forced to follow Solharn. They will live in an eternity of darkness. He will command their every thought."

"It's their sacrifice, one that they choose," answered Deo somberly.

The Chiling were now completely black. As if they were all following each other to oblivion, they rose up from Queen Elissa in small bunches and floated toward the stairwell.

Mary was crying as she turned with the others to watch the endless stream of Chiling make their way to their new master, to a fate worse than death itself.

"Quickly, Deke Brolin! The amulet of Rhol, may I have it?" came a serene, angelic voice from behind them.

The four turned toward the sound as if they were performing a synchronized act. Their emotions took over them; their voices were mute. They had come so far in search of the one person upon whom so many depended. They could see why she commanded so much respect. She beamed energy that revitalized you. She emitted a soft white aura which lit the room. Her long blondish, white hair flowed almost to her waist giving off a glow that only enhanced her soft, pallid complexion. Everything they had gone through seemed quite trivial as they stood in the presence of an angel, the angel of Rhol; Queen Elissa.

Queen Elissa stretched her hand out toward Deke.

"Please Deke, the amulet."

With both hands, he reached for the chain which had adorned his neck since he had arrived in this world, the chain that Kiran had given him to safeguard the Sacred Amulet of Rhol during his long journey.

Deke placed the amulet in her hand, leaving the chain dangling from her long, slender fingers. Queen Elissa did not respond as she put the chain around her neck. A blue circle of light began to form around her hands, not from the amulet itself, but from her. The circle kept expanding until eventually, it encompassed every one of the Chiling. Deke watched as their dark cores began to melt away. In mere minutes, the blackness in each Chiling was gone, returning them to their familiar glow.

With this task completed, Elissa placed her hand upon the amulet. One by one the Chiling floated toward the amulet and then disappeared within it, except one that hovered in front of her for several minutes before floating away up the stairwell. Deke could sense the sadness in Elissa's face following its departure.

"Deke, Deo! Quickly! You must climb the stairs. At the top, you will find Palto and Jayden. Jayden has been possessed by Solharn; he must be saved. Palto and his warriors need him. The Lealians' need him!"

"Your Majesty, is there another way, perhaps the Wall of Solace? Deke, he becomes…"

Deo did not have a chance to finish his sentence before the Queen jumped in.

"No, there is no other way, once I was freed from my bonds that energy dispelled and returned to me. The Wall of Solace no longer exists, and I doubt whether it would have helped anyway. I am sorry. There is no time for a longer explanation. Jayden will have to be taken out of his hypnotic state by Palto before Solharn's curse can be removed. His eyes are Solharn's eyes, and Solharn cannot know that I am free of my bonds, not yet. Please, Deke. We must hurry!" Elissa said, handing the amulet back to him.

Deke turned and ran up the stairs followed closely by Deo. When they reached the top, they could see that things had changed drastically since they had entered the cavern. The skies were black, rain and hail fell to the ground layering it with tiny balls of ice. Forks of lightning frequently crashed down from above. In the flashes of lightning, Deo and Deke caught brief glimpses of huge, powerful, black funnels of wind that stretched from the ground to the sky. It was horrifying to watch as they intertwined together, ripping and tearing into the ground, obliterating everything in their path.

Deke could see glimpses of Pegapires and Lealians fighting the Phits in the stormy dark skies. Every once in a while a glint of steel appeared as the blades of their swords reflected the glare of the lightning. The Phits attacked by the hundreds. Two Pegapires with their Lealian partners lay dead, sprawled out on the ground among several Phits. Deke felt devastated as he watched the rain wash the blood away from their lifeless bodies. It was a tragic day on Rhol.

"I've never seen anything like it!" Deo screamed through the wind. "They look like tornados or worse. They will destroy Rhol!"

"It must be the work of Solharn. Who else would be responsible for such utter mayhem and disaster?" responded Deke.

"I don't see Palto, Deke! Where is he? Where is Jayden?"

"Perhaps Palto was forced to flee with Jayden. Let's get back to Elissa and let her know what is happening out here!"

Deke was taking his first step back down the stairs when a voice boomed through his head.

"What is it, Deke?" Deo yelled.

"It's Palto. He's using telepathy. He's directing us into the trees to the east of the cavern. It's where he hides Jayden. He said that time is of the essence. His warriors need him and Jayden if they are to be successful against the Phits!" Deke screamed through the wind.

They found Palto in no time standing just beyond the first line of trees. Trickles of blood fell from several wounds that marked his body. Jayden was strapped to his back. His black eyes appeared lifeless, frozen in time as a result of the Pegapire trance Palto had placed upon him.

"Are you alright, Palto?" Deke asked.
"I am fine. These wounds are merely souvenirs left by the Phits. I was in no position to defend myself with Jayden on my back. Can you help him, Deke?"

"Yes, but first we must get him down and remove the trance he is under," Deke screamed through the howling wind.

"Very well."

Deke and Deo loosened the straps that bound Jayden to Palto and laid him on the ground. "I'm ready when you are Palto. We must act quickly. Solharn will see us through his eyes."

Palto nodded and walked over to Jayden. In seconds, Jayden was on his feet, laughing like a madman.

"You will not break her bonds boy, even if you know her whereabouts. You are too late. The darkness will become what little hope at life you have. You..."

Deke had heard enough from the voice he had become all too familiar with, the voice of Solharn. He struck Jayden with the current of energy that streamed through his hand from the amulet.

Ω

Deke instantly felt the power. He had missed the intensity of it coursing through his veins. He saw Solharn as he had never seen him before, hovering in the air over the Blackpool. Twisters and tornados formed all around him and disappeared just as quickly as he waved them away, unleashing them on Rhol.

"You have failed boy. You have failed to find Elissa. Otherwise, you would not be the one saving Jayden. It is over for Rhol, but it is not too late to join me, to be at my side. Together we will control the balance."

It seemed to Deke that he had been here before, perhaps in a dream. He thought about the power that Solharn commanded. Was it a bad thing to have such power? He had never had much of anything. What would it hurt to have a little bit of what Solharn had? Solharn began to move toward him lowering himself slowly from his perch in the sky. Deke did not move. He waited for him. Finally, he would have what he deserved.

Deo had retrieved Jayden's shield from Palto. He knew that soon Deke would be consumed with darkness, just as he had the previous times. He waited until he felt the darkness building up in Deke, until he felt his pain, and then he used the shield to slice through the stream of light thereby breaking the connection between the two. Palto was not prepared for what happened next. Deke was enraged and grabbed a sword from the Pegapire's, side all the while running toward Deo in a fury. Deo would not have escaped the wrath of his anger had Jayden not tackled him and removed the weapon.

Deke looked into Jayden's eyes. It must not have worked. Jayden was on top of him holding him down. Why weren't the others helping him?

"Are you okay now Deke?" Deo asked.

"Is Jayden okay?" Deke responded still wary of why he was being held down. He had no recollection of what had just happened.

Jayden stood up and held his hand out to Deke to help him up. Deke accepted the offer. It was the first time Jayden had the chance to take in his surroundings. "What happened? What has become of Rhol, and why am I back in the swamps?"

"Never mind Jayden, it is good to have you back. I will explain what you have gone through after we have defeated the Phits. Come! Our warriors need us," Palto yelled through the howling wind.

Jayden did not argue as he jumped onto Palto's back. "My thanks to you Deke. Now find a way to free Elissa. She is our only hope," Palto yelled as he flew into battle.

Deke nodded, a little confused. He had assumed that Palto knew she had been freed from her bonds.

"Come on, Deke. Let's get out of here!"

Ω

Mary breathed a sigh of relief when she saw Deo and Deke descend the last few stairs. They looked wet and cold but were fine otherwise.

"Were you successful Deke?" Elissa asked.

"Yes. But..."

Deke was unable to tell her what was happening outside because she simply continued. "I am sorry for being so abrupt earlier, but time was of the essence if I was to save the Chiling and you were to save Jayden. I could not let the Chiling fall into the hands of Solharn, and there was no time for explanations. They are safe now, so please allow me to explain myself," said Elissa.

"There's no need to apologize, Queen Elissa. We are just glad to find you alive and well, but please, I must tell you what Deo and I have witnessed and what has become of Rhol," responded Deke.

Elissa merely smiled.

"Please call me Elissa. I am told that you four have gone through many tribulations to come to my aid. Your passion has inspired the people of Rhol, and it inspires me. Even as I speak, the battle of Solace has been met with victory. Thanks to you, Jayden has been restored to his former self. I am confident that Palto and his small army will be successful in keeping the Phits at bay so as not to allow Solharn to learn of my resurrection."

"But isn't that what we want Elissa? Isn't that his greatest fear?" Deo asked.

"Solharn has no fear, child. He is obsessed with power, with revenge. His heart turned black long ago, and it has poisoned his very soul. He cares about nothing except his quest to become the all mighty, the new Creator, and he will stop at nothing to obtain that goal. We have come a long way in fighting against Solharn's depravity, but our biggest challenge is yet to come. That is why Solharn must not know about me yet, not before you understand what we are up against and how we can defeat him."

Deke was becoming a little stressed. Elissa had to be told what was happening to her world.

"Elissa, outside it is…."

"It is alright, Deke. I am aware of what you saw, but before we can act, you must understand more about what is happening. You must understand more about Solharn."

"I'm confused, Elissa. How do you know what's happening? How do you know about the war in Solace or for that matter, that Palto fights with the Phits outside this cavern?" Deke asked.

The look of sadness once again returned to Elissa's face.

"Because I was told Deke, I was told by Kiran."

Deke paused once again reflecting on the reason Kiran was dead. He wondered how it was possible that she could've told Elissa anything "...Elissa, Kiran, she is..."

"I know, Deke. She told me before she left us. She wished to remain in this world. Her journey was not completed yet. She was not ready to pass through the amulet. Selfishly, I am saddened to know that she no longer exists in our form. She was a faithful friend and confidant, but you must stop struggling with her death. Kiran knew more about this world than anyone and more about spirituality than most. When the Chiling came to the Realm of Solace to find refuge, Kiran spent every waking day trying to communicate with them. She knew that the energy contained within a soul was well beyond mere mortals. She quite correctly assumed that the curse Solharn had over me would be the most powerful one he had ever concocted. If it were to be broken, it would have to be done through the energy of the spirits, the souls, the Chiling. But Chiling can only communicate through a higher spiritual being, an angel for instance. She tried everything she knew, but it seemed that nothing worked. She would never be able to tell them what her belief was, the belief that they were my only hope should I be found. In the end, she did find a way. She became one of them, and in doing so, she saved you Deke. For Kiran, she fulfilled what she believed was her life purpose. She protected me. She saved me, and she died for me. It is I alone who will carry that burden, and it is mine alone to take, not yours child."

After listening to Elissa's eloquent words, Deke felt better. His guilt subsided knowing that Kiran, in the form of a Chiling, had found peace through death and then ultimately through Elissa.

"How does it all work, Elissa? The other Chiling, they seemed to evaporate within the amulet. Where did they go and what do they have waiting for them? What is the meaning of it all?" Deke asked.

"Those are questions that have been asked by many, and they are questions that you are destined to find the answer to. You must find those answers if you are to succeed, but it will take many years and many experiences before you have such wisdom. I can enlighten you somewhat. In fact, that is why we are here, hidden while Palto fights the Phits outside. You will need some answers if you are to understand the source of Solharn's power. Only then will we stand a chance of defeating him."

"The source you talk about, the source of his power, could we not destroy it so he can no longer obtain it?" Deke asked.

Elissa smiled. "To destroy the source of his power would be to destroy ourselves, along with the Balance of Five. It is not easy to combat something that you cannot destroy, and that is why Solharn has come as far as he has. You see, he uses us to gain his power. We are his never ending supply. His power is achieved through the energy of our souls."

Deke hung onto every word that Elissa spoke. Mary, Delca, and Deo were also completely fascinated, but they needed more information to comprehend the magnitude of what she was saying. Elissa did not disappoint them.

"Let me explain. The meaning of life has perturbed humankind for centuries when really it is quite simple. It is one's

258

existence in its purest form. If a person exists in the way they were meant to, then their life paths create positive energy, and that energy not only sustains life but creates it.

The worlds that we know, or at least which we are aware of now, they sustain themselves through energy. Not energy in the most common sense, but the energy that surrounds each individual, each living creature, the energy that is contained within the soul. It is that energy which lives on and which sustains life. The body itself is just a temporary vessel that is disposed of over time."

Elissa looked over at Deke momentarily. She could see his mind working to understand what she was saying.

"Yes, Deke. I can sense that it is becoming clearer to you. You are slowly beginning to understand what I speak of. The inhabitants of every planet are in fact the ones who maintain it and sustain it. The Creator merely conceived the venue, the planet on which we exist. After that, it was up to us to evolve into what we are today, and we did that by building positive energy around ourselves, through our very souls. It is the outer soul that is comprised of energy. You may have heard of someone having a good aura or good energy surrounding them? That is simply their souls, more precisely their outer soul growing much like your body does. It is the inner soul that controls emotion or one's nature. If one chooses an evil path, then it will create bad energy and vice versa. Your outer soul absorbs that energy. In simple terms, it becomes the external soul's food or nourishment. If your outer soul absorbs too much negative energy, that energy will become all consuming. It cannot be reversed making that person evil.

"The Balance of Five, the sustenance of life, the survival of each planet, really depends on the balance of positive or good energy versus negative or bad energy. Both types of energy are created by us, by our souls. It is a balance, one that is a struggle for many of our worlds. If the negative energy becomes the primary energy of any given world, then that world will eventually cease to exist. Slowly but surely, the planet will be unable to sustain itself. Earthquakes, floods, tsunamis, and tornados will make way for total annihilation. You may have already observed these things becoming more frequent on Earth.

"It was why the Order was created, the Order that Solharn was a part of. We helped maintain that balance and helped the inhabitants down the right path creating the positive energy that would support the planet and feed their souls. We, the Order, created religion as a way of keeping humankind on the right path. We designed it to provide a simplistic understanding of where we came from and a simple guide on how to live one's life. Religion worked. It served its purpose as it was meant to, but then to some degree, it took a turn for the worse. We learned far too late that Solharn had been meddling with religion for centuries. He convinced many leaders that religion could be used to manipulate people, to provide a faucet of money that would never run dry. Thus, some people began to use religion to make themselves powerful and rich. Solharn also turned different religions against each other. For many, religion became an excuse, a reason to fight wars and to kill one another. Some used its powerful message to gain great wealth and power by manipulating the people who truly believed. Solharn was instrumental in creating this religious dissension. He knew that if religion was followed worldwide, and if people followed it the way it was meant, then there would be peace and harmony amongst them. That would not work in his favor, and so he pitted religions against each other. It created hatred, anger, and greed which led to wars and violence, all in the name of religion. By the time the Order learned of his treachery, it was too late. We worked endlessly to instill the true meaning of faith and were successful to some degree, but the damage was already done. Even today religion is used by many to create wars and to gain wealth and power.

"Despite Solharn's efforts to undermine it, the balance remained intact, mainly because most still followed the right path. Positive energy still exceeded negative, but Solharn's influence is steadily eroding this balance. You see, when a person's vessel or body gives way to time, their souls become one. Positive energy moves on to form other life forces. Some call this reincarnation. This maintains the balance of each world, recycling the positive energy. Negative energy is cast out, sent to the Black Abyss.

"As you know, prior to Solharn being cast into the abyss, he managed to create a Blackpool on each world that would allow him to return to the planets. He did return, and by that time he had learned to manipulate the negative energy from the abyss. He was able to control it, using himself as the vessel. It created problems for all the worlds. Wars, unrest, violence and catastrophic storms occurred, but that was not enough for him. He wanted complete control, total power and to have that he had to learn how to harness the positive energy. I didn't think it possible, but he did it. He devised a way to steal a person's very soul by entrapping it, once he accomplished that he controlled that person's energy and used it to his advantage. This enabled him to tip the balance. By capturing the positive energy, he could use the elements to destroy the worlds. As we speak, he is slowly creating an imbalance where there will not be enough positive energy to combat the negative."

Deke was stunned. Had all of their struggles been for nothing? "Elissa, how are we to fight Solharn if he changes positive energy to negative? If he can steal one's soul, it's only a matter of time before he wins. We can't even destroy him. He is or was part of the Order, your Order."

"This is why you have to know where Solharn's power comes from Deke. We could not rush into a battle with him unless you all understood this. It is true; he cannot be destroyed. He must be sent back to the abyss, and the Blackpools destroyed. The Blackpools are the very foundation of his plan to destroy the Balance. Without them, he cannot return from the Black Abyss."

"But how do we destroy the Blackpools?" asked Deo.

"By using his own weapon against him," answered Elissa.

"The energy?" Deke chimed in.

"Exactly! You see Solharn has merely entrapped the positive energy, the souls of the unfortunate. He does not realize that he cannot change a person's soul or change a person's path. He can enslave it, but he cannot change who they are and what they represent. Good energy, positive energy will always be, just that. It cannot be reversed."

"So, to defeat Solharn, we have to free the souls he holds hostage," Deke exclaimed.

Elissa nodded. "Exactly Deke. Now, we are running out of time. All of you listen carefully. You must do exactly as I say!"

CHAPTER THIRTY-EIGHT

While the celebration of victory continued, Kaelyn made her way over to find Oisin. She assumed that he wouldn't be far from Phanthus. She had heard that the two had just been through a harrowing experience. They were probably celebrating their victory.

Phanthus was not hard to spot, and she hurriedly cut through the crowd in his direction. When she drew near the dragon, her heart sank. He did not have to tell her what had become of Oisin. She could see it in his face.

"Phanthus?" Kaelyn said trying to hold back her tears.

"I am sorry, Kaelyn. He would not leave. Even when he was the last one standing, he refused to go. He stood there fighting an impossible battle knowing that he would probably not come out alive, but he would not allow me to die alone. In the end, it was me that lived and he who died," Phanthus sadly responded.

"Where is he?" she asked, struggling to keep her composure.

Phanthus looked behind him bowing his head. "Over there, Kaelyn."

She looked in the direction Phanthus indicated. She couldn't see him, only Orulla who must have been standing over him, with her head bowed down. She had placed his sword in the ground above his head. This was a sign of respect in Leal to a fallen soldier. The sword would remain embedded in the ground for eternity marking the spot where a warrior of Leal died protecting others from the ravages of evil.

Kaelyn ambled over to him unable to hold her tears back. She had already lost Palvoy, the person she loved, and now she had lost a true friend, a friend that Palvoy had died trying to protect and one that she truly admired.

Kaelyn put her hand upon Orulla who was still weeping before getting down on one knee beside Oisin.

Her voice was broken while she spoke her last few words to her friend. "I will miss you, Oisin. You were a true Lealian, and you were true to others...to me...goodbye."

Her crying would not allow her to say anything else, so she did what any Lealian soldier would do for another. She placed her hand upon his face, closed her eyes and prayed that his soul would find the afterlife and find it well.

She had done this many times before, but this time she would not finish the prayer for she could feel something upon the palm of her hand. Ever so slightly she felt warm air tickling it. She pulled it back in shock.

"Orulla, Oisin breathes!" she yelled.

"Kaelyn, it is impossible with the wounds he has suffered. His chest alone was penetrated by three swords," Orulla responded.

"I know, Orulla. I know, but he is breathing! Look, look at the wounds on his chest. They are slowly closing, healing. I would not believe it if I was not here to witness it myself. Phanthus! Phanthus! Come here! Quickly!"

"What is it, Kaelyn?" asked Phanthus.

"He lives, Phanthus!" she excitedly yelled.

Phanthus couldn't believe it, but it was happening right before him. The wounds Oisin suffered were slowly healing. Before long his eyes opened, and he spoke.

"Phanthus, Kaelyn. What happened?" asked Oisin.

Phanthus was momentarily at a loss for words. The legends told by the Ancients were true. He would explain it to them in time, but for now, he just wanted to say his thanks for his life.

"To Oisin, may he live long in the comforts that Rhol will soon be able to offer him!" yelled Phanthus.

A great cheer could be heard across Solace, but the jubilation would not last long. Through the stormy weather, a Pegapire appeared in the distance carrying a Lealian warrior.

"Look!" cried Kaelyn. "It is Palto and Jayden!" More cheers rang out from the crowd that ran to embrace them as they landed but there would be no time for pleasantries. Palto immediately called for all the leaders. In minutes they gathered around him and Jayden.

"We have managed to hold the Phits down to the swamps. Our small army still engages them as we speak. We left the battle out of urgency to warn you of what approaches, of what we believe

Solharn controls, and what will probably destroy Rhol if he is not stopped. We can only hope that the boy was able to free Elissa's bonds, but it is looking dismal."

"Has she been found, Palto?" asked Phanthus.

"Yes, but Solharn's hold on her was stronger than anyone thought. The boy of earth and his friends are doing what they can. Unfortunately, we cannot wait. If she is not freed, then we will have to fight Solharn ourselves. The boy seems to possess powers which are beyond us. We can only hope they are enough to help us defeat Solharn. In the event they are not, we must preserve as much life as we can. Solharn has created significant storms which are making their way across Rhol. They destroy everything in their path. Tornados, lightning storms and torrential rains threaten to destroy us all. The storm you have been fighting in is but a mere glimpse of what is coming. Its full force will reach Solace in a short time. It has already devastated much of Rhol."

"What are we to do Palto?" Kaelyn asked.

"We have to get as many people as we can into the tunnels that lead to the Sacred Realm. It will be their only chance of survival. Issa, the Pegapires must work quickly. We must fly them to the entrance before it is too late."

"Over there!" shouted a Lealian warrior.

Behind them, a string of tornados, huge cycling torrents of wind, moved in over the mountains gathering size and speed as they devoured everything in their path.

"Quickly, gather everyone you can. Time is running out!" Palto yelled.

The Pegapires worked at a ferocious pace to get as many as possible to safety. If not for Phanthus they would not have been able to save everybody. He was able to carry great numbers on his back each time, giving them the advantage over the storm they needed.

Despite this, Palto's spirits were low. He looked out over the cliffs onto Solace. So many had fought so valiantly and died for their cause. It pained him to think it might have all been in vain. It was hard not to give up in defeat as he watched the beauty of Solace being torn to shreds at the hands of Solharn. It looked glum even for the people they managed to get to safety. What life would they lead in a world in which they were at Solharn's disposal?

"Where is your young rider, Palto?" asked Phanthus.

"He is with Kaelyn and the others. They are eagerly waiting for me to instruct them of our next move. I needed some time alone."

"I am sorry to interrupt," responded Phanthus as he turned to walk away.

"It is alright Phanthus. It's nice to have someone beside me that has been around for even longer than I."

"You look as though your thoughts are troubling you, Palto."

Palto did not respond; he merely continued staring ahead, watching as the storm grew larger gaining strength as it neared them.

"You and I have been around for centuries Palto. We have seen many things in our time. Things that one should never see, the extinction of a race, the struggle between good and evil, the struggle over power, over land that in the end was ours to nurture and protect. We have survived wars and hatred. We have fought against each other, killed for mere pieces of this world in a trivial struggle to cement our places in time. Yet, we always had one thing in common. We all lived here on Rhol. It is our world. We have come a long way Palto, for today we all fight together. We fight as one to protect what we have always cherished. I have seen things today that I never thought possible, new friendships forged. Perhaps today is our last day, but we will end our lives together, as one. It was not for nothing, Palto. It was for everything we should have been and are now."

"Your words, they are both heartfelt and genuine Phanthus, and you are right. Solharn tried to tear us apart, and instead, he has brought us together, and we will remain together as one, for Rhol. Let us end this."

Palto walked over to Jayden who was involved in a deep conversation with Kaelyn and Issa. Orulla and Oisin were also present along with Solko and Duffy. Phanthus slowly walked up behind them.

"Solko, Duffy, I am glad to see you safe. Solko, how is your sister?"

"She is doing well, Palto. She is attending to the wounded. She informed me that the Wall of Solace is no more. Its healing energies are gone."

"That does not bode well for us," responded Palto.

There was an awkward silence before he continued.

"It has been an honor and a privilege to fight alongside all of you. We have learned to work together and cast away our differences to save Rhol. As Phanthus so eloquently said to me earlier, we have become one. It is a bond that will last a lifetime. It is time to end this battle, to finish it before it finishes us. I have not received any word of Elissa, so I can only assume the worst. In any event, we can wait no longer. Orulla, I need you to stay here. I need you to take care of these people. To teach them what you know about the past and lead them on to a greater future, whatever that future may hold."

"But Palto," Orulla protested.

"I have my reasons Orulla, and I have given you your task," Palto sternly said, staring at her. She did not argue with her leader; instead, she turned and walked away in frustration.

"Issa, Solko I will need you to accompany me, to join the small army that awaits us in the swamps."

"I cannot speak for you three," Palto said looking at Kaelyn, Oisin, and Duffy. "Or for that matter you, my friend," Palto said glancing toward Jayden. "Of course I would welcome your company, but this decision is yours."

"Have you lost your senses, Palto? Of course, we are joining you. You are becoming far too emotional in your old age," Jayden said sarcastically.

Palto smiled. "It was a courtesy. I already knew the answer."

"Are you sure you will not change your mind about Orulla?" Oisin asked. "She has been my partner since saving me from the fields outside Kilto."

"Unfortunately, I cannot Oisin. But you deserve to know why. Orulla is too proud to tell you that she is nursing at least four broken ribs. She would not have the strength to make it. She tries to hide it even from me, but I have seen those types of injuries far too many times over the years to be deceived. Without the Wall of Solace to help her, she will be unable to fight."

"I did not realize. I should have done a better job protecting her."

"Do not blame yourself, Oisin. You were not with her. We were heading to help you in your fight to protect Phanthus. Duffy was well ahead of us, and I moved up the rear. At some point, I lost my footing and Orulla came to my aid. She placed herself in harm's way to save me from several Kaltaures. I have noticed her struggling ever since," Solko informed him.

"Then I shall remain here, with her and tend to her wounds," Oisin said.

"I was hoping you would ride with me, young warrior," Phanthus's voice boomed down from above.

"I am truly honored Phanthus, but I cannot leave Orulla, I owe her my life," Oisin responded.

Orulla overheard the conversation as she walked back toward Palto to apologize. "If it were you in my place, I would go Oisin. I appreciate your sentiments, but you will be of no use here. Go, ride with Phanthus. It is an honor which has never been bestowed on another living creature."

"Then it is settled," Palto said.

It took them much longer than expected to get back to the swamps. They couldn't take the direct route for the tornados that wreaked havoc in front of them blocked their way. They flew to the north of the mountains in a circle leading back to the swamps. It was a slow journey as they fought to avoid the worst of the storms.

They arrived to find that the swamps were now nothing but a wasteland of debris. The tornados had swallowed up most of everything, and everything they left behind lay twisted and torn, strewn over the ground around them. The rain had subsided slightly, and the tornados had moved on, taking their destructive paths to other parts of Rhol.

Bodies were strewn everywhere, Phits, Pegapires and Lealians alike. They had arrived too late. The storms and the battle had taken their toll. Palto swooped in low to the ground hoping to find some sign of survivors, but neither he nor Jayden could find any.

"The cavern, are you able to remove the debris, Phanthus? Perhaps some have sought refuge inside." Phanthus flew to the ground, and with one swipe of his tail, the opening was cleared. Jayden jumped off Palto and ran down the stairs followed closely by Duffy. They reappeared in moments.

"There is nothing, nothing!" Jayden yelled. "I should have stayed with them while you went to get help."

"We do not know what's happened, perhaps the boy and his friends escaped with Elissa," Duffy said.

"We would know if I had stayed, wouldn't we? Now we have no idea where they are or even if they still live!" Jayden yelled furiously.

"Jayden, please, your anger will not solve anything. We will simply have to keep looking," implored Kaelyn, trying to calm him down.

"We can fly in different directions, perhaps we will see them," Oisin suggested.

"We will see nothing. We can barely fly in this storm let alone see the ground from the skies. Look how long it took us to get here," Jayden shot back.

"And what would you suggest then, Jayden?" Issa yelled back angrily.

"Everyone, calm down!" Palto shouted. "It is not easy for any of us to witness our fallen warriors strewn across the ground and it certainly does not help to disrespect their efforts by arguing over their dead bodies."

Palto's words had struck a chord. Silence filled the air, the silence of mourning, the silence of not knowing. They felt as if they had been sucked into a void where nothing had changed. The wind still blew, and the rain still fell, thunder continued to echo across the skies, but they remained frozen in time waiting in the darkness for someone to break the silence. It was not words however that would renew their spirits. It was light, a light that pulsed with energy and one which charged their bodies and breathed life back into them; a light that burned blue. It was a Chiling which floated down upon them, giving them renewed hope.

CHAPTER THIRTY-NINE

Deke and Mary were holding hands. They walked along a path of darkness which brought them faint memories of years past. They had walked through the darkness before, down winding paths that led them to an escape from the life they were leading. A path they had made which they hoped would change their destiny, one that they could build their dreams upon, their hopes to live a normal life.

The path they walked down now was not much different, but it was a much bigger path that they walked today. It had a greater purpose, one which would not only change their destiny but the destiny of others, one where the dreams of many depended on how far they walked. It was a path that would lead to the hopes of others living a normal life. Yes, it was a much broader path, but it was still their path, their destiny and it would determine the fate of a world.

The smell of death drifted through the air becoming stronger the farther they walked. The ground crumbled in front of them trying desperately to hold them back. Trees and rocks caught in great torrents of wind flew all around them, spinning and turning with no particular place to go. Still, they walked, climbing the mountain that once was home to a little girl who loved to play along the shores of what once was a serene lake, Shimmer Lake. A lake, that was now home to a dark angel who was worse than death itself.

Solharn waited patiently for them. He could feel Deke as he neared. He could sense the power of the amulet. He snickered to himself knowing that if the boy still possessed the amulet, then he had been unable to free Elissa. Without Elissa's interference, Solharn would be able to convince the boy to join him, to follow his path. He relished the idea. He needed the boy or at the very least the amulet which the boy had, now more than ever.

They rounded the top of the mountain in silence, their hands tightly embraced. They were about to meet their destiny. It all felt oddly familiar to Deke. It was like déjà vu. He had seen this festering pool before, and he had watched Solharn manipulate it into the curse that was destroying Rhol. Strangely, his nerves remained intact. He could feel himself becoming stronger, a strange energy coursed through his veins making him feel as if nothing could stop him.

Mary obviously didn't feel the same. She kept up with him but the closer they came to Solharn and the turmoil that surrounded him, the tighter her grip became on Deke's hand.

"It will be okay, Mary," Deke said trying to comfort her.

"I'm fine," Mary lied. "He just looks so much more…lifeless, soulless, then the last time we met and the stench of death around him makes my stomach turn."

She was right. His face had changed from a pale white to almost entirely black. It bubbled as if something was fighting from the inside to break through his skin. His wings seemed to have no purpose any longer. Instead, black whisks of air swirled around him keeping him aloft. His fingers seemed to have stretched to an unnatural proportion, but it was only an illusion brought on by the strands of dark fluid streaming from the Blackpool into his body. His fingers were merely the portal. Slowly the strands of liquid began to shorten as he lowered himself to the ground.

"Concentrate, Deke. Remember her words," Mary whispered.

He hadn't forgotten them. Elissa had been very clear. Use everything you have at your disposal to occupy him, so his energy continues to diminish. The spell that he has cast over Rhol has already weakened him, but he is still much stronger than us, she had said. Deke only wished he had more at his disposal. They had been surprised to find that Palto and Jayden were not waiting for them when they emerged from the cavern, and could only assume they had died along with their fellow warriors. They had searched for survivors among the bodies strewn over the ground, but found none. Fortunately, they had not seen the bodies of Palto or Jayden among the dead, giving them at least a glimmer of hope.

"You are looking much better these days, Mary," Solharn laughed.

The sound of his voice sent shivers down her spine, and she could not help but gag from the stench of his breath.

"Never mind her, Solharn. We both know this is not about Mary!" Deke yelled.

"It is about whatever I want it to be, boy. Look around; I command Rhol now!" Solharn screamed through the darkness.

Deke noticed his voice had changed slightly. It was still a low whine of sorts, but it reverberated through the air. The more excited Solharn became, the larger the storms surrounding him grew. Lightning struck out all around him, waves of poison rose from the Blackpool and slithered their way up the shoreline, wrapping themselves around his feet.

Deke could hear Elissa's voice from deep within him. "Keep engaging him, Deke."

"Last time I looked, it was Queen Elissa who ruled this world!" taunted Deke.

"Elissa!" Solharn yelled, enraged at the suggestion. "Elissa will never see the light of day again. You were her last hope, Deke Brolin and you failed her. You all failed her! You could not have been prepared for the curse I imprisoned her within, even if you had the tenacity to find her. You are weak boy. You stand here before me with the Amulet of Rhol wrapped around your scrawny neck and think you, a mere mortal, can take Elissa's place. Think again, boy, and think carefully. Your future depends on it. The only reason I continue to allow you to grace my presence is because it humors me."

There was no better time than now, Deke thought. He signaled Mary, and together they began to concentrate, melding their minds together. Deo emerged as a Cawlaway and flew in behind Solharn poised to attack. Delca came in from above. She had decided to take on the form of a Balane, the animal that had once defeated her and left her at Solharn's mercy.

Unfortunately, Solharn had already predicted this trap. He stretched one arm behind him and one straight above, his eyes never left Deke's, his malicious smile never changed. A great globe of darkness flew from his hand and encompassed Delca. Solharn whipped her around as if she were nothing more than a brief annoyance to him. He laughed at Deke, antagonizing him.

"Let her go!" Mary yelled.

"As you wish," Solharn grinned.

He released her, spinning through the air, entrapped within the sphere of dark energy. She struck the side of the mountain, but not before the energy around her dissipated so as not to break her fall. Mary broke away from Deke and looked on in horror as Delca's true form took shape. One of her arms was twisted awkwardly backward, and her leg appeared to dangle aimlessly below her knee. She was not moving, but she was still breathing. Mary could feel her. She was still alive, but in desperate need of help. Instinctively, she ran to her aid.

Deo wouldn't reach Solharn either. He was within feet of him when he was met with a wall of dark energy that rolled along the ground toward him. He was too close to change his path and was hit with the full force of the black wall. It knocked him spiraling back, spinning helplessly through the air toward the depths of the Blackpool. In unison, Solharn arched his free hand to the ground releasing an orb of energy deep within it. The sphere tore a path down under the soil toward Deke. Rocks and debris became weapons, soaring through the air toward him. Deke was forced to run, forced to break his concentration.

Deo would no longer have the one advantage that may have helped him from the pool's vicious waters. He lost his size, but more importantly his wings, as he transformed into his former self and plummeted into the dark murky waters of the Blackpool.

"Deoooo!" Deke screamed in vain.

Deo disappeared within a rolling wave. He struggled to stay afloat, but the liquid was unlike water. It was thick; it felt alive. Tentacles of the dark liquid stretched over his body like tiny veins and began pulling him down into its depths. He began to experience extreme anger, numbness and a feeling of emptiness.

Deke could feel Deo's anger, his anguish, but at the same time, he felt a sense of extreme intensity, unbridled power. He could hear a familiar voice within him, Elissa's voice.

"Hold on, Deke. Do not be drawn into Solharn's trap. Your mind is your own, and only you control it."

Deo struggled to keep his head above the water. The tentacles had twisted around his legs binding them together. His arms were burning. He could feel the water on his face, feel it strangling him, pulling him in deeper and deeper. He took a breath of air and held it. He was quite sure it would be his last.

Deke suddenly felt like a part of him was gone. It was as if he had been abandoned. Solharn sensed this right away. He could see it in Deke's face just as he had seen it in the faces of the countless others who had lost part of themselves. Solharn loved to look into the eyes of his victims when he ripped their paladins, their spirit away from them. He knew Deke would be easily swayed now.

"You cannot defeat me, boy. Did you really believe that I would fall for the same ploy again? I knew exactly where your paladins were; you never stood a chance. You have been left to face me alone, brought here to save the world to which you owe nothing, the world that has used you to carry out an impossible task. It is not too late for you though. Think about it Deke. I am the only one that can help you reach your true potential. Join me, and we will control the balance. We do not need their help, but we can help each other."

Solharn was right. Deke was here alone. Nobody of Rhol was here to help him. They had left him here to fight the Dark Angel alone. He had waited a long time to find his path, the path that would lead him to the destiny he deserved. He began to walk toward Solharn. He had made his decision.

Ω

The Chiling that had led them to this place suddenly evaporated into the mist as they flew over the crest of Mount Sibileo. They had flown in from the opposite side of the lake. Had they come the other way, Palto never would have seen Deo fall into its dark waters. It was almost as if the Chiling had sensed the impending danger to a lost soul. Palto flew straight for him, but Deo was pulled under the water before they arrived.

"We have lost him, Jayden!"

"Not yet!" Jayden said diving into the Blackpool.

"Jayden!" Palto yelled while turning around to scour the black waters for any sign of him.

Jayden knew he had one opportunity. He dove as deep as he could, still cognizant that he would have to swim back to the surface

273

on a single breath of air. There was no point in opening his eyes. He would be blind either way. He could only hope that he had picked the exact spot where Deo had gone under. He was not disappointed as his hands felt the unmistakable feeling of hair. He had no time to be polite about it and pulled Deo to the surface by his mane. The waters were wavy. Jayden looked in desperation for Palto but saw only Phanthus. The dragon circled them once coming to a stop in midair, then lowered his tail into the water.

Jayden could hear Oisin yelling for him to grab on. He swam toward them, towing Deo behind. Oisin was yelling for him to hurry. He could hear strange familiar noises as he swam. He concentrated trying to recall the sound, a very particular sound...all of the sudden it came to him. It was the unmistakable sound of arrows slicing through the surface of the water.

He wondered where they came from and looked to Oisin for answers. He was standing on Phanthus madly stringing and firing, arrow after arrow, at a lightning fast pace. A sick feeling began to grow within his stomach, and he swam faster, using all the strength he had left to give. Finally, he managed to hook an arm around the dragon's massive tail. His other arm remained coiled around Deo. Oisin's bow did not relent as Phanthus began to drag them through the water towards the shore.

Jayden could see now what would surely have been a painful death for him and Deo. Floating on the water behind him, he could see that a great number of Freta had succumbed to Oisin's arrows. The remnants of them frantically pierced the surface of the water and dove back in trying to gather enough speed to close the distance between them and their prey. Jayden was more than happy to see that they could not keep up with the dragon's speed. The Freta were a vicious enough fish when they were not consumed with the dark liquid that now filtered its way through their gills. They were made up mostly of teeth, long needle like protrusions that were inches long. Their bones grew on the outside of their long slender forms making them look as if they had already died once and come back for more.

Jayden was relieved when he felt the familiar sensation of sand scraping his legs as they were dragged up onto shore. He released his grip on Phanthus and came to a rolling stop. Jayden quickly waved his thanks and ran to Deo's side. Deo was not moving and lay face down in the sand. He quickly turned him over surprised to find him laughing, laughing as if he were demented. His eyes were the color of coal, lifeless black specks that stared right through him.

Ω

Phanthus flew straight for Solharn, approaching him from behind. He could see that Deke was under his spell. He was walking toward Solharn in a daze.

"Oisin, we must distract the Dark Angel. I do not know whether we were able to get Deo out of the Blackpool in time to save him. Deke may have lost his paladin, and without Deo, his mind will be easily manipulated by Solharn."

The storms Solharn had created provided the noise Phanthus needed to move in undetected, and Issa and Kaelyn provided the distraction. They had seen Phanthus coming and knew he had a far better chance of causing damage to Solharn than they. Selflessly, they made themselves decoys by flying directly in front of him.

The distraction worked, but it would not have the effect they anticipated. Solharn had felt the heat of the fire behind him long before it reached its destination. He was able to create a vortex of sorts that sucked the flames into its cavity. Solharn was enraged, and Issa became the focus of his anger.

They were flying away, but they would not escape his wrath. Great orbs of energy formed between his hands and were catapulted toward them at an alarming rate. Issa maneuvered around the first three, but could not evade the fourth. It struck her wing causing her to spiral helplessly to the ground. She managed to slow her descent somewhat, but the impact would break her front legs and cause Kaelyn to fly off, somersaulting through the air. Kaelyn hit the ground and skidded across the dirt trying desperately to grab on to anything she could to slow her pace. It would be the last thing she remembered before slipping into unconsciousness.

Moments later, she awoke. Her entire body was aching, and blood covered much of her face and hands. Her nose throbbed from being twisted into such an unnatural position, and the skin of her

275

fingers looked as if it had been peeled back from her flesh. A short distance away she could make out the body of Issa, lying motionless on the ground and ran to her side. She had sustained the brunt of the fall. Her front legs looked deformed; her white coat appeared brown from the dirt and blood which covered it.

"Issa, Issa speak to me," Kaelyn begged.

Issa moved her head slightly. She was glad to see Kaelyn had survived. "Kaelyn, leave me. You must stop Deke. Solharn cannot gain possession of the Amulet or him."

"Stop him?" questioned Kaelyn.

"Kaelyn, you saw the same thing I did before we were hit. Deke no longer controls his actions."

"We don't know that Issa. We...."

"Kaelyn, you do know! You just don't want to admit it! Nobody wants to admit it is over, but it is, and Solharn must never possess the amulet. If it is given to him, he will be able to use its powers."

Kaelyn did not answer. She could not comprehend what Issa was saying to her. She did not want to comprehend it.

"Look at him, Kaelyn!" Issa shrieked. "Look at Deke! He is standing in front of Solharn. He is no longer in control!"

Kaelyn stood up from her kneeling position. "I will be back for you, Issa," Kaelyn said.

She could see her sword lying on the ground a few feet away and began to walk toward it. Tears streamed down her cheeks as she bent down and picked it up. She stood there looking at it for several seconds, wiped the tears from her eyes and then she began to run toward Deke.

Ω

"Phanthus, behind us!" Oisin yelled.

Phanthus turned hoping that he would not see what he had been dreading all along. He knew it was coming as soon as Solharn laid eyes upon him. They were the only creatures that were relatively his size and strength. To make matters worse, there were two of them, and they were both possessed with the darkness. Solharn had sent the Balane in pursuit of him.

It was not that he was afraid to fight, but these large animals were normally peaceful. They were not acting on their own accord just as he had not when he had been cursed with the same fate. Complicating things, even more, was the fact that the Balane were quite nearly extinct themselves. He could not fight something that did not act of its own volition. Nor could he end their lives knowing that he would be responsible for the extinction of their race. He could see Oisin was readying himself for battle. He was placing his arrows in front of him for easy access.

"Put your arrows away, Oisin. This is not a battle that we will be able to fight."

"But Phanthus, these creatures look crazed! They are not the Balane that we are typically accustomed to," he pleaded.

"You are right about that, but it is not their fault. They know not what they do. They are under Solharn's control. I will not be responsible for their deaths," Phanthus answered, maneuvering through the skies to avoid them.

"Okay, what are we to do then?"

"The only thing we can; lead them away from the others. The Balane cannot fly long distances so perhaps they will turn away eventually. Until that time, we will do our best to avoid coming into contact with them. Keep me apprised of where they are should they get close."

Phanthus continued to fly up and around the mountain cliffs and gullies surrounding Mount Sibileo in an attempt to avoid the Balane. He led them to the far side of the lake away from the others. Oisin kept him informed of how close they were getting, and Phanthus would adjust his speed accordingly while ripping over the mountain and back around. The Balane never relented; their minds were no longer their own. Oisin had seen a Balane before, but not like these. The red crimson colour surrounding their eyes seemed to be burned right into their skin. They had no control over their jaws which continuously snapped in the air searching for something, anything to clamp down upon. They were mad with hunger and hatred. They screeched and bawled as their bodies twirled and twisted through the air trying to get closer.

Oisin had to look again to be sure, but when Phanthus came around the last cliff, he could only see one Balane behind them.

"Phanthus, we have lost one of the Balane. Only one pursues us now!" Oisin yelled.

"Perhaps it turned ba... "

It had not turned back. It had come around the front of them and was hurtling through the air toward them. They were caught in between the two crazed animals. Phanthus dove quickly but he would not escape the Balane's jagged teeth which clamped down on his neck, sending him spiraling downward through the air.

Ω

Deke could feel the rage building up inside of him as the distance closed between him and Solharn. He tried to shut Elissa out of his mind, but he couldn't. "Deke, do not lose yourself. Remember who you are! Remember what you have learned about Solharn! Do not lose yourself."

Deke stopped and grabbed his head. "Stop it. I have not lost myself. I have been found. This is what I want; it is what I need."

"Who are you talking to boy? What are you waiting for? Come to me! Fulfill your destiny," Solharn droned.

Elissa's voice would not relent. "Do not listen to him, Deke. Remember what your focus is. Remember your true path."

"I've decided my path," yelled Deke as he started once again to walk toward Solharn.

"Yes boy, come, and our paths will join. We will be one," Solharn responded, thinking Deke was talking to him.

Deke reached out for Solharn's hand. Mary yelled for him to stop, but her voice was only a distant echo to him.

Ω

Deo hissed and rolled over taking Jayden with him, pinning him to the ground. Black veins branched out across his face. His mouth was open, and he was screeching. His breath smelled like a rotting corpse. Deo's hands were wrapped around Jayden's neck, choking the life out of him. Jayden struggled to breathe. He was slipping into unconsciousness and was seconds from death.

He thought he was dreaming as he watched a cloaked figure approach Deo from behind and place a hand on his shoulder. Deo immediately became silent. Jayden watched as the black veins slowly disappeared from his face and his eyes faded from black to their regular ashen grey. Air began to fill Jayden's lungs. He could breathe again. Deo still sat on top of him. Realizing he had done something horrible, he began to apologize profusely, but Jayden was more interested in the figure that he had seen.

"Deo, it is fine. I know it was not your doing but please get off."

Deo immediately rose apologizing once again. "Never mind, Deo. Did you see somebody? Anybody?"

"I saw only you Jayden, no one else," Deo responded.

Palto landed beside them. "Jayden, Deo. Are you alright?"

"We are fine. Did you see a figure by us Palto?" Jayden asked.

"No, only you and Deo. Why?"

"I saw somebody, something," Jayden answered.

"You can figure it out later, Jayden. We must move quickly. The others await us, and Deke needs our help. Quickly, both of you climb on."

Ω

With Deo's revival, Deke suddenly felt normal again, if only for a fleeting moment. He felt rejuvenated as if his outer spirit had returned to him. He could see clearly again and took a step back when he realized how close he was to Solharn. The words of Elissa came flooding back to him; they had meaning once again. No longer were her words drawn and incoherent. She was repeating the same thing over and over again trying to bring him back.

It wouldn't last though; it couldn't. Solharn's hold over him was too strong. He took a step toward Deke and stretched his hand out toward him. "Are you ready, Deke! Are you willing to begin the next phase of your life?" Solharn preached.

"I am," Deke responded.

CHAPTER FORTY

Palto could see that Deke was no longer who he once was. He had taken the amulet from his neck. He was going to relinquish it to Solharn. Palto realized that hope for Rhol was evaporating before his very eyes. Without the boy of earth, everything would be lost. They could not fight Solharn without him or Elissa. Palto could never relinquish himself to the Dark Angel. Nor could he allow the Sacred Amulet of Rhol to fall into Solharn's hands. That would be blasphemy.

It was apparent that Kaelyn had come to the same conclusion. He could see her running toward Deke with her sword poised to strike, but she was too far away to get to him in time.

Palto tried desperately to communicate with Deke through telepathy, trying to convince him to back away from Solharn, but Deke did not appear responsive. With a heavy heart, Palto came to a decision. There would be no time to save the boy and even if he could, what kind of life would he have. He was Solharn's now, and there was nobody left who had the power to remove that curse. No, Palto knew this boy well enough to know that he would prefer death to a life in which Solharn controlled him. He also knew Deo would never let the boy die, not knowingly. So Palto did not reveal his intention to Deo or Jayden as he made his final descent.

Ω

Solharn could feel the power of the amulet. It was so close he could practically taste it. "I am glad to see you have finally come to your senses, Deke. We will be an unstoppable force. You will have what you have always craved, a life with no worries in which you and only you command. You will finally have the life that you deserve. You possess an extraordinary gift Deke, and it will grow over time. Now, you depend too much on the Amulet of Rhol as the source of your power. You must learn to nurture your powers first, without depending on the amulet. Only then will you understand its full potential. Only then will you be able to manipulate its powers. It will make you the most powerful being in all of the five worlds. Isn't that what you want to be? Isn't that what you crave?"

"Yes, I can see it now. I had not realized it until this moment, but it is all I have ever wanted," Deke answered.

"Then you will have it, Deke Brolin, but first you must give me the amulet. It is too tempting for you to use and too valuable a tool to leave in anybody else's hand but mine. When you are ready, when I have taught you all you need to know and understand, then and only then, will I return the amulet to you and then you will realize your full potential, your destiny."

Deke reached for the chain around his neck and removed it. He did not notice Solharn drooling at the prospect of finally possessing one of the five items that would make him a king, a god amongst the minions that inhabited the five worlds.

Ω

Jayden was puzzled. His father had taught him everything about combat and war. He had spent countless days patiently explaining every technique a Pegapire uses in battle. His father had emphasized how important it was to understand them so that Jayden would be able to fight alongside a Pegapire, as a team, as one, as it was meant to be.

That was why he was confused. Palto was flying far too fast to be able to effect a rescue. His body was poised in such a way that it suggested he was moving in for a kill. His ears were pinned back, his wings were cupped, and his muscles were tense. These were all signs of an impending attack but he was not heading for Solharn, he was closing in on Deke.

"Palto, what are you doing?" Jayden asked.

Palto did not answer confirming that Jayden's memory had not failed him. "Palto, no! This is not the way to end this!" Jayden screamed.

"It is the only way," Palto answered.

"Only way to what? Jayden, what are you two talking about?" Deo asked.

"Palto, you cannot do this!" Jayden repeated.

"Do what?" Deo yelled in confusion.

"Kill, Deke! He is moving in to kill Deke!"

"What? Kill him! Palto, no! You are making a huge mistake. Listen to me!"

"I did not expect you to agree with my decision Deo. But my decision has been made," Palto retorted.

Deo was panicking. He was told not to mention Elissa under any circumstances for fear Solharn would find out.

"You do not understand, Palto...it is what was supposed to happen...Elissa..."

Palto would hear nothing of it. "Elissa is but a dream now, Deo. Deke could not save her. This war is over. It is the end."

He was nearing Deke at a ferocious pace. Deo could not believe that it had come to this after everything they had gone through, everything they had accomplished. It couldn't end this way.

"Jayden, do something!" Deo begged.

But there was nothing he could do. Palto would not change his mind; it was not in his nature. He was a leader, and as such, he would make the decision that he felt best served his people and he would deal with the consequences of that decision later. That's what made him who he was.

As Palto soared in for the kill, a blinding flash of light exploded in front of them. Palto was forced to change his course. The power of the blast knocked Deo backward. If not for his feet catching Jayden's legs, he would have toppled off the back of the mighty Pegapire. Jayden had managed to hold on. He was searching the skies trying to determine the source of the light that had suddenly pierced through the darkness. He looked past the place he had last seen Solharn and Deke. His eyes followed the ridgeline of the great mountain that formed the backdrop of their battleground. He was sure he saw something or someone standing there. He cupped his hand above his eyes trying to shade the light that was so desperately trying to blind him and confirmed what he had seen. There, high on the ridge stood a cloaked figure that remained motionless, poised against the rage of the winds that threatened this world. The same cloaked figure that he had seen before was once again revealing itself to him. This time, however, the figure did not gaze upon him. It gazed down upon what was the final battle of Rhol, the battle that would determine the fate of everyone.

Ω

Delca was in extreme pain, but she would live. Duffy had spotted Mary from the air and was desperately trying to protect her from the objects which the wind hurtled through the air toward them. He cringed as he watched a tree soar through the air just over their heads and come crashing down behind their place of refuge. Solko flew down to them immediately.

They all tried desperately to move Delca, but her body was far too weak and broken. A mere touch of her skin caused her to scream in pain.

"She cannot be moved. We will be alright Duffy. Help the others! Help Deke! I am not sure that he controls his actions anymore," Mary said desperately.

Duffy just smiled at her. "We will not leave you here to die like this," he said driving the Cortuc into the ground and creating a half dome shield around them. He could not have timed it better as a huge boulder broke away from the mountain and toppled over the shield.

Delca felt the effects of the shield immediately. Without the wind and the rain, she felt warm again, and her trembling body relaxed. Slowly her pain relented enough for her exhausted body to rest.

"Thank you, Duffy, Solko. I am indebted," Mary said.

"Nonsense," Solko said looking down upon her. "Everyone has a role on this day, and ours is here with..."

"Oh, god!" Mary whispered under her breath.

Solko could see that her expression had abruptly transformed from one of relief to one of panic. He turned to see what caused the unexpected change. He saw Issa, distressed and badly injured. She was trying frantically to slow her descent as Kaelyn fought to hold on to her. He watched in dismay as her body struck the ground with such force that it seemed unlikely that either would survive.

"Duffy, drop the shield! I have to help them!" Solko begged.

The shield vanished allowing Solko to escape its confines. He quickly leapt from the ground and took flight.

"Solko, look out!" Duffy yelled, but the wind whistling around Solko's ears prevented him from heeding the warning. He didn't see it coming, and was crushed instantly by a jagged boulder that fell from above.

"Duffy...I am so sorry...," Mary sadly said.

Duffy could not grieve at that moment. His anger toward Solharn had taken over his emotions. There was a long distance separating him from the cause of his anguish, but Solharn was not so far away that Duffy couldn't see him. The more he stared at the Dark Angel, the more his anger grew. This was Solharn's doing, all of it. He had wiped out Duffy's entire family and brought pain and misery to all who lived on Rhol. He had practically destroyed it. It seemed to Duffy that even Deke, who was now standing in front of him, had succumbed to Solharn's evil and now Solharn had taken Solko, his friend. He had to have his revenge, his reckoning with this scourge. He looked at Mary and then at Delca whom she was comforting.

Mary looked into his eyes and inquisitively called his name. The sound of her voice resonated through him. If he left them, they would die, but if he didn't, he would never have another chance to avenge Rhol.

He would not have to make the decision he was lamenting over, for a sudden explosion of blinding light burst across the terrain and continued over the mountain top taming the dark skies. The light gave him hope, if only just for a moment. For in those fleeting seconds he had caught a glimpse of what would be their redemption.

Ω

Phanthus managed to gain control once again, but the injury slowed his speed drastically. The Balane had still not given up their pursuit and were almost upon him.

"Oisin, I am heading for the ground. I want you to get off. I will deal with the Balane," Phanthus yelled.

"You mean you will die at the hands of the Balane. No! I will not leave you Phanthus!" Oisin screamed back.

"You are stubborn, Oisin. I owe you my life, and now I am paying you back. We cannot win, Oisin. I will not fight these creatures. There is no point in both of us dying."

"There is no point in trying to make it to the ground either, Phanthus. They are already upon us."

Phanthus swerved quickly to the side and turned in midair, all the while creating a circle of fire around them. The Balane swerved up and around the flames in an attempt to avoid them.

"Now, we are heading for the ground Oisin. Do not argue with me."

Oisin might have tried to argue, but he would not have the time as a wave of light encompassed them. He watched the Balane as they too reacted to the light. They seemed confused as to why they were flying. Their eyes once again returned to the familiar and soothing blue color. They once more seemed to be what he had always known them as, peaceful. Bewildered, they turned away from Oisin and Phanthus and flew back toward the Blackpool.

"Phanthus, they have retreated. The light, it has affected them somehow. Where is it coming from?"

Phanthus did not know, but the light had revealed something else to him. A stranger was standing high on a ridge of Mount Sibileo. The stranger wore a cloak that disguised their face and body making him wary of their intent. He maneuvered himself so that the mountain would hide them as he approached. He glided silently in from behind the shadowy figure, and landed a good distance back to allow himself time to react should he have to.

Oisin remained poised on the back of Phanthus. He too had now seen what had captured Phanthus' curiosity.

The cloak was the only movement that they could discern as it waved aimlessly at them in the wind. The individual it hid remained motionless, abnormally so. Phanthus walked forward, continuing to measure the distance that he would need to effectively mount an attack if it was required. As the distance closed between them, he became far less cautious. Something was drawing him in. He felt a connection of some sort. Before he realized it, mere feet separated them. Still, the figure had not moved.

"I am thankful that you recognized your true spirit, Phanthus. It could not have been easy considering what the fear and ignorance of others did to your heritage, to your family."

Phanthus was astonished. There was no mistaking that voice, the voice that was so pure, so calming and angelic. It was the voice that had spoken to his very soul the night Solharn had taken her away. It was the voice of Queen Elissa. Oisin remained silent while Phanthus spoke. He could not believe who stood before his eyes.

"Queen Elissa? How? How, did you come to be here? How did you escape?" inquired Phanthus.

She still had not turned or moved as she stared out over Rhol.

"I am sure both of us have stories to tell of a time when darkness consumed us and how we came to escape it, Phanthus. But those tales would take far too long to detail, and in the end, they would not matter. What really matters is how we use our newfound freedom to release those souls that remain trapped within themselves, fighting for an opportunity to escape what will eventually consume them."

"What can I do, Queen Elissa? Just say the word," Phanthus responded.

"Fly away."

"But why your Majesty? We can help! We want to help!" Phanthus begged.

"You will, Phanthus. You and Oisin both will. You are one now. You are Dragon Warriors."

"Your Majesty?" Oisin asked inquisitively.

"You were brought back to life by the tear of a dragon Oisin. A dragon can only use one tear in their lifetime to save someone, and

287

when that happens, it bonds them for life. It is a bond that can never be broken, not even in death," explained Elissa.

Oisin looked at Phanthus. "You did not tell me, Phanthus, that you sacrificed something so cherished to save me. Why?"

"It was not important Oisin. You were alive, and that was all that mattered to me. I did not want to burden you with having to choose between Orulla and me."

"I chose to ride with you Phanthus, and I still do, wherever that journey may take us."

"Then heed my words Phanthus, Oisin. You will fly to the people of Kilto, to their sanctuary. Even if all else is lost, they must be protected. They will be the last survivors of Solharn's fight for Rhol. They are also the most spiritual. Only they will be able to guide the lost souls who search for their salvation if I am gone. Protect them to your dying breath, protect them as your ancestors protected them and I will be forever grateful to you."

"Our ancestors?" Oisin inquired.

"Yes, your ancestors, the Dragon Warriors of Rhol. It is your heritage. It was what made you what you are now. The Dragon Warriors were guardians of the Kilto long ago, in ancient times. Each dragon had a warrior who rode with them before ignorance turned their fate around before hate nearly brought them to extinction, but ignorance fortunately failed. It forgot about you Phanthus, and you, Oisin. You come from a bloodline of warriors who died along with their dragons. That is why you never knew your parents or your relatives. It was forbidden to speak of. Both of your bloodlines are joined again. Now, you must go and fulfill your destinies, the destinies of your people."

"And you, Elissa?" Phanthus asked.

She turned and looked at them. "I will fulfill mine," she answered, evaporating before their eyes.

CHAPTER FORTY-ONE

Deke could still hear Elissa's serene voice guiding him, trying to ensure that his mind did not fall victim to the dark magic, the enticements, and the promises Solharn preached. She had told him that it would be the most difficult temptation he would ever face. She warned him that he would struggle with the decision whether to join Solharn or stay true to himself. She reassured him that she would be with him and that he would hear her voice guiding him, but she had also warned him that there would be times when he would not listen to her, that he would try desperately to drown her out. She cautioned him that, as the distance closed between him and the Dark Angel, the temptation of relenting to the darkness would become far stronger.

Deke held the amulet in his hand. He knew what he was supposed to do, what Elissa had told him to do, but was it fair? Was it fair to deny him a life of power, a place in history? That life was within his reach. It lay at his fingertips at this very moment. He could become more powerful than Solharn. He could rule the worlds. What harm would there be in that? He was a good person. He would not be too hard on his subordinates. Everyone would be satisfied with the life they led. They would worship him and if they didn't, then and only then, would he release his wrath upon them.

Elissa's voice was becoming much fainter now, a distant whisper in the back of his mind. Deke held the amulet in his hand, and he felt the power surging through his body as Solharn wrapped his long slender fingers under the chain. They were connected. The feeling was overwhelming and revitalizing. It was unlike anything he had ever felt before, a feeling that he had always yearned for. He could still just make out Elissa's voice. How dare she interrupt this moment with her trivial blabber.

"Concentrate, Deke. Do not forget what we spoke of. Do not forget the purpose of your journey. Do not forget why you made this your journey. Your fate lies with the light, not the darkness," Elissa's voice rang out.

What was she talking about? He remembered everything she had told him. He considered her warnings, but it was his choice to make and his alone.

Elissa could read Deke's thoughts. "You have not remembered everything Deke. You are right that the choice is yours, but you cannot make that choice until you have weighed it against all the choices you have already made."

She was desperate now, Deke thought. It made no sense. What choices was she referring to and what did it matter. He could barely hear her now, and it wouldn't be long before she was gone. Then he could concentrate once again on his new life, his new path.

Elissa's voice became broken and faint. "The path Deke, the reason...you...path...Mary..." and then her voice was gone.

Deke laughed. 'What path?" he said aloud.

Solharn looked at him strangely thinking, once again, that Deke was speaking to him. "The path? The path is through me Deke. Remember what I told you. You have much to learn, but with my mentoring, you would become everything that you have dreamed of. You must give me the amulet and then you can start to walk the path you seek, the path to power, the easy path."

That sounded very familiar to Deke, the easy path. Where had he heard that before? Elissa had mentioned a path...or a journey...or was it a reason for his journey? He was so confused. Why did Solharn's words bother him so much? What else had Elissa said? He asked himself, scouring his mind for answers. Mary, she had mentioned a person named Mary. She was his friend. Now he remembered. A lost friend, but he had found her. Yes! He had found her, and that was the reason he started this journey. That was what Elissa was referring to. He had tried to run away from her memory. He had taken the easy path. That was it! He had already walked an easy path, and that path led to a life of misery and loneliness. It was the next path that he had taken, the harder path, which had led him to his friend. That was the path that had brought him redemption. He did not want to take the easy path. He did not want anything to do with it, nor did he want anything to do with Solharn.

"Are you listening boy!" Solharn roared.

"Yes, yes I am," Deke responded.

"Well?" Solharn bellowed.

Deke would not answer. He couldn't hear Solharn anymore. He was in control. His mind was his own, and he would use it to follow his true path.

Elissa's voice spoke to him once again, and this time it was clear, clearer than it ever had been before. "Now, Deke. If you are still with me, now is the time."

He loosened his grip upon the amulet and looked down upon it lying in the palm of his hand. Then he released it, not the amulet itself, but the power within it, the energy of the souls. A great explosion of light burst through the amulet's core and followed its natural path.

The chain provided the necessary conduit to Solharn. The light streamed through Solharn's body and exited through his eyes and mouth. Anywhere the energy could escape, it did, and it did not stop. It exploded across the mountain, across Rhol.

Kaelyn had arrived bearing her sword, but it was no longer poised to strike. It just dangled in her hand as she watched what was transpiring in front of her.

Palto soared in behind her and stopped. His passengers jumped off, more than happy to feel the soil beneath their feet, but unsure of what was happening in front of them.

They could see that Solharn's energy was depleting and that Deke, who still held the amulet, was the source of his turmoil.

Solharn's speech was garbled, almost robotic. "You are too late, boy. You cannot defeat me. You will never defeat me. You may have released the energy of the souls and taken back that which was mine, but the power of the abyss will never be yours. It will never be at your disposal and will always be at mine."

Solharn fell to his knees unable to pull his hand from the chain that was fused to him, propelling the energy of the souls through his body. He bowed his head and placed his other hand upon the ground making it appear as if he was using it to support himself. He used whatever strength he could muster to call silently to the Abyss, the Blackpool. Slowly the dark liquid emerged from the pool and slithered across the ground toward his hand.

He would keep them occupied with his garbled banter as the darkness glided closer and closer to his fingertips. He laughed inside of himself knowing that they were oblivious to the wrath that he would unleash upon them in moments. He still was unable to move, but he could feel the energy of the Abyss as it inched its way towards his fingers.

They just stood there staring, waiting for him to surrender. They were all fools. Had they learned nothing about him, nothing about his power? They did not respect him as they all should have, but they would respect him soon enough, he mused to himself.

The dark liquid, the dark energy, wrapped its way around his fingers and gradually began to stream into his body. He was connected again to the dark power he commanded, to the dark energy that only he could conjure and control. He did not let on as his strength slowly returned. They were so easily deceived. He felt whole again. It was time to reveal to them all, that he could never be defeated. It was he and he alone who would command the balance.

Nobody could see the grin crackle its way across Solharn's face. He would take care of the boy first. It was a shame that he would have to die. He could have been such a useful tool. But Solharn knew he would have to break the connection between himself and the boy before he could unleash his unbridled essence upon them. For that to happen, he would have to kill him.

He pulled the chain toward him and lunged forward in the same motion. Solharn had not seen it coming. As he stared into those eyes, he knew that it was over, at least for Rhol. He had misjudged the situation. He had created what would be their redemption. He had defeated himself. It was over, and he only realized it when he looked into her eyes. The boy no longer held the amulet, she did. She had predicted that Solharn would call on the Blackpool, to regain his dark energy and with it, the power he so desperately craved. She had patiently waited for that very moment, timing it down to the last second.

In the boy's hands, the energy of the amulet could be unleashed. In the hands of an angel, it became the opposite. It became a portal that separated positive energy from negative. In the hands of Elissa, the amulet became a portal that dispensed with the energy of the evil by sending it spiraling into the Black Abyss and one that replenished and redistributed the energy of the good.

Solharn watched as the dark energy that he had conjured from the Black Abyss to form the Blackpool, to form his portal to this world, drained slowly from the lake and travelled through him, through his body. He had called for the darkness to come to him. He had conjured it, and then he had commanded it to consume the boy as only he could have.

He had not seen Elissa take hold of the amulet. Unwittingly he had sent the darkness to her. He had commanded the dark energy, and it had obeyed. It had travelled through him and found the most natural path to the boy, through the chain that Kiran had given to Deke to safeguard the amulet, but the boy no longer held the amulet, she did. She held the amulet, and in her hands, it was a portal. The portal could not be closed. Once the portal took possession of the energy it was connected to; it determined the final destination of the dark energy.

The Blackpool was no longer. Its dark waters were whisked away through the portal leaving Shimmer Lake whole again. The last thread of darkness wound its way toward Solharn from the lake. He looked at Elissa. He still could not fathom how she, someone so inferior to him, had prevailed. The last of the darkness disappeared as it siphoned its way through his fingers, through him and finally through the chain. His time had come.

"The abyss cannot hold me, Elissa. This is not finished," scoffed Solharn.

"It is for Rhol," she answered.

He could foresee what was coming next. He knew what he was, but more importantly what he wasn't. He no longer existed as he once did. He no longer possessed a soul. That was why he craved the souls of others. He was possessed with a dark malevolence and filled with nothing but the desire for power and supremacy. He was simply energy of the darkest kind, and as such, he slowly evaporated into the Amulet of Rhol.

CHAPTER FORTY-TWO

Throughout Leal, Aura and then further on to Tamon the light streaked through the dark skies illuminating them once again.

On Mount Kartago all the way through to Solace and right across Rhol itself, the light that was the energy of the souls cascaded across the land, releasing the energy which Solharn had ensnared.

The storms and the squalls slowly dissipated. They had reveled in Solace, utterly astounded, as they watched the light roll across the skies toward the tornados that were destroying their world. It was staggering to look upon the light as it ripped through the very core of each and every twister. The bluish color of the energy of the souls intertwined with the dark energy, swirling around in a bitter fight to overtake one another was something to behold. In the end, the dark energy succumbed to the energy of the souls, leaving for what was only a few seconds, a blue tornado that stood stationary before becoming a mere breeze drifting gently over the vast terrain.

The light overtook the dark. The positive energy entrapped in Solharn's shrouds of darkness was once again released from his control.

It would be something that nobody of Rhol would ever witness again, the positive energy fighting the dark negative energy. It was a battle of the souls, of good against evil. It was a battle that decided which way the balance would turn.

Elissa didn't believe that Solharn ever understood the power which Deke held, particularly since Solharn was not aware that Elissa had been there to guide Deke. But she had been there for Deke, and she had told him of his power to unleash the energy of the souls. She had instructed him that for the plan to work, the power of the souls would have to be sent through Solharn himself. Because Solharn had created the storms along with the portals to the Black

Abyss, only he could send the energy back to them. Elissa had instructed Deke that the amulet works through the body of whoever it was given to. Therefore, Deke had to give the amulet to Solharn, while still maintaining control of it to be able to unleash its power through Solharn.

It would all be for nothing, however, if the Blackpool remained. If the Blackpool was not destroyed, then Solharn would only return with more power and with more vengeance.

She had hoped Solharn would try to regain his energy and knew the Blackpool would be his only source. She counted on his thirst for domination and power, and it had worked. She had waited until the very moment when the dark energy had begun to stream through his body. She knew he would have to kill Deke to break the connection between the two, and to do that she knew that Solharn would have to send the dark energy to Deke. The only way to do that was to send it through the chain which connected them. The chain Elissa had given to Kiran almost a decade ago.

Elissa had a mere second of opportunity, a flash in time to take over the amulet; if she grabbed it too soon the advantage of surprise would be lost. If she waited too long, the boy would die, and all would fail. Her timing, however, would be impeccable. She had waited ten long years for that moment, ten years of suffering and torment at the hands of Solharn. She had waited patiently to see that moment, to see the look on Solharn's face when he realized that he had just defeated himself. Elissa had savored the moment.

Ω

Spirits were high when word spread about the defeat of Solharn and the return of Queen Elissa, but not everything was cause to celebrate. Rhol had suffered greatly at the hands of his wickedness. Many lives had been lost, and much of the beauty of Rhol had been destroyed by the storms, but Rhol would flourish again. They would rebuild their lands and their homes. Although their freedom had been regained at a great cost, it was worth it.

The Nightstalkers had been freed from Solharn's control once he was sent back to the Black Abyss. Elissa was able to use her powers to heal the wounded, including Delca and Issa. Sadly, she was powerless to help Solko. The rock that toppled on top of him had killed him instantly. Queen Elissa herself informed Preta that Solko died a hero saving this world. Preta was crushed, but Elissa convinced her to come to Mount Kartago to grieve with her, and to become her confidant and protector. She accepted and over time her grief diminished.

In the days that followed, many gathered atop Mount Kartago, at the castle where Elissa had devised her strategy ten long years ago. They had been invited to share in a small memorial for all the brave warriors who died in battle, and for the heroes who would never return home, but whom they would never forget.

Following the ceremony, Jayden looked around for Oisin. He had gone missing, along with Phanthus following the defeat of Solharn.

"Issa, have you seen Phanthus or Oisin?" he asked.

Issa hesitated momentarily before answering. "I have not seen either. Not since the battle at Mount Sibileo. Kaelyn, have you heard anything from them?"

"No, nothing, but I am sure they will be here. Let's join the ceremony."

It was the first time that all of them had gathered together in one place since the Dark Angel's defeat. It was a happy occasion and a time to reflect on the past. Palto now understood how the events had unfolded at Mount Sibileo, but he still did not understand why Elissa had not told him and the others of her plan.

She answered his question showing the utmost respect. "I am sorry Palto. I am sorry to all of you. There was no disrespect intended, but our plan was risky enough. The more people that knew of my freedom, the greater the risk it would have been that Solharn would find out. If he had managed to take control or possess any one of you, he would have known what we planned, and all would have been lost."

Palto nodded to her. He understood her reasoning after seeing what Solharn had done to Jayden and the others.

Queen Elissa turned to Deke. "I would like to thank you, Deke, and you, Mary. If not for you and your paladins, Deo and Delca, Solharn would have fulfilled what he thought to be his destiny. You have saved our world. We of Rhol are indebted to you."

Jayden shook their hands followed by Kaelyn. Duffy also thanked them before walking away in silence.

Although Duffy was trying to mask it, he was noticeably upset. Kaelyn could see that he looked alone and deep in thought.

"Duffy, are you alright?" she asked walking up to him.

"Oh, Kaelyn yes, yes I am fine," Duffy answered.

"You should be proud Duffy. Your valor played a huge role in defeating Solharn and his armies. You saved Preta, Mary, and Delca single-handedly."

"Thank you, Kaelyn. You are very nice to say so, but that is not what troubles me."

"What then?"

"My family...they are all dead. I have no relatives to speak of. Everyone I become close to ends up dying, and then Solko...I am afraid to get close to anyone," said Duffy as he paused for a moment before continuing, "I just don't know where my place is anymore."

"It is with us, Duffy. Come, let's join the others. Orulla and Preta are here. Perhaps they will lift your spirits."

"Yes, yes. Okay, Kaelyn."

They walked over and joined them in time to hear Deke asking Elissa what would become of Rhol.

"We will rebuild, and we will nurture what we have left. Rhol will return to what it once was, and it will prosper again. In many ways, it is already better. The many inhabitants of Rhol came together to protect each other, and protect the world which they call home against the ravages of Solharn. They worked as one, and hopefully, they will now live as one. That is what will sustain our world."

"What about the remaining Kaltaures, the Phits and the others who helped Solharn in his plan to destroy this world?" Deke asked.

"It will take many years for this world to become perfect but one day it will happen, and then we will have accomplished what we were meant to achieve; what all of our worlds must achieve. Once that happens, the Balance of Five will be one with each other. Until that time we will have to slowly work on fixing the imperfections of our worlds. We will try to work with the Phits and the Kaltaures. We will try to deal with their issues until eventually, there are no more issues. There will be no short term solutions or easy fixes. All we can do is try to live with one another. Perhaps one day we will not have to worry about having enemies or about the existence of evil."

"Well, at least Solharn is no longer," Duffy said cutting into the conversation.

A strange silence fell over the crowd. Palto looked toward Elissa. Most of them knew Solharn was far from gone but perhaps no one had told Duffy.

"He is only gone from Rhol, Duffy. He can, and he will return through the Blackpools on the other worlds, and he will be much better prepared. This war is over for Rhol, but it is just beginning for the Balance of Five, of which we are a part of. If Solharn manages to destroy one of the other four worlds, then ours will follow. That is how the balance was designed."

"Do the other worlds possess the power to stop him?" Duffy asked unaware of this gloomy revelation.

"Unfortunately, Beltic is only a year away from extinction. It barely sustains itself. The people of that world cling to a life in which they live in hiding while being hunted down by Solharn's armies. There is a small group that still fights for their world, but they have no chance of surviving without their ruler, Jobe the Seraphim who was sent to protect them," Elissa answered.

"What happened to Jobe?" Issa asked.

"I am not sure, but he no longer possesses the Amulet of Beltic. A Seraph would never relinquish the amulet willingly. Rest assured Solharn was behind whatever has become of him."

"How do you know this Elissa?" Kaelyn chimed in.

"I have many ways of knowing things child, but the obvious answer lies with the Sacred Amulet of Beltic. It is here."

"Where is it, Elissa?" Duffy asked.

"It is safe. The people of Kilto protect it, and they will continue to safeguard it until the person for whom it was meant retrieves it…or leaves it behind."

Elissa was looking directly at Deke. "You are that person Deke. It is your choice whether you continue on this journey or you return home. Because the Amulet of Rhol was found on Earth, I have the power through the Amulet to send you back there along with Mary."

Deke thought for several moments before speaking. "And if I choose to retrieve the Amulet of Beltic?"

"Then you will find yourself in Beltic against impossible odds. You will never be able to return to Earth again until you have located the amulet of your world."

"And what will happen if I choose to go back to Earth now?"

"Then you will never be able to leave Earth again. More than likely, Beltic will become extinct, devoid of life. If that happens, other worlds will follow the same path. Eventually, the balance will be unable to recover itself, and every planet in the Balance of Five will cease to exist. It is inevitable unless Solharn is sent back to the Abyss never to return. For that to take place, the other Blackpools must all be destroyed."

"Why me, Elissa, why am I the one that was chosen to follow this path and to determine whether the balance survives or doesn't. Why does the amulet even work in my hands?" Deke asked.

As she answered, he thought he could see her smile slightly. "I cannot say Deke. Only you can answer the questions that define your life."

He looked at Mary who gave him a nod of approval. They had no life left on Earth anyway. They had spent countless days in an effort to find a new path to follow, one that had meaning. So they would follow this one.

"I'm sure Kiran described the amulet to me once before but can you refresh my memory?" Deke asked.

Elissa did not question his decision. She already knew what it would be.

"It is that of a gold moon, and it represents birth. It can be found with the Kilto where their sanctuary lies. Ensure you learn everything that the Kilto are willing to teach you before you depart. It will be imperative if you are to succeed. They have a deeper understanding of the Universe surrounding the Balance of Five. Their knowledge will assist you in connecting with those who may help you succeed on your quest."

"But Elissa, nobody knows where that is. Nobody has ever walked upon that hallowed ground. How will he find it?" Jayden asked.

"There are some who know," Elissa answered pointing to the sky behind them.

They turned and followed her finger. In the distant sky, they could see a dragon gradually gliding toward them. Phanthus and Oisin had returned.

"Was your quest a success, Phanthus?" Elissa enquired.

"It was Elissa. And what decisions have been made in our absence?"

"I will let Deke speak to your question."

"We have decided to continue with the path we have already started down," Deke answered. "Are you to take us to where the Amulet lies?"

"It would be our honor. Before we go, however, we would like to say some goodbyes if we may," Oisin answered.

"Goodbyes?" Jayden enquired.

Oisin slid from Phanthus and approached Jayden. "You are the last one to know my friend. Please do not be angry with anyone but me. I asked Elissa and the others to allow me to tell you personally. You are my friend above all else, and I could not imagine you finding out any other way."

"What is it Oisin? What is wrong?"

"Nothing is wrong Jayden except that the path my life now leads me in will take me far away from the reaches of Leal. It has always been my legacy, my family's legacy. I just didn't know it until recently. I now understand where I came from, what my past was and who my family was.

"My family's heritage is that of a Dragon Warrior. That is why fate placed Phanthus and me together. Our paths were joined by our ancient bloodlines. Our families were sworn to protect the people of Kilto many centuries ago, and over the many decades that followed, our heritage was forgotten. People struck out against the dragons. They blamed them for horrible acts of violence and death. It was Solharn who cast the blame and convinced them to destroy the dragons. He needed them destroyed so he could get at the Kilto.

"In the turmoil of it all and sensing a rebellion the Dragon Warriors flew the Kilto, the most spiritual people of Rhol, to a place where nobody would ever find them, a sanctuary. If they chose to stay there, the Dragon Warriors believed that they would never be found and that they would always be protected. They were asked by the Kilto to live with them, but they refused out of fear that, although unlikely, they would be hunted down even there and the Kilto who they were sworn to protect would be placed in danger. So they returned in hopes of changing the minds of those who had been misled. It was not to be, however; they would not listen. They had been convinced that the dragons of Rhol had to be exterminated to protect themselves and their children.

"My relatives fought alongside the dragons in a desperate struggle to survive, to exist. They refused to leave them at the hands of such injustice. So, they too were killed by the swords of the ignorant and the misguided.

"Before that final battle, the Dragon Warriors agreed that they would protect their bloodlines. They chose a young girl and a dragon, no more than two years old. They told them nothing of who they were, or what their heritage was in order to shield them from the people who would accuse them and persecute them.

"The girl was sent to Aura where she eventually blended in. She married a Lealian, and they unknowingly kept the bloodline of the Dragon Warriors alive. Solharn however, learned of the bloodline, and he spent years exterminating my ancestors. He knew how powerful the Dragon Warriors would be if ever they realized their calling, and he knew they would oppose him. My mother and father did not understand why their families were being systematically wiped out, but they were not foolish enough to think that they would escape that curse. So, when I was born, they hid me away in the mountains. They were murdered a mere two weeks later. I was taken care of by a family of Brawltug. They honored my parents' wishes and told me nothing of my past. Out of fear that Solharn would learn of my existence, they would not let me leave the confines of their home. So there I stayed, ignorant of the ways of the world outside. One day they left to go out on one of their excursions. I waited for days for their return, alone and hungry, but they never came back. I set out on my own, wandering from place to place for years. Eventually, I found my way to Leal and was taken in by your father just prior to Elissa casting the protective field around it. I would be safe there for the next decade.

"The dragon lived a much harsher life. He watched as the last of the dragons were slaughtered. He assumed that the people that lay lifelessly beside them were simply casualties of the persons responsible for killing them. He did not know any better, as he was never told what his purpose was. The ancients hid him in a lair and told him that he needed to protect the bloodline of the dragons. He was told that he could never reveal himself to anyone until it was time, or else he would be responsible for the extinction of the dragons. As they left, he asked them how he would know when the time to reveal himself, had come. They had simply told him a legend. A legend about a dragon's tear, and that if the legend ever came to fruition, then he would know.

"Over the many years of seclusion hatred built up within that dragon. Solharn tracked him down, intent on destroying him to ensure that the Dragon Warriors of Rhol would never again reunite.

"When Solharn finally found the dragon, he realized that the dragon had no idea what his true heritage was. He also discovered, to his delight, that the dragon had a profound hatred for the inhabitants of Rhol. So Solharn did not kill the dragon. Instead, he saw the value in having this dragon work on his side, to fight with his armies and he convinced him to do just that.

"Over time the dragon eventually came to realize his true purpose through the compassion of a boy, and through the valiance of a warrior who refused to leave his side. That warrior gave his own life to try to save the dragon as his ancestors had done before him. The dragon gave that life back. That dragon was Phanthus, Jayden, and the warrior was me.

"We are the last in the bloodline that protects the Kilto. They are of great importance to the Balance of Five, more than anyone knows. We will stay with them and look over them, at least until the Balance is saved forever."

Jayden did not say much, he merely hugged his friend and wished him the best. He told them both that should they ever need his help he would be there for them. With that, the Dragon Warriors prepared to leave to fulfill their purpose, to follow their path.

"Wait! I want to go with them, Elissa. It would be my honor if you would allow me this request. I have no family left in this world. I only wish to help save what remains. I can assist the boy," said Duffy.

"I am quite sure you can Duffy, and I believe you will. Please, go with them and may the energy of the souls protect you all."

The night drew to a close as the full moon cast its glow over Mount Kartago. Palto stood beside Elissa, and they watched as

Phanthus flew his weary travelers to what would be the start of their most challenging journey yet, a journey that would lead them to the Amulet of Beltic and a new world.

"Solharn will be far more powerful and far more prepared the next time he comes in contact with the boy, Elissa. Will Deke be able to resist the Dark Angels temptations and remain on the path he follows?"

"Every path has its twists and turns that inevitably lead to a chasm, Palto. We can only hope that when he comes to one, he can find a bridge that will help him across."

For information on the release of books in the Deke Brolin series or
to contact the author, visit;

https://twitter.com/dbackus5

https://www.facebook.com/authordougbackus

http://dougbackusauthor.blogspot.ca/

www.ingramcontent.com/pod-product-compliance
Lightning Source LLC
Chambersburg PA
CBHW051412170626
46809CB00006B/2126